In The Mood

by

Paul Hupton

Bloomington, IN

authorHOUSE®

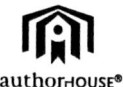

Milton Keynes, UK

AuthorHouse™
1663 Liberty Drive, Suite 200
Bloomington, IN 47403
www.authorhouse.com
Phone: 1-800-839-8640

AuthorHouse™ UK Ltd.
500 Avebury Boulevard
Central Milton Keynes, MK9 2BE
www.authorhouse.co.uk
Phone: 08001974150

This book is a work of fiction. People, places, events, and situations are the product of the author's imagination. Any resemblance to actual persons, living or dead, or historical events, is purely coincidental.

© 2007 Paul Hupton. All rights reserved.

No part of this book may be reproduced, stored in a retrieval system, or transmitted by any means without the written permission of the author.

First published by AuthorHouse 5/10/2007

ISBN: 978-1-4259-8251-5 (sc)

Printed in the United States of America
Bloomington, Indiana

This book is printed on acid-free paper.

In the Mood

by Paul Hupton

"How often have I said to you that when you have eliminated the impossible, whatever remains, however improbable, must be the truth?"

Sherlock Holmes addressing Dr. Watson in the 'Sign of (the) Four'.

1

Another time, another place

They said that it would only last a year at the most, those faceless civil servants I had learned to despise. A propaganda ploy to enlist the young and vulnerable I thought? The war was portrayed as a big adventure for those who had never strayed beyond England's coastline. A "jolly" I remember someone saying at the time, paid for by Winston Churchill. A quick visit to France, miss out winter in England, which wasn't a bad thing for most people given the employment crisis and poverty, and back home before anyone knew that they had been away. When a year came and went, quickly followed by another, the mood of the great British people changed to a more sombre one. Realization about the war wasn't far away and any notion of it being a great adventure quickly disappeared. The grieving for some had started within months of the declaration of war as once young smiling faces returned home in body bags; the lucky ones, as far as their families were concerned, still intact bodily.

For others it was arguably much worse. "Missing in action" had become a well-used phrase in those early months and would continue to be so for at least another three or four years. Neither lost or found, relatives were left in a state of limbo not knowing whether to grieve or keep their spirits up in the hope that their loved ones would return home some day. How many families were suffering or had suffered to date, I could only guess. Couples like John and I, married only a year. There was always a mixed opinion on the wisdom behind marriage during wartime. For us it was a conscious decision we made as the war took hold. We simply couldn't wait until it was all over. After all, when would that be? Nobody knew, not even Mr Churchill. We had to marry right away. There was no in-depth discussion about the perceived urgency; it was something we both understood and agreed on. Certainly, there wasn't an indication of what the war may have had in store for either of us. That would have meant acknowledging horrors that had been placed at the back and deepest parts of our minds. It was enough to accept, without the spoken word, that our time together could be short and that we should be happy, if it was only for a moment.

All these thoughts raced around inside my head as I walked arm-in-arm with John along the cobbled platform.

It was a cold bitter night for May, but for the last five minutes, I'd become quite oblivious to the biting effects of the northerly wind as it raced out of the tunnel entrance, just beyond the end of the railway platform. Far away in the distance, sirens announced the arrival of enemy aircraft, their monotone drone a familiar sound four years into the war.

"A penny for your thoughts darling?" John asked, squeezing my arm gently as he did. His breath bellowed out into the cold night air. With my petite 5'3" frame beside John's 6'2", heavy-set build, I had to crane my head back to see him clearly. We had been childhood sweethearts living in the same country village until John's father was forced to relocate further north, having been promoted by his employer. We were both just eleven years old when John and his family left the village and I cried non-stop for a month.

My mum tried her best to console me, bless her, but nothing worked. Then, six months later I received a letter. It was from John. Over the years we wrote regularly and even met a couple of times as our respective families found excuses to get together or mysteriously bump into each other on day trips to the seaside. One year when I was fifteen, I had planned – no, orchestrated – a cunning ruse to stay at a friend's house for a week during the school summer holidays. She lived a short distance from the Laines' family home. The only problem was my friend caught chickenpox the week before my visit and all arrangements had to be cancelled. Once again, I bawled my eyes out for a full week. Little did I know that alternative plans were already in place! I stayed at Calverly

Sands a few weeks later visiting my grandparents and guess who was also staying there that week on business…John Laine senior, along with his family. I sometimes wonder whether the whole business was contrived for our benefit. Perhaps John was as inconsolable as I was when we were apart. The thought made me feel warm inside.

"Betty darling," he persisted, patting my hand, "you're cold."

We stopped and he pulled his arm clear from between us, unbuttoning his RAF overcoat as he did. Bringing his arm and open jacket around at the same time, he wrapped both around my shoulders so that we were as close bodily as we could be. For a brief instant I felt safe. Safer than I had been since the war began with all the physical and mental torture that it had brought. But how could I ever be safe again? John was returning to duty after an all-too-brief spell of leave. Strangely, he had been unwell during his stay at home taking to his bed for a day at one point. Oh how I prayed that it would be something that would keep him with me longer. That was the selfish side of me. Seldom seen, but very much at the fore about two days ago. Why shouldn't I want my husband by my side as we had always planned when we took our marriage vows? Then I would see the propaganda messages about the war effort, radio bulletins from the BBC, individual acts of heroism, food rationing, and it wasn't long before those selfish thoughts were cast aside. I hated that maniac, Hitler. I hated him with a passion, like thousands of other women, wives and mothers, frustrated by the futility of war and sheer loss of life.

The teardrop was involuntary, yet hardly unexpected. From his limited line of sight, John couldn't see the tiny droplet and of course I knew that he must not. He needed all his resolve now. I blinked in a vain attempt to stem the flow.

"Oh Betty darling," John stopped, squaring up to me so that we were facing each other; my head was still bowed to try and hide my blurred vision.

"Gosh," I managed finally, staring up at him apprehensively. "The wind coming out of that tunnel is freezing. It brings tears to your eyes."

The fact that my lips were trembling and my voice was warbling did nothing to support my attempt to hide my true feelings. My Clark Gable lookalike, more so since the real Gable had himself recently become an Air Force pilot, pushed back the peek of his hat so that it perched on the crown of his thick black wavy hair. Even in the subdued light afforded by platform gaslights the twinkles in his eyes remained, those same twinkles that had melted my heart from an early age. His chiselled jaw slowly turned into a wide grin. He placed both his hands beneath my arms and gently, effortlessly, he picked me up until he could look directly into my eyes and I could look into his. The boy I had fallen in love with was still there underneath this raw masculinity, although the grin was a little more strained than usual. Pulling me forward those few inches, my feet dangling in mid-air like a puppet, he kissed me full on the lips. My arms quickly wrapped themselves around his broad shoulders, closing my eyes wishing that we were somewhere else; another time, another place.

Pulling us apart he smiled again, that strain still there now and in his eyes as well, a slight frown.

"I love you darling, I always have and I always will." He kissed my cheek and lowered me back down onto the station platform. His tone almost had a past tense feel to it, a final connotation that I objected to inside my head even though I knew I was being silly. I pulled at his waist until we were close again, burying my face into his chest.

"Why do you have to go John?" I blubbered, the tears now becoming uncontrollable.

"Oh darling," he uttered reassuringly, "I need to do my bit just like all the rest. You know that."

He pulled us apart, putting a finger under my chin, lifting my head as he did so that we were looking into each others' eyes once more. The wind howled again pulling ringlets of blonde hair from beneath my headscarf.

"I must look a sight," I said out loud, a forced grin playing on my lips.

John stroked my forehead, gently pushing my hair back into place with one hand, whilst reaching for his handkerchief with the other. He dabbed around my eyes and cheeks tentatively.

"You've never looked anything other than perfect to me darling," he said, trying his best to calm my increasingly agitated mood.

"Why now though John? You've only been home a week and you were supposed to have at least two weeks' leave," I protested. I knew the answer of course. It simply wasn't the one that I particularly wanted to hear though.

In The Mood

"Now you know the answer darling as well as I do," he said calmly, kissing my forehead and hugging me once more. "I can't discuss it with you, but it's an important mission. The Germans are sweeping across Europe at present and have to be stopped by fair means or foul."

Of course there was a heavy price to pay by allied forces. Nearly three quarters of John's squadron had been replaced, lost to the war within the last twelve months. Most of the replacements looked as if they should have still been at school, when John had shown me a photograph of his team soon after arriving home. John was an experienced squadron leader even though he was only twenty-seven years old. The RAF couldn't afford to lose many more with John's ability and equally couldn't afford to have them inactive where immaturity and inexperience was rife amongst the rank and file. It didn't take long for my thoughts to go out to the relatives of those brave young pilots wondering what they must be going through and to realise that their only chance of survival was having someone like John as their commanding officer.

I groaned again inwardly. The sound of a distant whistle emerging from the tunnel entrance cut short my self-pity. Wiping my eyes and blinking once more against the bitter wind, I concentrated on the blackness that was the tunnel entrance. Soon a train would arrive to take my love away, possibly forever. John noticed the grimace on my face and for a moment I felt ashamed of myself. What had been a world occupied by only the two of us for the last twenty minutes or so was in fact a busy railway station platform. The division between two sets of people was as psychological as it was physical. Close to the platform edge nearest to where the train would stop, eager excited families waited patiently to see husbands, fathers returning home on leave, as I had waited a week earlier. Under the cast-iron ornate canopy, several yards back, beneath hanging baskets bearing spring bulbs were more families huddled in groups of twos, threes and fours mainly, the focal point inevitably a man in a uniform returning back to the war. The stationmaster, a burly fellow, had become quite used to this and had taken to playing the accordion to welcome those returning home and to try and raise the spirits of those departing. Just at that moment, he appeared out of the ticket office strapping the accordion across his stout frame and was just about to play a jolly tune when John waved a hand at him.

"Excuse me darling, shan't be a tick," he smiled mischievously. He skipped across to where the stationmaster was standing and whispered something in his ear. The round-faced, middle-aged would-be musician nodded enthusiastically, before breaking into a melody that I instantly recognised as our tune.

"May I trouble you for this dance madam?" John asked as he returned, bowing and smiling like the cat that got the cream. He took hold of my hand and pulled me into a small clearing in between the crowds of people. I wondered what they would say.

"Perhaps John has had a relapse from his illness. Maybe he will have to stay at home after all." I said to myself in hope.

The twinkle in his eye suggested otherwise though. It was a typical gesture, one designed to make me feel at ease and take my mind off his leaving. Any worries about other people quickly disappeared and we began to waltz oblivious to everyone and everything around us. The hoot of the train ever nearer didn't stop us either. Round and round we danced until I stopped abruptly and began giggling like a schoolgirl. John's concerned look was followed by one of bewilderment. His mouth opened as if he was about to ask if I was all right, but this time it was my turn to surprise him. I placed the palm of my hand over his mouth, taking hold of his hand with my free hand, quickly slipping it inside my woollen coat. It rested on my plumper-by-the-week tummy and this time it was John's turn to chuckle.

"He's going to play for England at Twickenham when he is older," he announced, allowing his hand to rove across my tummy no doubt searching for the experience again.

"And what makes you think we are having a son?" I protested, mockingly. In truth we were just happy to have a healthy baby, whatever the gender.

Beside us and along the length of the platform, other couples danced now with us, their spirits lifted, if only temporarily. An army private danced with his daughter of about four, held aloft, firmly in his arms, she enjoying every minute of it. A young boy, unaware of the dangers that lay in wait for his daddy, sped past them on his tricycle ringing its bell, no doubt excited by a late night out and unconcerned about the reason for it. Another much louder hoot announced the arrival of the Edinburgh to London train on time at 8pm. Everyone seemed to stop dancing simultaneously and the hugs, kisses and squeezes began to mark the departure of some and the arrival of others.

"Take care John dear," I said, "God be with you."

We kissed and hugged again. John was strangely quiet now. Perhaps the good old English *stiff upper lip* was hard to maintain after all. He climbed aboard the train and I felt the strongest impulse to climb aboard after him, but I resisted for John's sake and for that of our baby. It was hard enough for him without me making it more difficult. I didn't even know if he was scared. I never asked. I suppose no one ever dared to ask their loved ones. If servicemen were ever allowed to have feelings and choices, the war would be over by now, possibly with the Nazis ruling the world. John pulled the carriage door closed behind him and then pulled the window down, reaching out for my hand.

"Now you look after yourself darling," he called, over the general mayhem of people boarding and alighting. "I'll be back before he…" he looked at me and grinned.

"She (the baby) is ready to arrive?" I corrected him.

"I've asked for special leave after this mission and Frank has assured me that it is in the bag," John said. He winked at me the way he always did.

I pressed my cheek against his outstretched hand, more to hide the tears that were welling up again inside. I felt his other hand caress the back of my head and our lips met again as he reached down for what we knew could be our final kiss. We parted eventually and John reached further and patted me lightly on the tummy, just as the wheels of the train began to spin and lurch forward.

"Now you look after your mummy and don't give her a hard time," he teased, staring down at my protruding bump. The train began to pick up some momentum and we both knew it was time to let go.

"Oh darling, there are extra ration coupons…" John started to shout now over the screeching sound of wheels against the tracks, before I interrupted.

"…Inside the soup bowl on the top shelf of the Welsh dresser in the kitchen," I finished off his sentence again. Through the steam I could see his all-too-familiar grin looking back at me followed by a shrug of his shoulders. The arrangements for my well-being during his latest spell of leave had been well-planned and rehearsed, given my condition. He couldn't help the leader in himself coming to the surface though.

"I've spoken to Jane. She is happy to help. Oh, the telephone number for the airbase…" John shouted again, now in full voice, some fifty yards away.

"…Is on the notepad on the wall near the front door," I shouted back through my tears.

"Call me – for any reason or get Jane to call me. Frank will get a message to me." John said, his voice straining against the backdrop of steam engine pistons hissing and shunting wheels.

"Oh, " he called. He waved, now more of a gesture than a coherent call. I stepped forward as if it would make a difference through the clouds of steam.

For a moment he disappeared from view only to reappear clutching a small package wrapped in brown paper presumably from his kitbag. He held it aloft too far away for me to even see what it was clearly. John shifted his attention toward our friendly stationmaster-cum-accordionist, who had just signalled for the train to leave moments earlier. John threw the package at him and he caught it, clasping it tight to his barrel chest. Words were exchanged as the train sped past and the man on the platform nodded understandingly. I tearfully waved a handkerchief and whispered, 'I love you,' to myself before the train left into the night. I stood watching as the last carriage disappeared into the inky blackness and found myself caressing my unborn baby. My baby was the only part of John that I had left now. I couldn't get that thought out of my head.

"Excuse me, it's Mrs Laine?" It was the stationmaster holding out John's package. "The young gent on the train asked me to give you this. He said to be sure that you keep it safe until he came home."

He passed the lightweight, soft package to me and I noticed a small tear. A piece of blue fur poked out through the hole and I smiled to myself in anticipation. It was a blue furry rabbit.

"John was still running with his little boy theory I see," I said to myself. I squeezed it to my chest – the rabbit a poor substitute for the man I loved.

"I promised your husband that I would see you home when he asked me to play the music for you earlier." He smiled; the rosy red veined cheeks and white beard gave him a Father Christmas look close up. "I'm just coming off duty now if you would like me to accompany you home?"

"That is very nice of you and very thoughtful," I managed, straining to read his name badge on the lapel of his jacket, "Mr Grimes, I only live at Henley Cottage, a short walk from the station entrance. Oh by the way, you play enchantingly." He blushed even more and we both made our way down the steps between the two ticket booths toward the station entrance. Even as we did I couldn't stop looking back to where I had last seen John.

Over the days that followed Betty had spoken frequently to John since his return to RAF Bellingham, but as the mission drew close, he became harder and harder to contact. She asked him about the mission repeatedly, even though she knew that he could not tell her anything. She hoped it would be cancelled or the war would end before the mission began, but this was just wishful thinking on her part. She had a terrible foreboding over the days that followed, something that she constantly put at the back of her mind and had dared not share with her husband.

2

Just the two of us

Jane Prentiss, a thirty year old cook with the village primary school, was putting her knowledge to good domestic use by baking her own bread for herself and the young mother-to-be, Betty Laine – her next-door neighbour. The newly rolled dough sat in steel baking tins waiting to be placed in the range oven, when it had reached the right temperature. In the background, on the kitchen mantelpiece, Vera Lynn sang White Cliffs of Dover out of a radio. Jane hummed the tune as she busied herself, tidying away mixing bowls, cooking utensils and carefully collecting any unused flour for another day. She had just cleaned her hands when there was a firm rap on her front door. She turned the radio down and unfastened her apron placing it on a nearby chair. It was a frightful night. Driving rain and gale-force winds had plagued the little village for most of the day.

"Who could possibly be out on a night like this?" she wondered. "Betty!" She shouted instinctively. She ran down the hallway to the front door fearing that her next-door neighbour might be in trouble or even in labour. Living on her own she was always concerned about strangers at her door at such a late hour and as she neared the glass pane she could tell that the figure behind it was too big to be Betty Laine.

"God knows I have enough to worry about with the Germans, " she said to herself.

She peered through the fan-shaped window in the front door and was relieved to see the distorted image of a rather wet and dripping Constable Fred Gorse wiping the rainwater from his reddened face with his handkerchief. She pulled back the bolts from the door and opened it.

"Evening Fred," she greeted him, the splatter of raindrops making normal conversation nearly impossible. "Whatever brings you out here on a night like this?" It was a pointless question, she thought, even as she asked it. He was a policeman with duties to perform and a beat to walk, irrespective of the weather or the war. "You should be sending someone younger out on nights like this," she continued, "like that nice lad you had with you in the park last week."

Her choice of words came out before she realised and she almost swallowed them with embarrassment as they tumbled out. She had taken an instant interest the minute she had laid eyes on Fred Gorse's young trainee constable and since that day she had tried her best to bump into him again, without much luck.

"Sorry Miss Prentiss, he's been given other duties outside the village tonight so you'll have to make do with an old relic like me." He grinned knowingly and for a moment she blushed.

"Come inside Fred, you'll catch your death out there," she offered, peering out at the night sky.

"Better not Miss Prentiss," he tipped his helmet as he spoke in appreciation. "Don't want to drip all over your floor."

He smiled and continued before she could protest. "Do you have a contact telephone number for Mr Laine your neighbour by any chance? Only I know that you're friendly with Mrs Laine and, well I wondered…" He smiled again expectantly.

She looked at him curiously. "Why yes Fred, but shouldn't you be speaking to Betty, I mean Mrs Laine, rather than me?" she replied. A sense of anxiety from her own question gripped her as she waited for a response.

"It's Mrs Laine that I need to speak to him about urgently," the constable answered, flipping open his notebook so that it was just inside the doorway and out of the rain.

Jane raised her hands across her face. "She has gone into labour hasn't she?" Jane could hardly contain herself. "Let me check my diary," she added, launching herself toward her handbag on the hall table.

"Begging your pardon Miss Prentiss, Mrs Laine has gone into labour early, on account of her fall," the constable added.

She stopped fumbling in her handbag, her eyes distracted from the contents inside and looked back toward the front door at the constable, his silhouette captured in the doorway, the rain pouring down behind him. Her face had changed from one of an excited schoolgirl back to a worried and concerned adult. Even in the darkened hallway, Fred could tell that she was shaken.

"I didn't mean to alarm you Miss Prentiss. Mrs Laine was found inside the telephone box at the corner of the lane not a half hour ago. I spotted her myself on my rounds. She is in the cottage hospital. I'm not sure about her condition, but the doctors want to deliver the baby tonight – complications or something they said. That is why I need Mr Laine's contact number." For a split second her mind was preoccupied with the welfare of Betty and her unborn child, before she resumed her search.

"Here we are Fred," she said gleefully. "This is his number at the airbase. Just ask for Wing Commander Frank Carter, John's commanding officer." She scribbled the number on a sheet of paper from her handbag and thrust it at him. Accepting the note gratefully he flipped over his notebook and slipped it back into his tunic pocket.

"Now come along Fred, you get back to the station, get yourself dry and give RAF Bellingham a call. I'm off to the hospital." Popping back inside briefly to turn the oven off, she grabbed her raincoat, handbag and umbrella slamming the door shut behind her as she left.

"I'm afraid the bread will have to wait," she said to herself.

The two walked hurriedly down the garden path, out through the gate and along the lane in opposite directions. Any concerns about walking along darkened country lanes, made even darker now by the wartime blackout, quickly faded as she hurried the quarter of a mile or so toward the little cottage hospital.

"Good evening, my name is Jane Prentiss. I am a close friend and neighbour of a Mrs Betty Laine. I believe she was admitted here this evening after a fall. She is also heavily pregnant." The young receptionist, a girl in fact, smiled back and began leafing through the large register in front of her. Jane eyed her critically. "Too much make-up, if you ask me," she said to herself. "And where does she get the money from to pay for it, I'd like to know, during war time?"

"Sorry, the name was?" the young clerk asked.

"Laine," Jane responded, her impatience filtering through into her voice. "Henley Cottage, Lowry Terrace."

"Ah yes, Mrs Laine is being examined now by the doctor. She will eventually be in Hounslow Maternity Ward in about an hour's time," the young clerk informed her, pointing to a pair of double doors bearing the same name behind Jane.

"Could I see her after the examination please?" Jane inquired.

"I see no reason why not, but I will have to check with Sister first. Please take a seat and I will come and find you." The clerk smiled and gestured toward the empty reception area. Jane took a seat, close to the open fire laying her damp raincoat on a nearby footstool to dry. Her

In The Mood

umbrella stood propped in the fire hearth for the same reason. Twenty minutes later she found herself reading the daily newspaper, the sound of background chatter from later visitors intermittently affecting her concentration, when she was interrupted.

"Excuse me, Miss Prentiss?" A stout looking authoritative nurse in a starched navy blue uniform stood a few feet away from where she sat.

"Err, why, yes," Jane replied removing her reading glasses and placing the newspaper back in its rack.

"You are here to see Mrs Laine I believe?" the nurse continued before Jane could elaborate further. "I am Sister Cunningham. I'm responsible for Mrs Laine's health and welfare at present while she is with us." Jane nodded in response, placing her glasses in her handbag.

"Would you like to step into my office for a few minutes?" The senior nurse gestured toward the openness of the reception area and other visitors that sat there. Jane collected her coat and umbrella and the two walked across to a small compact office at the head of the main entrance into Hounslow Maternity Ward.

Sister Cunningham closed the door as they entered. "Take a seat Miss Prentiss." Jane hung her coat and umbrella on the hat stand behind the closed door and turned to her host. As offices went this was hardly executive, more functional. A small wooden desk with an in-tray on top, a swivel chair that looked decidedly uncomfortable, now occupied by her host, and a single filing cabinet. A small blackout curtain covered what Jane assumed was the only source of natural light.

"I'm afraid it won't be possible for you to see Mrs Laine just yet." The senior nurse announced. Jane took the seat on offer, all manner of concerned thoughts racing through her mind.

"You are not a member of the family are you miss Prentiss?" something Sister Cunningham had gleaned from the hospital receptionist. She flicked through a file in front of her, occasionally looking up across the desk at Jane. She had an authoritative air to her that was a much-needed quality dealing with young and inexperienced nursing staff during wartime. Just now it was something Jane could do without.

"Well no, but I am the only one near to Betty in the village. She has no family, just her husband, John. Neither of them have any family. Both John and Betty's parents were early casualties of the war, so Betty had told me," Jane replied defensively. Sister Cunningham looked at Jane pensively as if toiling with some decision inside her head. "John entrusted Betty's safety and well-being to me, when he is not at home. I feel responsible if something is wrong," Jane continued as if consolidating her position.

"Ah yes, Mr Laine, the air-force pilot," Sister Cunningham repeated the name as if to change the emphasis. "We have had limited success in that direction," she replied fixing her attention on the page she was looking for. "The local police tried to contact Mr Laine's commanding officer about thirty minutes ago, but the airbase said he had left for the night on urgent business and he wasn't contactable." Sister Cunningham looked at the worried woman before her and thought for a few moments. She smiled for the first time, albeit awkwardly.

In The Mood

"I will probably be disciplined for this, but I am sure that you have Mrs Laine's best interests at heart?" She said closing the file again.

"Of course," what a question, Jane thought. After all, there is a war on and she was helping John as much as Betty.

"Whatever happened to Mrs Laine as a result of her fall has affected her mentally. Physically, she seems fine, although the doctors want to deliver her babies as soon as possible, before they become distressed." Sister Cunningham said, patting the file in front of her.

"Babies?" Jane queried.

"Why yes, Mrs Laine is expecting twins," came the reply. "She didn't tell you, I take it?"

Jane shook her head. "Oh gosh," she uttered, completely unprepared. She had a brief premonition of twins running about the place, banging on her front door to see Auntie Jane and being spoiled rotten. She smiled to herself lost in her thoughts, before remembering Sister Cunningham's other comments.

"I'm sorry, what do you mean *affected Betty mentally?*"

Sister Cunningham considered her next comment carefully before answering. "Mrs Laine appears to be in what we call a catatonic state."

Jane frowned, "What exactly does that mean?"

"Well I have limited knowledge in this area you understand." She smiled again apprehensively wondering if she should wait for Doctor Mason to explain the situation. "Err, I would say the reality around Mrs Laine has been closed out and she has retreated back into her own mind away from reality," sister Cunningham replied.

Jane stared at her host in thought rather than in expectation of anything further. "You mean she doesn't even know she is having twins?" Jane muttered eventually.

"At the moment, I doubt whether she even knows she is in the hospital. This was one of the reasons that convinced Doctor Mason to deliver the twins now, rather than as planned in two weeks' time," Sister Cunningham replied. She sat hands clasped in front of her allowing the news she had just given to sink in. Jane sat dazed in partial shock herself, happy about the twins, yet worried about their mother.

Poor John knows nothing about what has happened," she thought.

"Normally, only the next of kin would be allowed to visit her, but we desperately need a friendly voice to coax her back. Every little bit helps. Would you help us and Mrs Laine until her husband returns at least?" Sister Cunningham asked, a serious look now etched on her face.

"Why of course I would," Jane offered firmly, yet another unnecessary question in her eyes.

"I suggest that you go home and get some sleep Miss Prentiss. Mrs Laine is due to be operated on shortly. You can visit her tomorrow at 10am. We will continue to try and raise Mr Laine at the airbase in the meantime. Oh, and thank you for your help." The two women rose from their seats, Jane gathering her belongings and moved outside the office into the corridor once more. They shook hands before the Sister smiled and moved off into the maternity ward, whilst Jane made her way toward the main entrance in her own trance-like state. It was a lot to take in, along with the late hour. Betty's condition, John's continued absence, twins. The final thought at least ensured a cheery conclusion to her thoughts as the entrance door closed behind her.

ooooo

The following morning Jane arrived back at the hospital promptly at 10am. She had had a terrible night worrying about Betty, the babies, the operation and John. She was exhausted, yet determined to be there for her young friend whom she had grown very fond of. John as well for that matter; the whole family, in fact. She smiled inwardly. The thought of babies again brought a maternal flush from somewhere deep down, before her thoughts for some unknown reason turned to a certain young trainee constable. Her smile remained as she hurried through the main entrance. Her progress toward reception came to an abrupt halt, when her name was called from just outside the ward entrance.

"Miss Prentiss!" Jane, the receptionist and several other visitors looked in the general direction of the authoritative voice. It was Sister Cunningham, clipboard in her hand gesturing for Jane to come toward her.

"Good news Miss Prentiss. Mrs Laine gave birth to twin boys late last night, weighing 6lbs. 2ozs and 6lbs. 10ozs respectively. Both babies are doing fine, although," she paused for a few moments on reflection.

"Although what, Sister?" Jane asked worriedly.

"There is no change in Mrs Laine's condition and we still haven't made contact with Mr Laine." she concluded.

Jane stood motionless. "Poor little mites," she thought to herself, "and Betty as well?"

"Given Mrs Laine's condition, the babies are being cared for in a separate room, hopefully just for the first week or so," Sister Cunningham continued, to break the uneasy silence. Both women knew that was entirely dependent on Betty's recovery. They walked side-by-side along the main corridor toward a cacophony of baby cries from the ward ahead of them. The maternity unit was one of the few places where the normal odours associated with general hospitals – disinfectants and the like – were replaced by that unique odour only newborn babies bring. They passed toilet doors depicting his-and-hers with silhouette figures painted on them of Mickey and Minnie mouse. The corridor itself was covered in Walt Disney characters giving it a child-like, cheery look. Both Donald Duck and Mickey Mouse were painted on the walls either side of the inner doors bidding all who entered welcome like two comical centurions. Jane was tempted to continue until she noticed that Sister Cunningham had slowed to a stop outside a side room. Just before they entered, Jane decided to ask the one question she feared the most.

"What is the medium to long-term prognosis for Mrs Laine's condition?" Sister Cunningham folded her arms, holding the clipboard tight to her chest, pondering her own advice.

"The head of neurology examined Mrs Laine last night before the birth. He confirmed that she appeared to be in a state of shock, possibly caused by the fall itself and perhaps a worry that her child might be injured. We simply cannot be sure at this stage. Rest and recuperation with things familiar to her at close quarters might speed up her recovery was his initial advice. She will be kept in under observation for a few weeks and her children cared for. Of course Mr Laine would play a vital role during her convalescence, when he returns." Jane looked back at her solemnly. "Mrs Laine is in this room, Miss Prentiss," Sister Cunningham whispered quietly opening the off-white solid wooden door. Directly in front of them lay a motionless Betty Laine, her eyes staring at the ceiling of the little room never flinching once at the noise made by babies crying in the ward next door as they entered the room. A younger red-headed nurse in a much paler blue uniform stood beside the bed checking Betty's blood pressure.

"This is Nurse Andrews, Mrs Laine's nurse this evening," Sister Cunningham commented observing her junior member of staff. The nurse smiled at Jane and she smiled back. Her attention though was on her friend. An over-whelming feeling of sorrow came over her as she sat down beside the bed. Instinctively, she reached for Betty's hand and squeezed it gently.

"Betty dear, it's me, Jane," she whispered. "You have two wonderful baby boys! Yes that's right – two! Twins in fact! Won't John be surprised?" Tears welled up in her eyes. Neither the mention of twins or John's name had the desired effect. She remained totally divorced of any emotion or reaction.

"We will keep a watchful eye over Mrs Laine," came the reassuring response from the younger nurse, over Jane's shoulder. Jane's worried expression remained momentarily, her eyes reluctant to leave her vulnerable friend. She dabbed at her eyes, almost oblivious to Nurse Andrew's comment.

"Come let me take you into the next room," Sister Cunningham suggested, placing a reassuring hand on Jane's shoulder. "You can see John and Duncan, although they're fast asleep at the moment."

The names seemed to bring her out of her saddened state. "John and Duncan?" Jane asked with a whimper.

"Oh yes," sister chuckled quietly, "we had to call them something on the ward for the sake of their name tags. John was named after his father and Duncan after our head of paediatrics, Dr Duncan Mason." Jane turned back, patting Betty's hand.

"I'll pop back later and we can have a real chat about your new family." She climbed to her feet, her hand reluctant to let go at first and then the two women left the room. The room next door was blissfully quiet.

"It isn't always like this," Sister Cunningham whispered again smiling. "John is the one with the blue woolly hat, Duncan has the yellow hat."

"Oh, they are beautiful, wonderful, marvellous." Jane replied manoeuvring herself around each cot, until she could see the twins more clearly. "John looks just like his father and Duncan more like his mother. They look so peaceful, so unaware of what is happening around them. I suppose I couldn't hold one of them?" Jane asked hopefully.

"Perhaps tomorrow. They are settled at the moment," Sister Cunningham replied.

Jane smiled understandingly. "There will be plenty of time for that I suppose," she said, gently stroking the blanket covering each child. She turned to face the senior nurse once more. "Now I've brought a book, flask of tea and some sandwiches, so if you want to lead the way back next door I'll get started with Betty's recovery in two shakes of a lamb's tale."

Despite 24-hour care over the next few days, Betty Laine's condition remained the same. Her husband did not return to the hospital and there was no communication back from RAF Bellingham. The whereabouts of Frank Carter remained a mystery to the staff at the airbase. He had simply vanished the same night as Betty's accident and hadn't been seen since. His unauthorised absence was now causing concern within the hierarchy of the RAF given his knowledge of secret operations and a full-scale investigation had been launched to locate him. Even the local police were drafted in to help. To compound matters further, Frank Carter was the only contact with John Laine's squadron during their latest sortie over Hamburg, so the squadron's exact whereabouts was currently unknown to the remaining staff at the airbase. Any disclosure of information would have to be authorised by Carter. One thing they would say, albeit off the record, was that the mission was overdue. It was impossible to confirm this formally though without Wing Commander Carter. It was possible that John Laine's squadron had been reassigned on another mission since at the last minute requiring radio silence, but again without

Carter to verify this it was no more than conjecture and speculation.

It was the early hours of the following morning. The familiar sound of distant air-raid sirens filled the air providing a trigger for the hospital, like the rest of the village, to dim lights and draw blackout curtains. The distant noise of a spluttering, coughing engine seemed to be closer than it probably was against the stillness of the countryside outside the little cottage hospital. Patients rose from their beds alarmed and agitated. The less experienced, younger nurses ran around making comforting noises, even though it was clear from their reaction that they too were frightened. That night happened to be Sister Cunningham's turn on night duty supervising not only the maternity ward, but also the adult wards at the far side of the hospital. The commotion from Kingston Ward gathered momentum just as she arrived to do her rounds. She rushed inside raising her hands trying to calm patients and staff alike. She soon paused turning her attention toward the large French windows at the rear of the ward that led out on to the garden patio. Walking briskly toward them, anxious about the growing noise, she pulled the curtains back a few inches to maintain blackout status. Her eyes were transfixed by a flashing orb several hundred feet in the air.

From where she stood, it appeared to be above the open field at the rear of the hospital. There was no fixed pattern to the light; in fact it resembled a large rocket that one often sees on 5th November held in midair for those few seconds. One thing was certain, the ever-growing noise was coming from this glowing orb and it seemed

In The Mood

to be getting brighter. The realisation of what she was looking at suddenly dawned on her and her eyes grew wide and open at the portent of danger before her. It was a struggling engine, an engine belonging to an aeroplane. The central orb was now more like a ball of flames, sparks radiating out in all directions. The window frames of the hospital began to rattle furiously and once again patients began to scream and cower with fright. Those that could ran out of the ward taking refuge back in the hospital's reception area and outer wards.

The senior nurse could only raise her hands to her mouth and mutter, "God help us," through her tightly closed fingers, as the plane roared into the light afforded by a full moon as it shone across the hospital grounds.

"Down everyone – now! On the floor!" she called out, half turning as she did before, throwing herself down to the ground.

Seconds later, what would be later described as a Messerschmitt Bf 109 German fighter by RAF investigators, made an unscheduled stop at the little cottage hospital. The main fuselage of the German fighter first touched the ground just outside the hospital perimeter in a ploughed field. It exploded on impact, the force considerable and due in part to the munitions still onboard that were no doubt meant for London. The momentum of the wreckage carried it through the boundary fence as if it wasn't there. The next part of the hospital to be hit was the outbuildings. The boiler house and electrical supply were taken out as the wreckage raced forward relentlessly. Inside the main building the wards were plunged into darkness. There was more light outside now with the raging fire strewn across the hospital grounds. Sister Cunningham stumbled to her feet, the French windows shattered. She was covered in shards of glass and minor cuts. Pandemonium broke out in the ward. Patients screaming, babies woken in the far wards, she struggled to get her bearings.

"Nurse Andrews!" she called out in the darkness. "Nurse Andrews!"

"Yes sister," the voice came back from the end of the ward.

"My office now. You'll find a torch and a box of candles in the bottom drawer of the filing cabinet. Get them now," she barked, trying to restore some order. "Everyone remain calm, the danger has passed. However there is glass everywhere and I do not want any unnecessary cuts or falls through people wondering around in the darkness," she called out. In truth she expected the hospital to be busy enough after this without adding further injuries through general panic. "Nurse Andrews," Sister Cunningham called out again. The younger nurse had made it to the ward's inner door in the darkness just as her name was called a second time.

"Yes sister?"

"When you have fixed the candles I want you to get hold of someone from maintenance and get this glass cleared away, oh and some timber to keep the cold out for now," she called back.

"Yes sister." With that Nurse Andrews disappeared through the double doors into the blackened corridor beyond. A second equally large explosion caused the sister to jump back and she knew instinctively that the wreckage had hit the hospital maintenance shops behind the boiler room, where the hospital kept its emergency supplies of petrol for their ambulances. 45-gallon drums of petrol exploded and a number of acetylene gas cylinders fired out into the night sky like unguided missiles under the intense heat. She knew that it was a building guarded 24 hours a day, 7 days a week due to the value placed on fuel during wartime and her heart went out to those security personnel no doubt caught up in the blast. Restoring some semblance of normality some twenty minutes later, patients in the nearest wards to the fire were moved immediately into corridors at the far end of the hospital. The local fire brigade and other brigades called in from different counties arrived to try and bring the fire under control as it spread from buildings to the adjacent woodland. Local police threw a cordon around the area, taking control until army personnel arrived. The explosion shook the village and was heard in the next county. Hitler had come to their little patch of tranquillity.

The explosion had woken up every patient in the hospital and for the first time since arriving there, a young mother rose from her bed, wrapped her gown around her shoulders and put her slippers on as if pre-programmed. A blue rabbit sat peeping out of her dressing gown pocket. Her face was ashen, expressionless, her eyes cold showing no awareness of what was happening around her. Without a second thought, she slowly walked toward the French windows in her room and out into the night. Whilst every available body helped to combat the aftermath of the explosion, Betty Laine was making her way to the train station, to where in her mind, she thought John would be arriving home shortly. The sudden explosion, hissing and sound of air raid sirens had taken her back to when she had last said goodbye to her husband. It was John's time to come home again and she would be there to meet him. Somehow her mind, perhaps by pre-selection, had told her which direction to take toward the station. It was Tuesday, July 20th 1943 and unknown to Betty, passenger trains were not scheduled to stop that day.

Her progress was steady, only interrupted by curious onlookers who, unlike her, were heading toward the fire to lend a hand. Her nightclothes were enough to cause at least a few raised eyebrows. She walked up the steep hill oblivious to her surroundings, skirting around the perimeter of the park and back down toward the little railway station in the near distance. She cornered white rockery stones, which edged the lawn at the front of the station. Her eyes never altered their stare at any time. Only her smile became wider as she neared her goal. Blonde curls, long and loose, hung about her shoulders. She climbed the steps up to the station platform and walked between the two deserted ticket booths. The office, waiting room and platform were all empty. Undeterred, she marched on relentlessly along the platform expecting the train at any moment. The 10pm haulage train carrying tonnes of much-needed coal for the war effort was scheduled through the station within the next fifteen minutes.

Jane woke suddenly. Secondary explosions rang out and the normally darkened bedroom was alight with a soft orange glow. She jumped out of bed reaching for her dressing gown at the foot of the bed. Through the gap in the curtains she could see the glow in the night sky beyond the little park. There was something wrong, terribly wrong. Before she could dwell on what, another explosion rocked her back on her heels before she recoiled, her hands now pressed against the panes of glass of her bedroom window. The need to maintain blackout conditions was somehow no longer important. Whatever had caused it; the origin was close to the hospital. With many other villagers, she rushed out into the night partially dressed fearing the worst.

"What more could go wrong for this couple?" she thought as she and droves of other people swarmed along the country lane toward the blaze. The scene appeared as absolute carnage. There was a smell of burning aviation fuel everywhere and general panic broke out amongst the disruption. People made human chains from the hospital to the pond on the outskirts of the park using buckets and bedpans, anything that would hold water, dousing areas where burning embers had travelled to spread the fire's death and destruction. She made it to the main entrance, ignoring the protestations of firemen, military police and the fire itself. Reaching out she caught the nurse by the shoulder.

"Excuse me, Nurse Andrews isn't it? Do you remember me? I visited Betty Laine yesterday. You were in her room at the time – I'm Jane Prentiss, her neighbour?"

"One moment please," the nurse replied. Two burly men carrying tools and large sheets of plywood had caught up with the nurse by this time and stood just behind her. "Take that wood inside to Kingston ward please and secure the broken windows in there. See Sister Cunningham if you are in any doubt." With that she pointed toward the main entrance and the workmen disappeared inside.

"I'm sorry," the nurse stopped and looked at Jane curiously for a few seconds, no doubt reflecting on a rather long day and the many patients and relatives that had passed through her hands, then a look of recognition. "Why yes Miss Prentiss." The nurse placed both her hands on Jane's shoulders and squeezed them gently. "Don't worry Miss Prentiss, Mrs Laine and the rest of the patients in the maternity ward were not directly affected by the explosion. They've been moved to safer areas away from that side of the hospital. They may be a little shocked, but they will be fine." The nurse's comment was good news in itself, but Jane had already surmised this from the devastation and its proximity to the maternity ward.

"Do you know where Mrs Laine may have been moved to?" Jane asked. Nurse Andrews clearly had her hands full and had no idea where Betty Laine was.

"Well I'm not sure. I've spent the last half-hour outside with the ambulance crew – I'm sorry I can't be of more help," nurse Andrews replied. A call from inside the hospital for more nursing help prompted a further apology from her before she disappeared inside and out of sight. Jane stood bewildered, unsure of what to do next.

"Excuse me, did I hear you say Betty Laine?" The voice came from a heavily built middle-aged lady with a bucket of water in one hand and a broom in the other. Her pale skirt and matching blouse were now covered in thick soot. Her sleeves were rolled up over her elbows and her size of frame was not helping her cause as she moved awkwardly. She seemed to lose more and more of the water as she moved from side-to-side. The broom was used for beating out smaller fires. Now she was content just to put the bucket down and lean on her broom while she took a breather.

"My daughter gave birth at the same time as Mrs Laine. I've never met her you understand because she was so ill, but I am aware of whom you are talking about. I've just seen her heading down the road, out of the village. I didn't realise that she was better although she did look in a world of her own and she didn't seem to react when I spoke to her. She will catch her death dressed like that." The older lady spoke as if she had to get all the information out in one breath.

"Thank you!" Jane snapped, before hurrying away from the hospital in that general direction. She passed scores of people running toward the hospital until she came to a crossroad.

"Oh bother," she said. "Which direction would she have taken?" An aircraft warden caught sight of her as he carried out his duties.

"Evening Miss. Are you lost?" he queried. "You're the second person I've seen tonight heading off in the wrong direction," He gestured back toward the raging fire beyond them. "At least you're better dressed Miss."

"What did you say?" Jane asked, the last few words grabbing her attention.

"Err you're better dressed – coat and shoes. The other girl was in her night cloths and slippers." Jane pondered again as if collecting her thoughts.

"It had to be Betty," she said to herself. "Which way did she go?" Jane insisted.

"Who?" The warden's attention had moved back toward the orange glow a mile or so away."

"The woman in the night clothes?" Jane asked, her impatience-gathering pace.

He pointed up the lane in the distance. "Up there Miss, toward the railway station."

"But, it's closed," Jane said out loud. "What on earth is she…oh God no!" she called out. The warden watched Jane make her way towards the railway station, puzzled by the action of both women in quick succession. She reached the station entrance and paused, breathless, holding on to the signpost depicting the station's name. Most of the village was at the fire by now and she could hear the commotion in the distance. The sound of the approaching freight train caused her to spring forward and she climbed the few steps up to the ticket office entrance. She froze when she saw that the chain between the two ticket booths had been removed.

Staggering out onto the platform, she gasped for air again, her chest heaving, grabbing hold of one of the cast iron canopy supports, and cursing her poor fitness. She looked left first, then right. At first Jane couldn't make out what she was seeing. Whoever it was was on all fours reaching out for something hidden from Jane's line of sight. Then another gust of wind from the oncoming train out of the tunnel caught the unseen object and it bobbled into view. The figure, still on all fours, turned and followed, now at ninety degrees to Jane's line of sight. Jane could tell that it was Betty, crawling like a baby. Each time she had the little blue rabbit within her grasp it seemed to move again just out of reach, as if tied to

In The Mood

an invisible wire, pulled by an unseen tormentor. Now it sat upright on the edge of the platform and Betty was oblivious to the danger.

"Betty," Jane shouted, her voice no competition for the piercing whistle coming from the black tunnel. She began to run toward Betty, but it was no use, the train was already thundering out of the tunnel drowning out any further warnings that Jane shouted. Betty finally grabbed the little soft toy, a smile broadening across her face as she did.

"I've got him John, I've got him." She whispered to herself as she pulled it to her neck where it nestled, just as the train thundered toward where she crouched. Jane was still fifty yards away when the suction from the train as it roared passed pulled both mother and rabbit beneath its wheels.

Jane cried out in horror, falling to her knees. "No! What about your babies? What about John?"

3

The late Jim Stevens

It was a bright sunny late October morning. The sky was blue and clear with only a few fluffy white clouds far off on the horizon. The air was crisp and a light frost covered adjacent fields and trees alongside Willenbury Bypass.

Only the road itself appeared untouched due to the salting from the night before. The fresh autumnal air breezed in filling the cab of long-distance lorry driver, Jim Stevens. It was a welcome relief as he drove down the A413. He had been feeling a little queasy all morning. First it was a touch of indigestion, followed by a dizzy spell as he was tying down his load back at the depot. He put it down to his usual early morning fry-ups and overworking doing double shifts – one shift officially with his employer, the second a spot of moonlighting with a local security firm. Money was tight at the moment since his wife had been made redundant. Margaret Thatcher's second term in office some eighteen months earlier had effectively closed the local car factory where she worked, so every penny counted. The pains and dizziness were getting worse though. Even he had to admit that. Joyce had wanted him to give up his second job, even begged him at one point when the pains put him in hospital, but he had got used to the extra money.

"Maybe next month," he said to himself, as he had done countless times before. "I'll get some more pills from the quack in the meantime." He winced once more, holding his chest, the sudden movement causing the long and heavily laden trailer to stray sideways. A car blurred out its horn and not for the first time that morning, the long thirty foot trailer strayed from the inside lane out toward passing cars.

"Kiss my arse," he growled through the window at the offending driver, then blurred out his air horn, holding it down for several seconds. A twinge across his chest ensured that he let go soon enough and he rubbed it again vigorously, it becoming the object of his cursing now. The HGV swerved once more as he corrected its position, the movement exaggerated due to the load of steel girders, meandering like the tail of a rattlesnake. Other cars joined in with their chorus of disapproval, some choosing to hang back in trepidation. This time he chose to wind down his window further and offered a hand signal that you wouldn't find in the Highway Code. Again the exertion influenced the huge trailer once more and this time it wasn't about to recover easily. Both wizened hands gripped the huge steering wheel pulling hard, the face of the driver beginning to turn red with the effort.

Traffic was slowing up ahead as more traffic entered Willenbury Bypass at junction 2. Several cars were already anticipating the danger posed by the erratic heavy goods vehicle and had pulled smartly on to the hard-shoulder creating a lane for the now wayward HGV as it ploughed on. A number of cars were buffeted, some swatted like flies, their bodywork crumpled like tissue paper and tossed on to the adjacent roadside verge and central reserve. A reduction in the speed of the HGV was barely noticeable, its momentum contributed to in no small part by its load. The steering wheel itself moved from side to side of its own volition with involuntary spasms. Leaning on the door slumped with his face against the window was the lifeless face of Jim Stevens. What he perceived to be mild indigestion was the early onset of heart failure. Whether his altercation with other drivers had finally pushed him over the edge would never be known. By some stroke of good fortune, the huge HGV seemed to steer itself between stationary queuing cars down the slip road until it left the road at an awkward angle launching itself toward the traffic light junction below the bypass. Again, the lights turned to red at the most opportune moment and traffic stopped just before the HGV came thundering across the junction.

In The Mood

The bang that followed was heard five miles away, it was later reported, by school children gathering for morning assembly. The HGV's diesel tank ruptured and ignited on impact, the ensuing fire engulfing the driver's cab, which sat directly above it. What was left of the cab was now wrapped around one of the bridge columns and unrecognisable. The load of steel girders en route to a local development snapped their harnesses, their own momentum carrying some forward and some sideways. A 15-foot main span girder simply carried on travelling passing through the mangled cab, ignoring the fire that was now raging there hitting the bridge column head-on like a battering ram.

Drivers from nearby cars raced across the road only to be beaten back by the intense heat from the blaze. Some sat in shock watching the nightmare as if it was a film on TV. In the distance the wailing of emergency services were already alerted to the situation and were struggling to find a way through the early morning rush hour traffic. Cars pulled to the left or right to allow police, ambulance and fire brigade through parting like Moses with the red sea. Traffic police were among the first of the emergency services on the scene cordoning off the area, effectively closing the road below the bridge, it now becoming a potential crime scene. Firemen mobilised their hoses using water supplies from their machines whilst others looked in the immediate vicinity for connections into the local water system for additional supplies. Ambulance crews moved between stationary cars starting with those most badly injured before moving on to those suffering the aftermath of shock.

Four fire engines trained their hoses on the blazing cab. Large clouds of steam hissed back at them as the cold water met the red-hot twisted metal until the fire, slowly vanquished, was brought under control. A steady stream of people were being escorted from the scene in what was now a constant convoy of ambulances and medical related transport commandeered as soon as the scale of the accident had been confirmed. Fortunately, preliminary reports would show later that no one other than the HGV driver was killed due to the way the driver had apparently kept control of his vehicle – or so scene of crime investigators thought at the time. The emergency was far from over though. Fire Chief Stedman's assessment of the situation rendered the bridge structurally unsafe and county engineers were quickly engaged to confirm or deny Stedman's observations. Willenbury Bypass was immediately closed in the meantime. Traffic was steadily directed on to diversion routes and it was hours later before traffic queues subsided and the accident site was left for forensic examination. It was only when the cab and debris were cleared that all operations were stopped and CID murder detectives were called in.

4

Mind games

"If it's the last thing I do, I'll nail that bastard!" Philip Graves tightened his grip around the steering wheel of his racing green MG BGT as he entered Delamere Road. He slammed the gear stick into third accelerating forward to where he was late for an appointment with his old friend, Giles Prenton-Smythe. Sleep deprivation over the last few days was catching up with him making driving hazardous at best. He blinked feverishly through rainwater as it cascaded down the windscreen, his attention caught momentarily by the rear view mirror, which now reflected his gaunt features. Bloodshot eyes with darkened hollows stared back at him belonging to a face he hardly recognised. His normally clean-shaven face now sported at least three days' growth. His hair was collar length, much longer than normal. Grey curls fell down across his forehead and he tried in vain to sweep them back as he freed one hand from the steering wheel. He felt like shit, he thought, and he certainly looked like it. The sound of raindrops splattered heavily on the canvas roof pushing surplus amounts of rainwater that had gathered there over onto the windscreen. He put his thoughts of Adam Gray, the subject of his cursing, to one side, trying to concentrate on the parked cars that flanked both sides of the road. He wiped the windscreen vigorously with his handkerchief to clear the condensation and recognised Smythe's office on the brow of the road up ahead.

He was unsure now on reflection what he expected or wanted from Smythe, even though he had requested the meeting. He couldn't turn to the Met for help, even though it catered for such needs. No, he decided that it would send too many tongues wagging and harm his career irrevocably, although it had occurred to him that that might have happened already. Discretion was needed and his old friend Smythe could provide that he was certain. The main hurdle had always been admitting that he had a problem to himself. At first he denied it to others around him and then more importantly to himself – then the nightmares began. He needed help, possibly psychiatric help, and fast. His initial self-denial that he needed help, his increasingly hostile behaviour and obsessive loathing for Chief Superintendent Gray had eventually earned him a suspension. During the few weeks that followed he began to analyse his bizarre behaviour himself eventually deciding to talk to a psychiatrist, one he could trust and one divorced from the Met and Gray's influence.

"Are you going mad?" he said out loud at his reflection in the mirror. "Is Gray worth it? Is he really even at fault here?" he paused as if not wanting to contemplate his next thought. "Am I at fault for what happened to Tony? Is that what the nightmare is telling me?"

The thought stayed with him for a few seconds before his attention was diverted back to the road ahead by a Border Collie appearing from between rows of parked cars. It yelped startled retreating back from where it came as Graves hit the brakes hard causing the sports car to aquaplane dangerously close to the canine visitor. The dog scampered away through the rain none the worse for the near miss, but Graves froze, visibly shaking, the car now stationary, his hands trembling as he let go of the steering wheel. He watched the dog disappear behind a garden wall in the distance and for once he envied its uncomplicated existence. A car horn from behind him brought him back to reality and he pulled away once more completing the last 500 yards or so of his journey.

Graves had only seen Smythe a handful of times since the pair had relocated to London with their respective careers. The very last time was at his father's retirement party. The thought of his estranged father and his suspension from the Met at that moment only heightened his resolve to get to the truth behind Operation Wharf. If anyone could help him now without attracting any further attention of London's Metropolitan Police force it was Smythe.

He brought the sports car to a gradual stop, parking just outside the main entrance to Talbot House. Grabbing his raincoat from the back seat, he launched his leaner than usual 6'2" frame toward the front door, sluggishly skipping through puddles of water, using a copy of *The Times* newspaper to divert any more rain from his head. A portly looking concierge dressed in a long, blue double-breasted coat and a matching coloured hat met him as he climbed the steps. The peak on the concierge's hat was pulled down so that it sat almost on the bridge of his nose. He looked Graves up and down initially, no doubt choosing his words carefully.

"Sorry sir, you'll have to move that," the concierge said. Only his eyes, just visible beneath the peak, seemed to move indicating toward the MG. Graves flashed his warrant card without a response. "Oh," the concierge reacted understandingly, stepping to one side. Graves was in no mood for a little Hitler. Gray was bad enough and he had no time for cheap facsimiles. Five minutes later he was inside the plush offices of Dr Giles Prenton-Smythe DHP, DCH, FICH. Melissa, Smythe's delightful secretary, announced his arrival showing him through into Smythe's office.

The genial face of Smythe smiled back at Graves as he entered the room and for a second Graves could see a brief look of shock in those pale blue eyes. Perhaps his demeanour warranted a shocked reaction, he wondered. Smythe quickly corrected himself as he became conscious of Graves's disconcerting stare.

"Well Phil it's good to see you. How long has it been since we were in the same company – at least a year?" Smythe said answering his own question. "You are looking well. Did you find the place all right?" He smiled at Graves, his hand outstretched which Graves took and they shook briefly. Dressed in a Savile Row suit set against his tanned, lean frame and slightly greying hair, Smythe looked more like a man at least ten years younger than his age, rather than his guest who if anything looked much older. Graves folded his raincoat and dropped it on to the nearest chair, while Smythe propped himself against an ornately carved antique Chippendale desk, surveying his own success like a peacock preening its feathers.

Life had treated Smythe very well over the last ten years since he qualified as a psychiatrist in 1975, much better than it had his old school and university chum Philip Graves, an opinion that was solidifying more and more with Graves as he took an impromptu tour of Smythe's office. It had nothing to do with recent events with his partner, Tony McDowell and Gray, just a fact of life when it came to public and private sector employment. The opulent office denoting the modern successful and professional man, took graves aback, as he tried to curb his personal frustration. It had certainly changed since his last visit. The only thing that gave away the fact that the room was a psychiatrist's private consulting room was the couch, positioned within the one and only window in the room, a bay window full-height and big enough to take the couch. On a smaller side table, next to the couch, sat a tape recorder and a notepad in readiness for the next consultation.

"Giles," Graves managed, "stop humouring me. I look as rough as a bear's arse. Oh and I did find your office easily, after all I am a detective." Graves continued to walk around the room, his eyes never focusing once on his host, but on the tasteful décor of the room.

"I obviously made the wrong career choice at university," Graves said, briefly stopping, his eyes taking in every potted palm tree, bookcase and thick shag pile carpet. His eyes focused on some rather expensive looking prints of England's south coast shoreline. He adjusted the frame of one of the pictures slightly, whist noticing the reflection of Smythe behind him in the plated glass.

"Henry Moore I think?" Graves said without turning to address Smythe.

"Why yes Phil. Are you familiar with his work?" Smythe asked quietly surprised by Grave's knowledge of seascapes.

Graves ignored the question, letting his frustration get the better of him. "While I'm risking my neck defending the general public for a pittance, like a good public servant you've been raking in ten times as much if your office is anything to go by. Not fucking bad for listening to sad, weak-minded, more-money-than-sense patients," Graves turned as he spoke his features remaining unchanged. The ever-present smile on Smythe's face receded slowly. It had been a little under twelve months in fact since the two men had shared a conversation in the flesh, but even so there was something in Graves's whole body language that suggested something deeper than their respective career choices was bothering him. Even at school Philip Graves only ever became obnoxious, bordering on insulting, when he needed help or advice. He didn't like asking for either as Smythe recalled so whatever had brought him here this wet October afternoon must be important and obviously against Grave's usual inclination. Smythe watched Graves as he moved toward the settee at the centre of the room.

"Stop analysing me Giles," Graves blurted out, conscious of Smythe's now quiet observation. He sank into the soft leather, resting the back of his head against its brow. The coolness of the leather was a welcome relief to the tension building across the base of his neck. "Do you remember at university when you needed guinea pigs for your psychology thesis?" Graves asked. Smythe nodded. "You had a way about you designed to put them at their ease – just like the look on your face now," Graves added, finally managing a smile, remembering that he was there to get help from Smythe, rather than persecute him. Smythe grinned back thankful to see more of his old friend once more. Walking around the other side of his desk, he retrieved two tumblers and a bottle of single Irish malt from one of the drawers.

"Neat as I remember?" Smythe asked, waving the bottle at him. Graves nodded. Smythe sat in the armchair opposite placing both drinks on the marble coffee table between them. "You're not here to admire my office Phil. Nor do I believe that you are here to challenge the fees I charge, even if you think I'm making a killing," Smythe said casually, crossing his legs. "On the telephone you seemed agitated, angry despite my agreeing to invite you over at short notice. I conjured up an image in my mind during our telephone conversation and that image became lifelike the minute you walked into my office so why don't you tell me why you are really here Phil?" Smythe probed, sipping his whiskey. He relaxed back into his chair balancing his glass on the chair arm. Graves looked at Smythe the defiance almost visibly draining from his face. He took a long drink before speaking.

"Tell me Giles, what do you know about nightmares?" Smythe stared back at Graves intently before smiling pleasantly the way he always did with his patients to put them at their ease.

"Well it's not my speciality really," he replied almost evasively. Graves stared back at him unflinchingly. "Well," Smythe said furtively, "dreams or nightmares, as I am sure that they can appear to be to some people, are products of the human psyche, a facet of the mind and personality. They are very rarely a literal representation of a person's thought processes or experiences, rather they are more symbolic," Smythe explained.

"You will have to break that down into plain English Giles, I'm just a simple copper," Graves replied bemused.

"Very well," Smythe said contemplating a scenario in his head, "let's say, hypothetically, that your nightmare involves you speeding in a car along a country lane, your speed increasing all the time. You want to slow down, but something is stopping you. Inevitably, you lose control and that is when you wake from your nightmare," Smythe gesticulated with his hands as he stood now and moved about the room. He paused before a bookcase, retrieving a well-thumbed reference book from the top shelf. Flicking through several pages he found what he was looking for.

"The interpretation of this dream may well be that you are, shall we say, burning the candle at both ends, metaphorically speaking. In other words, you are living your life too fast and you need to slow down, possibly for the sake of your health. It could be your body, mind or both telling you to slow down and relax more," he continued.

"I wish my nightmare was that simple a translation." Graves replied. "What about recurring nightmares?" This time Smythe stopped pacing, a non-committal look played across his face before he glanced at his watch casually, placing the book back in its place. He turned to where he had left his cigarette burning in the ashtray on his desk.

"The more frequent the nightmare the more acute the anxiety I would say," he replied drawing on the last half-inch of his Embassy Regal. He watched Graves fidget as he took in the last comment. Checking his watch again discreetly he sighed inwardly resigned to having an unexpected consultation. "Oh well, the afternoon's rain would make a decent round of golf impossible anyway," he said to himself. Lifting the telephone on his desk, he waited a few seconds.

"Melissa, I don't want to be disturbed for an hour, so hold all my calls please?" Replacing the receiver, he turned back to face Graves, as he sat back in his chair.

"Describe your nightmare Phil," Smythe asked. Graves was visibly appreciative.

"It always starts the same way. I'm somewhere dark, there is an unpleasant odour and I'm going down, down somewhere," Graves muttered, looking into his whiskey glass. "There isn't anything discernable, no shapes just shadows amongst the darkness." Smythe decided in his own mind to take things one step at a time.

"What can you smell during your nightmare Phil?"

"Dampness, urine, decay, rotting food – all mixed into one sickening smell," he replied. "It feels cold or perhaps it's just the thought of the smell and dampness and the places you would associate with it?" he took a drink from his glass as if to drive the coldness away and shivered as the whiskey made its way down the back of his throat. "At this point I always recall hearing voices. Something compels me to find out whom they belong to. I don't want to, but it feels like an invisible force is pulling me forward. I never quite recognise the voice and yet I know it. I seem to get just to that point and then…" Graves hesitated. Smythe cocked his head to one side expectantly.

"Suddenly the darkness is replaced by a blinding white light. I still can't see anything because the light is so intense. Strangely, I'm not cold any more. The voice, a single voice, now comes from the light and it's screaming at me. I always wake up shortly after."

"And how frequently do you have this nightmare?" Smythe inquired.

Graves sighed wearily. "Every night now for the last six months on-and-off."

"So since that unfortunate incident involving your ex-partner?" Smythe replied cautiously, unsure of the reaction he would get. The death of Tony McDowell had never been mentioned since their conversation had begun and yet…then the realisation hit Graves.

"I had heard that you severed your links with the Yard about the time we last met Giles – obviously not?" Graves said indignantly. He was more annoyed at his own sloppiness in truth. "I take it you still hold a commission with the Yard?"

Smythe gave a resigned look. "You're right, the Yard dispensed with my services a year ago, but I occasionally get called in for the odd consultation," Smythe admitted. Smythe had established himself over the last two years as one of New Scotland Yard's private psychiatrists. Work was sporadic and often interfered with his daily practice, but it was worth the effort and a useful addition to his portfolio when drawing in new clients.

"Then you probably know about my little disagreement with Adam Gray?" Graves continued. Smythe stood and walked to where his cigarettes and lighter lay. He offered one to Graves, but he declined. Tapping the box with the filter end, he walked around the screen to where his couch stood considering it for a moment. Turning back to look at Graves he gave an understanding look. Before Smythe could respond the full implication of what Graves had said began to sink in. "And you know about my breakdown?"

"I meant to call you Phil, really, I just never got around to it. I was hearing rumours of a speedy recovery and before long you were back at your post. I thought about giving you some space and seeing you later. One month led to another then I heard stories of a relapse. You were acting oddly, hardly sleeping. You had a conspiracy theory about McDowell's death and it involved Gray. I have to say that the Yard appears to have been supportive throughout. You were offered sick leave only it led to confrontations with senior officers even higher up than Gray. I believe you were suspended to help you try and get yourself together Phil, mainly because you wouldn't take the sick leave that was on offer. You refused to seek medical or psychiatric help, both of which are standard procedure after the trauma you suffered following McDowell's death. When I got your telephone call after months of not hearing from you I suspected that there was a connection." He lit the cigarette and took a long draw on it, blowing the smoke out toward the partially open bay window.

"I was asked to see you as a patient by Gray. I declined the offer though. I said I was too busy," Smythe continued with a conciliatory comment. Graves lifted his head angrily. Smythe anticipated the reaction and was already on the offensive. "He isn't aware that we know each other. I'm not producing a report on you after this session and this is not a fit-up. You called me remember?" Smythe pointed out coolly, realising what was going through Graves's mind. Graves drained his glass unsure what to believe or think anymore. He offered no comment either way.

"What happened Phil? How and why did you manage to piss your superior off so much to earn yourself a suspension?" Smythe asked. He tapped the spent ash into the ashtray on the coffee table. He knew of course. He just wanted Graves to explain matters in his own words.

"That's where you come in," Graves replied. Smythe frowned. "I want you to hypnotise me Giles. I want to know what really happened that night when Tony McDowell died?" Graves announced. Smythe smiled until he realised that Graves was serious.

"Come on Giles, it's what the Yard wanted – me to see a shrink," he added.

"It's hardly what they had in mind Phil and certainly not something I get too involved with these days," Smythe replied trying to distance himself from the suggestion.

"Unlike your university days then?" Graves interjected.

"The thing about hypnotism Phil is it may unearth truths that could shatter your beliefs and make matters much worse for you," Smythe volunteered.

"I take it you're referring to Tony McDowell's death, that maybe it was my fault?" Graves replied sternly.

"No not necessarily, but you are not entirely sure about what happened yourself that night or you wouldn't want me to hypnotise you." Smythe reminded him.

"It's a risk I'm willing to take, if only to rid myself of this nightmare," Graves said thoughtfully.

"The death of your partner and your nightmare may not necessarily be connected." Smythe pointed out.

"What have I got to lose other than my sanity if I do nothing?" Graves said shrugging his shoulders.

"OK," Smythe said acceptance, in his tone. I know something of what happened through hearsay mostly. Why don't you tell me in your own words?"

Graves looked at Smythe cautiously. He had to trust his old friend, he'd known that all along. Smythe's continued involvement with the Met though placed a different complexion on things.

"I work with the Serious and Organised Crime Squad based at New Scotland Yard, mainly dealing with Class A drug seizures coming into London," Graves explained. "I was involved in an undercover sting operation over a two year period. It was a combined European operation involving many forces including Interpol. The operation was so secretive it only involved four people from inside the squad. It concerned the largest shipment of heroin that the country has ever been subjected to," Graves explained.

"A very short chain of command," Smythe said.

"At the time it was just a means of keeping the chain of command and the Met's general involvement as short as possible to protect Tony's cover story. Tony was our man on the inside and I was his contact and liaison with the Yard. Gray had overall command on day-to-day operations whilst Assistant Chief Constable Waring sanctioned the operation and was dealing with his counterparts in Europe strategically getting the most out of the operation. Months of preparation had resulted in matters being brought to a head one night six months ago at Canary Wharf on the Isle of Dogs. On the night of the operation senior officers were selected and briefed on what to expect." Graves began to fidget again, agitated at the memory. Smythe looked at him intently, willing him to continue.

"Tony had learned when the next shipment was due. We had a bonus as well, which was one of the main reasons behind the decision to act that night and bring our operation to an end. It would be the first time that buyer and supplier would be found in the same building during the exchange of drugs and money. There was some disagreement about how the heroin had been cut. The quality was much lower than the price would suggest and so they had decided to meet and test the sample together on the night of the exchange. Risky on their part, but a necessity according to Tony." Graves became solemn as he retraced his memory. "It all went wrong somehow. They found out about Tony and…" he hesitated briefly," they tortured him. I will never forget his screams Giles, just like screams in my dreams," he commented. "There has to be a connection. We were supposed to have backup, an armed response unit that Gray was tasked with supplying, but it never arrived," Graves almost spat the words out and then he seemed to retrace his thoughts.

"No that isn't strictly true, they turned up at the wrong warehouse and scared the shit out of two tramps sleeping rough. I tried to reach Tony," he was wringing both hands now feverishly, reliving the memory, "but the bastards had set fire to the building. It went up in flames in a matter of minutes then the roof collapsed. I only just got clear myself staggering through a side door that I forced open in a blind panic. I had a few minor burns and smoke inhalation as I fell into the Thames," Graves concluded, his hands covering his face as he shook uncontrollably.

"I can understand why you feel guilty Phil, that's a natural reaction. Is Gray at fault here though?" Smythe probed. Pulling his hands clear, Graves looked at him incredulously. Smythe held out a placating hand.

"I'm just getting matters clear in my mind Phil, as a neutral observer you understand? I have no axe to grind here," he said. There was an uneasy silence as both men considered the implications.

"What do you hope to gain by this Phil? Your friend is gone, sad as it is I know," Smythe continued.

"Justice at the very least – justice for Tony's wife and daughter. Exposure of the 'old boys' network that exists between senior officers at the Yard when cock-ups occur."

Graves rubbed both eyes vigorously. "Oh I don't know, I'm not really sure anymore. I just know that it isn't right." Graves had subconsciously moved forward to the edge of his seat.

"You just reminded me of your father there for a moment," Smythe said cocking his head slightly to one side again as if the comment was to inject some much-needed light-heartedness into their conversation. Instead Graves took on a defensive posture, his eyes glaring back at Smythe at the mention of his estranged father.

"Oh," Smythe managed holding both hands up apologetically this time, as he stood, now conscious of the rift that obviously still existed between father and son.

"What does 'Oh' actually mean?" Graves asked defensively.

"Nothing Phil. I perhaps foolishly thought you had patched things up with your old man since we last spoke. Judging by your reaction maybe not?" Smythe pulled out another cigarette patting his waistcoat pocket for his elusive lighter.

Reginald and Philip Graves were never really close like a father and son. Reginald brought his son up as any caring father should, but there was a bond missing between the two, one that should have existed from birth and evolved with time, quality time spent with each other through a child's formative years. They never played sports together or shared the same interests other than the police in later life. Even that joint interest was short-lived. Unlike his relationship with his mother, which was close and affectionate, his father was more distant as if resentful of the mother and son bond. It was something he'd only become aware of, as he became an older teenager. By this time their relationship was already strained and distant. On the odd occasion that they were in the same company it was easier to stay quiet and put up with the ritual before slipping away, back to his flat in London. His mother was always there though acting as an emotional buffer between both the men in her life.

In later years as his career took off with the Met they saw less and less of each other. In a way it suited them both. His father had his mother's attention back and Philip Graves was free to pursue a more exciting career in London's Metropolitan Police Force. He didn't resent his father he just found it difficult to talk to him. He became more of an acquaintance over the years that followed than a father and yet he was his father. Some sort of bond existed, but it was getting finer as each year rolled by. Philip had joined his father in the force from school as a young trainee constable in their hometown. It was one of the few things that father and son shared with a passion over the coming years until young Graves decided that uniform work wasn't for him. He needed something more challenging than plodding the streets. It wasn't that his father objected he just felt that his son was running before he could walk. Ambition was something that Graves senior had never pursued too forcefully himself in the past, but his son was a different matter. He had the ability to climb the ranks, but all in good time.

Graves junior passed his sergeant's exams in 1968 whilst working in the local CID. Still not Content with his progress, his limited experience and colloquial ways of a backwater town, his ultimate goal had been to join

London's Metropolitan Police Force at New Scotland Yard, which he did having passed his Inspector's exams in 1975. He was transferred a few years later to the Serious and Organised Crime Division of the Yard, at the same time leaving the family home. Philip had said that it was time for him to find a place of his own, after all he could afford it and job relocation demanded it and in truth the daily atmosphere between father and son was getting steadily worse. It all just sort of happened with his transfer to New Scotland Yard. Smythe had followed him quite by chance soon after to work as a junior consultant in a practice in Harley Street.

Of course Graves senior took the issue personally, an affront to his role as father, mentor and role model. The physical distance between the pair only helped to emphasize the emotional split that already existed. His mum was a different story. Fiercely protective, proud and supportive of her son in all of his endeavours, perhaps at the expense of her own relationship with her husband. No doubt another cause in the rift between father and son. There had always been fierce competition for the affections of wife and mother. During the last ten years his mum had visited his flat twice a year alone. The only time the family got together regularly was at Christmas at the family cottage. Even then the atmosphere was always strained, the event nothing more than a ritual lasting three days at the most.

Smythe stood upright and then paced slowly toward the couch and stood looking out of the bay window. His thoughts centred on hypnosis as a reliable technique for Graves's purposes. Hypnotism was something he initially

In The Mood

got involved in at university as a party trick, then as a means of generating extra cash for people wanting to give up smoking or lose a stutter or weight. As his consultancy had flourished with more mainstream psychiatry and with the advent of hypnotism becoming more showbiz orientated, Smythe decided to distance himself from such practices. Graves on the other hand was well aware of Smythe's past achievements and latent abilities.

"There is no guarantee that I could bring this nightmare business to a satisfactory conclusion Phil and even if I could it would take time, certainly more than one session," Smythe suggested trying in vain to put Graves off the idea. Graves rose from his chair and walked slowly toward where Smythe was standing. He pulled the Venetian blinds closed without being invited, turning back to Smythe as he did.

"Well I'm in no hurry following my suspension Giles and I have nothing to lose, other than my career and my mind if I don't come up with any answers."

"You may not like what I find Phil." Smythe warned him again.

"Anything is better than this Giles. I need to know. I need to prove what I know, that Gray is guilty of gross negligence," he stopped momentarily, "and I also need to stop this nightmare one way or the other."

"And what about your role in your friend's death Phil? Are you ready for what the truth might be? Maybe the guilt you are feeling is down to your involvement or actions, rather than Gray?" Smythe asked tentatively. It was a thought that Graves had pushed to the back of his mind since his nervous breakdown six months earlier.

Even so he knew Smythe could be right. Lying down on the couch he relaxed and breathed steadily and evenly.

"I understand what you're saying Giles, but my mind is made up, I need to know," Graves replied looking directly at the ceiling. Smythe looked at him understandingly.

"Okay Phil, let's see what we can find out then."

5

Out of arm's reach

Chief Inspector Jim Chambers paused outside the door of Julia Goldsmith's office, secretary to Chamber's boss, Chief Superintendent Adam Gray. His eyes focused on the brass nameplate in front of him, adjusting his tie and shirt collar in the reflection. He let his mind dwell briefly on past events over the last six months, culminating in this meeting today.

"Well Chambers," he said in hushed tones, "you wanted the job at any price and you got it. Whether the powers that be saw you coming is of no consequence now. You've made your bed…" Despite the combined mood of self-pity and defiance, he was still filled with a sense of foreboding. He had been dragged into an argument – one that was fast becoming very public and potentially very damaging to his career. He was fast regretting his promotion and his subsequent transfer to New Scotland Yard's Serious and Organised Crime Squad. Yes he was aware of the circumstances of his appointment to replace Tony McDowell, but not the issues surrounding McDowell's death and certainly not the public scenes and outbursts between Gray and Chamber's newly suspended Inspector, Philip Graves. The job advert had been conveniently light on those details. The poison chalice had been offered to Chambers and he had accepted it, albeit unknowingly.

Operation Wharf had happened just before Chambers arrived on the scene, a fact that seemed to escape senior management at the Yard. He had spent his time since as referee keeping the peace between Graves and Gray, neither of them enjoying his loyalty exclusively.

"You could say that I am caught between a rock and a hard place," he muttered again lowly, his breath steaming over the nameplate. He looked around secretively up and down the corridor as if his comment might have been overheard. He had no wish to be here and there was no real reason why he should be as far as he was concerned. Gray wanted to distance himself from Graves and as Grave's superior officer Chambers had to administer Gray's will, whilst trying to act fairly. He didn't know how much truth there was in Grave's accusations.

"Perhaps Gray was drinking excessively six months ago? Maybe Gray had been negligent in his duties? If he was, there was no evidence now," he said to himself.

"Either way, Gray had yet to be reprimanded and the more time slipped by the less likely it was that he would be." Chambers raised his clenched fist to the door panel and thought again.

"Maybe Graves was still suffering from depression after McDowell's death and the part he may have played or thought he had played? Who knows?" With that thought in his mind he tapped the large oak panelled door. The two men were on a collision course though and Chambers was the man tasked with keeping the peace until Gray's imminent retirement in three months' time. Even if Gray were negligent, in three months he would be gone along with any dirty linen surrounding Operation Wharf, as long as Graves could be kept quiet. His stomach churned once more at the challenge as he passed through the door.

"Morning Jim," came the stern greeting from across the long, narrow room. The obvious lack of warmth in the welcome made him groan inwardly. At the far end, the owner of that greeting, Julia Goldsmith, busily hit the keys of her typewriter. The distant fragrance of Chanel N°5 filled the room, a scent that Julia was noted for wearing by a number of officers, usually after the Christmas party. Its fragrance intensified as Chambers made his way toward her. She looked over the glasses on the end of her nose at him. It was a tried and tested technique that she used to impose authority on any unwary guest – a sort of first-line of defence before entering Superintendent Gray's office, only Chambers knew her too well by now. He walked toward her, passing the adjoining door into Gray's office, his eyes momentarily distracted, before placing his hat and raincoat on the stand beside her desk. His briefcase remained with him like a treasured possession. His mind was still preoccupied with thoughts of the day's meeting. For now, Julia would have to make do with a slight nod of the head in her general direction. After a few seconds he turned looking directly again at the door of Gray's office.

"He is in I take it?" he asked eventually, his Geordie North-east accent always an interesting contrast to that of his London colleagues. He knew full well that Gray would be. Over the last six months or so that Chambers had worked for Gray, he was always in the office on time, sometimes even when he was supposed to be on holiday regardless of Graves's claims. Gray was and as far as Chambers knew still an insomniac. A prerequisite for the post Chambers had thought with the condition becoming more acute the higher one climbed up the career ladder at the Yard, although the passing of Gray's wife five years ago no doubt played its part. It was one of the reasons Chambers had chosen not to pursue the post on Gray's retirement.

"Philip Graves is suspended, what more do you want?" She said coldly, bypassing his question. Her immaculately manicured fingernails, painted pillar box red turned the ribbon vigorously on her typewriter at the same time barely disguising her annoyance. For a few seconds he objected to her suggestion that he was a party to Grave's suspension, but he let it go.

"What makes you think I'm here to discuss Philip Graves?" Chambers replied, trying his best not to be drawn on what after all was a personal matter and very

In The Mood

sensitive to deal with. He shuffled across to one of the easy chairs between the secretary's desk and the door into Gray's office. Unbuttoning the jacket of his three-piece suit, he collapsed into the chair and allowed himself to sink into its soft upholstery. His briefcase sat prominently on his lap. His eyes never left Gray's office door throughout the conversation. He hadn't slept for eighteen hours and it was impacting on him physically and mentally. The suspension of Philip Graves was expected, but it had left Chamber's team short-staffed and he and his other officers were beginning to pay the price. She lifted a buff folder from her in-tray and allowed the loose pages to flap about as she thrust it toward him. He recognised it instantly as a personnel file, presumably Graves and requested for by Gray in advance. Chambers looked at her sheepishly.

"OK," he said quietly, "if you think Phil is being treated harshly, who do you think is at fault here between him and Superintendent Gray – off the record of course?" He kept his voice low and barely audible, conscious that Gray sat only several feet away behind the closed door. For the first time since knowing her, Julia appeared a little ruffled and uncomfortable. More than once she opened those ruby red lips to speak only for them to fall silent. Instead she chose to tap her front teeth with her pencil as if toying with the question in her mind. "Come on Julia," Chambers insisted still quietly, but with more urgency in his voice. "Fair's fair, you've been at the Yard for, oh, five years I'd say from what I have been told."

"Six years," she corrected him.

"Alright six years then. You've been Gray's personal secretary for two of those years and you have known Graves socially and professionally for most of those six years. I expect that you are loyal to both for different reasons." She looked at him accusingly, yet kept silent. "Perhaps you were involved in some way with Operation Wharf, albeit on the periphery?" Chambers continued, now convinced that Julia Goldsmith was hiding something of material importance. It was the last reference to Operation Wharf that seemed to unnerve her the most.

"Surely she was interviewed at the time?" Chambers asked himself, whilst focusing on the slightly agitated secretary. "What is it Julia? You know something don't you?" Chambers asked her, his voice slightly higher now as he pressed for information that he thought she had.

"Why no," she protested, her own attention now drawn back to her nail file inside her handbag. She pulled it out and busied herself determined not to make eyeball contact with Chambers. Undeterred, he leaned forward out of his chair and decided subconsciously not to press too hard just in case she chose to tell Gray later.

"Julia, the reason Phil is in trouble is because he opened his mouth without any corroborating evidence regarding his accusations. If you can help him, if you have anything that can help him would you be willing to speak up?" Chambers asked, one eye on Julia and one eye on the door into Gray's office.

In her eagerness to help her one time lover and friend, she had implied or suggested that she knew more. She had a reputation as a personal secretary to protect, and a degree of loyalty toward, her boss. Without that she would be finished career-wise.

"And what of Phil anyway?" she asked herself. She hadn't seen him in months, in fact only after that bloody drugs operation at Canary Wharf went wrong did he come looking for her to spread some dirt on her boss. "Yes that's right," she continued in her mind. With each second she was convincing herself that she had said enough. She stood pushing her chair back in one motion, revealing a short, tight-fitting mauve skirt. The contrasting coloured blouse hung loose about the waistband. Matching mauve stiletto shoes completed the stylish fashion accessories. She pulled at the short skirt and marched across briskly toward the filing cabinets. She seemed more her old self by now and Chambers realised that he had lost the initiative. He wondered about pressing her further, but his thoughts were interrupted by the sound of the intercom on Julia's desk. The deep Glaswegian voice of Superintendent Gray resonated from the black box.

"Julia, tell DCI Chambers to join me when you have finished chatting. Both the DCI and secretary eyed each other instantly, wondering if Gray had overheard their conversation, before she rushed across to her desk.

"Very well sir," she replied, clicking the button.

"Can you give him the personnel file for Philip Graves and ask him to bring it in with him please?" The intercom clicked and fell silent again. Chambers spotted the file that Julia had shown him minutes earlier now sat prominently back in her in-tray. He waved it at the now seated secretary and carried it with him through into superintendent Gray's office.

"Morning sir," Chambers said as he entered the room, closing the door behind him.

"Come in Jim. Drop the file on my desk." Gray stood with his back to Chambers staring out through the window at the London traffic below. "One thing I will not miss when I am retired, Jim, is the traffic." He turned as he spoke and settled down behind his teak leather topped office desk. The small watering can he had been using to feed his prize Geranium was put on the adjacent filing cabinet. He stared directly at Chambers and for a second or two; Chambers was convinced that Gray had heard every word that he and Julia had been talking about.

"What is your honest opinion of Philip Graves, Jim?" Gray inquired out of the blue, his voice was cold and without emotion. His eyes briefly fixed on Chambers then changed their focus back to the file on his desk.

"As a policeman?" Chambers asked. His boss gestured affirmatively.

"Well as you know I only became the head of the team following Tony McDowell's death six months ago." Chambers stared at the man before him expecting a reaction, but Gray continued to leaf through the file quietly. "I would say he is sharp, professional and career minded – at least he was until…" His voice faltered.

"Until his DCI died during an undercover operation that Inspector Graves blames me for," Gray volunteered without lifting his eyes from the file.

"Sir, I think the events leading up to and after the death of DCI McDowell would be enough to unnerve anyone," Chambers replied in Graves's defence.

"It's not just that unfortunate incident though is it?" Gray added. He relaxed back in his chair both elbows on the chair arms, the fingers of both hands clenched together across his chest. He left the file open before him. Whatever Graves's claims, Gray's face was showing all the symptoms for someone use to drinking heavily over the years. That combined with his rather large waistline and breathlessness, no doubt abetted by his pipe smoking, hardly depicted the image of a modern, healthy, lean Metropolitan Police Force.

"I have had at least eight or nine complaints about Graves and his increasingly odd behaviour – one from a senior officer above my rank," Gray continued, his voice gaining in decibels as he spoke. "It has been a long time since I had to eat so much humble pie in one go," he growled across his desk.

"Yes sir," Chambers replied, reigning in his support for his Inspector. He had only known Graves for as long as his short reign as the current head of the team and he started to feel that his show of loyalty for his junior officer might be ill-founded. Whatever their differences, Graves's treatment of the Assistant Chief Constable's wife during a garden party designed to raise money for the police charity had hardly endeared him to senior management. Even Barbara McDowell, Tony's widow, was beginning to tire of Graves's attempt to hound Gray into oblivion. Gray leaned forward lifting his pipe from the ashtray where he had left it smouldering. He tapped the barrel on the edge of the ashtray using a dead match to scrape out the remaining ash and stale tobacco.

"Apart from the death of McDowell would you know if anything else has happened to Graves to make him change so much over the last six months? Anything recently in his private life?" Gray asked. Chambers looked at his boss curiously. Was Gray fishing and if so why? He had Graves where he wanted him, perhaps not for as long as he would have liked, but nevertheless…

"When you asked me what I thought about Philip Graves, I immediately thought of him as a policeman. I never really knew him socially," Chambers replied. "After McDowell died he took it hard by all accounts. I understand that he refused to see the force psychiatrist, but that is not unusual in itself. I can make some discreet enquiries if it might help?" Gray looked up across the open file directly at Chambers. He closed it slowly and gave out a deep sigh.

"The force is sympathetic to Graves's nervous breakdown and his troubled recovery, of that there is no doubt. Having said this, I cannot have a loose cannon at the Yard. His past psychiatric profile, which pre-dated Operation Wharf, concluded that there was something in his make-up, which made me decidedly uneasy about his role in my team – period. McDowell begged to differ, so I bowed to his opinion as Graves's commanding officer. Now I'm convinced I was right all along," Gray volunteered.

"Yet another revelation, this time about Graves that he wasn't aware of?" Chambers said to himself.

"Until he demonstrates a vast improvement in his conduct I am unofficially putting him out of arm's reach for the good of the Yard's reputation and his own," Gray continued. Chambers looked puzzled.

"Sorry sir, how do you mean 'out of arm's reach'?"

"An old friend of mine, a DCI, that I came through the ranks with owes me a favour. He is in charge of CID, which takes in the village of Willenbury and several others about an hour's drive from London. I have explained the situation to him discreetly and in confidence and he has agreed to accept Graves on a three month secondment," Gray explained.

"Willenbury? Why does that ring a bell?" Chambers said to himself. His mind drifted as he pondered his own question.

"If you are wondering why I chose a small parish in the middle of nowhere, the choice was quite deliberate. Willenbury is also where Graves's parents live, where he was born in fact and spent his youth before following his old man into the local force there. I want him to take some leave, perhaps spend some time adjusting with the local CID. If he proves himself he can return here afresh, ready to take on new challenges in his old post." Chambers wondered if it was Gray's genuine intention or whether he just wanted him out of the way until he had retired. Whether Graves was fit to return or not would be the last thing on his mind after three months, retired and back in Scotland.

"He will not like being sidelined sir. He will view it as a poor reflection on his ability as a senior officer, probably viewed as a backwards step career wise by senior staff as well," Chambers responded.

"Frankly, I don't particularly give a damn about Graves's likes or dislikes. I want him on less stressful duties in familiar surroundings with helpful faces to provide support both inside and outside the work environment. Then we can talk about his return," Gray said using his pipe as a pointer to drive home his point. An uneasy silence followed until Gray broke it. He looked hard at his junior officer.

"Now I think we're done Jim," Gray said, closing the file. "We're are in agreement aren't we? Philip Graves will revert to a spot of gardening leave for six weeks and then resume his official duties at Willenbury's CID," Gray recapped. "That should remove the stigma of a suspension. However, if he proves difficult I will extend his present suspension and make sure he stays away for the foreseeable future."

"It will leave me short-staffed sir, particularly with the recent increase in haulage hijackings and spate of armed bank robberies," Chambers protested meekly.

"I'll sort that out Jim, don't worry," Gray assured him. Just then there was a low tap on the door and Julia Goldsmith popped her head inside.

"Excuse me sir, I'm sorry to disturb you, but I have some news that may be pertinent to your discussion." Both men looked at each other then back at Julia.

"We were just finishing Julia. What is this urgent news then?" Gray asked obviously intrigued by the interruption.

"Well, I've just spoken to Philip...I mean Inspector Graves's mother. She needed to contact him urgently. Apparently, his father has been attacked and is in intensive care at the local hospital. It's quite serious and, well, she was ever so upset sir," Julia's eyes wondered as her attention switched to thoughts of how Graves would react to the news.

"Thank you Julia, be sure to pass the message on to Inspector Graves right away," Gray acknowledged. With that she disappeared back into her office pulling the door closed behind her.

"Capital!" Gray said in a rasping Scottish accent, recognising that fate had presented him with an unlikely solution. In his mind, Graves would have to return home now and take some leave to be with his mother and stricken father. He of course would represent the compassionate employer extending this leave on compassionate grounds, at the same time keeping Graves's out-of-arms reach as he had intended all along. The minute the word left his mouth he was already regretting it. He turned his gaze slowly back toward where Chambers sat. Chambers stared back at him, an incredulous look on his face.

"That didn't quite come out right," Gray was quick to correct himself. "What I meant is we both know that Graves will be against any talk of secondment back home – well now he might welcome it." Despite Gray's attempt to placate his point of view, Chambers was already beginning to suspect his motives even more and perhaps Gray's true role in Operation Wharf.

6

Under the influence

"Where are you now Philip?" Smythe's softly spoken voice pierced the hypnotised mind of Philip Graves as he lay on the psychiatrist's couch in Smythe's office. Smythe had moments earlier taken Graves back to that fateful night six months earlier. "Philip," again Smythe's voice much softer still. "Can you describe where you are to me first?" Graves furrowed brow and tightly closed eyes gave away a troubled response.

"Large," Graves managed as if checking his words first in his mind. "Large building, dark corridors. Need to find the stairs. I've got to get to Tony – he needs my help. He's been in here far too long." Smythe had already pressed the tape recorder at the start of the session. Now he hurriedly made notes annotated with his own thoughts and reaction for digesting later after the consultation.

"Why are you in the building Philip?" Smythe asked. His questions were general in nature and designed to ease his subject into a line of progressive questioning.

"To help, to help Tony. They have him," Graves answered.

"Who are they Philip?" Smythe asked.

"Men, up to no good. They will hurt Tony again, I must stop them," Graves shouted, his voice steadily rising. Smythe observed him curiously. The language Graves was using seemed out of context and a strange choice of words, but he did nothing more than note his observation at this point.

"So you are inside the building Philip. What happened next? Don't forget, you are safe, no one will harm you now," Smythe said reassuringly.

"I'm hiding behind a curtain at the top of the stairs leading to the basement. It's so dark, just the moonlight coming in through the window." Graves wiped his face with his hands. "I am sweating I am so frightened. I hear voices down inside the darkness below." The experience was obviously very real to him in this state, real enough to actually cause him to physically relive it.

"Was it Tony's voice you heard Philip?" Smythe asked, prompting Graves steadily.

Graves shook his head. "Can't tell, it's muffled, someone is crying," he winces, "crying out for help and I know that Tony is down there. I'm supposed to help him." There was a tremor in Graves's voice that Smythe had to dispel if he were to take Graves to the point where he accepted his own innocence or guilt in what happened that night.

"Everything is okay Philip, you are quite safe talking to me," Graves seemed to relax. "Now what did you do next?" Smythe pressed as much as he dare.

"I had to be brave and put the danger to the back of my mind and help Tony," Graves replied, his voice easing slightly, his breathing steadier compared to the panic from earlier.

"Where were your police colleagues at this time?" Smythe asked.

"Police colleagues," Graves replied, a perplexed expression had returned to his face.

"Yes, your fellow officers. They were assigned to your operation with you." Again Graves was silent as if he really didn't understand the question. Realising that he was in danger of losing his patient, Smythe cut short this line of questioning.

"Never mind that for now Philip. You made your way down the stairs – then what happened?"

"I walked slowly down the stairs toward the basement. The light was very dim and it took a few minutes for my eyes to adjust. There was a door at the bottom and I could see some light coming from behind it. I stopped and listened for a moment to see if there were any voices behind it and I suddenly heard another scream. The sound seemed to carry and I knew that Tony would be there. I tried the door handle and slowly opened the door," Graves answered.

"What do you see Philip?" Smythe asked, trying to take the edge off his own curiosity.

"Candles! Lots of candles lining the walls on both sides of the corridor. Some on stands, some in alcoves in the walls." Graves left leg kicks out at some unseen object.

"What have you seen Philip?" Smythe inquired.

"Rubbish, boxes and…rats. There are half eaten chicken legs and chips in the rubbish and the rats are helping themselves. I don't like rats and I wave a candle to keep them away from me. They scamper back to their hiding places. The corridor has many doors, but only the end door has the sound of voices coming from it. I can't make it out at first as I move slowly along, one eye on the rats and the other on the door. I can hear laughing now coming from behind the door, tormenting, jeering laughs. Another scream and this time I know it is Tony behind the door. I recognise his voice." Graves's body was becoming tense as if he were about to spring from the couch.

"Take it easy Philip, try and keep calm. You are amongst friends here, there is nothing to be afraid of," Smythe assured him. Graves continued without any prompting this time.

"I hit the door hard with my fists as hard as I could. The voices just get louder though. I picked something up, to hit the door with - a piece of wood. I hit it and hit it and shout through the door to let Tony go."

"And?" Smythe continued. "You are doing very well Philip, remember there is nothing to be afraid of." Smythe spoke with an assuredness in his voice that seemed to have the desired effect.

"The door opened. A man lunged forward and tried to grab me, but I was too fast. He stumbled past me into the corridor and I caught him on the back of his head with the wood. He fell along the wall before crashing into the pile of rubbish knocking over one of the candle stands. The rats run for cover back down the corridor into the darkness." Graves looked calmer at the memory. "I turn and for a brief moment I saw Tony. He was tied up and screaming through a gag tied over his mouth. Before I could react, someone behind the door slammed it shut again in my face."

"Why didn't you use your gun? You carried side arms for this operation." Smythe asked. Again and just like before the question remained unanswered. Instead Graves threw his arms across his face and grimaced. He peered through his open fingers, his eyes wide open with terror, despite the hypnosis.

"Smoke," he blurted out. "Thick black smoke, flames raging along the walls toward the ceiling. The rubbish and the man, they are alight. I hear his screams now, the man's arms waving trying to put out the fire and then he falls to the ground, his voice is quiet and he is still."

"What did you do Philip?" Smythe inquired. "Remember you are perfectly safe here, the fire can't touch you," Smythe said.

"I turned back to the door and banged on it loudly shouting, 'fire'. The shouting from inside the room just got louder like before. They either didn't hear me or didn't care," Graves replied.

"What about the fire?" Smythe asked.

In The Mood

"The fire – it's spreading quickly along the corridor. I'm trapped? No maybe if I run as fast as I can, I can jump over the burning man." Graves's animated actions emphasized what he was experiencing. "I did it but my clothes are on fire," Graves's voice was shrieking and Smythe held him firmly down on his couch. "I need to put the fire out – roll about on the floor quickly. Yes that's better, now the stairs, must get to the stairs." By this time Graves was moving erratically on the couch as if reliving every moment.

"Okay Philip, take a few deep breaths and try and calm yourself. You are in safe hands here, the fire has gone," Smythe told him. Graves took the instruction without question. His body took on a more relaxed pose now.

"Where are you now Philip?" Smythe asked.

"I, I…" Graves stammered, his face etched with frustration. "I'm in hospital," Smythe checked his watch and decided that the session should end on that note.

"Now Philip, I will count to three and click my fingers and you will awaken safe, relaxed and contented." Questions still needed answering about the organisation of the team and the backup by armed officers, but these could be done by traditional inquiry. For now, his job was to help his patient to accept that he was not to blame for the death of his partner. This would take more than one session though, Smythe was certain of that. "One, two, three," Smythe said, counting out loud. Graves's eyes immediately flickered before he opened them. He looked about him momentarily before he fully grasped where he was.

"Are you starting our session now?" Graves inquired.

"Already done old chap," Smythe replied, patting his notepad then pointing to the wall clock across the room. An hour had passed since Graves had lain down on the couch. Graves regarded the psychiatrist with a puzzled expression. Smythe smiled back at him.

"Don't worry, its quite normal for a patient under hypnosis to be unaware that a consultation has taken place after the event."

"Well," Graves announced, expecting earth shattering developments, "did you find anything out?" Graves's eyes followed the psychiatrist as he ejected the audiotape from the recorder.

"First impression and knowing very little about the case you were working on, I would say that you were deeply troubled by the death of your friend. This appears to go much deeper than anyone else probably realised so far. Graves was unimpressed and indicated as much in his reaction. "Don't rush me Phil," Smythe said. "It'll take more than one session before I get at that part of your memory we need to get access to. Suffice to say there was something odd that happened. Your mannerisms were a little peculiar to say the least."

"What do you mean?" Graves replied.

"Oh, peculiar language that you use and you seem to be avoiding certain questions about police operations on the night your partner was killed and the use of side arms," Smythe explained. Graves swivelled his legs off the couch and stared at the blinds covering the bay window.

"You may be right Giles, but how do I get Tony's cries for help out of my head and the nightmare and what about Gray?" Graves pleaded.

"It won't happen overnight Phil. We need to carry out some more regression therapy here. I will need to access the case files, the police command and control logs," Smythe continued.

"Gray will love that," Graves replied groaning out loud.

"I could always take Gray up on his offer officially and take your case and use that as a ruse to get the information?" Smythe suggested warily. Graves continued to stare into space, his mind somewhere else.

"Whether Gray was at fault has yet to be determined. You need a rest, take some time off. Take your mind to somewhere pleasant – a holiday in the country or abroad perhaps?" Smythe volunteered. Graves frowned at the suggestion. There were a number of people at the Yard who would be happy to see the back of him and this might provide them with the ideal opportunity.

"I'm okay Giles. Work is the best thing for me right now, it will keep me sane, besides my new DCI needs my support and experience," Graves replied. "Can we pencil in another session Giles? I need to know to straighten myself out and hopefully move on," Graves was standing at the window now, pulling at the blinds he stared vacantly at the passing traffic below.

The question remained unanswered as both men were distracted by a knock on the door. Smythe's secretary put her head inside the room.

"I'm sorry to disturb you sir, but there is an urgent phone call," she declared.

"That's okay Melissa we're just done for the day," her boss replied. "I'm sorry Phil, but I'd better get that call now if it is urgent," Smythe said half-turning toward his secretary.

"I'm sorry sir, the call is for Inspector Graves, it's New Scotland Yard," she announced shifting her eyes toward him.

7

The return home

The phone call was unexpected, given that its origin was New Scotland Yard. He hadn't advertised his intention to see his psychiatrist friend for obvious reasons and yet he had been found. It had taken over an hour of phone calls before Julia Goldsmith located Graves systematically working through an old diary that he had left behind during one of his less than frequent visits to her flat. Despite her thoughtful, tactful tones over the telephone there was no easy way of breaking the news about his father. Up until the phone call Graves was sure of the extent of his feelings toward his father. He simply didn't have them any anymore. They had dissolved with time to a point where he was little more than an acquaintance.

The prospect of more arguments, more flare-ups had filled him with dread when Giles had suggested a visit to the country, to the family home. Now he wasn't quite so sure. His poor mother deserved better. Now the man whom he had respected from a distance as a fellow policeman, but rarely in a father and son relationship, was in intensive care at the local general hospital. A massive stroke brought on by a blow to the head was the diagnosis. Julia had given him only brief details over the telephone, basically what she had been told, but it was enough to convince him that he needed to be there.

"Giles would appear to have got his own way recommending a break in the countryside, although the circumstances were hardly conducive to rest and relaxation," he said to himself as he laboured through the rush hour traffic. He'd called briefly at his flat for a suitcase and stuffed it full of clothes. By 6pm he was heading north away from London. The heavy rain had died away to a fine drizzle until it finally stopped around 6:55pm. Traffic had initially been heavy heading out of London despite the newly constructed M25.

Dotted about the countryside he could see several points of light as the day moved into dusk, more so having left the motorway, as the car meandered through the unlit country lanes. The nightmares that had plagued his sleep had been just that up to now, but he was getting drowsy. It had been a long day with little quality sleep from previous nights, really since his suspension from the Yard. The same nightmare was getting more and more real with each episode so that he was becoming reluctant to sleep at all. The more the journey became mundane and uneventful, the more fatigue began to invade his weary mind. Up ahead, a small fire attended by several youths marked the early onset of Guy Fawkes Night, only a week away. The bonfire behind them guarded no doubt night and day from would-be predators. He wasn't sure whether it was the sight of the little campfire that triggered the episode or just general tiredness. Soon after passing it and not that far from the parish boundary marking the entrance to Willenbury, he suddenly wasn't in the car anymore. A man engulfed in flames appeared to be lunging toward him to make contact, screaming in agony. The scene was well known to him though and he instinctively moved to the left.

"No, no, not again, not now," he cried out in his mind. The body collapsed just beyond him as it had so many times before and he knew from experience that he had seconds to turn and leave. Leave without Tony McDowell who was in the room beyond as he had done so many times before in his nightmare, leaving his partner to perish. Unable to visualise the torment any longer he turned to run back up that familiar long dark corridor only this time as he leapt clear of the flames he was back in the front seat of his car. The car was already leaving the narrow country lane. His reactions were certainly not those of a man fatigued and in need of sleep. He pulled the steering wheel hard trying to correct his position, to get back on to the lane.

The recently surface dressed country lane sprayed new chippings to the left as he applied the brakes hard. The attempt was futile though. Locking the front wheels the MG began to slide sideways picking up more momentum as all four wheels made contact with the grass verge. The car was spinning now like a child's fairground ride fortuitously on to a wider expanse of grass where the roadside verge had broadened out locally. The smell of freshly cut grass, exaggerated by the skidding car filled the car's interior through the open driver's window. He pulled hard at the handbrake trying everything possible to bring the car under control, when suddenly it hit something firm, yet the impact was cushioned. He allowed his head to fall toward the steering wheel where it stayed for a few minutes, before pressing back against the headrest.

"Nightmares were now becoming hallucinations during my waking hours," he thought. This was a new dimension he hadn't anticipated and it could so very nearly have cost him his life. The MG was now facing the direction it had travelled in when it left the road. A figure-of-eight pattern lay between where he sat and the lane he had left tracing out the last few minutes of his struggle with the wayward car. The lane appeared quiet with no lights in either direction suggesting that no one else was involved. He thanked God at least for that small mercy. The car had come to rest against a number of large silage bales probably stored there by the local farmer that day ready for collection for the approaching winter. Another few yards to the right and the car would have hit one of the dry-stone wall pillars that marked the entrance to the adjacent field with more damaging consequences.

In The Mood

He climbed out of the car, stumbling, even more grateful now that no one else was involved; that he was in one piece and that the damage to his car was minor, in that order. He sat on the car bonnet taking in great gulps of night air. He had a short way to drive now, but the incident had shaken him. Looking back toward the lane before him, the lights from the MG picked out the lane and what lay beyond it. He hadn't noticed that a substantial boundary wall had replaced the normal tree-lined verge on the opposite side of the lane. Opposite where he sat, slightly off-centre were two large and rusting wrought iron gates. A loose chain hung around both more to keep the two gates together than to offer any sort of security.

"It's just as well I didn't swerve to the left," he said to himself, breathing a sigh of relief.

Glancing at his watch he quickly checked the damage before climbing back into his car and carefully negotiating his way back onto lane. He gave the scene one last consideration in his rear view mirror. He reached the village outskirts without any further incident five minutes later, pulling to a stop at the familiar cenotaph that marked the entrance to the west approach to the village. The cenotaph would soon be covered in poppies and wreathes and for a second his mind recalled one of the few times father and son had talked on a subject at length without arguing. The headlights of the car shone against the stone monument highlighting those that fell during both wars. Nodding and tilting his hat, he paid his respects and continued his journey.

Ten minutes later he was passing through the centre of the village, beside the park and beyond the pond, along the village high street passed the Rope and Anchor pub. At the northern end of the village he took the familiar right fork to Willenbury hospital, arriving there a short time later. He stood taking in the front of the building, momentarily disturbed by the arrival of an ambulance and the hospital's next patient. Surprisingly, his natural aversion to hospitals remained in check, with no appreciable signs of any panic attacks. He passed through reception, checking his father's whereabouts as he did. The smell of disinfectant and other odours normally associated with the medical profession lingered in the corridors reminding him of exactly where he was. The words 'Intensive Care Unit (ICU)' from the hospital receptionist brought a sobering thought over him as for the first time since speaking to Julia he began to realise the seriousness of his father's condition.

A short while later he reached ICU, pausing briefly, reflecting on what he might be met with and how he might react. He wondered about the circumstances behind the attack on his father and why a constable hadn't been posted at the door, anger beginning to invade his tired mind. He peered through the little window panel in the door, initially catching sight of the bed inside. He traced its length almost reluctant to see the inevitable. Several monitors surrounded the head of the bed, each active no doubt tasked with a different role. A lone figure he recognised as his mother sat close by, her head resting on the bed sheets, a right arm thrown protectively across her life-long partner. He pushed his unkempt hair back, suddenly conscious of the way he looked, adjusting his tie and then squeezed the door handle gently, pushing the door open, not wishing to disturb either parent. There was plenty of time for that later. His mother was only resting. She reacted to her son's entrance turning her head only and managing a look that reminded him of the one he initially got from Smythe earlier that day.

"Oh, Philip, you came," she whispered, the joy in her reaction just about contained under the circumstances. She held out her free arm, not wanting to leave her husband's side for a moment and Graves walked across to her. She hugged her son as mothers do, not wanting to let go, letting her emotions get the better of her, though out of joy this time. Her face was damp from the constant flow of tears, giving it a redness and puffiness over and above her normal appearance. "Oh, Philip I'm so glad that you came so soon. I tried my best to get hold of you. The office said you had taken some leave. I didn't know what to do and then I remembered that nice young lady that I met at your flat the last time I was there and that she worked with you. She said she would get a message to you. She rang me back an hour or so ago to say you were on your way. You'll never know how that lifted my spirits," she said thankfully. She pushed him away briefly raising a tentative hand to his face.

"You look tired Philip and what about these whiskers?"

"I've been a little busy mother, you know working undercover, getting into the part?" he said his eyes drifting from her to his father.

"It's not your appearance that worries me Philip, although I've seen you tidier. It's your eyes," she said now focusing on them.

"How is he?" he asked, partly wanting to know and partly to change the subject. She would only fret more if he explained his predicament at work, his nightmare, and she had enough on her mind at present. It suited him for now to offer up a little white lie. She turned her attention back to the bed a look of guilt on her face for feeling better, if only for a few brief seconds. Reginald Graves lay on his back. A facemask aided his breathing, which appeared to be adequate for the moment.

"You mean how is your father," she corrected him.

"Yes, I'm sorry," he said, "how is father?" he replied craning over the head of the bed, trying to get a better look.

"He's been like this for the last five hours. The doctors say his condition hasn't worsened, but then it hasn't improved either. He had a blood clot at the back of his head where he was hit. They have relieved the pressure following an operation this evening. He has yet to regain consciousness," she replied. She slipped her hand inside her husbands and squeezed it gently, no doubt hoping for a reaction. "Why Philip? Why?" she said, dismay in her trembling voice. "You know what your father is like. He never carries cash around with him, he's known and respected in the village so why was he attacked?" The tears started to roll down her heavily lined face again and she wiped them dry with her damp lace handkerchief. Graves moved nearer to her now, placing a comforting arm around her shoulders.

"I can't answer that question just now, but I aim to find out." Whatever their differences, he was his father and at the very least, a fellow officer. He had already decided on the way up from London to find out more about what had happened. After all, there was only so much he could do over the next day or two, whether his father recovered immediately or not. Hospitals always made him feel uneasy at the best of times. He never knew why, they just did.

"What was he doing? Where did it happen?" Graves urged her as quietly as he could. She looked at him hesitantly as if she was undecided whether to answer the question in full or even in part.

"He…" her voice broke as she looked back at her husband. "He was on his way home from work, so Gary said," she replied, shaking her head in disbelief. "It wasn't even dark. He'd sound the car horn as he drove past the front of the cottage and I waved to him through the window just the way we always had," she fidgeted, her handkerchief between her hands and now the subject of her concentration. Graves looked beyond where she sat considering his father, trying to picture the all too familiar scene. What she had described he himself had been witness to over many years as a young boy, even took part in several times as he use to race out the front door down the garden path around all the other cottages to try and get to the garage at the rear of the cottage before his father. Sometimes he beat him, although he always thought that his father had allowed him to win. He smiled at the memory. "I found him unconscious fifteen minutes later," She continued.

"You said 'work' and 'Gary' in the same context?" Graves asked questioningly. She looked straight ahead now, her own comment bringing to life what might have happened the previous night. Her mind was barely picking up the fact that her son was there now, but the question seemed to get through eventually.

"Gary Swallow, your father's old boss," she replied, her eyes finally moving to where he stood. "You remember Gary don't you?"

Graves moved around the private room now mulling over matters in his mind, rather than answering the question. It had been a long day full of shocks and surprises. This one currently didn't make any sense at all. Of course he remembered Gary, his old Inspector. Why should he be involved though?

"I don't understand, what has Gary Swallow got to do with things anymore? Father retired twelve months ago," Graves said, his voice stern and in control as if he was interrogating a suspect.

"Please don't be angry son," she replied," he was just doing a little job for Gary to help out at the station. There are a lot of people off with the flu at the moment and this strange case has just come up, your father wouldn't go into the details, you know what he is like. He just locked himself away in his study, delighted to be of some use." She tried to continue further, but Graves was already feeling anger and frustration building up inside him again. This time his father's welfare was the farthest thing from his mind.

"You mean to tell me Swallow still has him running around as his lap dog? Not only that, this work may have been the cause of his assault." Graves voice was growing in volume with each word and hardly helping his father's recovery.

"Please, please don't be angry son, your father," she pleaded looking directly at him then at her husband. His mother had the ability of conveying more in a look sometimes than in the spoken word.

"Look mother, I don't mean to be angry or shout, but this was your time together, to get away, relax, put your feet up. What does he do? He scuttles off back to the station to see if there are any odd jobs he can do, while you are at home alone." Graves shook his head, his voice still louder than it should have been and now attracting the attention of passing medical staff outside in the corridor. "If there is a potential connection between the attack on him and the case he has been working on, why hasn't Swallow put a man on the door?" he barked, almost oblivious to the fact that he was shouting at the person he had come to ultimately protect and support. His mother merely stared at him. In her eyes the questions were unimportant now, the deed was done, the questions could wait.

"Excuse me, I'm afraid I'll have to ask you to leave sir." A male auxiliary nurse appeared at the door addressing his request at Graves forcefully. "Only one guest to see the patient at any time, even if you are a relative. Given that I can hear your voice at the end of the corridor, I respectfully suggest that it should be you sir that leaves, if only for the sake of the patient." Graves looked at his father and nodded accepting that his temper had got the better of him.

"Philip come and see your father tomorrow, he might be much better then," she suggested moving across to where he stood squeezing his shoulders to sooth his frustration. "You will stay at the cottage won't you?" she asked as they made their way toward the door.

"I had planned to take a room at the Rope and Anchor," he said as they linked arms.

"Nonsense," she scolded him. "You'll sleep in your old room – I've prepared it. I'll ring you if there is any change."

"You're staying then, all night?" he asked her.

"I wouldn't have it any other way," she said smiling for the first time as they both stepped into the corridor. "Do you remember Mrs Martin from next door?" Graves nodded. "She asked if she could help in any way. I said you might come home later today, so she said she would put a sandwich in the fridge for you just in case. There's tea, coffee and milk as well just where it has always been, just help yourself." She pressed a shiny brass Yale key into the palm of his hand and closed his fingers around it, not unlike when he was a schoolboy with his pocket money. "Now off you go, I'll be fine with a blanket and an easy chair. I have everything I need now – change of clothing, toiletries, thanks to Mrs Martin. Now don't worry, I'll ring if I need you or if there is any change." He brought her close and hugged her gently as if she might break. She responded in a similar way pulling him down to her level to kiss him on the cheek.

"I don't know what the story is about the way you look Philip and I'm not sure that I want to know. You will find a spare razor in the bathroom cabinet. You're not undercover now," She teased his whiskers playfully, before disappearing back inside the private room. It was no use, she had spoken in that tone of hers and he had to do as he was told.

ooooo

The old cottage hadn't changed much over the years. Perhaps the darkness and shadows were being kind to it. Graves pushed open the garden gate and heard the distinctive squeak and for a moment he was swinging backwards and forwards on it again as a boy of seven. The cottage garden was looking a little overgrown which surprised him. His father had always been a keen market gardener in his youth, growing his own produce and plants from seed, which ensured that it was always well stocked and tidy, something he was proud of.

"Maybe his new part-time duties with Swallow had kept him too busy," he said to himself scornfully. The old timber frame around the front door looked as tired as the Wisteria it was supporting. He fumbled for the key that his mother had given him back at the hospital, just as he noticed the familiar loose brick, central above the door and three courses above the doorframe. Smiling to himself, he popped his mother's key back inside his overcoat pocket. After some initial reluctance, he pulled the brick from its resting place and put his hand inside the hole tentatively, his smile quickly turning into a grin. The key he had used for emergencies in his youth had remained there after all this time.

"Not exactly clever for a policeman," he thought as he let himself in. He flicked the light switch behind the tied-back curtains used to cover the doorway from drafts at night and two wall lights lit up the front room, one in each alcove either side of the gas fire. His father's grandfather clock was the only noise that he could hear. The room was cold and cheerless without people to give it character and atmosphere. He walked around the lounge taking in familiar sights as well as some new ones. His mother had finally got her new three-piece suite and a dining table that she always wanted. His father's rocking chair remained in its usual place, beside the fire and directly in front of the television. The writing bureau that he had sat at many times doing his school homework was still a prominent feature in the far corner of the lounge.

The hatch in the wall was the boundary between lounge and kitchen. He wondered about the place, choosing to retrieve his roast chicken and salad sandwich left by Mrs Martin initially from the fridge, occasionally biting into it as he moved around the cottage. Memories came flooding back, some good, some not so good. At the bottom of the winding staircase he looked up visualising the upstairs before he clicked the downstairs lights off and made his way up to his room. The troubles of the day were catching up with him and he suddenly felt drained and tired, climbing upstairs the final draw on his reserves of strength. Whether he would have an uneventful night was hard to say. He crashed onto his old bed, thoughts of the day arranging themselves inside his head. It was hardly how he had expected the day to unfold and for once since his chat with Giles Prenton-Smythe, he had an opportunity to reflect on their earlier discussion. The plate already discarded it wasn't long before he found himself questioning the attack on his father again. It had been so brutal and unnecessary. He decided he would pay his old Detective Chief Inspector a visit the following day and ask him about that very question. They were the last thoughts he had in fact before he fell, exhausted, into a deep sleep, a sleep that would be devoid of his usual nightmare, thankfully.

He awoke to the sound of birds singing in the grey sycamore trees just outside his bedroom window. Sunshine cascaded in through the window and it was as it always had been when he was a youngster. It was a pleasant place and time to be a boy and he had fond memories in his early years. The whole atmosphere of being home again in his old room alone put things into a different perspective. It was only as he rose from his bed that he noticed he was fully clothed, so tired the night before that he didn't even have time to undress. Thoughts of his father forced their way into his mind. He needed to contact the hospital to check on him and his mother. He wasn't disturbed during the night by a phone call, so he'd assumed that things were OK. Fatigue had kept him soundly asleep and for all he knew though the telephone may well have rung. Stepping out on to the landing with the intention of calling the hospital, he noticed that his father's study door was slightly open.

"Strange I didn't notice that last night," he said to himself. "Even stranger that the door is unlocked."

Pushing it open for the first time he peered inside. This private domain, protected, guarded by his father even during his youth was nothing more than a desk, chair and a filing cabinet. It was a small box room with a tiny window. No wallpaper, just plaster painted a combination of vanilla and beige. It measured little more than three yards square. A filing index sat prominently on top of the cabinet and behind that, mounted on the wall, a board with old newspaper clippings pinned to it, each making reference to cases his father had been involved in and surprisingly, some of his own as well. He suddenly felt the oddest of sensations – that his father might have been proud of him all along. He sat on the swivel chair, turning right then left considering the room. There was something strangely satisfying about it all and yet it was something of an anticlimax. On the desk lay a number of papers, doodling mainly from what he could see. His dad was hardly a sketch artist and had never shown any natural abilities in that direction, but these weren't half bad, he thought. He lifted what appeared to be the best of the bunch and held it up to the light.

"Well maybe it's a new hobby since he retired?" he thought. "Hardly worth keeping me out the room for though." The comment was made deliberately tongue-in-cheek. He was only too aware later in his own career of his father's involvement in graphic assault, murder and suicide cases to know that his exclusion from this room was for his own good as an impressionable youth. How cruel and ironic now that he should be the victim of such an assault. He was just about to turn his attention to the filing cabinet when the phone rang downstairs.

"Mother," he called out. He leapt out of the chair leaving it spinning, leaping two stairs at a time, and grabbing the phone in one movement. "Hello mother," he shouted down the phone expectantly.

"Philip is that you?" the male voice on the other end of the telephone replied. Graves hesitated, trying to place the voice. "It's me Gary, Gary Swallow," the voice continued.

"Gary, sorry, I've just woken up. I'm a little disorientated. It's been a while," Graves said putting his hand to his forehead.

"Yes, you can say that again. I was ringing to see how your father is, expecting your mother to answer?" Swallow replied.

"I actually thought you were my mother when I heard the telephone. She stayed with father overnight at the hospital and I came home. I arrived here late last night," Graves replied. "He has been stable since the operation and I didn't get a phone call during the night so hopefully, all is still well?"

"Fine Phil, that's good news. I won't keep you long just in case she rings and finds the line engaged. Why don't you pop in for a chat when you can spare a moment? Despite the circumstances, it would be good to see you after all this time," Swallow suggested.

"Thanks, I'd like that. I would also appreciate discussing just what my father was working on for you," Graves replied. He needed to understand the circumstances surrounding the attack on his father and Swallow would have some of the answers. He also wanted to know why his father was still working after he was officially retired. No sooner had he replaced the phone when it rang again.

"Hello Philip?"

"Mother, are you OK? How's father?"

"He is resting dear, no real change. He had a settled night, probably more than I did." She tried hard to hide the worry and weariness in her voice.

"Did you manage to get any sleep at all?" he asked, concerned about the tone of her voice.

"A little son, a little," she replied.

"I'll come up to see you and father later today. Gary Swallow wants me to call in at the station," he told her. He could sense the dismay in her voice.

"Please don't give Gary a hard time dear," she said. "Your father would have badgered him until he gave him something to do, you know what he is like?" she begged him.

"I promise you mother I won't and I'll be with you later with a change of clothing and some supplies.

"Okay dear, we can work around having one person in the room at a time," she conceded. He replaced the receiver. The thought of visiting the hospital again sent a shudder through him.

"I've just enough time for a quick shower, the shave I promise mother the night before, and a bite of breakfast," he thought to himself.

8

The macabre find at Bedford Bridge

"Come in Philip, you're a little early, but not to worry." The broad figure of Gary Swallow had been pacing behind his office door just as Graves passed through the incident room, a custom he was known for when he was thinking. He held out a welcoming hand as Graves walked in and he took it shaking it briefly. Graves smiled politely. Until he knew why his father was out of retirement and involved in one of Swallow's cases he reserved the right to let old acquaintances be rekindled.

Graves looked directly at Swallow before allowing his eyes to wonder about the office. It was only a few seconds before he found what he had sensed upon entering the room. Behind the door, partially out of sight, sat a heavily built man, carrying a substantial paunch. Graves guessed him to be around forty years old. He was dressed in a grey checked two-piece suit and sported a full beard and thinning straight hair kept in place by copious amounts of Brylcreem. He glanced up momentarily at Graves before resuming his note taking.

"Can I introduce acting DI Tom Wheldon, Philip?" Swallow continued. "Philip is a former sergeant from this nick Tom. He's a DI now based at Scotland Yard." Swallow said looking at Wheldon. The two men exchanged pleasantries. "Tom has just been briefing me on a curious case we have had forced upon us, literally. I won't bother you with the details just now. Tom is just about finished," Swallow continued eyeing his junior officer. Wheldon made no attempt to leave the room until he was ready. A new DI on the scene was threatening to undermine his new temporary status and he needed to know why Graves was really at Willenbury CID.

"Would you be related to Reginald Graves?" Wheldon asked, the introduction eventually bringing him out of his shell. Graves nodded as he took his seat. "I'm sorry to hear about your father's injuries. He is well thought of and liked here," Wheldon said. There was something about Tom Wheldon that Graves didn't like that he couldn't put his finger on, something disingenuous in his voice and manner, but this sudden show of support and respect for his stricken father was appreciated.

"Thank you," Graves acknowledged, "he's holding his own at present. He doesn't give up easily though so we are hopeful." With that Wheldon left the office, closing the door behind him. Graves sat down opposite Swallow peering at each other between columns of case files stacked on Swallow's desk. Graves recalled the events of the night before in his mind.

"I spoke briefly with my mother last night about the attack. I didn't want to drag up memories of what it must have been like for her. Not surprisingly, she wouldn't tell me anything at all and eventually I didn't like asking anymore," Graves said, bending the truth somewhat.

Swallow considered Grave's demeanour, "She's probably exhausted and worried Phil, it's understandable."

"I would say that she also knows me and doesn't want me to get involved." Graves speculated.

"Well you are your father's boy Phil," Swallow commented.

"What does that mean exactly?" Graves queried, a change in his tone evident.

"Nothing to get wound up about Phil," Swallow said defensively. "One of the reasons your father was doing work for me after his retirement was his problem with letting go. I thought I could give him some minor duties to wean him into retirement permanently. You are very much like him in that respect. If you get involved in this, you won't let go until you've wrapped up the case, probably single-handed." Graves could sense the inevitable truth in what Swallow had said and reined in his planned verbal attack.

"I can't do anything at the hospital. They'll only let one guest at a time in to see my father and that will always be my mother. She doesn't like to leave him," Graves explained.

"I don't know what to say Philip. Just being there is often enough for some people, even if it is in the next room and primarily to support your mother," Swallow replied, keeping his eye on Grave's body language.

Graves straightened in his chair, conscious again of why he was visiting Swallow. "Who found him Gary?" Graves asked intent on finding out the details.

"Your mother Philip. I thought you knew?" Swallow offered guardedly. Swallow suspected that the question was aimed beyond the obvious and he was right.

"I mean which officer attended and who gave the prognosis on his injuries?" Graves replied irritated by Swallow's evasiveness.

"One of my young constables, a DC Colin Morgan, arrived at the scene within minutes of the station being informed by the doctor attending to Reg's injuries," Swallow confirmed, still reluctant to be forthcoming with information. "See here Phil, I know where you are going with this. There's nothing you can do that we aren't already doing ourselves. He was one of our own you know? It was just a mugging that went seriously wrong. There is nothing more to it." Graves merely looked back at Swallow waiting for a complete answer. "OK, your mother's first reaction was to call Jack Rowan, given that they only live a mile apart from each other and I presume because he is an old friend of your parents. He was the attending doctor prior to the ambulance arriving," Swallow confirmed reluctantly.

Graves seemed a little surprised at first. "I had thought that Jack would have been retired as well by now?" he asked, familiar with another ex-colleague from his days at Willenbury CID.

"You must be joking Philip," Swallow quipped, picking up the buff coloured file that he and Wheldon had been discussing the contents of when Graves first walked in. "Even HM Coroner's Office are short-staffed these days. Jack is on some kind of annual contract with them until they can find someone suitably able and qualified. The arrangement seems to suit both parties for now." This need to work beyond retirement was catching and for a moment Graves thought about what he would do when his time came and he found himself strangely understanding his father's and Rowan's position. Swallow threw the file across the table between the stacks of case files and it slid to a rest just in front of Graves.

"That was Steve Tranter's case, a DI like you in my team. He's just been admitted into hospital with a perforated duodenal ulcer, according to his wife, when I spoke to her over an hour ago. A little bit inconvenient," Swallow groaned gesturing to the stacks of case files balancing precariously on his desk, "but it's presented one of my sergeants with the opportunity to shine. That was he who you've just met. We were just discussing progress – mainly Jack Rowan's on site. He's been out there for two days now processing the evidence."

"Two days? Jack must be getting old. I always had him down as a lab-rat rather than a field operator especially during the colder months," Graves replied, wondering if they were talking about the same man.

"I suggest that you look at the file first Phil before passing any premature judgement." Swallow commented, leaning back in his chair. "It's rather an unusual case to say the least – a road traffic accident with a difference. Suffice to say the media are giving me a hard time over progress because we had to close the bypass and the road below it. It's causing daily chaos in the village and on surrounding roads. Both roads are supposed to be open by tomorrow," Swallow said without any real conviction.

"I heard the news reports on my way here this morning, but I hadn't realised the scale of the traffic disruption. It must have been a major incident." Graves offered.

"Read the file Philip. Take it with you and see Jack. I presume that was your next intended course of action anyway?" Swallow asked. Graves looked back at him without comment. "I thought as much."

"Thanks Gary," Graves said rising from his chair. "I'm sure the case is interesting, but I only need to see Jack about my father's condition." Graves commented turning toward the door, he left the file where it lay. Swallow walked around his desk, scooping the file up in his hand, offering it to Graves once more.

"You asked on the telephone yesterday about the work Reg was involved in, those minor clerical duties I had him sorting out for me." Swallow reminded him as he offered the file back to him again.

"Oh yes," Graves replied half-listening to the question and half looking at the buff file again, which Swallow was intent on him having. "I'd forgotten about that."

"Well, it was this case," Swallow confirmed patting the file. Graves's face changed markedly at the news and this time he gripped the file as if it were his own record. "Now before you read too much into this Philip he was doing nothing more than collating and filing case notes, reports and transferring evidence for Tranter and Jack back to the station. That was it, nothing suspicious, just straightforward police work," Swallow explained as he squeezed the door handle leading back into the incident room. Graves regarded his former boss carefully, choosing to reserve his judgement.

"Morgan!" Swallow called out the name in a low commanding tone across the incident room. "Can you come inside for a moment please?" The question was aimed at a tall, fair-haired uniformed constable busily tapping at the typewriter on the desk where he was sat. Swallow closed the door and turned his attention back to Graves. "Take Morgan with you to see Jack. He could do with the experience and he will get you on site without any problems. For Christ's sake don't compromise the crime scene or Rowan will have your balls on one of his operating tables. Give the file back to Morgan after your visit – I need it for several media interviews this evening." There was a light tap on the door and the gangly figure of DC Morgan stepped in.

"Philip, this is DC Colin Morgan. Morgan, this is DI Philip Graves. His father..." Swallow was about to say.

"Is Reg Graves – yes the whole station knows sir and DI Graves's background at Scotland Yard," the young constable added. Graves wondered briefly whether the trouble between him and Superintendent Gray had filtered through yet, then quickly dismissed it. "Pleased to meet you sir," Morgan said offering a welcoming hand.

"Morgan," Graves replied shaking the hand on offer.

"Morgan, after I speak to the team in a few moments I want you to take DI Graves to see Jack Rowan at the accident site at Bedford Bridge please and stay with him until about 5pm. I want you back here with that file by 5:30 at the latest," Swallow informed him handing the file to Graves.

"Sir," Morgan replied dutifully. The two men paused in the doorway, Morgan choosing to walk on ahead to sit with his colleagues and await Swallow's formal announcement.

"DC Morgan?" Graves said, the name suddenly registering as he looked back at Swallow beside him.

"Yes," Swallow said resignedly. "It's the same Morgan that found your father – no coincidence that I should choose him to take you to see Jack – so just go easy on him. You would have caught up with him sooner or later. Oh and as far as the team is concerned you are here as an extra resource if you want to get involved in any investigation regarding your father. I intend to formalise this now at the team meeting while you are here." Graves tapped the side of his head with the file in appreciation and both men disappeared out through the door into the incident room. Wheldon called his team to order, already enjoying his new bout of authority.

"Before we start our team meeting, Detective Chief Inspector Swallow would like to say a few words. Sir," Wheldon gestured to Swallow to step forward and address the team.

In The Mood

"Thank you Tom. As you all know, Steve Tranter has been rushed to hospital earlier today with a suspected perforated ulcer. I'm sure you will all join me in wishing him a speedy recovery." There was general acknowledgement and agreement around the room. "Steve will need rest and recuperation after his operation, which means he will not be back for the foreseeable future. I know the department is under great pressure at the moment so I've requested additional resources. Sergeant Tom Wheldon will continue as acting Detective Inspector, as will Detective Constable Parker in the role of acting Detective sergeant," Swallow announced. General banter broke out amongst those gathered along the lines of congratulations.

"OK settle down now," Swallow said. "As I've already said at a time when resources are stretched we are very lucky to have the help of an experienced DI on temporary leave from New Scotland Yard. Can I introduce DI Philip Graves?" Graves had found himself a wall to lean against and a filing cabinet to rest his right arm on. He gave a friendly wave of acknowledgement to the crowd of junior officers following Swallow's announcement. "Most of you will know his father Reg Graves and may have even been mentored by him in your time here. You will also be aware of the vicious attack on him." The jocularity ebbed immediately. "Phil is here primarily to offer support to his parents. However, I know some of you will deem what I have to say next as unusual at best, but I have agreed to Philip looking into the circumstances surrounding the attack on his father," Swallow continued. Once again there was some unrest amongst the audience some of which was no doubt aimed at the wisdom of allowing someone emotionally attached to a victim to get involved in a case of this sort, no matter how stretched the resources.

"I've asked DC Morgan to help DI Graves in any way he can, whilst still acting as a an integral part of this team." Swallow kept silent for a few moments to hear any dissenting voices. "Right that's it. Can you all speak to DI Wheldon and DS Parker about your duties please?"

The audience broke into little huddles to discuss the news and the volume of the background noise rose accordingly. Graves was already making his way to the back of the room at this point to where Morgan was waving a set of car keys discretely over the general chatter.

Swallow motioned to Wheldon in the meantime and the two slipped discretely back into Swallow's office for a quiet word.

"Tom, I suspect you above anyone else feel that what I've agreed to here with Philip Graves is foolhardy." Swallow said sitting down heavily in his chair.

"With all due respect sir, you've been around long enough to know what happens when someone with emotional attachments to a victim in a case gets too involved," Wheldon replied taking the seat opposite.

"Yes I am painfully aware, that is why I wanted a quiet word and why I want you to keep an eye on him and what he gets up to. He doesn't know it yet, but he is here technically on secondment from the Yard, despite his father's condition. He will have some compassionate leave to use as he sees fit. He will be here a little longer than he thinks, which can only be good for the station, given Tranter's condition." Wheldon visualised his temporary

In The Mood

promotion being curtailed by Graves's presence and inwardly began to take an even greater dislike to him.

"Sir, I don't understand. Why is he being seconded here?" Wheldon queried.

"You don't have to understand Tom. I've told you all you need to know. Now get your team out there and find me Reg's attacker and wrap up that bridge incident," Swallow replied gesturing to the door. The fact that Superintendent Gray had pulled in a long-standing favour of Swallow to get Graves out of his hair for a while was on a need-to-know basis and Wheldon didn't need-to-know. Wheldon on the other hand knew there was a missing piece of puzzle here and he had his own way of finding out. If there was any chance he could dislodge Graves back to the Met in the short-term, it would only add to the opportunity for him to continue to act as DI for an extended period. He left Swallow's room with that thought alone on his mind.

ooooo

The traffic in Willenbury village centre was heavier than Graves had ever seen it. Sure it had been a few years since he had been there, but hell's teeth, it wasn't even rush hour yet.

"I'm beginning to see why the media is giving Gary a hard time," Graves remarked as the Ford Granada moved along at a snail's pace.

"Sir the traffic congestion, it isn't always like this." Morgan had one eye on the queue in front of him and one eye on his new charge beside him. The young lad was keen, Swallow had warned Graves earlier. Now he had a man from the Yard to work with, he might be a little too keen to please. He no doubt suddenly had ideas about his own career prospects.

"Yes, Gary warned me about the bridge incident." Graves patted the file with palm of his hand without attempting to open it. I expect the work currently being undertaken by the 'Ripper' is also a contributory factor to the delay, although I'm still puzzled as to why he is still out here." Graves spoke aloud whilst admiring the odd shop window and general hustle and bustle of the village high street.

"Ripper sir?" Morgan looked at him curiously.

"Never mind constable," Graves said dismissively.

"Sir, may I speak frankly?" Morgan asked.

"Be my guest constable, I'm only passing through here, as it were, so let's get our relationship off on the right foot shall we?"

"You see sir, when DCI Swallow asked me to assist you I have to admit my first reaction was how fortunate I was working with someone from New Scotland Yard," Morgan explained.

"I feel a but coming." Graves said staring out the windscreen ahead.

"Well I more or less guessed I was chosen because of my involvement in the attack on your father and well, that was fine sir, I have no problem with that," Morgan continued as if becoming increasingly uncomfortable. Graves turned his attention to his young driver expecting more. "It's DI Wheldon sir. I sense he resents your presence here just as he has been made up temporarily to Inspector."

"I'm a threat to making his post a full-time appointment. Is that it?" Graves guessed.

"I suppose so sir. Either way, I officially report to DI Wheldon as part of his team whilst I'm detached and helping you, however briefly. I find myself serving two masters one of whom I will serve long after the other has returned to the great metropolis," Morgan pointed out. "He expects me to keep him informed of your activities sir, I'm afraid."

"Point taken constable," Graves conceded. "I'm here first and foremost for my parents Morgan, that's it. I would like to understand the circumstances behind the attack on my father though. I suppose it's the copper in me. Once I have that understanding I would be more than happy to let you and Wheldon get on with it. I'm not interested in this or any other case I can assure you no matter how interesting DCI Swallow thinks it is." Thoughts of Gray and his job at the Yard flashed through his mind fleetingly as he thought about a rapid return to his day job.

"Fine sir," Morgan replied with a smile, "glad to have your understanding. As far as progress to date is concerned, DI Wheldon has two officers making discreet enquiries with your mother," Graves looked at the young constable uneasily knowing his mother's fragile state, "and Dr Rowan about the night of the attack. He has four officers looking at house-to-house enquires, to see if anyone has been hanging around the area suspiciously or knocking on doors. DC Rogers is currently based at Hendon Mews going through old case files at the police archive to see if there are any cases over the last five year period when your father was on active duty, to see who was involved and whether they are around now or recently came out of a spell in prison. Rogers is also looking at cases where the same modus operandi was used resulting in a similar attack," Morgan explained. "As yet, no weapon or any real evidence has been found at the scene, but we are widening the search area as we speak. Another three officers joined the search today sir, that makes ten to date," Morgan continued.

"Remind me to thank DCI Swallow for committing so many of his resources the next time I see him," Graves replied.

"You know the old saying sir, if we don't find anything substantive to go on within the first 48 hours, then we start to lose the trail. Also, your father's colleagues deserve some credit sir. DCI Swallow has committed resources during normal working hours, any overtime is being worked for nothing by the team – your father was a well-liked officer and a genuine friend to many of those out there looking for his attacker," Morgan explained.

"More the reason why we need to find this bastard and quickly," Graves replied, reflecting on the father he perhaps didn't really know as well as his fellow officers did.

"The weapon sir," Morgan paused as if unsure about broaching the subject.

"I'm listening," Graves interjected, noting Morgan's nervousness.

"It seems we should be looking for something with a dish shaped profile…like a hammer," he said the word with some trepidation, but Graves gave little emotion away.

"Okay Morgan I get the picture. What is Wheldon doing about the potential connection between my father's attack and this case?"

Morgan looked at him oddly. "I don't understand sir? How does this case fit in with the assault on your father?"

"I must admit, I find it extremely doubtful that a straightforward road traffic accident could result in a brutal attack on my father, despite his involvement." Graves pondered. "It's just a loose end."

"You haven't read the file yet sir have you?" Morgan asked. Graves looked at the case file on his lap and shook his head. "And DCI Swallow hasn't explained the unusual nature of the case to you?" Morgan continued. Again Graves shook his head.

"Not enough time son. I think he thought you and Jack Rowan would fill me in along with a look at the file," Graves commented.

"Well perhaps I should start from the beginning?" Morgan offered. Just then a vista opened up before them and Bedford Bridge could be seen in the distance.

"The bridge up ahead holds up the bypass as it passes over Willenbury valley. One of the supporting columns was hit the day before yesterday by a heavy goods vehicle. The damage is extensive and army engineers requested temporary supports to be erected before Dr Rowan could carry out his examination in more detail. They're partly installed now, but both the bypass and the road below remain closed in the meantime. That is why the traffic is so busy on this road sir – it's part of the designated diversion route. It's all in Inspector Tranter's notes sir," Morgan volunteered, pointing at the file on Grave's lap.

"Army engineers?" Graves replied.

"Yes sir. Royal Engineers based at Chippenham Barracks. The engineers had to take immediate action apparently. The local council has some sort of contingency plan with the Barracks when emergencies like this happen. They have the kit, the county council doesn't," Morgan explained further.

The Granada picked up a little more speed as they approached the huge structure now in the near distance. It looked odd as they approached the roundabout beneath it closed and no traffic at all using the bypass above. The huge supporting columns, some eighty feet high, stretched out in full view across the length of the valley, all except one. One of the columns, whose foundation was in the roundabout itself, was completely enveloped in scaffolding and sheeted out to prevent prying eyes from gaining access and to preserve the accident scene. The Granada pulled to one side of the queuing traffic just beside a row of cones and Morgan pressed the horn to attract the attention of a local traffic policeman. The uniformed policeman recognised Morgan immediately pulling several cones to one side to allow the Granada through. Morgan parked on a stoned area in between a bright red Volvo estate and an army jeep. Graves recognised Jack Rowan's car immediately.

"Passed its sell-by date just like its driver," he said to himself. The jeep he guessed belonged to the army engineers who busied themselves beyond the sheeted out area in the background. Both men stepped out of the car, Graves distracted by the engineer's activities.

"Sir, " Graves turned and looked toward Morgan. "You will need to wear one of these." Morgan had disappeared momentarily into the boot of the Granada and had reappeared with two hard hats. He waved one at Graves.

"Is one of those absolutely necessary?" Graves protested. "If the bridge falls down while I'm under it, a fibre glass hat won't save me."

"Sorry sir, site safety. The bridge is fine without traffic on it, but there is just a chance that lose debris from the crash might work its way free. Even a pebble at eighty feet can cause a lot of damage." Morgan looked up at the full height of the column before offering the spare hat to Graves. He accepted it reluctantly. The two made their way towards the scaffolding at the base of the bridge column.

"Oh sir," Morgan offered as they walked side-by-side. "Be wary about touching anything or doing anything without asking Dr Rowan first. He hands out bollockings for fun. I met him when we attended to your father and he was fine out-of-office hours. On the job some say he's a little old shit with a big opinion of himself."

Graves smiled wryly. "Thanks for the warning. I've had it from DCI Swallow already. Jack and I go back along way," Graves replied, trying hard not to stand in anything unpleasant. Morgan looked a little apprehensive, wondering if his comment had offended. "Perhaps I should have looked at the case notes after all," Graves thought. He was still curious as to why a laboratory dweller like

Jack Rowan would be out here, especially after a few days in the cold, when he could have delegated the job to an underling that he wasn't fond of. Then there were those questions about his father's present condition. The hospital was being cagey about his father's prognosis and he needed a second opinion from Jack, one he could trust. He went to pull back the heavy plastic sheeting when it moved back all on its own. From inside popped a small round man, about 14 stones in weight, 5 feet 3 inches tall with craggy features and a grey sallow complexion. Graves knew him to be at least 66 years old and was already lighting up a thin roll-up cigarette as he stepped outside the enclosure. Graves appeared in his line of vision unexpectedly.

"Morning Jack, Gary Swallow said I'd find you out here. I thought they would have put you out to pasture years ago." Graves grinned at the much smaller man, who by this time was coughing uncontrollably and bent double at the sight of Graves. "I see you're still smoking that weed of yours." Graves gestured to the thin roll-up between Rowan's stubby fingers.

"Well bugger me," Rowan managed after some effort as his coughing subsided.

"I'd rather not if it is all the same to you and certainly not in public," Graves replied dryly.

"I very nearly didn't recognise you with that hat on. What brings Scotland Yard out to the sticks? You struggling for work or some interesting cases?" Rowan teased. Graves grinned back at him ignoring the wind-up. "But of course, Reg," Rowan continued his mood and voice changing.

"Haven't you had enough of this Jack?" Graves asked dodging Rowan's questions. "You should be relaxing, taking it easy, growing tomatoes or something." Graves knew from past experience that 'Jack the Ripper' as he was known in the local force at Willenbury when Graves worked there, lived for the job, but his health had never been great. "There must be some young blood out there chomping at the bit to take over."

"Don't be a cheeky bastard. I'm good for a few years yet," Rowan chastised him.

"If you cut out the weed," Graves added, trying his best to see beyond the much smaller man and inside the sheeted area.

"Do shut up, you sound like my wife. I came here to get away from all that sort of thing," Rowan replied, moving as Graves did to block his view as best he could. Graves's height advantage made it virtually impossible though.

Sparring over with Graves had to admit that after the last six months it was good to see a familiar dependable face from the past.

"Would you like to put that marijuana out?" Graves asked. Rowan could be a pain in the arse at times, but he was always the consummate professional at his job.

"You were right just now, I am here because of my father," Graves said quietly. "DCI Swallow told me you attended to his injuries and incidentally, thanks for that. I've been to the hospital and there's no real change. All they will tell me is he has a serious head injury."

"I'm truly sorry about your father Phil. He is as well liked within the community around here as he is in the force. I can't believe that anyone would commit such a savage attack." Rowan remarked, eventually giving up the ghost on keeping Graves from seeing beyond him. He sat down on the only piece of crash barrier that had been left intact after the crash. "I suppose you think you will get more about Reg from me." Rowan remarked reading Graves like an open book.

"Come on Jack, this is my father we're talking about," Graves protested.

"Too little, possibly too late Phil if you ask me," Rowan said alluding to their strained relationship. The jibe didn't seem to register with Graves. He merely stared at the elderly pathologist. His expression said it all forcing Rowan to elaborate further.

"OK, OK, there's not much more to tell you Phil. Your mother had apparently seen him drive slowly passed the front window of the cottage, as always. He gave the car horn a honk and she waved back. She began to get their evening meal out of the oven while your father put the car away in garage behind the cottage. After ten minutes or so he failed to show, so she went out the backdoor to see what the delay was. She found him slumped against the garage door. He must have been opening the door when he was hit from behind," Rowan explained the account tallying mostly with his mother's version.

"What was your medical opinion about the attack?" Graves pressed further.

"Are you sure you want to go through this just now?" Rowan challenged him. Graves nodded. Rowan sighed, squinting against the morning sunshine. "I'd say it was vicious, not particularly consistent with robbery of a man

In The Mood

in his late 60s," Rowan said, shaking his head in disbelief now as he recalled the detail. "The force behind the blow may well have fractured his skull, which is why I suspect there are complications at the hospital. To my mind it was totally unnecessary. A younger man could have easily overpowered him and taken whatever he wanted." Graves turned to face the young detective constable standing slightly behind him.

"Was he robbed?" Graves inquired. Morgan pulled out his notebook, anxious to get his facts correct.

"Your father had no cash on him sir, according to your mother, so we are unsure about a motive just yet, although the car radio was ripped from its place. The briefcase he was carrying was thrown several feet from the car, the contents missing."

"It wasn't unusual for my father not to have any cash on him. He only carried what he needed, a trait from when he was much younger when cash was a scarce commodity," Graves reasoned out loud. He paced up and down between Rowan and Morgan for a few seconds then stopped suddenly. "The contents of the briefcase?"

"Just some photographs of the site and a draft report for this case for DCI Swallow to look at the same day, so Tranter said before he went into hospital, " Rowan commented.

"Did he act strangely that night, as he left the site?" Graves asked.

"He looked a little vacant and preoccupied at the time now you mentioned it. I did ask him if he was okay. He said that he was and left a little earlier than usual," Rowan replied.

"The gold dress watch, tucked in his waistcoat pocket, it was my grandfathers." the inference from Graves was obvious and the question directed at Morgan. Morgan feverishly looked through his notes twice before confirming that there was no sign of any such watch. It was Jack Rowan that spoke though.

"It was still there Phil, I gave it to your mother. She needed something of your father's to hold on to while they assessed him at the hospital – sorry son," his last remark was aimed at Morgan for potentially misleading his investigation.

"Whoever is responsible is either a bungler or this was made to look like a robbery for some other reason, a poor attempt at that," Graves reasoned out loud again, ignoring Rowan's poor judgment over the watch.

"Why should anyone want to have a go at your father Phil other than for money?" Rowan asked. Graves remained silent, lost in thought.

"Maybe he had some enemies from his time on the force?" Morgan interjected.

"It's unlikely son. Reg Graves spent the last five years of his working career training people like you. Hardly what I would call frontline exposure and five years is plenty of time to seek any revenge wouldn't you say?" Rowan replied.

"Unless it was someone with a grudge that was recently released from prison and the timing was just coincidental or perhaps he or she deliberately waited to spoil his retirement." Morgan replied. Graves looked at Rowan as if expecting a rebuttal, but he merely shrugged his shoulders. "I'm already looking at this angle with

Sergeant, I mean acting DI Wheldon and DC Rogers sir," Morgan confirmed. Graves's eyes wondered beyond the two men now focusing on the sheeted out area around the bridge column.

"My father was working part-time for DCI Swallow up until the attack I believe." Graves said out loud and not necessarily at either colleague. They both nodded in agreement. "Swallow also said that this was the case he was working on with DI Tranter and you Jack." A mixed look of curiosity and confusion reigned over the faces of Rowan and Morgan, before Rowan realised where Grave's thought processes were taking him.

"I know what you're thinking Phil and you're way off base. Do you know anything at all about this case?" Rowan queried.

"Very little. I was meant to read the file on the way over, but I got chatting to my chauffer here and the traffic queues were not as bad as we expected," Graves said. Rowan looked back at Graves resignedly.

"Right follow me and pay attention to my instructions to the letter. I think we should put this line of inquiry to bed before it gets started," Rowan insisted. "You'll find overalls, overshoes and gloves in my car." He threw the keys at Graves. "Get yourself kitted out and I'll take you inside." Five minutes later, protective clothing donned, Rowan pulled back the plastic sheet and the trio entered the cordoned off area. Inside the lack of natural light was compensated for by the use of large floodlights powered by portable generators used by both Rowan and the engineers outside. Even so, the light cast many shadows around the base of the bridge column giving the immediate environment an eerie, cold feeling.

"Right, a quick summary," Rowan said out loud. "An heavy goods vehicle carrying steel beams from Bentley Steel Fabricators left the dual carriageway above us and down the slip road outside. It came to a rest against that column over there," Rowan said pointing to yet more plastic sheeting attached to the surface of the concrete column.

"There were statements given by drivers saying that the cab and its trailer were moving erratically just before it crashed into the bridge sir," Morgan added. "The driver was also seen slumped against the window by the time it entered the roundabout by a number of other drivers sat in stationary traffic at the junction below the bridge?" Graves had only moved just inside the area and stopped when he could see the full extent of the damage.

"The resulting fire caused by the fuel tank rupturing and the sheer force of the impact has left the bridge in a weakened state," Rowan continued.

"The driver?" Graves asked, as if the question did not require further explanation.

"He is the least of my problems. The fire put pay to any serious *post mortem* conclusions. The body was burnt to a crisp. If he didn't die before the crash he would have been killed on impact. You may get some corroborating evidence from the driver's wife or his doctor when you make contact regarding his health and any medication he was on at the time." Rowan suggested. The reference to a fire and the evidence made Graves uneasy. Fleeting visions of that fateful night at Canary Wharf filled his mind again and he gripped nearby scaffolding to steady himself.

"Are you feeling OK sir?" Morgan asked quietly. Rowan was moving ahead and hadn't seen Graves stumble. Graves glanced back at Morgan without comment and Morgan took that to mean he was fine and to mind his own business.

"What makes you think that he was married?" Graves asked making his way closer toward the shrouded the column.

"A distorted wedding ring from the heat of the blaze, which we managed to retrieve from his left hand." Rowan answered.

"Hardly what I would call a special case Jack and certainly not one I would have thought would keep you occupied for so long. In any case the driver has long since gone so why are you still here?" Graves commented, his stare strangely attracted now to the sheeting covering the damaged column.

"Come and take a look at this and maybe you will understand better then." Rowan suggested. "Be careful where you stand and what you touch," Rowan said, reinforcing his earlier comments. The trio moved forward, ensuring that as little damage as possible was caused in the process. Rowan pulled at the second sheet around the damaged column with more vigour this time and it came away from the surface of the concrete. The wreckage from the crash had long since been removed, but in its place was a cavity, about four feet from the base of the column, where solid concrete should have been. Only the steel reinforcement remained making the hole look like a cell window into a prison on one of those Spaghetti Western films. The artificial light merely created a more dark shadowy area behind the bars and Rowan invited Graves to look more closely with the aid of a torch.

"I assume that this hole shouldn't be here even if it has been hit by forty tonnes of heavy goods vehicle?" Graves asked as he stepped forward over the loose rubble, gingerly leaning forward, supporting his own weight. Satisfied that he could kneel down and free one of his hands, he took the torch from his clenched teeth and shone it in between the heavy meshed steel reinforcement. His revulsion jarred him backwards and he fell against a roll of surplus sheeting that had been left behind by Scene of Crime Officers. His eyes moved sharply from the now dark cavity back to meet Rowan's stare a few feet behind him. The two exchanged glances without saying a word, before Graves clambered back to his feet and moved, more slowly this time, back to the damaged column. Morgan was fully briefed on what lay inside the cavity and made a conscious decision to stand his ground.

Graves shone the light much sooner this time as he approached the hole to lessen the inevitable shock. The white bloated face of an adult appeared to be sat crouched on its knees, the hairless head leaning directly on to the inner face of the rusting steel reinforcement. The facial features were indiscernible, the eyes long since gone. What was left of the upper tongue still protruded through the teeth and lipless mouth. The opening below the nose was stretched, giving the mouth an exaggerated clown-like appearance. The whole body was covered with an unknown coating that glistened against the torchlight.

In The Mood

There was a nauseating smell now seeping through the opening and he raised his handkerchief to try and persuade the contents of his stomach to stay put.

He moved the torchlight around the edge of the cavity. In some areas the hole was a tight fit, as if the concrete itself had formed around the body. In other areas there was more of a gap. There were indentation marks from the reinforcement where they made contact with the face suggesting pressure had been applied from above or behind the body. A rusty piece of corrugated metal lay on a slight angle, directly above the crouching body, appearing to touch both the neck and back. A steady flow of rainwater cascaded from a pipe cast into the concrete directly over the head of the body. Graves allowed the beam of light to move around the body now picking out more detail where he could. The remainder of the drainpipe exited the column through a hole at its base.

"The smell is the body beginning to corrupt and decay at an accelerated rate due to the exposure to the elements I suspect. That's why I need to get it out of there before all the evidence turns to mush," Rowan explained over Grave's shoulder. "Do you remember what I taught you all those years ago Phil, you know, in my lab classes?" Rowan continued as Graves examined the inside further, mesmerised by the macabre sight.

"Mostly," Graves replied. "Then again I was one of the few that didn't faint with your demonstrations," he replied, straining to see something below the body.

"Do you remember a one-off class I gave on a subject about human tissue preservation, partly on a substance known as Adipocera, a form of preservation dependent on certain environmental conditions being present?" Rowan asked, his chest wheezing with the effort as he crouched beside Graves. "Similar to mummification in preservation terms."

Graves turned and looked blankly at his former pathology lecturer.

"Not particularly. It sounds bit like Latin from my limited education?"

"Well done my boy," Rowan slapped a hand on his knee. "Glad to see you learned something in my classes."

"Fascinating," Graves commented dryly, thinking that this was a pathologist's thing to get excited about. "What is the significance Jack? All I can see is an anaemic adult, probably male, possibly strangled or crushed judging by the expression on the face. The only oddest thing though…"

"Yes," Rowan said, prompting him further.

Graves took out a biro from his inside jacket pocket and gestured at Rowan with it. Rowan nodded guessing his intention. He held out the pen and gently rubbed it along the left arm of the body. Retrieving it he held it up to the torchlight. The glistening texture of the unknown substance seemed to hang from the pen like melted candle wax.

"The body, all of it in fact seems to be coated in this stuff," Graves said turning the pen as he did in the limited light. "It has a slimy texture," he concluded, rubbing it between his gloved forefinger and thumb.

Rowan smiled, "I've spent the last day or so researching a rare condition associated with the preservation of corpses buried in certain types of environments."

"Adipocere?" Graves said out loud and Rowan nodded. "It reminds me of embalming." Graves commented, turning the torchlight back to the body.

"Not quite," Rowan said studiously. "Oh the outcome is similar, but the preservation with Adipocere is not by design. Adipocere forms when anaerobic bacteria in the digestive tract consume the body fat of a corpse. The microscopic bacteria excrete Adipocere and other ammonia type gases. The skin saponifies effectively coating the skin in a layer of wax-like substance known as Adipocere – *adipo* meaning 'fat' and *cere* meaning 'waxy'. It essentially acts like a form of mummification sealing the body, given the right environmental conditions."

"Such as?" Graves asked, dropping the pen into an evidence bag.

"Constantly damp or wet conditions, free of insect and rodent infestation," Rowan replied with raised eyebrows toward the cavity. "You see that broken pipe at the back of the head?" Graves nodded. "That's a broken highway drainage down pipe leading up to the gullies on the bypass above the bridge. The bridge sits in a low spot on the bypass as it crosses the valley. No doubt hundreds of gallons of water have passed through this hole in the past, eventually draining away during dry spells." Graves used the torch beam to pick out the watermarks around the perimeter again. "Adipocere can form within a matter of weeks or months after death and preserve the body for hundreds of years. The preservation here is remarkable, relatively speaking. I should be able to tell you the age, sex, height, teeth from dental records - assuming they exist somewhere to match against - and perhaps even a fingerprint or two. Oh, and I feel certain that I will be able to tell you eventually when he died – give or take a day or two. There even appears to be the poor fellow's clothes beyond the body, which may yield further clues and information," Rowan explained further.

"So you can use a preserved body like this to estimate the day that death occurred?" Graves inquired.

"Not exactly," Rowan said, a mischievous smile playing on his face. "How else would a body have found its way into a bridge column behind all that reinforcement, other than during construction? From memory I'd say the body has been in there for twenty-five years. The month and day will hopefully come later, but young Morgan here shouldn't need me to work that one out. Try the village library archive. It should have copies of old press cuttings about the opening of the bypass. "

"Twenty-five years," Graves whispered almost to himself, before taking a closer look. "Poor sod," Graves managed, eyes fixed on the pale smooth bloated face.

"I shouldn't have thought that he or she suffered much though," Rowan volunteered without any prompting. He shone the torchlight again at the corrugated metal directly above the head and back of the crouching body. "Of course I can't confirm anything until I carry out a formal *post mortem*." He rubbed his stubbly chin with his free hand, having second thoughts about saying anything further.

"Come on Jack, spit it out," Graves pushed, his policeman's curiosity getting the better of him, despite his initial disinterest in the case.

"I suspect that the contorted look on the face and the missing tongue is due to the impact caused by the weight from above," Rowan paused again and gazed up as if through the plastic sheeting to the full height of the column supporting the bridge. "I'd say approximately eighty feet. County Engineers told me that the concrete above the steel plate would have been poured in liquid form when placed, quite weighty as well. It would have solidified with time of course. Death would have occurred much sooner, fortunately for our victim."

"I assumed that he had been pushed in there during construction?" Graves said surprised.

"The body was definitely placed there," Rowan replied. Graves looked at Rowan disbelievingly. "OK Phil, assuming that you are correct for a moment, why has the body not sustained more damage in the fall, particularly," Rowan reached for his briefcase, "as there are no defensive marks or abrasions on the body suggesting it was pushed. I doubt whether I will find any fractures either, unless they are over twenty-five years old," he continued. "Quite apart from this I decided to use a boroscope to get some pictures around the back of the body before we attempt to get it out of there. I was concerned that some of the evidence might be destroyed in the process. The results were conclusive." Morgan gave Graves a perplexing look.

"It's a flexible tube basically with a tiny camera on the end that allows pictures to be taken in awkward and confined spaces," Graves explained.

"These are the pictures that we took as soon as we got access to the body," Rowan said passing them to Graves. "The degree of magnification can be deceiving and make objects larger than they actually are. You can clearly see though that the hands and feet are bound together from the photograph. You can also see the way the knots have been tied, they look unusual to me, or should I say, less common?"

"So it is murder?" Graves said. Both policemen were about to press Rowan further when Rowan held his hands up.

"I've said enough. Wait until I've done the *post mortem*. I will know more then.

"Why did the fire not affect the body? Graves asked.

"The impact on the column was enough to weaken the thin layer of concrete covering the cavity. Concrete also has a tendency to explode under extreme heat. That combined with rapid cooling from water hoses ensured that this thin layer of concrete fell away after the fire was extinguished," Rowan explained.

"How the hell are you going to get him out of there?" Graves inquired.

"Slowly and carefully," Rowan replied firmly as if to emphasize that he wouldn't be rushed. "Once we have the temporary army trestles erected to support the bridge I intend to have these bars burned away to create a hole big enough to ease the body out. I will need a thorough investigation of the cavity itself and the surrounding concrete and I want that metal plate, ropes tying the hands and ankles – knots intact – everything material to the case. We need to be as quick as possible before time begins to catch up with the body." Graves found the whole business mildly diverting from the real reason for his visit. He was about to leave Rowan to get on with what he does best, when the pathologist produced one more photograph from his briefcase that would change everything. "What do you make of this Phil?" Graves held the photograph up against one of the large floodlights. "Again the quality isn't brilliant. I should get better definition once the body is out and I've cleared the Adipocere," Rowan added.

"It looks like a faded imprint of some kind." Graves commented. It looked familiar to him though he couldn't place it immediately.

"This came from the right arm of our victim ghosting through the Adipocere. I believe it to be the image of a tattoo. Again, I'll confirm this back at the lab," Rowan replied.

"It's a Second World War ship, a Royal Navy frigate I think." The voice was that of DC Colin Morgan who was standing looking between them. Graves and Rowan both turned and looked at the young policeman in unison and surprise. "It's too small to be a destroyer. There are more gun turrets on smaller frigates than destroyers because it gave them more manoeuvrability. The two funnels at the rear of the ship also suggest a frigate," Morgan continued. He smiled and then looked uncomfortable about the revelation. "Oh, I use to build them as a boy. I still have over twenty Second World War battleships that I made myself." Morgan confided albeit less enthusiastically.

Graves mused over the information in his mind for a few seconds. "Is there anything unusual about a ship like that?" he asked looking directly at Morgan. He was beginning to remember why it was so familiar.

"Not that I am aware of sir. It was one of a number that I made," Morgan replied, relieved that the spotlight had left him momentarily.

"Look Phil, what is bothering you?" Rowan interrupted, witnessing a look on Graves's face he hadn't seen in twelve years.

"Like you I'm not sure Jack. My purpose coming here today was to find out more from you two about my father's injuries, how he was attacked his involvement in this, this…weird business," Graves could find no other words for it. "I'd almost agreed with DCI Swallow that this case was nothing more than a coincidence," he mused again, his thoughts lost once more, his mind elsewhere. Rowan looked at him strangely.

"Oh, its just that my father's papers in his study at home, he'd been doodling or at least it looked like doodling. There was a pretty fair sketch of a ship on several sheets of paper. Some I think were early attempts until he appeared to get it to look like what he wanted. What I saw in my father's study is very similar to this tattoo despite the waxy substance. I couldn't tell you how old the sketch was, but it is an uncanny resemblance," Graves replied. "Do you have any other photographs developed Jack, any better defined than this one?" Graves inquired.

"Not of the tattoo Phil, they're in for development back at the lab," Rowan replied. Graves looked at their newly elected seafaring expert Morgan, turning his attention now to the photographs of the knots. Morgan stared blankly at them before admitting that they meant nothing.

"Mind if I borrow these Jack? I know someone who might shed some light on the tattoo and the type of knot at the same time. Someone I've dealt with in the past,"

In The Mood

Graves volunteered. "Oh and can you keep me informed of your findings please from the *post mortem*?"

"You can have the photographs as long as Swallow and Wheldon have no objections and you don't shout about it, but might I suggest that you concentrate on your father's health Phil? He has a serious condition and you should be close by at the hospital, not gallivanting around the place looking for answers where there maybe aren't any. What is done is done. Let Wheldon and Morgan handle things," Rowan told him firmly. Graves thought about his mother's similar comment briefly.

"I'll bear that in mind Jack. Can you get a photo to me of that tattoo when you have removed that stuff from the body? The drawing and the tattoo may well turn out to be unrelated, but until they are..." Graves said without finishing the sentence. With that the two policemen left, leaving Rowan to prepare for the removal of the body.

ooooo

Graves had spent the remainder of the day at the hospital, the first fifteen minutes trying to get through the front entrance. Each time he froze. There was no logical reason that he could point to. Eventually he managed to summon enough strength and willpower and he clambered upstairs. He had managed to see the doctor in charge and the prognosis on his father wasn't favourable. There had been little improvement overnight indicating that his father was becoming solely dependent on the machines and monitors around him. The operation to relieve the blood clot would have been successful in most cases on a much younger man. An elderly man would always pose a risk, especially under general anaesthetic. His fate was now down to rest and recuperation and a good degree of willpower to live. This man whom in truth he had revered quietly all his life and yet argued with for the last ten years was slipping away and only now he was beginning to feel uncomfortable about the potential loss and those years of wilderness.

There was a change in his mannerism that even his mother noticed. He had left finally just before midnight, at his mother's insistence, to get some rest, that in reality they both needed. Even so, his mind was restless both during the journey back and during his sleeping hours. Despite his wish to leave matters to Tom Wheldon and his team whilst he attended with his mother at his father's bedside, his natural loathing for hospital environments and policeman's curiosity were influencing his thoughts and actions as he drifted finally off to sleep. He had decided on a course of action over breakfast the following morning. Again there were no phone calls during the night, which hopefully signified good news. He'd promised his mother the night before that he would carry out some errands – paying bills, that sort of thing – during the course of the day, which had given him an ideal opportunity to follow up on his suggestion to Rowan the day before. He would seek a professional opinion on the photographs that Rowan produced and then hand the feedback over to Wheldon while he returned to the hospital, at least that is what he told himself. As he left the cottage mid-morning he was greeted by the accommodating constable Morgan, parked outside the family home like a 24-hour one-man surveillance team. Graves had joined him, wondering if this was Swallow's idea of keeping in touch with the movements of his former sergeant.

"Where to sir?" Morgan chirped, opening the door to the Ford Granada for Graves.

"To see an old acquaintance about a knot and a tattoo," Graves replied mysteriously.

9

Public Records Office

The personnel records of ex-servicemen, those soldiers, sailors and airmen no longer on active service or deceased are kept in archive at the Ministry of Defence's Public Records Office at Hayes, Middlesex.

Graves had had one reason to call there in his career once before involving a missing child and a pilot from the Second World War. The Yard had received a tip-off that the body of a child abducted three weeks earlier could be found in a lake on the outskirts of London. In actual fact the child was found dead in a barn several miles away

In The Mood

from that location a week later. Police divers did, however, recover the body of an RAF pilot and the wreckage of a spitfire on the lakebed. Graves had the job of tracing the relatives of the missing airman. In actual fact he found the task most interesting as well as gruesome and gained a valuable insight into the archive material stored at Hayes. He hoped to be suitably impressed with a second visit today.

The dark blue Ford Granada pulled off the A312 through Hayes town centre and parked opposite the front entrance to the records office. It was bright and sunny again, although nothing like what lay inside. Public Records offices always reminded Graves of libraries and museums. Everyone speaks in hushed tones and there is a smell of age and varnish about the place, like an old boys' club.

"If I am not mistaken," Graves volunteered, hands-on-hips, tucked beneath his jacket, as he scanned the front elevation of the building, "we need to enter through the main door and turn right to reception. I had hoped to see someone who was very helpful the last time I visited here, but it seems he retired last year, so I was told when I rang this morning. I've arranged to see a Captain Handby who has taken overall responsibility for the upkeep of the records and the ten or so staff working here," Graves explained to Morgan as they mounted the steps to front entrance.

"Why exactly are we here sir?" Morgan inquired, slightly bemused.

"I want an informed opinion on the tattoo as well as the type of knot used, especially the tattoo," he replied.

"Hopefully, I should get both from Handby." The two passed through the front door and turned right along a gloomy corridor flanked by high-sided sash-type windows, which let surprisingly less light into the building than they were perhaps designed for. The long corridor, Graves guessed it to be several hundred yards from his last visit, was interrupted at the end by a reception desk, which acted as a focal point where two similar corridors also converged. Slightly elevated, it was imposing to visitors and gave the occupants behind it a sense of authority. Of the two ladies behind the mini-fortress, it was the older of the two that greeted the policemen.

"Good morning gentlemen, can I be of assistance?" The lady in her late fifties dressed in a tweed skirt and matching short jacket, lifted the glasses that were dangling around her neck as she spoke to get a better view of her guests.

"I hope so, I have an appointment for 10:30 with Captain Roger Handby My name is Graves, Detective Inspector Graves of New Scotland Yard." Graves thought about explaining his rather unique involvement in what was to follow, but then decided to allow the good Captain the opportunity to ask instead. Perhaps he would overlook the question with some luck. The receptionist looked officiously at the two policemen over her half-rimmed glasses without reaction as if she had seen it all or been witness to it all before. She glanced at her colleague initially before she sat down on the swivel chair behind her and fingered the large desk diary that occupied most of the counter between her and the policemen.

"One moment and I will see if he is available." She closed the book and reached for the desk telephone. "Hello sir, Agatha here at the front desk. I have two gentlemen here to see you," She looked up across at the duo again. "They say they have an appointment with you for 10:30, but there is nothing in the diary." She paused for a moment as if receiving instructions. "Why yes sir," she exclaimed," the police – here, whatever next?" She stopped talking abruptly. "Right away sir, I'll bring them now." Graves heard the line go dead on the other end before Agatha put her phone back on the receiver. "If you will follow me gentlemen, Captain Handby will see you now." She appeared from behind the walnut counter retaining her stern look, her height dropping at least a foot as she stepped off the platform. Morgan's smile was more derisory than pleasant and she scowled back at the younger police officer. They walked briskly passed at least six large double oak panel doors on each side along the narrow corridor, none betraying what lay within each room, only silence. She stopped two doors from the end, the door in question bearing the name 'Captain R Handby' on a brass nameplate. Tapping lightly on the left-hand door she listened intently for a response.

"Enter," came the officious response and she grasped the brass door handle as if her life depended on it. The door swung open and both Graves and Morgan were led into a large room with a uniformed man sitting at the far end behind an equally large writing desk. The name 'Captain R. Handby' stood prominently on the edge of the desk facing anyone entering the room. The room itself, as with most civil servant buildings, seemed disproportionate in size for the job it appeared to be employed for. The only furniture in the room beside the ornate writing desk were two filing cabinets three spare chairs and an umbrella stand, currently unoccupied presumably due to the change in weather today. All could have been accommodated in a room a third of the size.

"Come in Gentlemen and take a seat, I'm Captain Handby. Detective Inspector Graves I presume – we spoke on the telephone early this morning." Handby was already standing gesturing to the chairs strategically arranged around his desk. The feet of both men echoed as their footsteps moved along the varnished oak floorboards. Graves shook hands with Handby across the table. Handby's distinctive blue uniform was immaculately pressed with creases where you expect them and sharp enough to cut your finger with. A Terry Thomas type moustache partly covered a small scar running between his upper lip and left nostril. Square jawed and with pale blue eyes he somehow didn't look like a regular navy officer. A hat and cane lay side-by-side on the table next to an empty in-tray and a half full out-tray. Agatha squeezed passed both guests, scooping up the contents from the out-tray and left closing the door behind her.

"Good to meet you Captain Handby," Graves replied. "It is always nice to put a face to a name. This is Detective Constable Morgan."

"Constable," Handby commented. "Have a seat gentlemen and pray tell me, how I can help you? I was rather intrigued after your call to have New Scotland Yard visiting us." Graves looked coyly at Morgan deciding to keep the little subterfuge intact for now. Graves took the nearest chair.

"It's as I explained to you on the telephone really, not much more to add," Graves offered casually. "We are investigating a suspicious death at the moment involving a body that looks as if it has been dead for twenty-five years. I don't think I am speaking out prematurely, " Graves continued, having noticed Morgan's piercing stare. "I can't go into specific details you understand, well not at the moment, but there are some characteristics of the body that I was hoping your predecessor would help me with. I hadn't realised he had retired," Graves explained.

"And you thought that I could help you instead?" Handby replied. Graves smiled hopefully. "Glad to Inspector. Please, fire away."

"The body," Graves continued," was found tied and bound in a distinctive way." Graves took out a plain brown envelope from his briefcase and pulled out four of the five photographs inside. Each picture gave a close-up view of the rope used to tie the hands and legs. "I'm far from an expert in these matters, but the knot appears unusual." Graves asked. "These photographs were taken using a boroscope camera. Handby took all four photographs and arranged them on his desk in front of him. His eyes moved from one to the other initially without comment. Finally he spoke.

"I can tell you what kind of knot it is Inspector, but you could have found that out speaking to any cub scout," he suggested. "I thought at first it was a Constrictor knot, but now I'm convinced we are looking at a Strangle knot." Handby continued, turning the photographs around several times until he was satisfied with the perspective. "Constrictor and Strangle knots are very similar in appearance and in what they are used for in practice. The strangle knot is much neater in appearance and leaves minimal marks on whatever it is securing. Obviously, if that object were hard or firm it wouldn't really matter which knot was used. Each would be as effective. I'd expect less impressions on the skin with a Strangle knot than I would with a Constrictor knot. You see Inspector," Handby referred to the wrists on the picture, "it may not be of any consequence, but it could have been a conscious decision on the part of the killer." Handby suggested. "The Strangle knot is common on seafaring trips to secure cargo and stop it moving around as the ship rolls from side-to-side. With more typical, everyday knots, even a Constrictor knot, the load would eventually strain the rope and knots to the point where the load would work its way loose. The strangle knot, however, becomes tighter the more the load tries to wriggle free – hence the name."

"Only in this case the load was a human body," Morgan pointed out.

"Yes Constable and equally as prone to wriggle free if given the opportunity and circumstances, so I would say a deliberate choice by the victim's captor – someone who knew his knots," Handby continued, passing the photographs back to Graves.

"So we are looking for someone with a knowledge of sailing and how to tie knots?" Morgan pressed.

"Oh I doubt it will be that easy Constable," Handby smiled. "Any cub, scout, mountaineer, fell walker, abseil enthusiast, camping enthusiast or mountain rescuer would probably know all about the more obscure or unusual knots." Morgan scribbled notes furiously as Handby spoke. Without answering Handby, Graves pulled out the remaining photograph and passed it across the table.

"I'm afraid that the quality of this picture is not much better. I was wondering if you could identify this type of ship. It was in the form of a tattoo on the arm of our victim." Graves explained. Handby opened a drawer in his desk and pulled out a large magnifying glass. With the reading lamp aimed at the photograph, he moved the glass in and out until he had it in focus.

"The profile looks familiar for some reason," Handby commented without taking his eyes away from the glass.

"It looked like a frigate to me sir?" Morgan offered, keen to have his earlier observation confirmed.

"Not quite my boy. If we are to make a positive identification…" Handby replied leaving the question unanswered. He moved over to his filing cabinet and reached inside the top-drawer shuffling books and reports to one side until he had what he was after. He pulled out a large A4 size book, the sort you find in libraries that are for reference use only. "Here we are," he said triumphantly, 'Wyatt's Brief History of the Royal Navy – Second World War Edition'," he read out eagerly like a schoolboy with a comic book. Both Graves and Morgan listened intently, letting Handby indulge himself. "This gentlemen is the collector's bible concerning seafaring warfare of the Second World War. Every Royal Navy vessel ever designed, whether launched or not is covered in some detail inside this book. Now let me see," Handby said flicking through various pages until he found what he was after. "Ah yes, a Town Class Cruiser gentlemen." He seemed to pause unexpectedly as if having second thoughts. His pale blue eyes glazed over and for a few brief seconds he was in a world of his own.

"Captain Handby…you were saying?" Graves prompted him.

"Oh my apologies gentlemen," he replied visibly embarrassed. "I haven't had call to discuss this particular ship for, oh, 30 or 40 years." Why it should have such an adverse effect on him was obviously his own business and he was keeping it to himself. "Your tattoo gentlemen I think you will agree is based on this ship. There were 17 commissioned of the 1910 version and 10 of the 1936 version and as far as I know they were all in service during the Second World War. Each carried a compliment of 750 men, with 6-inch guns and powered by gas turbines with a top speed of 32 knots. They were quicker than the larger destroyers and used to great effect tracking German U-boats." He passed the open book across the desk to Graves, followed by the photograph of the tattoo.

"See for yourself gentlemen. The outline of the ship in the book is a very close resemblance to your tattoo, do you not think?" Handby asked. Both men had to agree.

"Would it seem too much of a generalisation to say that most sailors had tattoos of the ship they served on?" Graves said speculatively.

Handby looked at him unsure and then a look of understanding spread across his face.

"If you contain your hypotheses to ordinary seamen and exclude ranking officers I would say that the majority got around to it sooner or later. It was some kind of code

In The Mood

they had, pride even, and another way of narrowing the search if they were lost in battle," Handby explained. "If you are trying to identify your victim by this line of inquiry though I would say that without a ship's name as well it would be like looking for a needle in a haystack. Even with the right ship it would be a challenge to identify one man."

"We fully intend to have more details from the body, following the *post mortem*. Perhaps we might pay you a second visit then?" Graves suggested.

"By all means Inspector, only happy to oblige," Handby replied, standing as he did. The trio shook hands before Graves and Morgan left. On the way back to Willenbury, Morgan finally broke the silence.

"Did you get what you were after sir?" Morgan asked, turning the steering wheel right off the A312 as they joined the M4 motorway.

Graves looked out through the front windscreen momentarily lost in thought about what was happening back at the Yard and his father's condition all at the same time.

"Sir?" Morgan said, trying to get his attention.

"Sorry Morgan, my mind was a little preoccupied. Until we have the *post mortem* results we can only act on the evidence at hand. Yes I know I could have had the knots identified by others much nearer to home, but the tattoo was a little more specialised and I needed someone with knowledge or an eye for warships to confirm type and model, which he did, fortunately, although I have a feeling that we are not finished yet with Captain Handby," Graves commented.

Graves hadn't realised that he was gradually being drawn into the case despite his best endeavours to be at his parent's side. The Granada made its way along the M4 toward the M25 interchange when the car radio crackled into life.

"Come in DC Morgan over," the voice on the other end of the radio called out.

Morgan picked up the microphone, " This is DC Morgan receiving, over."

"Morgan, this is DCI Swallow, is Inspector Graves with you, over?"

"Yes sir, over."

"Tell him that Jack Rowan would like to see him at the County Laboratories, lab room 4, as soon as possible. Rowan managed to get the body out late yesterday and more evidence has been discovered that he feels will be of interest," Swallow responded.

Graves found the case interesting and yes, the tattoo had intrigued him as far as his father was concerned, but he had no burning desire to visit Rowan's lab, where all manner of dissection was no doubt taking place. Morgan eyed him expectantly, poised with the radio handset. What the hell Graves thought, the lab was on the way back anyway. Graves nodded silently at his driver.

"We will be there in about 35 minutes sir, over and out." Morgan said, and then the radio fell silent.

ooooo

Just over thirty minutes later Morgan pulled the car into a parking spot marked 'Visitors only' at the rear of County Laboratories. The old building had started off life as a hospital in its own right during the Second World War. Time and technological advancement had eventually caught up with it over the twenty or so years that followed and it was reassigned to house and process the deceased of those bodies that were of interest to the Coroner's Office. As one of the Coroner's staff carrying out *post mortem* examinations, the Labs had become Jack Rowan's residency in recent years. Once inside and past security, they made their way down to Lab room 4. Graves stood outside the lab entrance apprehensive about entering, as he always was when it came to forensic pathology. He always found it difficult to regard the body of a dead person to be nothing other than a carcass or cadaver to be taken apart at will to discover why it had stopped working, then to see it put back together, usually rather crudely. Rowan would always call him in just when the examination was at its most gruesome in the past and he had no reason to think that anything had changed. Morgan stayed even further back with no wish to take the invitation presumably for the same reasons.

"Come in Phil, don't be bashful, and bring young Morgan in with you. There are gowns just outside the door," Rowan called through the microphone as he stooped over his present case on the mortuary slab. His attention turned back to the subject at hand, a twenty-one year old road traffic accident victim. The familiar squint and frown returned to his face as he lifted the majority of the victim's rib cage out of the torso and on to a nearby tray for weighing.

"This one is nothing to do with you Phil, so you can speak from a safe distance if you prefer." Rowan continued his eyes catching a fleeting glimpse of the pair as they approached him. "Can I have a photograph please?" Rowan called out, standing back away from the body as he did. A technician appeared from the sideline and clicked a few frames off with a Minolta camera.

"Jack," Graves called out. He stood several feet away on what he considered the right side of the body away from Rowan's handiwork.

"I'll be with you in a few seconds Phil," Rowan assured him without being deterred from his goal. His right arm seemed to disappear into the young man's chest cavity. Graves winced turning slightly to focus on something else, anything.

"What else did you glean from the body Jack?" Graves asked. "Any clues as to who he is?" Rowan retrieved his right forearm, slowly the sound resembling a serving of red cherry trifle being pulled from a deep bowl for the first time. The colours involved also seemed appropriate. He turned and placed the heart from the body onto a separate tray close by.

"Get that weighed for me please and record the information," he asked his assistant. He turned to face Graves, smiled and then moved toward the sink at the far end of the room. "OK Phil, you're late. I can give you ten minutes – I need a fag," Rowan said without pausing. "A bit of a rush job, poor kid's related to the Mayor." He removed his gown, hat and over-shoes en route. Peeling off his surgical gloves he threw them into a disposal container. He washed his hands vigorously, whilst considering his thoughts carefully before speaking. Morgan had recovered by now and stood a few yards behind Graves. Turning, he stood leaning on the sink facing Graves, finishing wiping his hands on paper towels. He stared at Graves, one of the pre-rolled cigarettes now lit between forefinger and thumb, waving at both policemen toward the exit. The three men walked slowly out the room without further conversation until they were outside.

"The body was that of a man in his 40s. He was tied and bound from behind at both the wrists and ankles as we discussed earlier. The rope knot is distinctive as we also discussed earlier," Rowan explained.

"Yes we know it's a Strangle knot," Graves interrupted.

"Well done detectives," Rowan said sarcastically, then irritated at losing his train of thought. "The rope itself is of a certain quality and particularly tolerant of calcium chloride. We found traces of calcium chloride inside the fibres along with some silica deposits." Morgan looked across at Rowan puzzled. "Salt and sand my dear boy, sharp sand that you find at the beach rather than softer, building sand from a quarry. The fibres also had a pigment change caused by time and the cyclic flooding of the chamber in which the body was contained. Some of our clever boys up the corridor here have been mixing a cocktail of chemicals to bring out what was originally there. The results are due back any time now, which was the main reasons I called you," Rowan explained.

"What about the body itself?" Graves asked.

"We have dental evidence now – two missing wisdom teeth – but obviously without something to compare against they're of no value. You might want to check local dentists in the area with practices going back over twenty-five years, but judging by their general condition, I would say this chap was not very keen on oral hygiene. There appears to be an unusually shaped scar tissue on his forehead." Rowan gestured with his finger tracing the shape of a horseshoe on his own forehead. "He has a fracture of the right femur, an old fracture probably done as a child. Similarly, I managed to retrieve a partial thumbprint, where the skin tissue remained uncorrupted, which you should be able to run through your databanks back at the Yard. My only concern is that the case goes back twenty-five years. Even if the Yard has these prints for whatever reason, they may not be on the computer yet. It may take some time to get through all those record cards, but at least you have a start. Oh, if you are interested?" Rowan continued pleased with himself about something "The condition of the body made conventional printing of the hand useless. We simply couldn't get the level of ridge definition to show up a clear enough print." Rowan paused as if expecting a prompt and Morgan duly obliged.

"I don't understand?" Morgan said. "So how did you manage to get a partial thumbprint then?" Rowan tapped his nose gently.

"The skin residue we found beneath the body," he described graphically, "when I laid it out on the mortuary slab, the majority of it was in tatters except for the hands. They must have separated at the wrists near where the ropes had chaffed into the skin and simply slid off the hand with time. I put the skin glove over my gloved hand and pressed it home as if it was my own print," he continued gesticulating with his hands. "I should have a final report to give to you before you leave once I insert a paragraph about the chemical composition of the rope," Rowan concluded.

"What about the clothes?" Graves asked.

"Nothing of any significance. Whoever murdered him had the presence of mind to remove all distinguishing labels. Pockets were empty, not so much as a bus ticket. The style suggests the late1950s or early 60s, but we knew that already from the age of the bridge. The *post mortem* examination confirmed my suspicion. The third Cervical Vertebra and fifth Thoracic Vertebra were broken completely and coincident with the ribbed pattern from the metal on the back and neck of the body," Rowan explained.

"What does that mean exactly Dr Rowan?" Morgan asked.

"The neck and backbone were broken basically my boy, caused by a large weight coming into sudden contact at both locations. The ribbed steel panel appears to have been placed there as a means of supporting the wet concrete as it was poured, as I suspected at the time. County Engineers described it as 'permanent formwork' when used intentionally. A sort of sacrificial means of supporting fluid concrete until it hardens. The panel appears to have buckled though under the weight and sudden impact, severing the neck and backbone at these two points. We found tissues between the teeth, which indicate that the tongue had been bitten, clean through by the force. The facial features are consistent with sudden death grip and impact. I would say that he was dead seconds after the metal plate made contact," Rowan explained further.

Graves considered what Rowan had described before speaking. "So this backs up your murder theory," he said, " but to what end?"

"I believe that is your job Phil or should I say Wheldon's job. I only deal in facts," Rowan reminded him.

"Why is he naked?" Morgan interrupted.

"Humiliation before death, slow torture through cold temperatures had he survived that is," Rowan offered. "It's an old Gestapo tactic. Again, I can only present the facts as I see them. Interpretations and where they may lead is your department detectives," Rowan said with a knowing look.

"Doctor Rowan," the call came from the door leading back into the lab occupied by one of Rowan's assistants.

"Ah, Richard," Rowan called, "you have the results from the rope analysis?"

The spotty-faced technician walked across the forecourt toward them, several sheets of text and plotted graphs in his hand. "Here you are sir, all done."

"Just give me the highlights Richard," Rowan remarked. "That is all they are really interested in," he remarked referring to Graves and Morgan.

"Right you are sir," he replied. "The faded pigment on the rope turned out to be letters. Some were random letters and some of the letters made out a word – a name in fact sir. There was an S, H and an M, sir. We had to try something different for the word until we made out the name 'Ulysses'," the technician explained. The brief summary seemed to unlock something inside Graves's head.

In The Mood

"If we maintain our focus on a maritime theme you could rearrange the letters so that you get HMS – HMS Ulysses. The rope could have come from a ship bearing that name and if I'm not mistaken," Graves said thoughtfully, "a Town Class Cruiser."

"Like the tattoo on the victim's arm?" Morgan added.

"Precisely Morgan. Maybe, just maybe our victim was once a serving member on a ship called HMS. Ulysses," Graves explained.

"The name on the rope doesn't necessarily mean he was a serving sailor on the ship though, assuming the ship exists," Rowan pitched in.

"Perhaps, but it's our best lead so far and worth looking into," Graves replied. "I think a visit back to see Captain Handby might prove fruitful this time now that we have a ship's name to work with. Perhaps I'll check with the Royal Navy first and see if it existed before bothering Handby again." The two men thanked Rowan for his efforts and left. The return trip to Hayes would have to wait just now. It was late afternoon by now and he needed to be back at the hospital as he had arranged the night before. He would visit Handby alone this time. Morgan had more pressing duties with that partial thumbprint and dental records. He'd given him a contact name at New Scotland Yard to talk to about tracing the print on their database.

10

HMS Ulysses

The previous night had brought little improvement at the hospital. A specialist neurosurgeon had taken a look at the brain scans of Reginald Graves, but this brought little change other than to wait for some sign of improvement. It was 2am by the time Graves had left the hospital and 2:30am before he arrived back at the cottage. Despite being exhausted, he had a restless night. The nightmare that had invaded his every night's sleep, and day if his trip home was anything to go by, was back with a vengeance. Having made a quick phone call to the Royal Navy at Plymouth the night before, he arrived tired and weary and already late for his appointment with Captain

Handby. Fortunately, Handby had agreed to see him the following morning at short notice. Parking was abysmal exaggerating the lateness of the hour. He rushed through to the reception area as he had the previous day fearing the worst from Handby's helpers.

"Ah, Inspector Graves is it not?" Agatha announced, an air of superiority in her voice confirmed that he was indeed late.

"Yes good morning," Graves answered slightly out of breath. "I'm here to see Captain Handby again urgently."

The lady behind the counter looked at the appointments register, then at Graves and back at the register. "I'm afraid you're thirty minutes late Inspector. Captain Handby does like punctuality otherwise he insists on organising another appointment. He is a busy man you know," she told Graves like a schoolboy caught outside of school grounds after the register had been taken. Graves imagined the clear desk in Handby's office and had to bite his tongue before he spoke.

"Yes I'm sorry about that, the traffic is terrible this morning," he said bending the truth somewhat. She looked him up and down again, his tired demeanour not helping his cause and then lifted the telephone receiver.

"Captain Handby, Agatha on the front desk, I have Inspector Graves here again to see you." She spoke slowly as if he was hard of hearing. "Yes I told him about being late sir," she raised an eyebrow in Graves's direction, "something about the traffic being terrible today sir." The telephone went dead soon after she received her instructions. "Okay Inspector if you will follow me?" she asked.

"I'll be fine thank you, I know the way," Graves replied already heading down the hallway toward Handby's office. Agatha followed him with one of her stares until she finally resumed her duties. Graves tapped on the door, intending to walk in directly but the slightly pompous voice of Handby passed through the door before he had the chance.

"Enter!" Graves stepped inside. "Ah, Inspector Graves, back so soon. What can I do for you this time?" he announced. "Have you more evidence now?"

Graves marched across the room and took the same seat as the day before. "I have a little more information now – and I must admit, sooner than I anticipated yesterday. The rope that I showed you yesterday, the one with the Strangle knot?" Handby nodded curiously. "We found a faint trace of a coloured dye within the fibres of the rope. We were able to make these faded areas more pronounced and the dye represented letters and a name in fact – HMS Ulysses." Graves commented. Handby reacted oddly to the news. His friendly outgoing personality changed and he became introverted and thoughtful, yet he offered no immediate comment.

"I've checked with the Royal Navy this morning on the way down here, one of the reasons why I was late arriving, and they said that it was common practice to name-stamp MOD property in that way suggesting that there was once a commissioned vessel called HMS Ulysses. The officer that I spoke to at the navy base ran a check on the name. He described HMS Ulysses in exactly the

In The Mood

same way that you did yesterday – a Town Class Cruiser, commissioned during the Second World War. He also said that if I wanted anything specific about its crew that I should visit the archive at the record office at Hayes," Graves explained holding out his hands animatedly, "so here I am again. What do you think your records can tell me about the crew of the HMS Ulysses?" Handby's features visibly changed even more as Graves described what the forensics lab had found, but again he kept silent. Instead, he stood and limped awkwardly to the window as if in deep thought almost oblivious to Graves being in the room.

"You know the name don't you?" Graves said quietly reacting to Handby's surprising behaviour.

"I cannot help you Inspector," Handby eventually replied. He continued looking outside the window not offering to address his guest directly at any point.

"I'm sorry I don't understand." Graves replied. "If you have records of servicemen serving on the Ulysses, it might help us to identify the body we found. I admit it's still a long shot, but we have little else to go on at present," Graves explained.

"I'm afraid the Ulysses went down off the coast of Singapore in October 1943 with all hands," Handby said slowly and deliberately. "It cannot possibly have any bearing on your investigation Inspector, regardless what your lab has found out."

Graves observed his host momentarily, taking in Handby's change of mood in a matter of seconds. "You seem fairly certain of your facts if you don't mind me saying Captain Handby?" Graves asked, trying hard not to antagonize his host.

"My father was the Second Lieutenant on the Ulysses Inspector. I was only sixteen when the ship went down." Handby said, still staring out of the office window.

"Oh I am sorry," Graves said feeling insensitive. He hadn't quite lost his own father yet, but that potential loss and gut-wrenching pain was growing inside by the day. Just then there was a tap on the door and the younger receptionist, Edwina, appeared, complete with silver tray, teacups and a plate of ginger nuts.

"Excuse me Captain Handby, Agatha thought you might like a nice cup of tea." Handby turned, the self-assuredness returning to his face, he managed a strained smile as Edwina poured the tea.

"If I could help you Inspector I would believe me, but the personnel records of HMS Ulysses and many others like it were destroyed or given back to the surviving relatives nearer the time that these ships were lost. This one was way before my time here." Handby explained, accepting his cup and saucer and a ginger nut from Edwina.

She beat a hasty retreat leaving the two men to speak freely. "I'm sorry if I brought back painful memories." Graves replied.

"Not to worry Inspector, it was a long time ago and quite frankly, an uncanny coincidence. Needless to say the name Ulysses came as a shock so long after the war," Handby said with an awkward smile. "I'm afraid I have to go out Inspector just now – a dental appointment unfortunately," he continued, having second thoughts

In The Mood

about his biscuit. Graves returned the smile thanking Handby for his help once again. Finishing off their tea, both men left together. Handby left directly, leaving Graves to speak to Edwina who was waving discretely to catch his attention.

"Excuse me Inspector Graves," she said pulling his arm so that they were gently out of earshot from her colleague, Agatha. She ushered him into a side room that seemed to go back some distance. The name on the door said, 'Records'. "I couldn't help overhearing earlier. Captain Handby was quite right Inspector, about the general records from the Second World War, but we tended to keep hold of medical records. Some as far back as the First World War and as recent as the Falklands War. Some of them are museum pieces now you know and we have been asked to preserve them for that reason. It is something to do with relatives' right to know, particularly after the most recent engagements. Some of the older records are in archive within this building."

"Do you think you have the records for HMS Ulysses? " Graves asked, hope in his voice.

"It's possible Inspector, we haven't carried out a clean sweep since I began working here twenty years ago," she replied.

"A 'clean sweep'?" Graves queried.

"Yes a sort of rationalization of records by taking out the older ones and putting them into deeper storage, those less likely to be of interest to anyone over the passage of time," she smiled. "Please, take a seat and I'll see what I can do on Captain Handby's behalf. I heard him say that he would help you if he could and I know that he was in a hurry to leave for his appointment, so I will see what I can do," she said. With that she scurried off into the back of the room disappearing through a door at the rear.

It was a full hour later when she emerged cradling a dated looking file referencing box, about the size of a large shoebox. She placed it on the small desk in front of him reaching for a cotton cloth hanging on a hook behind the door and gently brushed it along the surface of the lid pushing copious amounts of dust into the waste paper bin below.

"Sorry about this Inspector. The archive really does look like an archive when you delve this far back. There must be at least thirty years of dust on this box, allowing for some initial use just after the war," she explained. She lifted the lid cautiously as if she expected it to fall to pieces revealing an equally dated card referencing system inside. Cards denoting every letter of the alphabet sat prominently upright with yellowed paper sheets between each card. "I wasn't able to find actual records for individuals serving on HMS Ulysses, I could only find the card referencing record itself that they used in the past to locate the actual records stored here," she continued. "It's only a brief summary, although you may find it useful Inspector. I should be able to give you the headlines for an individual – basic vital statistic details including a forwarding address, but that may be of little use to you by now, around forty years later, I would have thought. Now then, what exactly are you looking for?"

Graves pulled the box around to get a closer look. "I'm not entirely sure." He said tentatively. "Fingerprint details, dental records, basic physical statistics as you said

– something that matches the details of my victim in the case I'm involved in."

"Well let me see," she said out loud. "The first card of these old box systems always had a nomenclature showing what the symbols meant on each card. If I'm not mistaken, we could narrow down certain reference cards to male or female, height and probably age. That should focus your search and then you can look for specifics." she suggested. She looked at Graves as if having second thoughts. "Do you really think that you will find your victim inside this box?"

"Maybe," he replied cautiously. "We have other lines of inquiry that other officers are following at present. I have, err, personal and professional reasons for following this line of inquiry. I also knew Captain Handby's predecessor from a previous case. Ironically, he retired last year, hence my introduction to Captain Handby.

"Ah you mean Major Goddard – a lovely man," Edwina volunteered.

Graves nodded in agreement. "I'm just concerned that I might be inconveniencing you, I am willing to commit some time here sifting through potential candidates," he suggested, trying to be helpful.

Edwina shrugged her shoulders," Agatha has left for the rest of today and Wednesday is our quiet day anyway. I'll make a cup of tea – you could be here for a while." she smiled and left. A few hours and several cups of tea later and Edwina reappeared. It was 4:30pm and the office was due to close for the night. Graves had completed his interrogation of the file referencing record and found one name that met the scant information from Rowan's *post mortem*. In particular a reference to a left femur fracture and the removal of two wisdom teeth as well as matching vital statistics suggested that the identity of the body in the bridge was that of Robert Benson. Born 1918, it would make him 25 years old on the Ulysses and 42 by the time he met his demise at Bedford Bridge. The age was about right from Jack Rowan's examination. A thumbprint could remove any remaining doubts something they would pursue later. Strangely, the card was hidden with three others inside an envelope lying face down beneath all the other reference cards. The envelope was marked, 'DEMOBBED 1943'. There was no forwarding address or next of kin noted.

"Any idea what this might mean?" Graves asked her.

"Well I suppose the way it reads," she replied, shrugging her shoulders.

"Yes, but I've been sat here for fifteen minutes wondering why you would demob experienced servicemen during the height of the war." he asked, still wrapped up in his own deliberation. "There is no other information on the card to explain why," Graves said out loud turning Benson's card.

"No, but there is more information on this card," Edwina commented looking at one of the three remaining cards from the envelope, she offered it back to Graves, "nothing to say why, err, Jeff Woollsey was demobbed, just a forwarding address. There is nothing at all on the reverse side of Jack Turnberry and Charles Grundy's records though."

"Woollsey, Jeff," Graves read out from the card, "next of kin a Miss Jessica Woollsey, Crandon Hall, Lake

District, Cumbria. Nice part of the country," Graves said turning the card once more. "Could I impose on your kindness just a few moments longer?" he asked with a hint of pleading in his voice. "I wondered if I could have a photocopy of these records before I leave please." Handby's clerk smiled and duly obliged, disappearing along the adjacent corridor into the first door that she came to. Five minutes later she returned with good quality copies tucked inside a transparent folder. He thanked her for her help as they both headed toward the main door making small talk when Graves paused.

"What happened to servicemen after the war?" he asked. She gave him an odd look, shrugging her shoulders again.

"What I mean is, after the war soldiers, sailors, pilots: were they left to find employment when they were demobbed? Graves said clarifying the motive behind his question. "There must have been a huge demand for work when the war was over."

"There were employment agencies tasked with finding jobs for ex-servicemen," she replied. "The Hadley was local to this area of the country." He eyed her curiously. "The Hadley Employment Agency, Inspector, was based about eight miles from here and covered a 100 mile radius finding work for demobbed servicemen after the war."

"So the Hadley would have dealt with finding employment as far away as a small village like Willenbury?" he said to himself trying to make the tenuous connection with his home village and Benson before he met his demise. "Tell me more about this Agency." Graves asked as they passed through the main entrance.

"It is or rather was an employment agency in the 1940s and 50s. The company and building have long since gone. The Wild Boar Pub stills stands opposite the site and a few of the former employees still drink there," she volunteered, "well the ones that are still alive and possibly some that aren't, as local ghost hunters would have you believe."

"I'm impressed by your powers of recollection Miss Bradley," Graves replied, "though I'm not complaining."

"My father worked through the Hadley initially after he was demobbed himself in 1945 Inspector. I use to meet him with my mum at teatime from school just up the road from their main office. You really need to have chat with Charlie Grimshaw. He was the General Manager at the Hadley at the time. He is a regular at the Wild Boar. He still drinks there according to my aunt who cleans there," she told him. One good deed deserved another in return for her help he thought to himself. Offering Edwina a lift home might yield even more information.

Later he called in at home briefly to gather more supplies for his mother before calling at the hospital. His visit was uneventful as far as his father's condition was concerned. Even his own anxiety attacks were kept in check this time. All that he could do was offer moral support to his mother who appeared to be becoming more frail with the passage of time, no doubt contributed to in no small part by the lack of improvement in her husband's condition.

He awoke the following morning with the thoughts of the previous day's inquiry at the records office firmly fixed in his mind. Despite Handby's reluctance to help for personal reasons, Edwin Bradley had on the other

In The Mood

hand been very helpful. The information on the medical cards for all four men demobbed in 1943 was patchy at best, but he expected Benson to be the man entombed in the bridge and he also appeared to be closely linked to three other men named as being demobbed with him at the same time.

"If he or Morgan could trace one of them," he thought to himself, "it might help them find out what happened to Benson and the significance of the tattoo and his father's drawings back at the cottage.

He sat beside the telephone in his parent's cottage spinning the photocopy of Benson's medical record between his forefinger and thumb, letting it tap on the table, deliberating over his next move. His decision to give Edwina a lift home had also paid off as the Wild Boar Pub was only a mile off her route home. If he were to locate Charlie Grimshaw the likelihood would be that he wouldn't show until lunchtime at the earliest at the Wild Boar. Even if he found Grimshaw, the trip may turn out to be a wild goose chase; or boar chase, he smiled to himself.

The more he considered his options the more he was convinced that he needed to see Rowan and probably another ex-colleague, Ray Brightwell, first to consider the corroborating evidence he had discovered at Hayes. He promptly jumped into his car, heading due south toward County Labs. Quarter of an hour later the MG was parked behind one of the outbuildings and Graves was making his way down the darkened corridor that divided each laboratory from its neighbour. The last lab on the right was producing some heated discussion. He could make out Rowan's voice clearly – he was the one making all the noise. Edging toward the door he could now see Rowan and his guest. Graves recognised Ray Brightwell immediately from his previous time at the station. Rowan swung around just at that moment catching sight of Graves in the corridor outside. He waved at him to come in. It was only when Graves was inside that he sensed a familiar third presence, a presence he had sensed before.

"Phil, you know Ray don't you?" Rowan said gesturing to his sparring partner. Graves nodded at Brightwell. "Do you know Tom?" Rowan continued. As in Swallow's office, Wheldon sat farther back, out of sight, no doubt listening to the debate. Wheldon gave a friendly gesture before Graves's attention switched back to the overhead projector that both men had been stooping over during their lively discussions. "I take it you're here for an update on the final *post mortem*?" Rowan asked, first looking at Graves and then at Wheldon.

"Well no actually, but now that I'm here," Graves replied. "I recall you mentioning the business about the skin glove when we spoke last time?" Rowan nodded. "You managed to get a print off it as I recall?" Graves asked. Wheldon sat passively in the background choosing to listen rather than partake.

"Well it's Ray's area of expertise as you know and it was a partial print. That is why he is here this morning. Unfortunately, young Morgan hasn't been successful locating a match. I believe he's even had Interpol carrying out a search," Rowan replied. Brightwell looked frustrated by the lack of progress. Clearly he felt that his time was being wasted by incompetent detectives, a trait in his personality Graves recalled from his past experience working with him. Wheldon on the other hand seemed to be enjoying the spectacle.

"Do you have a photocopier Jack?" Graves asked.

"In the corridor – you passed it on your way in," Rowan replied.

"Two more minutes Ray and I think I'll have something for you," Graves commented as he looked at the size of the print on the overhead projector. Shortly afterwards he reappeared with four pieces of acetate film separated by blank sheets of A4 print paper. He moved over toward the projector to where the image of Rowan's partial thumbprint was projected onto a white screen. He pushed it slightly to one side and introduced one of his acetate films alongside.

"Do me a favour Ray and give me your professional opinion on any similarities between these prints?" Graves asked. Brightwell walked across to the screen, pulling his glasses from the top pocket of his lab coat.

"Can you adjust the focus please?" Brightwell asked. Graves turned the lens clockwise, then anticlockwise. "That will do thank you," Brightwell said.

"As I was saying to Jack, before you arrived Phil this is a typical central pocket loop despite the missing upper portion. You can see how the ridges focus at the centre of the pattern radiating out like the ripples in a pool of water. The print that you produced just now is a double loop characterised by the reverse S-shape of the ridges. Even a layman can see that they belong to two different people," Brightwell explained. Neither Wheldon nor Rowan offered any comment, looking bewildered. Graves stared hard at the first print trying to recall the brief few minutes previously when he copied the documents in the corridor before realising he'd given Brightwell the wrong print. Pulling out the remaining acetate films he spotted what he was looking for and passed it to Brightwell.

"Sorry Ray try this one," he said thrusting the copy toward him. Brightwell took the film replacing Graves's first specimen with it. Brightwell chose to stare at it before pushing the two prints together until they overlaid each other exactly. "Gentlemen, I would say we have a match in my humble opinion," Graves smiled, pleased with himself. Tucked under his arm was the copy of the medical form for the print in question. "Here Jack, your turn. Does anything look vaguely familiar to you?" Graves passed Rowan the form as he walked over to the screen where Brightwell was less than impressed with the theatrics.

"Judging by some of the additional detail on this form," Rowan said tracing a finger across the card," I would say I can concur with respect to the broken femur, dental records and vital statistics."

"How long have you had these records?" Brightwell asked almost demanding an answer.

"Since late last night. I played out a hunch and found Benson's details at the public service records office," Graves replied. "Why and how I won't go into just now." Brightwell looked at him glumly, not happy with the reply, but knowing he wasn't getting anything else.

"Benson?" Wheldon suddenly found his voice, as Graves appeared to be making greater headway than perhaps he had hoped for. Graves looked back to where Wheldon sat less smug than he was before.

In The Mood

"Yes, Robert Benson, ex-sailor serving on the HMS Ulysses, demobbed in 1943, lucky for him," Graves explained.

"Rather strange to be demobbed during the height of the war?" Rowan seemed to have picked up on the odd fact as well. "In fact, to my knowledge I can't think of a scenario that would allow it, unless he was battle fatigued. In any case, why was he lucky?"

"The ship was torpedoed three months later off the coast of Singapore, all hands lost," Graves replied. "Benson and three others were demobbed in July 1943 and it saved their lives."

"It seems his luck ran out in the end," Wheldon quipped. "Is there anything else on the record like an address or next of kin?" Wheldon asked aiming his question at Rowan who was still examining both sides.

"Nothing, just basic physiological information, sex, date of birth, that sort of thing," Rowan replied. Graves smiled inwardly. Woollsey's details were a diffcrent matter and something he chose to keep to himself for now. He had left Woollsey's record back in his car for safekeeping, telling Morgan of his intention to keep this information to himself. Morgan wasn't happy, but he agreed to keep quiet for now. In truth, Graves felt like taking the case forward himself if only to thwart Wheldon's attitude, but he only needed to satisfy himself about any potential connection between this case and his father's sketches.

"Well I'm afraid I have to dash gentlemen," Graves said moving toward the lab exit. "Tom, can you tell Gary Swallow that the body in the bridge has been identified as Robert Benson? Oh, and thanks for your efforts Ray,

Jack," he called out waving a hand of appreciation and with that he was gone. The dry atmosphere in clinical environments always made him thirsty and he knew just where to go for his liquid refreshment.

11

The Wild Boar

The Wild Boar public house looked like a typical workingman's pub from the outside. Situated on the corner of York and Wardle Road, it intruded on both. Graves parked his car more or less where he and Edwina had stopped briefly the previous night. A large board swung to and fro in the autumnal breeze, a picture of said wild boar snarling at any passing pedestrians. A tired hanging basket kept the board company, its contents no longer in bloom. The half-glass, half-wood double doors on the corner opened inwards and an elderly man sporting a long worn-out overcoat and a dirty baseball cap staggered out into the sunshine, barging over empty milk bottles along the way. His lank, grey hair was tied in a ponytail through the back of his cap. He squinted covering his eyes with a fingerless glove from the glare of the afternoon sun, before continuing his unsteady progress along the pavement.

The darkness briefly revealed through the open door was in stark contrast to the unusually sunny autumn day. Given that it was late afternoon, he'd chosen to seek out Charlie Grimshaw before considering the need for a lengthy trip up to Cumbria to see Jeff Woollsey's relatives, regardless of the obvious attraction to such a picturesque part of England. After all, Jeff Woollsey may not have had anything to do with Benson and maybe Grimshaw could confirm this one way or the other? It was a long shot, given the time that had elapsed, but one worth pursuing as far as he was concerned.

No doubt the pub looked significantly different thirty years or so ago, Graves thought to himself as he crossed the street. He stepped inside only to be met by a smoke filled, heavy atmosphere. Two stocky built, greasy haired youths, probably too young to be there legally, stopped their darts game and glared in Graves's direction. Three pensioners – well, Graves guessed them to be pensioners – lifted their heads from their domino game momentarily. They considered Graves with equal contempt before returning back to their game. Two young girls pored over the jukebox in the corner. Both were dressed as if they were much older than their years. It didn't take a New Scotland Yard Inspector to work out that the boys and girls were together. They paused, giggling at Graves giving him a coy look and a sly wink. The landlord appeared from the cellar trapdoor behind the bar.

"What can I get you?" he growled, wiping his hands on a grimy bar towel.

"Something definitely out of a bottle," Graves said to himself. "Err, Britvic 55 please." He sat on the nearest barstool, considering the room's occupants once more before asking any questions. His interest sat before him, the three elderly domino players. From Edwina's description he guessed that the dapper gent dressed in a checked shirt and bowtie was Grimshaw. His bottle arrived.

"I'm after some information," Graves announced accepting the orange juice and offering payment.

"Are you the filth?" the landlord replied.

Dress code for staff working at the Wild Boar was certainly informal. The landlord's short sleeve shirt revealed matching tattoos on both arms extending from the wrist and disappearing beneath his shirtsleeves at the bicep toward the shoulder. Beneath it peeping out at intervals between the strained buttons, a rather grey looking string vest. A pair of denim jeans hung as they always do on men with large waistlines or pot bellies at hip level, barely covering their backside and low enough to let their stomach hang over it. A large buckled belt seemed unnecessary in this instance, but he wore one anyway.

"Am I the filth?" Graves thought to himself giving the landlord's attire the once over again, that's rich! "Your mark of respect is touching," Graves replied

"I don't talk to the filth," he snarled, saliva trickling down his bearded chin.

"How about vice?" Graves asked, looking at the mirror behind the publican where we could see the reflection of both teenage girls. "Maybe I should ask my colleagues to pay you a visit," he added.

"What do you want?" The landlord said slamming a tray of glasses down in annoyance in front of Graves, sending most of them tumbling.

"That's better," Graves replied, keeping his voice low. "I'm looking for Charlie Grimshaw I believe this is his local?" Graves turned again to get a better look at the three pensioners.

"What do you want with that old fart?" the landlord mumbled from behind him.

"That's between Mr Grimshaw and I," Graves said, spinning back around on his stool so that he faced the burly landlord again. The barman scowled back at Graves before his bloodshot eye changed direction toward the trio of domino players in the corner of the room. Graves collected his drink and moved along the bar to a stool that was within earshot of the three men. His movement caused a brief pause in their game again, which Graves took advantage of.

"Mr Grimshaw?" The man in the bowtie regarded him inquisitively. The smoke from his cigarette drifted across his face like a blue gaseous cloud. He offered no response one-way or the other. Graves took silence as confirmation. "I'm Inspector Graves of New Scotland Yard Mr Grimshaw. I need a quiet word," Graves continued sipping the orange juice from his bottle. This time all three men turned and stared up at Graves. The mere mention of the word 'police' always seemed to bring out a defensive streak in people even when they had nothing to hide. The phrase 'New Scotland Yard' added a further dimension though. Grimshaw's colleagues had decided to act on his behalf and promptly rose from their chairs before heading off toward the exit. Graves took one of the now vacant chairs, without invitation, looking directly at the man in the bowtie.

"OK Inspector, you've managed to spoil my game, you have my undivided attention. I can assure you I have an alibi," the older man drawled out sarcastically.

"Relax Mr Grimshaw, I am investigating an old crime and I believe from what I have found out to date about it that you could help me with my inquiries." Graves replied.

"Oh, is that so?" Grimshaw eyed Graves suspiciously. "What is this crime and how old exactly Inspector?" he asked.

"Oh, 25 years ago," Graves replied. Graves observed the older man as a grin erupted across his heavily lined face.

"Inspector, I have trouble remembering what I did yesterday," he managed finally as his chortling subsided.

"You were the General Manager of the Hadley Employment Agency during and after the war, err, 1941 to 1955 so I have been told," Graves said checking his notebook, details found out by Morgan from Companies House in Cardiff earlier that morning. Grimshaw drew deeply on the last half inch of his cigarette, running his thumb along his jaw as if using the delay to gather his memories. He blew the contents of his lungs up above him coughing loudly as he did. He took great gulps of beer from the glass in front of him to try and put out the fire he had just started inside his throat.

"You've done your homework Inspector, but what can you want from me?" he croaked. "I didn't kill anyone."

Graves sighed, "I'm interested in someone you may have found work for back then, an ex-serviceman," Graves said.

"You have got to be bloody kidding me surely," came the reply, "do you know how many ex-servicemen were looking for employment after the war Inspector? I found work for hundreds for five years after the war." His dull grey eyes now stared back at Graves with ridicule.

"I didn't say anything about after the war did I?" Graves corrected him.

Graves flipped through his notebook, occasionally glancing across the table. Grimshaw looked back at him thoughtfully. "The man I'm interested in is Robert Benson, aged 25 in 1943. Ex-Navy, approximately 6 feet tall, he had a tattoo on his right arm of a WW2 ship. He had a small scar on his forehead shaped like a horseshoe." Grimshaw pulled a second Senior Service from the packet in front of him. He tapped the filter end on the tabletop pensively considering the information.

"Ex-Navy, 1943," he replied. "The scar about here shaped so," Grimshaw gestured to his own forehead," and a ship's tattoo on his arm?"

"You recognise the description don't you?" Graves interrupted impatiently.

"Well," Grimshaw began, "your facts are familiar Inspector. Had it not been for the fire I probably wouldn't have remembered this fellow Benson though. His name doesn't ring any bells." He took another long drink from his glass, choosing it now in preference to his cigarette, draining the contents. Graves looked at him quizzically. One thing at a time he thought to himself.

"Enlighten me please Mr Grimshaw if you will?"

"Well Inspector, Benson fits the description of an ex-sailor that I found work for, but he was one 1 of 4 men as I recall. I don't recall Benson's name as I said, but one of his friends Woollsey, I remember him quite clearly. The other two men," he shook his head.

"Turnberry and Grundy," Graves added without prompting. Grimshaw shrugged his shoulders noncommittally. "They all had the same tattoo though as I recall. In those days Inspector, especially during the war, hired help from physically fit men was at a premium. Four young men looking for work in wartime – it was like Christmas Day come early for me. I didn't ask about their circumstances. It was none of my business. Then again the bonus that I got helped to persuade me to keep my nose out. They were an unusual quartet though." He paused reflecting over past memories.

"How do you mean, 'unusual'?" Graves asked keen to milk his guest of all helpful information.

"It's coming back to me now slowly. They appeared in my office one afternoon with no prior warning. You see, Hadley was one of only three agencies in the South of England that had a commission with the Ministry of Defence for finding employment for men leaving any of the armed services, usually injured I might add while the war was still in full swing." Grimshaw suddenly felt a twinge of guilt about his own role or lack of it during the war.

"The quack told me I had a heart defect at the time so I never left England. Ironic isn't it, I'm still here at 80 years of age, smoking 60 a day. Anyway, I digress. The war was still in full swing in 1943 as you know and here I had four apparently healthy males being demobbed prematurely. I would normally have been notified in advance if any work were coming my way, but not in this case. I seem to recall asking that very question of one of the men and he said that they had heard about the agency through hearsay amongst other servicemen. In other words the MOD hadn't sent them at all, despite their valid papers. Most unusual as I recall, still they kept the real reason to themselves and I didn't inquire further." Graves scribbled notes down as Grimshaw spoke about his memory now in surprising detail. "They didn't seem to be too concerned at the time as I recall about what job they wanted to do as long as they stayed together, at least that was the impression that I got from the older chap with the scar, your man," he explained.

"Benson," Graves volunteered and Grimshaw nodded.

"Despite the shortage in service staff, it wasn't easy to find work for them all with the same employer. Benson or Woollsey," he paused again frowning, "yes it was Woollsey. He wanted a particular location, which really tied down my options. Woollsey wanted to work within a ten mile radius of a village…Wildon or something like that," Grimshaw said.

"Willenbury?" Graves volunteered.

In The Mood

"That was the name. He never said why. He was really insistent as I recall," Grimshaw added.

"So that is how Benson happened to be associated with my home village," Graves thought to himself. Putting that thought to one side for a moment he questioned Grimshaw further. "But you did eventually find an employer I take it? You mentioned a fire before," Graves reminded him.

"Yes I got a call from an old friend whom I had found work for in the recent past back then. The place needed odd-job men prepared to do general duties such as gardening, cleaning, heavy lifting, that sort of thing," Grimshaw explained through a haze of blue smoke.

"Do you recall the name of this employer?" Graves pressed.

"I shall never forget it Inspector, Harrington Orphanage, on the outskirts of Willenbury." Graves's reaction was enough to prompt Grimshaw into action.

"You're familiar with the place?" he asked.

"Yes I know the village intimately," Graves replied. "The orphanage, though, escapes me. How did you know about it Mr Grimshaw?"

"You see my fellow domino players that left?" Grimshaw asked. Graves nodded. "The smaller of the two men, that is Harry Gold. He is a year older than me. He was a caretaker at the orphanage in 1943. He wanted to come home and work nearer to London at the time, his family were there during the blitz and he was worried about them. Just at that time the orphanage needed more staff rather than less so I got Harry back in return for four new starters. It was an unfortunate time when more and more kids were losing their parents to the war and ending up in places like Harrington. It was outside London and far enough away for evacuees you see, so places like Harrington were popular with the Government."

Graves gaze took him back toward the door where Harry had left five minutes earlier. "I wouldn't bother chasing him Inspector. His attention span is virtually zero. Even dominos are a real challenge these days. You wouldn't get anything worthwhile from Harry – take my word for it," Grimshaw said, pre-empting Graves's own inclination. "What he told me about that place would make your hair stand on end," Grimshaw added.

"For example?" Graves took the bait.

"Fraud, theft, misuse or misappropriation of food rations and child abuse. You name it, it was going on." Grimshaw stared into his glass and then looked at Graves raising his eyebrows as he did. Graves read his thoughts and ordered a second round of drinks.

"Did you not recall any of your employees from that place?" Graves asked.

"It wasn't good business shall we say to pull people out of employment, especially if they didn't want to be pulled, and these four were quite happy," Grimshaw gave Graves a wink and tapped the side of his nose. "After the war the orphanage continued as it had before and this little quartet stayed on as well. It was a nice little earner from memory until the fire," Grimshaw explained.

The landlord interrupted the two with their drinks. He gave the pair an unfriendly stare, letting it linger on Grimshaw no doubt annoyed at him for bringing the 'old bill' into his delectable establishment. He left as he had arrived abruptly banging the bottle of orange juice and pint of beer on the table between the two men. Graves waited until he had returned behind the bar.

"Yes you mentioned a fire earlier?" Graves reminded him.

"Ah yes, the fire, "Grimshaw pondered. "It must have been 2nd June 1953. I'm sure of the date. Old Ed' Hillary had just conquered Everest a few days earlier and the celebrations over the Queen's coronation were in full swing. The orphanage couldn't have a street party like the rest of England, so they had a garden party.

"What do you remember about the fire Mr Grimshaw?" Graves pressed.

"Sketchy, only what I was told at the time by Eric Gallagher," Grimshaw replied. "Eric spent six months there up until the fire."

"Maybe I should be speaking to Mr Gallagher," Graves suggested, slightly frustrated and wanting to get to the point.

"You could try I suppose, but you would need a medium and some sitters," Grimshaw replied dryly.

"OK, tell me what he told you," Graves asked with a sigh.

"I got him a job at Harrington Hall in 1953. The orphanage had got its own bus from a generous benefactor and they needed a driver. Eric had trained during the war so off he went temporarily until I could find someone local to the area. Me and Eric have been mates ever since up until his death five years ago." Graves gave him an impatient stare about the unnecessary detail. Grimshaw pulled at his collar and bow tie, clearing his throat. "They were never sure about how the fire started. The place would have been a real fire hazard if it hadn't leaked so much when it rained. I seem to recall reports of the fire taking hold below ground level and spreading upwards toward the ground and upper floors." He paused momentarily, drinking from his glass.

"Were there many casualties?" Graves asked, taking advantage of the quiet few seconds.

"Thankfully, the majority of the kids and staff were still outside tidying things away, although some children were still inside. Smoke and flying embers affected some as I recall. Other than that there were five men and one child that perished that night." He blew a smoke ring, watching its progress before it lost its shape and disappeared. "It could have been much worse, but for one brave copper," he continued. "His lady friend was the cook at the orphanage. She apparently telephoned him off-duty at home – so they said at the time – and he raced around there to help. He got the children that were left inside out of the dormitories to a safe place and carried out first aid. He tried to reach the cellar where the victims were trapped, but he was too late. He suffered burns himself I think and he was decorated for his efforts." Grimshaw was rambling again.

"That's all very interesting," Graves offered. "After the fire, do you remember what happened to Benson and his friends? Were they involved in the rescue? Did you find them work elsewhere? " Grimshaw stubbed the remainder of his cigarette and stared once more now at the empty chair beside Graves.

"Maybe I wasn't as clear as I should have been earlier Inspector? Benson was one of the men who died in the fire, that's why I remembered him, " Grimshaw added.

"But that's...not...possible!" Graves rocked back on his seat at the news. His mind retraced the events over the last 48 hours. "Was Jack Rowan wrong?" he said to himself. "What about the others – those he was demobbed with?" Graves pressed Grimshaw still dazed and bemused at the revelation. Grimshaw turned and stared directly at Graves without comment. After what seemed like an age the reality suddenly dawned on the policeman. "Wait a minute, you're not telling me they all perished in the fire?" Graves said incredulously. The man in the bowtie merely nodded, his features lacking in any sort of reaction. Graves sat numb and dumfounded at the news. Did they have the wrong identification for the man in the bridge, just when he was so sure? Was Jack Rowan's partial print at fault? Thoughts were colliding inside his head one after the other. "Are you sure that they all died in the fire?" Graves asked.

"Forty years ago," he shrugged his shoulders, "I could be wrong, yes, but it is unlikely, given the high profile the fire attracted at the time. You can check the local newspaper library if you don't believe me." Grimshaw added. Graves held out a placating hand as if to assure him that he did believe him.

"Yes, it's all coming back to me now," Grimshaw said straightening in his chair." Another reason I recognise these men was more due to Woollsey, on account of his sister Inspector," Grimshaw continued. "I managed to get an address at the time of the fire for Woollsey. The other three seemed to have no living relatives and certainly no one that I could contact. I contacted the Woollsey household at the time of the fire and even they didn't want anything to do with their son except his sister. I think the family came from near the Lakes District in Cumbria. Anyhow, Woollsey's sister came down for the inquest – a very attractive lady if you ask me." Grimshaw smiled to himself lost in his lurid thoughts.

"What about Benson and the others?" Graves inquired.

"No one ever came forward for them Inspector or to claim the bodies. It's as if they never existed," Grimshaw replied downing the last of his beer. "What little belongings that they had I stored. Eventually, I gave them to a local charity."

Graves didn't press any further. He had the Woollsey address in his notebook from Edwina Bradley and now Grimshaw had corroborated it independently. Whether he needed it was open for debate. If Rowan stood by his examination then Benson had effectively died twice. His efforts to try and explain the significance of the tattoo and his father's sketches had only resulted in a deeper mystery, which he was beginning to regret. He thanked Grimshaw for his help and then left. It was nice to get out into the fresh air, even though his clothes reeked of cigarette smoke.

A trip to the North West of England would take the best part of the following day, effectively preventing any sort of trip to the hospital, unless he managed to squeeze in a short visit later in the evening. Mentally, he had made his mind up to go to Crandon Hall as soon as

In The Mood

old Charlie Grimshaw had finished his account of what happened at the orphanage fire in 1953. He would visit the hospital that evening as usual, keeping his trip to Cumbria to himself for now. Just why it had to be him visiting Crandon Hall he wasn't too sure himself. There was something inexplicable now driving him along to bring matters to a satisfactory conclusion, something he was having trouble understanding himself, never mind being able to explain it to his mother. For now he would keep her in the dark about his trip and hope that she would remain that way long after his return.

12

Crandon Hall

Getting out of London to the countryside was a pleasant change, but the Cumbrian Lake District was something much more. Even the M6 appeared quieter the more northerly the car travelled. By the time Morgan had pulled off on to the local road network it was almost a pleasure driving. Approximately twelve miles west along the A590, Graves spotted the sign announcing Crandon Hall, two miles ahead.

In The Mood

His decision to make the long trip north followed an intense discussion and debate with Jack Rowan. The pathologist had conceded to his first ever re-examination in his career, albeit reluctantly. The suggestion that he got his conclusions wrong had prompted him to work through the night. The results were conclusive and the same. The mystery surrounding Benson's death and that of his friends in 1953 deserved further investigation and warranted a trip to Cumbria to see Woollsey's relatives, even if they weren't pleased to see him. After all, if Benson didn't die in the fire then someone took his place. Morgan steered the Ford Granada along the access road until their progress was halted by a pair of wooden gates denoting the entrance to the grounds of the hall. Pushing them open, they continued along the snaking gravel driveway, passed lush green fields with grazing sheep, until the drive broadened and a large Edwardian stone house appeared in the foreground. Morgan brought the Granada to a stop inside the turning circle.

"Well, not quite what I was expecting," Graves admitted. Having parked the car, Graves stepped up to the large door and pressed the bell. A few minutes later the door opened and a frail, elderly lady appeared, her expression a little vacant and preoccupied.

"Excuse me, my name is Inspector Graves. I'm here to see Mrs Woollsey. We spoke briefly on the telephone yesterday." The old lady gave him a confused look. She stood motionless dressed in a grey twin-set skirt and top and a thick, black cardigan. She wore slippers on her feet and her arthritic hands fiddled with the pearls around her neck. She was well nourished for someone of her age, slight frame and quite small set against the huge oak door behind her. Graves looked to his sergeant as if he could expect some support.

"I am Mrs Woollsey, "she stammered slightly. She began to smile, clasping both hands to her cheeks eventually converging over her mouth. "You look just like Teddy. Teddy is my brother you know. I come out here each morning to wait for the postman to see if he has a letter from Teddy – you know, from Africa. He is a desert rat you know? Dreadful code name, but he didn't choose it – I can't say anymore – top secret don't you know," she looked about her as if to give the comment some added weight of secrecy. She had fixed her gaze on DC Morgan who in turn looked behind him to see if anyone else had approached from behind.

"Are you the postman?" she continued focusing on Morgan's uniform. "Have you brought me a letter?" She stopped abruptly and became quite distressed. "Oh no," she said, her voice quivering, "is it a telegram? Is he not coming back?" She pulled a white cotton handkerchief from her cardigan sleeve and began to cry into it.

Both Graves and Morgan looked decidedly uncomfortable, Graves more so. His investigation had taken him a few hundred miles north to follow up on a lead with a woman who was perfectly lucid over the telephone. Now in the flesh she was anything but lucid. Talk of a war that ended over forty years ago, as if it were still being fought? He held out a hand of comfort, but she was having none of it. She stepped back against the door holding out a hand defensively, her voice becoming more agitated. "You're German agents sent here to get my Teddy's secret papers?" she cried.

Graves wondered if he should just leave and let her calm down of her own accord, when the door opened inwards and a hand appeared on the old lady's shoulder. A hand that appeared to have a soothing effect. The owner of the hand quickly followed and a much younger, taller, slim and dark haired woman came into view. For a few seconds the family resemblance was quite uncanny. The younger lady turned without addressing the two men and put her head through the door out of sight. Her voice was high enough to be heard from the drive outside and yet had a tone of control and refinement.

"Mrs Dobson! " she called out. "Mrs Dobson!" There was a brief, muffled response, before a smaller plump lady in a maid's uniform appeared in the doorway. "Can you take my mother back to the library please Mrs Dobson and remind me later to have a better lock put on this door?"

"Of course Lady Woollsey," the maid responded.

"Lady Woollsey?" Graves said to himself surprised.

The old lady was ushered back inside before the familiar-voiced Lady Woollsey, returned to greet her guests. She gave them both a quick look over as she spoke.

"I am sorry gentlemen, my mother has not been well for some time now."

"That was a polite way of saying the old lady was as nutty as a fruit cake," Graves thought. Neither he nor Morgan got the opportunity to respond.

"You do not look like travelling salesmen to me, so you must be police detectives?" she said, folding her arms against the chill of the day.

"Yes," Graves replied, "and you must be Mrs, or should I say Lady Woollsey, that I spoke to yesterday?"

"Inspector Graves I presume?" Graves nodded.

"This is Detective Constable Morgan," he added.

"I apologise for the slight deception on my social standing Inspector, not that it is important. It has been twenty-five years since I spoke to a third party about my brother. Even back then I was always plain Jessica or aunt Jess depending on whom I was talking to. The reason is of no concern to you though Inspector," she said the last sentence in such a way that the subject was not up for discussion. "On the telephone you mentioned that you wanted to talk to me about Jeff?" she said, changing the subject.

"Yes, your brother, that's right Lady Woollsey," Graves replied. Rather than invite them into the house she guided the pair down toward a garden path edged by mature box hedge beach trees so that it felt like Hampton Court Maze.

"I hope you don't mind, but I thought that the summerhouse would be better for our conversation. I do not want my mother upset about the mention of my brother you understand? She has trouble with reality at the best of times," she explained. They continued down the path to an old-fashioned summerhouse that could have housed a small family of its own. She unlocked the door and stepped inside leading the way. "I also felt that a chat about Jeff would be more conducive in the right surroundings," she said half-turning around as she did. Graves and Morgan followed her inside and were met by family photographs and memorabilia scattered across numerous work surfaces, tables and walls. She motioned toward a settee under the window and both men made themselves comfortable.

"I understand Lady Woollsey perfectly," Graves said, taking in the sight.

"Tea gentlemen?" She asked. "Ice, Lemon, Earl Grey?" She said, busying herself with cups and saucers.

"Earl Grey would be fine please," Graves responded. Morgan declined her offer. She pushed a stainless steel kettle under the cold tap.

"You are in luck gentlemen. I was only in here yesterday otherwise there wouldn't be any tea here at all," she said as she turned to face them both. "Now gentlemen," her tone becoming more serious," have you found my brother after all this time and if so is he…" she struggled with the word, "dead?"

"I don't understand Lady Woollsey. Your brother died in 1953 – I believe in a fire where he worked at the time? I was led to believe that you attended the inquest into his death?" Graves prompted her, interested by her reaction.

Lady Woollsey considered her next comment more carefully. "Come, come Inspector, I see no reason for a 300 mile journey just to tell me what I already know if that were true, unless of course it's because you have found him and traced him back to the family home. He is dead is he not?" Her voice trembled as if she expected what she felt was the inevitable answer.

"Are you saying that your brother didn't die in the orphanage fire Lady Woollsey?" Graves asked evading the question. She stood motionless choosing not to respond. Graves decided not to press further. "We are investigating the body of man who is definitely not your brother. However, we have found a link between your brother and this man." Graves could almost feel the relief in her sigh. "Your reaction intrigues me Lady Woollsey," Graves added.

"Oh, in what way is this man linked to my brother Inspector?" Her voice had regained its composure. She cursed herself inwardly at the way she gave away information on her brother so cheaply passing Graves his cup and saucer.

"I now understand that your brother and this man, Robert Benson," she seemed to react to the name, "worked together at a place called Harrington Orphanage between 1943 and 1953. Both men were also Navy servicemen during the war serving on the same ship off the coast of Asia," he continued. She took the words in more carefully this time over the brim of her china cup.

"How did you find me Inspector?" she asked changing the subject slightly again. "You did not mention this on the telephone."

"The man we are investigating – it is a suspicious death." That was putting it mildly, Graves thought. "We traced Benson through his service record using fingerprints and dental records. He was one of four men, including your brother, discharged before the end of the Second World War, again the reason for this is unclear." Graves said watching her body language. "As I said before

In The Mood

I understand that your brother was one of six victims of a fire at Harrington Orphanage in 1953, according to my investigations. The orphanage is just outside a village called Willenbury, about an hour's drive north-west of London. The other victims were Robert Benson, Jack Turnberry and Charles Grundy, coincidentally, the same men that your brother was demobbed with. The fifth man was never identified as the rest of the staff at the orphanage were all accounted for, according to archive records," Graves continued. "The sixth body was that of a child." Graves paused allowing the information to sink in. Benson has been confirmed as the victim of our suspicious death, some seven years after he was supposed to have died in the orphanage fire with your brother." Graves fixed his eyes on the face of his host looking for a reaction. A single tear ran down her face and she wiped it dry across her cheek with the back of her hand.

"Jeff never spoke of Benson out of choice and if he had to, it was in anger and hatred. The other two men, I can vaguely remember. They were good friends of Jeff. They all joined the Navy together. Benson joined later so Jeff said at the time. I learned as I grew older that all four had one thing in common," she said controlling her voice. "Let's say they preferred the company of their own sex and leave it at that. I believe their parents lacked understanding of their nature, and hounded them all, possibly out of embarrassment and fear of ridicule into the armed services. Jeff was no different. My parents thought that a spell in the armed forces would make or break him – and it nearly did break him. Of all the places to put him though – the Navy! Then Jeff and the others met up with

Benson and fell into bad company. He was a loathsome man who preyed on young vulnerable children – boys in the main."

"What did happen on HMS Ulysses?" Graves asked eventually. She looked at him squarely before shuffling magazines that did not necessarily need shuffling.

"You understand that Jeff and the others were very young and impressionable and easily led back then. They were no more than boys themselves, but Benson was twenty-five and had served in the Merchant Navy briefly before." Graves gave a reassuring look and waited for her to continue. "As I said earlier, Jeff had always been effeminate and preferred the company of his own sex from an early age. His friends were the same, except Benson, oh he had a liking for the same sex, but he was a nasty, vindictive excuse of a man more than capable of inflicting pain and suffering on younger victims." Her cup and saucer rattled as she relived the past. "From what Jeff told me, Benson paid one night in Singapore harbour for a young male prostitute to visit the ship, whilst it was Jeff's watch. Jeff turned a blind eye," She hesitated taking in gulps of air.

"Well to cut a long story short, Benson battered the lad to within an inch of his life for demanding payment in advance. Singapore authorities got involved and the international press. Benson was disciplined. Jeff and his two friends were implicated and received charges against them as well." She stood and placed her now empty crockery back on the tray, facing the window overlooking the lawns.

"The Navy top brass decided to make an example of them all weeks later and had them thrown out rather than court-martialled to try and limit any ensuing scandal. The national gutter press here in England managed to get hold of the story and quoted the names of those involved. Poor mother had a breakdown and has never been the same since. Incidentally, Teddy was her brother, killed in the Second World War," she added by way of an explanation for her mother's odd behaviour. "Father passed away ten years ago vowing never to speak to Jeff again and he never did." She leaned heavily on the low windowsill for support, her face inches away from the windowpane, her breath steaming up the glass.

"I never stopped loving my older brother though whatever his shortcomings. I was just twelve at the time of the fire. My parents had packed me off to boarding school, but little did they know it was only a few miles away from where Jeff was working." Graves gave Morgan a surprised look. "He managed to get the employment agency to get him work near my school. I used to see him and his friend at the weekend. We use to go to the pictures or the park or even swimming. I knew that his friend was more than just a friend, even at twelve years old. He was as happy, though, as I had ever seen him. We agreed never to tell our parents and for a while everything seemed fine." She turned facing both men again, her composure restored.

"He would never let me come to the orphanage. I don't think he trusted Benson too much, even though I was a girl. His preference was for young boys, although I got the impression from Jeff he would take whatever was on offer – even me. I have a picture of them together taken just after they arrived to work at the orphanage," she explained. "I use to keep it out of sight in the past but since father died and now mother stays mainly indoors I keep it there on the mantelpiece." She pointed to where a black and white photograph sat above the dormant hearth. Graves walked over and picked it up, taking in the features of each man.

"You surprise me Lady Woollsey having such an unsavoury character as Benson so close by, even though your brother is in the picture. I would have thought you would prefer to distance yourself from someone who had such a damaging influence on your brother, perhaps cut him out of the photograph altogether as a last resort?" he remarked.

"You misunderstand Inspector, there are only two reasons why that picture sits there in full view. The first one is the picture was one of only a few means of identifying Jeff when he disappeared. Unfortunately, to no avail. I suppose I put it there years ago after father's death and it has stayed there ever since," she said.

"And the second reason Lady Woollsey?" Morgan asked.

"The second reason, Constable, is Benson isn't actually on the photograph. He's behind the camera. You see I couldn't recognise him if he were to walk in here this minute." Graves looked at her quizzically, placing the frame back on the hearth. "Oh, the fourth man in the picture Inspector – Jeff's friend I referred to earlier, Franco Russo," she explained smiling at his sudden realization. Graves passed the photograph to her and she stared intently at it. "One day in early June 1953 I met Jeff as we had arranged the week before. Jeff was broody as I recall looking back now. Eventually he told me that he would have to go away for a while, that we could not meet again for some time. He would come to me eventually though. I was not to believe what would be said about him in the days that followed. I was not to tell anyone about our little chat. I asked him over and over again why. Was it something I had done? He said no and he could not discuss it further. Franco was leaving with him," She replaced the photo back on the hearth.

"We parted that day with a great sadness. It lasted a day or so then I decided to see him at the orphanage, to insist on an explanation. It was a Tuesday night, fairly mild and dry weather as I remember. What I thought was a pink sunset in the distance as the bus approached the outskirts of the village, was in fact a raging fire. We were being diverted with all the other traffic along an alternative route, so I jumped off at the next stop and ran across a farmer's field that fronted the orphanage. There were at least six fire engines trying to bring the fire under control. Ambulances were tending to men, women and children from the orphanage. Most of the children and staff were outside in a makeshift tent for the injured by the time I got there. I remember climbing over the fence and running forward toward the fire only to be blocked by the fire chief in charge. I was already crying, screaming for Jeff. It was mayhem.

The fire was out of control quickly catching hold of the remaining East, West and North wings. The fire brigade could only train their hoses on the flames and try and prevent them from spreading beyond the grounds." She moved across to the hearth and touched the same picture running a finger over the glass, her saddened eyes caught in the reflection. "It was 6am the following morning before senior fire officers could survey the damage. A full nine hours since the fire had caught hold," she managed a strained smile. "My mother found out about me being there and was very angry with me." Graves looked at her in surprise. She noticed and guessed his thoughts.

"Oh, she didn't find out about Jeff. I made up a story about visiting a friend from school nearby and that I got caught up in the aftermath of the fire. It was some days later that I learned of the victims. Surprisingly few, but significantly my brother, Benson, Turnberry and Grundy all died in the blaze, along with a child." She moved around as if collecting her thoughts, her hands clenched, squeezing the life out of each other. "You see, my brother and his friends lived at the orphanage in rooms below ground level at the end of the South wing – where the fire started. I was devastated, angry then sad for months and I could not tell my parents why. You see I promised Jeff that I would never tell, whatever happened. I would not tell them about him, unless he said so."

"The worst was over," Graves said to himself and yet she was struggling to continue and then he decided to prompt her further. "But then he turned up again and everything was alright?"

"Yes, but how did you know?" she asked, a little unprepared.

"You asked if we had found him earlier, so I presume that he didn't die in the fire after all, like Benson and probably the others. You must have known that." Graves replied. As to why they went to such elaborate lengths to fake their deaths and conceal their continued existence from their families had yet to be determined.

"They all survived didn't they, all four?" She nodded. "You know one thing concerns me above all else Lady Woollsey," Graves looked at her sternly. "Let us not lose sight of the fact that there were five adult bodies and that of a child that perished in the fire, burned beyond all recognition. If your brother and his friends carried out this plan they effectively killed those people, whilst putting countless others at risk."

Despite her natural inclination to jump to her brother's defence, she knew he was right. She had asked herself the same questions over the years and never reached a satisfactory conclusion. Her brother had never told her any details about the fire later and she offered no defence now.

"How did he make contact with you Lady Woollsey?" Graves asked his question designed to ease the mood a little.

"It was twelve months later. I was on medication and had not started back at school since the fire. My first school class on my return turned out to be a nature ramble through the woods behind the school. Pupils were paired off and told to gather various leaves and insects for classification back at the school lab. I was paired off with Cynthia Gittings-Smith, a real busybody. She wanted to know all about the fire and my involvement. In the end I told her to leave me alone. After twenty minutes I stumbled across the old oak tree where I use to meet Jeff at the weekend. I sat down for a rest and began to cry as

I remembered all over again. As I rocked backwards and forwards, two hands came around my face from behind," she mimicked what she was describing, "one hand over my eyes and the other over my mouth. I kicked and punched out until the dirty-gloved hand let go. A tramp stood before me, dressed in tattered clothing with long straggly hair and an untidy beard. His unmistakeable blue eyes set against his pathetically unnourished frame gave him away though. I must have passed out with shock. When I woke up Jeff was sat opposite me eating half my packed lunch."

"'Sorry Jess, I didn't mean to startle you,' I remember him saying, smiling through that horrible matted beard. I said 'Is that you Jeff?' I was really angry. He just nodded as he munched on my apple. He just said that 'he told me he would come back, no matter what I might have heard', alluding to his reported death later in the fire." She paused reflectively. "'The fire,' I said to him, 'they said that you were dead.' He just said 'That was the general idea'. Then he said 'It was touch and go in the end, not what they had planned. The fire got hold too quickly'." She looked uncomfortable now. "I told him that I remembered some people were killed, bodies had been recovered, what was left of them. If not Jeff and the others then who? No one else was reported missing apart from a young child. I said 'What about the people that were killed, the bodies they recovered, and the state they were in – if it wasn't you, then who?' Even in this pathetic state I could tell that he was saddened, more than I have ever seen him before. He told me eventually that Franco died in the fire."

"The fifth adult body," Graves replied. She nodded.

"He gave me a partial explanation about how the old building caught fire too quickly. How he had lost Franco as a result," He said, nothing about how or why they had to escape in the first place. "I remember him telling me tearfully that Franco wasn't supposed to be there in their plan, but the fire was started prematurely, during one of Franco's frequent visits, a horrible coincident. Jeff and Franco had put some money away in Franco's name at the bank to use after the fire, but he couldn't get access to it after Franco's death so he lived rough, begging until in desperation he made contact with me. I gave him my pocket money and for the next twelve months, I helped him as much as I could, selling ornaments and furniture from the house here," she told them.

"What do you recall about this Franco character?" Graves asked.

"Mediterranean extraction, dark, good looking, uninterested in girls though, that sort of thing," she replied. "We met as frequently as we could over the next 6 to 7 years. Jeff finally managed to get the money that he and Franco had saved. School exams dictated my time though as I prepared for university. Jeff soon made contacts, even with his new identity. I think it was more to do with one of his other friends getting him work." she recalled.

"His new identity?" Graves replied.

"Why yes. Jeff took the name Tim McDonald." Morgan scribbled the details in his notebook. "His two friends survived with him. I'm not sure about Benson. I think he thankfully, dropped out of sight from what I remember from Jeff on the night of the fire. I never heard him mention him again in open conversation," she remarked.

"Turnberry and Grundy, did they change their names as well?" Graves queried.

"Err, yes Inspector, but I couldn't tell you what their new names were. I saw them briefly with Jeff when he was back on his feet and that was that," she responded furtively. Graves thought about the implications on Benson's murder and Woollsey's apparent disappearance before gesturing to his host to continue. "Jeff got a job in local politics eventually, thanks to Margaret's father. Margaret was his girlfriend at the time, which was a great relief to me from his past relationship with Franco," she admitted. "They were married in the winter of 1957. I suffered a bout of pneumonia, no doubt brought on by a student protest I had been involved with that year on nuclear weapons when I was soaked during a rally. I missed the wedding as a result.

My father was insistent on me making a full recovery before I was allowed out again. They were still completely unaware of Jeff's existence, never mind his marriage. He did not want his new bride learning about his family, with the exception of me, and even I was economical with the truth about the family history." She stopped as if trying to catch a past memory. "Just one moment Inspector, I think I have another picture somewhere here." She walked across the room to a writing desk. Unlocking a drawer she pulled out a faded album and produced a single photograph, which she passed to Graves. He sat looking at an old black and white picture of a couple in their 30s holding a baby. "That was taken almost ten months after they were married, Jeff and his wife Margaret and my niece, baby Estelle. I say baby, she must be nearly thirty years old herself now." Graves handed the picture back to Lady Woollsey.

"Do you have an address for your sister-in-law?" Graves asked. She looked at him cautiously. She did not believe that anything could be gained from disturbing her brother's family and became protective all of a sudden.

"You will not find anything there to tell you where Jeff is – or should I say Tim? Both Estelle and I have looked more times than I care to remember and I have not been in touch with my sister-in-law and her daughter for nearly seventeen years," she replied, trying to put him off.

"Why is that?" Graves inquired.

"I stopped looking," she explained awkwardly, "I stopped looking because it wasn't healthy for my niece at her mother's insistence. I didn't know, but during a spell in between our investigations she had a nervous breakdown when her expectations over finding her father were dashed. She was only twelve at the time, just like me I guess when Jeff left the first time around. Margaret asked me to stay away for the sake of her daughter's sanity. Besides, I also thought that if Jeff wanted to be found, he would appear as he had last time – the trouble is he never did," she said sadly. "I can only relate to you what Margaret told me," She winced knowing that she had effectively talked her way into giving him the address of her sister-in-law. "Margaret said that Tim got up that morning as usual for work. Oh, after a few years he had climbed to the dizzy heights of prospective Councillor for the town he had chosen to put his roots down in, Chetley."

Graves knew the village well. Its parish border made it the next community north of Willenbury. It wasn't as large as Willenbury, although equally as quaint. "Margaret's father had been the Mayor there some years earlier and still had contacts. My brother could charm the birds off the trees and he did, a quality he inherited from father," Lady Woollsey commented melancholily. "He had been a little nervous and aloof for a few weeks Margaret said.

"A little like he was with you before the fire?" Graves asked.

"No, I would say not, according to Margaret's account. He flew off the handle the day before he disappeared when she queried him about sizeable amounts of money leaving their joint bank account. I remember Margaret saying that it crossed her mind that he might have found another woman. I was more concerned that it might have been a man at the time," Lady Woollsey exclaimed almost comically.

"Was there anything more specific that your sister-in-law pointed to?" Morgan added.

"Not really, he just went from a loving husband and father to a distant stranger in a matter of weeks. I myself saw him a number of times briefly over the last three months before he disappeared. He tried to hide it from me, but I have to agree with Margaret. I tried to get him to tell me what the problem was. He just smiled and said, 'Not to worry, things will be different next week, back to normal, trust me, you know how to do that sis don't you?' He winked at me, but it just wasn't the same as it was when I was twelve. It was something in his voice, his eyes and his mannerisms." She wept a little, dabbing her eyes.

"It was the last time I spoke to him. I'm sorry Inspector." Graves allowed her to settle.

"Thank you for your time and help Lady Woollsey. Could I trouble you for that address now? I'm afraid I need to ask your sister-in-law a few more questions." Lady Woollsey gave a sigh of acceptance.

"She still lives in Chetley. She has a cottage called Little Crandon, named by my brother after this place," she said resignedly. "My sister-in-law knows nothing of me and my family here. Jeff never wanted her to know and have her visit and uncover memories about him best forgotten. As far as she was concerned I was Jeff's little sister from the North, Jessica McDonald. We were the only two remaining siblings from a family hit hard by the last war." Graves thought about the elaborate hoax for a moment.

"May I also borrow your photograph please? I promise to return it within a day or two. As you say, there is very little by way of identification and although dated, we have some clever people at the Yard that can age the features of everyone on this photo to what they may look like now, almost forty years later," he said, gesturing to the photograph on the hearth.

"So your sister-in-law is Margaret McDonald and you to her are just plain Jessica McDonald as far as she is concerned?" Graves asked, clearing things up in his mind. She nodded without speaking handing him the photograph and for once Graves began to see the full implications of the plot put together by the quartet. As to why they should take such drastic measures had yet to be explained, if it ever would be.

"Do you really think that you could locate my brother after all this time Inspector?" she queried almost reluctant to hear his reply.

"Anything is possible Lady Woollsey, especially with the intelligence systems we have today in modern policing," he tried to reassure her. Morgan glanced at his boss more sceptically. The two men were just about to leave. "Oh Lady Woollsey," Graves asked," that particular boarding school, it seems a little out of the way for someone based in Cumbria? Most people would never have heard of Willenbury let alone…"

"St. Bernadette's, Inspector," she finished off his sentence. "Before my mother met and married my father and moved to his ancestral home here, she lived about two miles outside of Willenbury and she went to school at St. Bernadette. She loved it there and had happy memories and thought I should go there too," she shrugged her shoulders in a matter of fact way. "Jeff knew even before he joined the Navy that my parents had reserved a place for me at St. Bernadette. That's why he insisted on taking the job at the orphanage, or at least that is what he told me."

Graves smiled appreciatively and the two policemen bid their host a final farewell and headed south down the M6 motorway. With Morgan driving, Graves settled down for the long journey back, pulling his hat down over his eyes. The trip north had started off as an opportunity to find out more about Robert Benson through the Woollsey family. Instead of helping to explain matters, it merely confused them further. The thoughts whirled around inside his head until in the end he could not make any sense of them at all. He shut them out and drifted off into a deep sleep.

13

Visit to Little Crandon

Graves and Morgan had returned home late after their trip to Cumbria. Reg Graves had remained stable throughout the day. He called in at the hospital on his way home and spent some time with both parents, although he received a frosty reception from his mother. Mrs Graves had duly noted his absence all day and she struggled to quell her anger. He attempted to make conversation, but she avoided him at every attempt. He eventually left an hour later, his tail between his legs, unsure of his longer-term involvement in the case.

It was late the following morning when Graves and Morgan arrived at Little Crandon. They passed through the white picket fence gate and along the flagged slate footpath up to the solid wood front door. Graves stooped below the low eaves of the thatched cottage roof and gave the bronze doorknocker a firm rap against the nameplate, 'Little Crandon'.

"Touch of déjà vu hey sir?" Morgan volunteered alluding to their trip to Cumbria. He made no attempt to keep his voice low whatsoever. Graves put his finger to his lips without uttering a word.

"Hello," came a female voice from what appeared to be the back of the cottage. They both moved away from the front door in opposite directions, taking a gable-end each to investigate. It was Graves who discovered the side gate to the cottage leading into the back garden. As he reached to try the latch a very attractive woman in her late 20s opened it. She was dressed for manual work in dark green overalls and large gauntlet type gloves and boots. Her hair was held in place by a bright, multicoloured bandana. She had a look of Lauren Bacall in her heyday, even more so the way she leaned on the gate post like a security guard barring their entry. In her free hand she had a pair of secateurs, which she playfully waved around for effect. By this time Morgan had joined Graves and stood behind him grinning like a Cheshire cat at the more than welcomed distraction, whatever her attire.

"Can I help you gentlemen?" she drawled, again using the gardening tool as pointer. The voice was almost a perfect match for the body. Her eyelashes flitted up and down as she spoke. This was a woman who was used to getting what she wanted. The gesture just washed over Graves, but Morgan just stood there, almost with his tongue hanging out. Graves half-turned and gave him a serious look. Morgan, a few years younger than the lady at the gate, pulled himself together delving into his notebook to distract himself.

"Good morning," Graves replied, touching the brim of his hat as he did. "My name is Graves, Inspector Graves, and this is DC Morgan."

Morgan managed a controlled, "good morning," his grinning now in check.

"Police," she said, her laid back posture hardly betraying what would be a little disconcerting for most people. "My, my, three parking tickets hardly warrants an Inspector and a detective constable surely," she teased. Her eyes moved from Graves to Morgan. "Although I can try harder next time if you and your *constable*," – there was a slight overemphasis on the word 'constable' in her voice – "promise to come again." Morgan wisely chose to ignore her flirting, despite his obvious interest and scribbled furiously in his notebook.

"Actually Miss?" Graves had already guessed this was Estelle McDonald, but he had chosen to keep her aunt out of the investigation as far as Estelle and her mother were concerned for the time being.

"McDonald Inspector. Miss Estelle McDonald." Again she flashed another look at the increasingly uncomfortable Morgan, who at last had something of interest in his notebook. "Not a bad guess Inspector, considering I'm wearing gloves." She draped her arm over the gatepost and opened the gate partially, the secateurs now limp in her hand.

"Just a guess Miss McDonald I can assure you." Her aunt hadn't confirmed the marital status of her niece and probably didn't know anyway, so it was a genuine guess. "I am here to talk to you about your father." This time her stance changed from its relaxed repose, to one of uneasiness. She pulled the gate further closed behind her as if it would offer further protection for what lay behind it. The secateurs took on a more menacing role and her eyes became intense going from the extremes of self-control to hatred and insecurity in a matter of seconds. Before she could say anything, another voice called out from behind her, a much older sounding female voice, a little tired and weary yet still full of authority.

"Estelle, who is it dear? Either invite them in or send them on their way," the voice called out.

"OK mum," Estelle called back, her gaze never leaving both men for a moment. She stood back from the gate pushing it open as she did and gestured to the two policemen to walk through. The self-assuredness and playful tone in her voice had been replaced by something much harder and colder. "I would appreciate you not upsetting my mum Inspector. She is not a well lady," she said as the trio made their way to the back of the cottage. As they turned the corner at the rear of the stone building they were met by an old English cottage garden with mature borders filled with late flowering perennials, intermingled with home-grown vegetables. Hazel weaved fence panelling gave the garden a secure private feeling as well as protection from the ravages of an east wind that blew across Chetley Moor in the distance. Estelle was in the process of pruning back the late summer growth in readiness for winter, with her mum supervising. A large sycamore tree created shade at the bottom of the garden from what had turned out to be another gloriously sunny autumnal morning. Beneath it an elderly lady sat in a wheelchair.

"Who is it Estelle? You shouldn't be inviting strangers in at the drop of a hat." She stammered slightly and then coughed delicately, before sipping her drink again.

"It's OK mum," Estelle smiled nervously, wondering what her mum's reaction would be. "These two gentlemen are policemen. They have come to talk to us about dad." The old lady's eyes never flinched from her daughter. Graves had already guessed by now that this must be Tim McDonald's long-suffering wife, her expression gave away nothing at the news. "This is Inspector Graves and Detective Constable Morgan mum," she broke the uneasy silence. Eventually, the old lady looked at Graves directly as if trying to judge him on appearances only. Unlike her sister-in-law, Jessica Woollsey, any emotion toward the disappearance of her husband was a complex mixture of a sense of loss cancelled out by something altogether colder, something Graves had sensed in Estelle McDonald's manner moments earlier. She looked at Graves cagily.

"Good morning Mrs McDonald," Graves said, holding out a hand. The elderly lady shook it instinctively.

"I take it you have found him after all this time?" the old lady's eyes squinted with a piercing stare. Graves briefly remembered Lady Woollsey's exact same reaction.

"Mrs McDonald, our inquiries relate to another incident, which recently came to our attention. It involves a man whom we believe knew your husband when they served in the Navy together. This man appears to have disappeared a year or so before your husband did. We came across him quite by accident nearly a week or so ago through our inquiries."

"Oh," she said, her voice almost betraying disappointment. Her eyes maintained their piecing stare. "Did this man mention my husband?"

"Unfortunately Mrs McDonald, we found the man concerned, twenty-five years after he died, the same year that he disappeared. " The old lady was alert enough to register the comment and gave him an odd look.

"I'm sorry Inspector, my hearing isn't as good as it use to be. Did you say you found him twenty-five years after he died?" Graves nodded. "Pray tell me how did you find me from the body of man who had been dead for twenty-five years? She inquired, obviously much sharper than her years and condition suggested. Graves thought about trudging through the events of the last few days and decided his time might be better used pushing forward with the investigation.

"It's a long story Mrs McDonald. Suffice to say we got to you through your husband's sister."

"Jessica," she said, banging the half-empty glass down on the garden table. "I haven't seen her since we gave up looking for Tim – oh, it must be approaching seventeen years ago."

"Auntie Jess," Estelle said out loud with glee. "I haven't seen her since..." Estelle's voice became silent as if she

In The Mood

suddenly remembered something long since buried. Her mum noticed her change of manner and interrupted her.

"Never mind that for now Estelle." Her mum's voice was enough to snap her out of her thoughts.

"Err, yes auntie Jess, she used to bring some lovely presents and take me to the park for ice cream when I was little. Do you have her address? She never did tell us where she lived and dad would always change the subject when we spoke about it."

"Lady Woollsey lives in Cumbria," Morgan blurted out the news before Graves could react. Both women stared back at Morgan in shock. Graves looked at his colleague almost in equal dismay. Having said he would try and keep Lady Woollsey's secret intact, Morgan had unintentionally let the cat out of the bag.

"Estelle can you take me inside please? I am getting a little chilled out here. In the meantime could you repeat what you just said my boy?" Mrs McDonald asked. Morgan was already regretting his outburst and stared at Graves for his intervention as the two walked toward the cottage behind mother and daughter. They walked straight into the kitchen, Estelle pushing her mother's wheelchair. Graves spent the next half hour briefly explaining her husband's family history, as Lady Woollsey had explained it to him. Although pressed by the elderly lady, he wouldn't tell them why such an elaborate hoax had been played over the McDonalds' brief married life. In truth, he wasn't sure himself. That would be Lady Woollsey's problem to sort out now, thanks to D.C. Morgan.

"I suppose I never really knew Tim, or should I say Jeff, at all." The old lady reasoned as she negotiated her wheelchair next to the range fire.

"So my Auntie Jess is a Lady," Estelle could only repeat over and over again. Her real surname didn't seem to register. She paraded around the kitchen as if the news had given her a regal air. "And I'm her niece," she purred.

"Do you mind having a look at this picture for me Mrs McDonald?" Graves asked. She glared at him.

"Don't you mean 'Woollsey' Inspector?" she said angrily; her anger not really aimed at Graves, but real just the same. Graves offered no response, just an understanding look. The old lady settled herself taking the picture.

"Your sister-in-law kindly gave it to me. It shows your husband months after he left the Navy. I have been led to believe that the men in the photograph worked with your husband for a time together after the war. Do you recognise any of them? Unfortunately, the man we are investigating – Robert Benson – is holding the camera." He wasn't sure if the information was of any use given that Woollsey had changed his name to McDonald after the orphanage fire. Benson would surely have a different name as well.

"Estelle, pass me my reading glasses dear," her mum asked her. She used them like a magnifying glass rather than putting them on her face. "This was a long time ago Inspector. It predates my knowledge of my, err, *husband*." The word almost became stuck in her throat. "The one person you referred to is completely unknown to me, but

In The Mood

for some strange reason, the other two men look vaguely familiar from the distant past." She passed the photo back to Graves.

"The man on the left is Charles Grundy. The chap alongside in between him and your husband is Jack Turnberry," Graves replied. Again these were unlikely to be the names that they were using, even if she did know them thirty years ago.

"They could have been some of Tim's cronies from that time Inspector. I could have met them at a function, I suppose," she said frowning. "You see, Tim supported many causes as a local councillor and he used his influence to get other more well-off people to contribute at charitable functions. They could have been supporters." She paused for a moment as she tried to remember. "Estelle dear, do you still have that old shoe box with your dad's things in?" Her daughter gave a non-responsive look without admitting or denying whether she had the box or not.

"Oh come, come child," her mum scolded irritably," I know you have it. I may be an invalid and unable to climb the stairs, but I do know that not all your dad's belongings were thrown out and burned. I was happy for you to have the box and its contents as a keepsake, despite how I feel he betrayed us both." Estelle bowed her head and slipped upstairs to her bedroom as if she was a child again, sent there for being naughty. After a few minutes she returned with an old battered shoebox displaying a company name that had long since gone out of business. She passed the box over her mum's head and muttered an apology. Mrs McDonald merely put her hand over her daughters and gave it a playful squeeze. "Now then," she said out loud, "where is it? Ah," she said soon after with satisfaction. She pulled out a more recent photograph, still in black and white though, but displaying styles of dress common to the late1950s. "Here are the men in your photograph Inspector, some years older I would guess. The place is the Town Hall steps in Willenbury."

"Are you certain Mrs McDonald?" Graves asked.

"Why yes Inspector. I am the one behind the camera this time." She recalled a smile returning to her pale lips. "My memory isn't what it used to be. I was sure that the names were different to those you mentioned Inspector and I was right. See for yourself they are on the back of the photo," she explained. Graves turned the picture. "You see, I only ever met them once and this wasn't that occasion," she continued. "The exact year escapes me I'm afraid. I used to take my new camera out on the odd occasion and take some photographs of the park opposite County Hall in Willenbury for my geography class. I was a schoolteacher you know. That day I just happened to see the three of them together from a distance. I took the picture before shouting to Tim, but a large delivery truck blocked my view as I recall. By the time the truck moved on they were gone. I met them only once about a month later when I had had this picture developed and wrote their names on the back of this photograph. Yes it's coming back to me now. It's been buried amongst hundreds of other photos ever since."

"Frank Hewitt and Ted Gould?" Graves read out as he turned the photo.

"I'm afraid I can't remember which one is Gould and which one is Hewitt," She replied quietly.

"Would you mind if I borrowed this picture and had it copied please Mrs McDonald?" His question was clearly aimed at the old lady, but it was the younger Estelle who gave him a guarded look. "I promise to have it back with you by tomorrow," he said, turning his attention to the younger of the two ladies.

Estelle nodded reluctantly and Graves passed the photograph to Morgan. "I appreciate that this is painful Mrs McDonald, but when your husband left you, well," Graves struggled to say the words until they were said for him.

"He left me for another woman, Inspector? After twenty-five years I've come to terms with his infidelity, although I blame myself from time to time for not reading the signs, not that there were any from what I remember," she added calmly. Estelle gave her mother's hand a squeeze of comfort this time. "The day my husband left us – disappeared would be too kind – he left me a note." She frowned as if trying to recollect the content in its exact detail. "As I have already said, it was a farewell letter Inspector. It was brief and to the point. Basically, he said that he had met another woman, that he was sorry. 'Try to forget me and give my love to our daughter.' He didn't even say her name. That was it." She reached into her cardigan pocket and pulled out her handkerchief, cursing her lack of self-control after all this time. "I could take him leaving me, but Estelle, that was unforgivable," she murmured. Graves wondered why Jessica Woollsey hadn't thought to mention the letter. Perhaps Margaret McDonald had never told her.

"Mum, you shouldn't upset yourself like this," Estelle said, comforting her.

"You don't understand Estelle. The man I knew as your dad, my husband and the man who wrote that letter could have been two different people." The old lady sobbed quietly into her handkerchief. Clearly even after twenty-five years the emotional wounds were still open and quite deep.

"Is it possible Mrs McDonald? Could someone else have written the letter?" Morgan asked. A second disappearing act wasn't out of the question. Morgan and Graves had both discussed the possibility since leaving Cumbria. Both women looked at Morgan aghast. He continued, relentless, though. "Do you still have the letter?"

"I burned it a long time ago, but the letter was definitely his handwriting." she replied. She looked at the young policeman again as if the full implication behind Morgan's question had just dawned on her. "It had to be," she continued, a faint hint of desperation in her voice. She began to become agitated and breathless. The question had for the first time in twenty-five years raised doubts about a man she had despised since that day, but for whom she still obviously held some secret affection, secret from her daughter, at least; for her sake.

"We are obliged to ask questions that take us off in different directions Mrs McDonald. More often than not, they just help to fill in the background and any gaps. I am sorry if we suggested anything to the contrary," Graves added, trying to ease her discomfort whist giving Morgan one of his stony looks. The young constable got the message and promptly shut up. "What do you recall of the weeks leading up to your husband leaving? Was he acting normal?" Graves asked, remembering what Jessica Woollsey had said.

"He was quite thoughtful, not exactly depressed, but distant at times as if his mind was somewhere else. He was reluctant to go to work, which was unlike him. I remember asking him if he was all right and could I help or do anything. He just flew into a rage and bit my head off – the first time since we were married. We were losing money out of our joint bank account. It went on for months and then a week before he left he changed back into the man I married. He said that every thing would be all right very soon. I remember he hugged me and kissed my forehead and he was gone." She touched her forehead where the kiss had obviously happened all those years before. "The letter arrived through the door a few days later," she continued.

"And you are sure that it was your husband's handwriting?" Morgan again pushed the question.

"Constable!" Graves said sharply.

The old lady sobbed again. "I don't know, I think so, oh I can't remember." She began to cry mournfully. Graves didn't wait for Estelle to jump to her mother's defence.

"Thank you for your time, both of you. I am sorry if we upset you both with our questioning. You have both been very kind and understanding." Graves picked up his raincoat and hat, gesturing to Morgan and they both made their way to the front door.

"I will see them out mum, you stay by the fire." Estelle squeezed her mum's shoulders and followed the two policemen out. "Inspector," Estelle called, keeping her voice as low as possible so that her mum couldn't hear. Graves turned expecting to hear a well-deserved lecture. Still clutching the old shoebox under her arm, she placed it on the telephone table in the hallway and removed the lid. She fumbled through various papers and photographs until she found what she was looking for. She took out a folded piece of A4 paper from behind an old photograph of herself as a child and thrust it at Graves. She had one eye on him the other was looking behind her to check where her mum was. "You might find this useful, Inspector, in answering constable Morgan's question, and I for one would like to know your professional opinion. Now please before my mum wonders what we are talking about. She is upset enough. The authenticity of this farewell letter was taken at face value at the time and dad was convicted of adultery in her mind on the strength of it. To think it might be a forgery never occurred to mum, me, or Aunt Jess," she whispered as the trio walked out of the front door back up the garden path.

Graves put the sheet of paper into his soft leather briefcase as they reached the gate. "I'll be in touch," he said turning.

"No, I'll be in touch," Estelle corrected him. "I want to avoid upsetting mum again." Graves smiled understandingly and both policemen bid her farewell as they climbed into the waiting Granada. The cottage door was already closed as both men took stock of their discussions before setting off.

"Even if the letter is a forgery, why should anyone want to carry out such a trick?" Morgan said out loud.

"Yes I noticed you were keen on labouring that point," Graves replied with a lingering look. "Why indeed."

"What about the money sir?" Morgan continued, trying to recover his position. "Perhaps McDonald was being blackmailed and ran out of money and decided it would be easy to disappear." Morgan was quietly challenging his own thoughts now. "But why get someone to forge a letter on your behalf?"

"Let's not jump the gun," Graves interrupted. "We need to establish a motive and opportunity first. If I am not mistaken," he reached into his briefcase and pulled out the sheet of paper again and photograph, placing both side-by-side on top of his briefcase. "It's a pity we don't have a copy of Tim McDonald's handwriting prior to his disappearance to compare this with," he said staring at the letter.

"So you think it is a fake?" Morgan asked.

"It's possible," Graves replied. "The week before he disappeared all seemed well. It doesn't make any sense. As far as the authenticity of the letter is concerned it's impossible to say without a specimen to compare against.

Perhaps Lady Woollsey can accommodate us." he speculated. "I expect Ray Brightwell to be able to give us an opinion on the nature and characteristics of the person behind the pen though, which may help."

"Sir, I'm not sure where this is going in terms of Benson." Morgan replied as he pulled out on to the main road.

"Neither am I at present Morgan, but our friend at the bridge died in a very particular way. He was placed there, which means there may have been more than one person involved considering his size or some elaborate lifting equipment was used." Graves suggested.

"McDonald and his friends in the picture?" Morgan suggested.

"Possibly," Graves replied

"I get it," Morgan shouted. "They killed Benson, then panicked and decided to disappear just in case the body was traced?"

"Well that is where your logic falls apart Morgan. The body may not have ever been found, at least not in their lifetime, had it not been for the accident," Graves reminded him. "Killing someone that way comes with a great risk of discovery as Handby pointed out. The bypass was new at the time, but the older road below was still open to traffic and therefore visible to a great number of people even at night. No, this method of killing, the environment, it was important to the murderer and quite deliberate. We need to find Tim McDonald, Woollsey, whatever, one way or the other and rule him out of the investigation, ideally him and his two friends," Graves continued. He never took his eyes off the photos while he spoke. A further ten minutes passed without further conversation. Morgan occasionally glanced at the senior officer as he studied the photograph on his lap.

"Something else of interest sir?" he asked finally.

"The photograph is very interesting," Graves replied. "You see the thing about photographs is they tell more of a story in the background sometimes than in the foreground."

In The Mood

Morgan looked puzzled. Just then the Granada slowed to a stop as it approached traffic lights on red. "Get this picture to Ray Brightwell and ask him to copy it and then enlarge the copy about ten times normal magnification in this location." Graves circled the area with his finger as Morgan took a brief glance. "There is something in the background that looks familiar, the motif on the sweater that they are all wearing. Concentrate on the motif. It definitely looks familiar to me but I can't place it. As I said earlier, I want Brightwell to look at the letter as well. I want a handwriting appraisal of the type of person who might have written this."

"Yes sir," Morgan replied pulling the Granada out on to the A413. "How about a bite to eat sir, oh and a pint? I'm starving," Morgan pleaded.

"Oh very well," Graves replied. His mind drifted back to the photo on his lap and that motif. Where the hell had he seen it before?

14

The McDonald Interviews

Later that day Morgan had returned to the station, having called in enroute at the County Labs to see Ray Brightwell. The photo enlargement would be done by close of play that day, but the handwriting assessment would have to wait until the morning. Morgan had agreed to meet Brightwell after lunch the following day when he was sure Graves would be back at the station. He was making his way back from the staff canteen when he heard his name called.

"Morgan!" The detective constable stopped in his tracks. The voice was unmistakeably that of acting DI Tom Wheldon. Wheldon stood at the top of the second floor stairwell, a smirk lurking behind all that facial hair. "I've been attending to a potential lead in the case downstairs until you returned. She preferred to speak to you and she awaits your pleasure in reception." He gestured below by nodding his thinly covered balding pate, whilst his bushy eyebrows moved up and down rapidly. "And she can pleasure me any time," he added, the smirk still playing on his face. "Come and see me when you have a moment. I want to know all there is to know about our esteemed DI Graves and his activities on this case." He didn't wait for a reply and carried on his accent toward the incident room on the second floor.

Morgan hurried downstairs to the ground floor and along the corridor past several interview rooms toward reception. Looking beyond other colleagues in his line of sight through the glass door at the end of the corridor, he moved from wall-to-wall as he made his way trying to get a clear view, but he could only see the portly figure of Sergeant Watkins, the desk sergeant for the day. He knew in his own mind who he was expecting to see from Wheldon's reaction a few moments ago. He squeezed the door handle catching sight of visitors and policemen alike through the little window panel in the door. Estelle McDonald sat in an easy chair in a provocative pose, wearing a short denim skirt. The skirt just about covered her and everyone else's embarrassment. The jacket worn open, barely contained her ample bosom, something Morgan had appreciated earlier at Little Crandon, despite her overalls. A low cut blouse with just the three buttons up the front barely contained the matching pair. He took a deep breath before entering. Her hair was swept back and up and tied in a bun at the back of her head, unlike the bandana that she wore earlier. She immediately saw Morgan as the door opened and beamed a welcoming smile at him. She straightened in her chair before rising to meet him. Her rosy red lips parted and she rolled her tongue between them as she held out her hand.

"Miss McDonald," Morgan managed, trying hard not to squeeze the life out of her. "What a pleasant surprise, so soon after our visit." She eyed him at close quarters this time still apparently pleased with her initial assessment of the young officer earlier that day.

"Is there somewhere you can take me constable?" she purred, her eyes never leaving him, her flirting from their earlier meeting still at the fore. Her eyes seemed to twinkle with mischief and for a moment he wasn't sure if this was part of some elaborate wind-up, possibly involving his colleagues.

"They could all be watching this on CCTV cameras back in the control room," he said to himself. "Oh, yes of course," he managed with some effort.

"Yes to talk. I have some additional information for you about my father, slightly more recent." The twinkle subsided as fast it had appeared with the word 'father'.

"Oh yes of course," he replied, looking over his shoulder at sergeant Watkins for inspiration.

"Interview Room 2 is free," Watkins offered.

"Fine, thank you sergeant," Morgan replied. There was a buzz before Morgan pushed the security door and the

In The Mood

two retraced Morgan's footsteps from a few moments ago. She walked behind him seeing him from a different angle this time. Morgan recognised the old battered shoebox from their earlier encounter, held tightly again under her left arm. Once Inside, she sat down at the interview table placing the box in front of her. Morgan had asked WPC Winton to attend in line with station procedures.

"Coffee or tea Miss McDonald?" Morgan asked.

"No thank you. I can't stay long. Just enough time to show you a second letter and a number of other items that I kept without my mum's knowledge," she added, keen to emphasise the point. She opened the shoebox taking out a single sheet of paper and passed it over the table. "I found it last night tucked inside some other papers. I thought it might help you compare it with my dad's farewell letter." Her eyes welled up as she spoke, the memories of a little girl still trapped inside this adult version. For a few seconds her self-confidence escaped her and she was vulnerable, something Morgan hadn't seen before. He picked up the letter without speaking and read through the content.

"I'll take it to the lab and see if they can verify that they were written by the same hand," he replied thoughtfully.

"Thank you," she replied, the smile returning to her face. He looked her up and down again conscious about what he was going to ask her next.

"Your father has been missing for twenty-five years. In a way I can understand your need to know what happened, but," his words were followed by an uneasy silence before she gave her own interpretation.

"But its unlikely he will be alive. Is that what you were going to say Constable Morgan?" she asked. He looked at her uncomfortably.

"It's OK, I just need to know one way or the other. It floored my mum when I was only twelve years old. I still remember her crying herself to sleep. I just remember a loving father who use to read me bedtime stories and played with me in his spare time," she replied.

"I'm sorry, I didn't mean to upset you. I just didn't want you to get your hopes up too much," Morgan said. There was that little-lost-girl look in her eyes again. "We will do what we can Miss McDonald. You go home and look after your mum and I will contact you if there are any developments." He offered a hand more in gesture than to make any physical contact. She stood, tall and slim with curves in all the right places.

"You didn't really say why you were investigating my dad, did you?" she asked, her mood changing to one of inquiry. Morgan considered her youthful features for a moment. His boss had chosen to keep this from both mother and daughter until they had more evidential corroboration.

"I'm really sorry Miss McDonald, but I can't discuss the case with you at present." Her eyes became sad again and Morgan felt guilt overcoming him.

"Look Miss McDonald we have reason to believe that your dad may not be dead and I do stress the word, 'may'," Morgan offered. The fact that Tim McDonald might be involved in the death of Robert Benson he kept to himself. "That's all I can say for now. We have a draft report in preparation, but its early days." She looked at him helplessly the air of self-assuredness no longer evident.

"You will…you will tell me when…if, you find him won't you?" she stammered, holding back the tears. Morgan nodded sympathetically. "Thank you," she said as she got up to leave. She left the shoebox in Morgan's care. He saw her back to reception and out of the station. There was something about Estelle McDonald that disturbed him, something in her personality and body language and behind those big brown eyes that made her unpredictable, a Jekyll and Hyde type character. What he didn't expect was confirmation of his concerns so soon after she had left the station.

He collapsed into his chair, emotionally drained after his conversation with Estelle McDonald. The look on her face, a sense of pleading for help and information had sapped him of his resolve and he was glad to see the back of her before he cracked. Grabbing a coffee from the percolator, he relished a sudden quiet spell and an infuse of caffeine. As luck would have it, the phone rang just as these thoughts passed through his mind. He lifted the receiver.

"DC Morgan?" the voice said on the other end of the telephone.

"Yes," Morgan groaned.

"DC Harris, front desk," Morgan rolled his eyes again. "I have a lady in reception to see Inspector Graves. I've explained that he is out, so she asked for you. It's a Mrs McDonald. " Morgan was partway through drinking a mouthful of coffee, half-choking at the news.

"What the devil is she playing at?" he said dabbing at the coffee stains on his tie. "I've only just seen her not five minutes ago," he said to himself. "Tell her I'll be down directly please." Replacing the receiver he bounded down the stairwell a second time to the ground floor. There were plenty of other things he could be looking at he reasoned as he raced three steps at a time, but Estelle McDonald was certainly one of the better options. He smoothed his blond hair as he made his way along the corridor again self-consciously pausing for a few seconds behind the door. Taking a deep breath, he entered reception. His efforts were wasted. An elderly lady sat in a wheelchair in the centre of reception. DC Harris had already organised tea for her and she sat sipping Darjeeling from a china cup.

"Mrs McDonald?" Morgan announced surprised, "I believe you're here to see Inspector Graves?" he said slowly and deliberately gathering his thoughts. "Unfortunately, he's been called away. I would be happy to help if I can." Morgan offered as he sat down on one of the chairs normally occupied by members of the public. He was recovering now from the initial shock of coming across Mrs McDonald senior so soon after her daughter's departure. The old lady placed the empty cup and saucer on her lap before Morgan relieved her of her burden.

"I would like to speak to you about my daughter Constable Morgan," she said. Morgan looked uneasy as if caught off guard by the question. "It's OK son, I saw her leave before I came in," she continued.

The comment did nothing to dispel his uneasiness about the topic and the underlying tone in her voice, as if he was being implicated in something. His discomfort must have found its way on to his face as the old lady picked up on his expression of innocence.

"Don't panic my boy, I just want a private word concerning my daughter and her relationship with her dad," she explained taking in the relief on his face.

"Interview Room 1 is free," Harris said gesturing toward the corridor that Morgan had appeared through. Morgan pushed Mrs McDonald through into the room asking WPC Averill Winton to sit in on the interview along the way as she had earlier with Estelle McDonald.

"No need to make this formal constable," she suggested, "it's just a call to give you fair warning about my daughter." She paused taking in Morgan's confused look. "Tell me constable, what did my daughter say to you?"

"I'm afraid I'm not at liberty to discuss information disclosed by other people about the case, even if that person is your daughter Mrs McDonald," Morgan replied. "You will have to talk to her about that".

"Oh come on my lad. Let's not be coy about this," she said a little annoyed.

"I'm sorry Mrs McDonald I cannot tell you," Morgan said a little more forcibly.

"OK if you must play these silly games, I'll tell you what she said and if I'm broadly correct you won't need to interrupt," she remarked. Morgan gestured affirmatively deciding to humour the old lady. WPC Winton observed passively, her role one of observation only. "My daughter constable has never really recovered from her dad's disappearance. She was an extremely impressionable youth at the time. She has spent a great deal of time trying to track him down over the years. Once, when she was twelve, she thought she had found him, on the South Coast somewhere, Brighton I think." Morgan wondered if he should be noting all this, but decided not to for now. "She had a nervous breakdown soon after. She was admitted to a psychiatric hospital after she tried to cut her wrists weeks later. She was in that place for six months, during which time she nearly throttled a nurse for keeping her locked up, albeit for her own safety." The old lady paused, remembering unhappy family memories. "She has stabilised over the years; or so I thought. I'm afraid all this talk of locating her father again may have change that."

"How do you mean exactly Mrs McDonald?" Morgan probed.

"I'm not sure. Last time she had terrible mood swings. Sometimes she was quite content and happy with her lot in life, the next very angry and often violent, but never toward me. I saw the signs back then only after they were explained to me by her psychiatrist…and I saw them again briefly last night at home," she explained further. Morgan fidgeted wondering what these behavioural traits might be when Mrs McDonald spoke again. "She brought you something to look at didn't she? Something of her dad's, something I thought I'd destroyed all those years ago," she asked. Morgan's silence only confirmed her suspicions.

"Be careful my lad and treat my daughter with the utmost caution. I may be old and frail looking, but I'm not the one you need to treat with care," she suggested. "I'm afraid for her mental health. If she thinks you are on to something concerning her dad she will hound you in any way she can to get at the truth. Keep her at arm's length for your own sake as well as hers." That last sentence had a sense of menace about it that Morgan didn't care for. It merely confirmed his own intuitive opinion now of Estelle McDonald. He was about to ask why when there was a knock at the door and Philip Graves walked in.

"Ah, Mrs McDonald, D.C.Harris told me you were in the station. I hope Constable Morgan has been making you comfortable?"

The old lady swivelled her wheelchair around toward the door in his direction. "If you would be so kind Inspector?" she said, gesturing toward the door. Graves moved to one side. "No doubt constable Morgan will fill you in on the detail, what little there is. A bit of a one-sided conversation if you ask me," she glared as she manoeuvred herself out into the corridor.

"Err WPC Winton will see you out Mrs McDonald." Graves motioned to the WPC and she hurried out in to the corridor in hot pursuit. "Now constable, would you care to enlighten me about what that was all about?" Graves said pulling up a chair.

"Well sir," Morgan said reflectively," it was a very odd visit, as if she was warning me...us I should say, to stay clear of her daughter. To be guarded about Miss McDonald asking questions about her father at the very least," Morgan explained. Graves looked expectantly as if there was more to come. Morgan went on to explain Estelle McDonald's medical background as a youth and her mother's worries and concerns. It all appeared to confirm what Lady Woollsey had said previously in part.

"We only saw her the once and I didn't pick up on anything of that nature," Graves said out loud. "Perhaps it's just a mother's protective way, although Miss McDonald must have been through a lot in the past as a child," Graves speculated out loud. Morgan looked a little disconcerted until it dawned on Graves why.

"Estelle McDonald's been here as well hasn't she?" he barked." That's why her mother called in at the station."

"I could hardly turn her away sir, it wouldn't seem right under the circumstances," Morgan replied awkwardly. The two walked back to Morgan's office, Morgan giving a word-for-word account of his conversation with the younger, Estelle McDonald this time. By the time they sat facing each other at Morgan's desk, Graves was in full possession of the facts.

"Do you have the box that she brought in?" Graves asked. He didn't expect to see anything of any significance, but then again you never know, he thought to himself. Estelle McDonald must have been on a fishing trip, choosing to target the one person she thought she could get more information from – the young, impressionable constable from their last meeting at Little Crandon cottage.

"Here you are sir, a letter that Miss McDonald says was written by her dad to her headmaster, but was never posted. It was drafted the year before he disappeared. There are some family pictures taken just after Miss McDonald was born. They look like a happy couple sir, it's hard to think that it could all go so wrong." Just then Graves noticed a small imitation silver box, hidden beneath the bits of paper and photographs.

In The Mood

"Hello, what have we here?" he said out loud.

"Just a cheap souvenir sir and a dated one at that. She said it is a music box that her father brought back with him from Singapore. Miss McDonald said that her dad use to open it at night and let it play until she fell asleep. "The quality of the tune is pretty poor given its age." Graves placed it on the desk in front of him and lifted the lid. It played a little jingle, a section from a much larger composition, the sort that dated and cheap music boxes play, out of tune and at a different pitch than the original melody it was taken from. For a moment Graves thought he recognised it. Not just the tune, it reminded him of the past, perhaps a favourite of his mother he thought.

"Its just a bit of cheap reproduction sir, of no real value," Morgan said dismissively.

"I wonder…" Graves said to himself, trying to place the tune's familiarity.

"Philip," the call came from Gary Swallow at the end of the office. From the tone of his voice he was much happier than the last time the two had exchanged words. Graves tipped the lid of the music box shut and put it and the shoe box back in Morgan's desk drawer.

15

Motif

It was late that same day and Graves had intended to drive straight to the hospital. Instead his mother had left him a message asking him to call for some supplies from the cottage on his way, which gave him the ideal opportunity to stop off and see Ray Brightwell about Margaret McDonald's picture. He had to confess to being curious about the letter as well, especially now he had a comparison courtesy of Estelle McDonald, but that would have to wait until the following morning. Earlier, he had briefed DCI Swallow about his inquiries and progress. Swallow was under severe pressure now to issue something more positive to the media even though the road above and below the bypass had reopened. Graves had agreed to produce a draft report over the next day or two to inform Swallow and to provide the basis for a media briefing. A

In The Mood

short while later he found himself back at the labs heading toward Brightwell's office.

"Evening Ray, I believe DC Morgan dropped some photographs off with you first thing this morning for enlargement. He seemed to think you would have them ready before you closed for the day?" Graves inquired. The red haired bespectacled lab technician dressed in customary white coat had moved his attention away from the microscope on the bench in front of him, allowing the glasses propped on his forehead to drop down on to the bridge of his nose. He squinted as Graves approached him for the second time in as many days.

"Graves," he nodded nonchalantly, "I presume you are not going to pull a stunt like the other day?" he suggested, referring to their earlier encounter over the fingerprinting episode.

Graves shook his head. "No I'm as much in the dark this time as you are. Did you manage to do the enlargement yet?"

"Yes as a matter of fact, nothing too special. In fact fairly straightforward despite the age and condition of the print," Brightwell replied. He placed his hand over an array of photographs on his workbench away from Graves's prying eyes. "That's for another customer," he said firmly, " your photograph is over here." Brightwell led him to the overhead projector that they had used the previous day and flicked the switch to the on position. The equipment hummed as it projected Margaret McDonald's photo on to the pull-down white screen at the front of the room. "That's the section of the photo that DC Morgan asked me to enlarge," Brightwell indicated recapping.

"Beside it is the original picture to allow you to get some perspective from the enlargement. You were quite correct when you said that each man wore the same sweater and you were also correct about the motif," Brightwell said almost disappointedly. "However, due to the angle of the shot and the way the men were stood at the time the photograph was taken, I couldn't quite get a clear definition of the motif from the enlargement." Graves looked at the photographs more intently across the screen. There was something desperately familiar with this motif, yet he still couldn't place it. Brightwell followed him silently a smile playing across his face. He was enjoying his time in control.

"However, I guessed what you were after and so I also enlarged this area here on the ground showing the bags that they were carrying." Brightwell produced a second enlargement to increased magnification, replacing his earlier effort. "This is twenty times normal size and as you can see, there is one racket visible, well at least the handle of the racket poking out of this chap's bag. I've been able to get an impression off the base of the handle, which I guess is the same motif that is partially hidden on the men's sweaters.

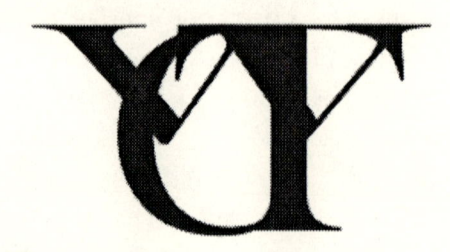

You can certainly see the partial similarities once I orientated them the same way on the screen," Brightwell explained. "Some of the lines are made up of different colours if that means anything, possibly a combination to make up the whole?" The comment was enough to jog Graves's memory as he realised why it was so familiar.

"Combination to make up the whole!" Graves said to himself, seizing on Brightwell's comment and then it all fell into sharp focus. "Thanks Ray. I believe I know where I have seen it before now. I will pop back in tomorrow, if that's OK and you can take me through your thoughts on the handwriting comparison please." Brightwell suggested late afternoon of the following day, as the two men walked toward the lab door. Graves paused suddenly remembering Estelle McDonald's second letter from earlier. "Could you also have a look at this letter and compare it with the one that Morgan gave you?" he said retrieving a brown envelope from inside jacket pocket. "I want to know if they are by the same hand."

"I'll see what I can do, but I am busy at present," Brightwell replied with a sigh.

"I know I can depend on you Ray," Graves said trying not to sound too patronising. The two then left the lab, Brightwell back to his office and Graves heading toward Willenbury General Hospital.

16

Willenbury Tennis Club

The following day Morgan called for Graves at the cottage at 9:30am sharp.

"Right Morgan, we're off on a little trip," he exclaimed. "Take us to the west of Willenbury along the A677, approximately three miles. I am going to show you that motif from Margaret McDonald's photo," he said, brimming with his own cleverness. Twenty minutes later and the Ford Granada weaved its way around several potholes along an unadopted track that seemed to be going precisely nowhere and then it suddenly swung around an old oak tree, the track dropped to a much lower level and about a thousand yards ahead it broadened out into

In The Mood

a neatly maintained car park, half full of cars from their approach angle. At the head of the car park was a 2 storey Victorian stone building, its walls dripping with climbing ivy. Graves had told Morgan about his brief meeting with Ray Brightwell and the motif that Brightwell had pulled from the photograph whilst they were driving. As the car cleared the old oak, Graves had asked Morgan to pull over to the left, just before the car headed down the steep slope toward the car park. Graves retrieved Brightwell's enlargement from his briefcase and gave it to Morgan to consider.

"Tell me Morgan, having told you about the motif and now that you have the photograph, can you tell me anything significant about the building up ahead?" Morgan took his time, looking about him before giving Grave's a blank look. "What about the flower bed fronting the building?" Graves asked. There was still no reaction from Morgan. "OK then constable," Graves said emphasising the need to be more observant. "How about the roof?" he continued. Morgan looked even more bewildered.

"Different coloured tiles sir, winter flowers in the flower bed, other than that, I can't see anything of significance," he replied.

"Lift the photograph and shift your line of sight between it and the building in the background." Morgan did as he was instructed until his look of confusion was replaced by one of surprise and slight embarrassment. Both the flowers in the bed and the tiles on the roof were in the pattern as the motif on the picture.

"I knew I recognised that pattern from somewhere," Graves exclaimed. "Its actually three letters superimposed on each other. 'W', 'T' and a 'C' to give you that odd pattern, which became the club's motif in the 1960s," Graves explained.

"Club sir?" Morgan replied as he edged the Granada forwards now down the poorly maintained track in low gear.

"Yes Morgan, welcome to Willenbury Tennis Club. Strictly members only, unless you represent her majesty's boys in blue of course," Graves said grinning. Parking the Granada beside what Graves now called the Clubhouse, both men entered heading directly to the reception desk. The two storey building comprised members' changing rooms with access directly to the rear of the building and the six grass tennis courts. A member's bar and a central reception area were located to the right and centre of the main entrance, whilst meeting and storage rooms took up the remaining space.

"Excuse me my name is Detective Inspector Graves. This is Detective Constable Morgan. Can we speak to the secretary of the club miss?" Graves asked. The young lady presiding over the reception counter tutted audibly putting her freshly brewed cup of tea to one side.

"Would it be about the break-in?" she asked, her eyes now fixed on the younger of the two men. Graves was getting use to this by now.

Graves shook his head, "No I'm not aware of a break-in, I just need to speak to someone in authority." She gave him a derisory look before quickly looking through the register in front of her.

"Er Mr Tyson is on Court Number 1 checking the tension in the net before this evening's semi-final. He's

In The Mood

the Club Secretary. Can I get someone to take you down there?" She offered; her tone was as hard as her look.

"No thank you," Graves replied. "I know the layout of the courts fairly well." Back outside at the rear of the building this time Graves turned immediately left with Morgan following in his wake. The hedgerows that divided each grass court stood erect, turning brown as winter closed in. From a slightly elevated position they could see all the courts in one panoramic view.

"From memory the courts were not set out as you would expect. Court 1 is the farthest away, whilst Court 6 is this one just in front of us," Graves said, as if talking to himself rather than Morgan. Now then, if we skirt around the perimeter there should be a rear gate leading to Court 1." Graves was already walking briskly as he spoke retracing his steps he had taken as a boy a long time ago. As they cornered the last hedgerow they saw a man exiting through the gate in question. He was hardly dressed in whites, more casually dressed, and for manual work. "Mr Tyson," Graves called as they approached.

"Yes, can I help you? Are you members of the club? The courts are booked all week and in any case you should speak to reception." He pulled the gate closed behind him, his attention now fixed on the squeaky hinges of the gate.

"I'm Detective Inspector Graves, this is Detective Constable Morgan. We would like to speak to you about some of your club members," Graves displayed his warrant card as he spoke.

"Oh, I'm sorry, I thought you were prospective club members," Tyson replied, slightly embarrassed. He gestured to both men back towards the clubhouse. "I'll take you back to reception and we can have a look at the records there. Can you be discreet with our members' privacy though please?" Tyson said pushing on just ahead, the sound of gravel crunching beneath his feet.

"Actually sir," Morgan said, "I think discretion won't be a problem."

Tyson half turned, a bemused look on his face.

"What DC Morgan means Mr Tyson is we would like to see your members' records for specific years, namely years 1958–1962," Graves clarified.

A look of curiosity changed to one of a smile. "Oh, I see. I was in university over that period Inspector." He looked at Graves as if this was enough to get him off the hook.

"That's as may be sir. Do you have archive records of past members around that time?" Graves pressed. He of course knew from his youth as a junior member that such records existed then, but were they still around now he wondered.

"I must admit Inspector it is a duty I have neglected in the past," Tyson said, as the threesome walked back up the ornamental steps towards the clubhouse.

"How do you mean neglected sir?" Morgan asked.

"Oh I have maintained records here from when I joined as club secretary in 1970 to present day, constable. I have to rationalize my time. Pressures of the job as I am sure you can appreciate. I can't vouch for records before 1970." They reached the clubhouse entrance and Tyson turned before entering. "So on reflection, I doubt that I can be of any practical use to you." There was an air of superiority to his tone that was beginning to frustrate both policemen.

"So what happened to the records established by Bill Naylor when the club opened just after the war?" Graves asked enjoying the uncomfortable look now on Tyson's face.

"Ah," he said surprised, "you knew our esteemed groundsman and unofficial historian?" Tyson queried as he turned and they entered reception.

"I knew of him. I was just a junior member here at the time. I once saw his work though, me and several other boys. It would have been about 1965," Graves volunteered.

"Hmm," Tyson pondered, as if in deep thought." I keep my records in filing cabinets in the office area behind the reception desk." I suppose anything predating my involvement before 1970 would still be in the Reading Room."

"The Reading Room? Of course," Graves repeated the name. "I'd forgotten all about it." Turning right from reception, they continued along a short gloomy hallway to a door at the rear of the building.

"It's seldom used these days," Tyson said, unlocking the door then pushing it open. Even the club secretary looked surprised to see the depth of records stored there. "I'm sorry if I seemed to be a little unhelpful. We had a break-in a few days ago in this very room, although I reported it as much for insurance purposes you understand, I have had no visit from the police about it."

"I can only apologise Mr Tyson. I'll look into it back at the station," Graves replied, glancing at Morgan. "Was anything taken?" Graves asked as he looked about the circular room.

"It was just malicious damage, probably kids. Nothing was taken just a window broken." Tyson pointed to an ornate stain glass window now partially covered by a piece of plywood. "Now gentlemen, could I leave you to your investigations and ask that you are careful please? Some of the records are quite old and fragile. I will be in reception if you need me." With that he left both men, disappearing back along the corridor. The room had a musty odour to it, despite the fresh air seeping in from the broken window. The atmosphere was depressing and uninviting, hardly conducive to someone sitting in a room carrying out research for an indefinite period, in spite of its name. The room had a single arch window. Its partially stained glass limited the amount of natural light that was allowed through. With this oppressive atmosphere, it was a wonder if anyone came here at all.

Down the centre of the room were three wide desks set-up as if a meeting were to be held. Lining the walls on racks were large registers and judging by their size and how far they protruded from the wall, Graves guessed them to be A3 in size. The leather binder of each book was arranged in alphabetical order starting from the door entrance and continuing around the outer wall of the room. Each volume had letters of the alphabet and dates stamped into the binding. Not surprisingly the books changed to a cheap looking plastic version as they approached the 1970s. The shelves contained the club's whole membership since it began in 1945 until 1970 when Tyson presumably took over. Old Bill Naylor was a thorough man. Not only did the registers cover past members, they also catalogued the courts, type of grass used, frequency of mowing, hedgerow planting and pruning. There were designs plans for the court layout and one for construction of the clubhouse itself. Even the sewer system servicing the clubhouse was recorded there.

"Where do we start sir," Morgan asked? Graves placed his brief case on the desk nearest to him opening it at the same time. He produced Margaret McDonald's photograph and a magnifying glass, placing the photo on the desk beside his brief case.

"Switch on the light Morgan please," he asked, leaving Morgan's question unanswered. Morgan duly obliged, the fluorescent tube blinked twice before lighting up the room. Graves used the glass to scan the picture.

"Sir?" Morgan pressed.

"Do you recall what Margaret McDonald said when she described the circumstances about when she took this photograph?" Graves replied, smoothing out the surface of the picture a little more with the back of his hand.

"Only that she took the photo without her husband's knowledge, part of a school geography assignment or something," Morgan replied retracing his thoughts. Graves considered his DC thoughtfully.

"She had started work at Chetley Junior School the same year and I know from my own memory at the time that it opened as a new school in 1957. Also, the man in the background behind our trio just leaving the building is holding a copy of what looks like the Daily Telegraph." Morgan took the glass and looked at the photo.

"Yes sir, but the date is obscured. Even Brightwell wouldn't be able to do anything with that," Morgan observed.

"Quite right, Brightwell said as much at the lab" Graves replied his eyes now roaming along the shelves of volumes above their heads. He saw the record he was after and moved toward it. Morgan watched, a confused stare playing across his face and not for the first time. "Check the headline Morgan on the front of the paper and tell me what you see?" Graves continued pulling a register from its resting place.

"It looks like the name Munich and then something else partly obscured beginning with 'Di'," he replied.

"There is only one event that was synonymous with Munich in the late 1950s and it nicely ties-in with the opening of Chetley Junior School twelve months earlier and that was the Munich air disaster," Graves said, content with his deduction. Morgan still looked confused. "1958 Morgan, Manchester United football club lost 7 of their team in a plane crash from a total of 21 passengers," Graves explained further. There was still no reaction from Morgan. "Never mind. I suppose it was a little before your time. The important thing is it places the photograph around 6th February 1958," Graves concluded, "Which is why I am interest in members registers for 1958," He said showing Morgan the date stamp on the binder. He carefully placed the folder on the table beside his briefcase. "I suggest that we work forward toward 1962, until we have personal details for Gould and Hewitt. With some luck, they may both be in the 1958 edition."

"And Benson sir?" Morgan added.

"I wouldn't hold out too much hope, but by all means check. From all accounts Benson wasn't liked and there is nothing to suggest yet that he was still involved with the other three after the fire," Graves reasoned. "At this stage their involvement in Benson's death is purely conjecture."

He was already thumbing through the 1958 members' register, until he came across the letter 'H'.

"Here we are," he said flipping over Margaret McDonald's photograph to check the names once more. "Frank Hewitt, he became a member in January 1958 according to the summary page at the beginning of the folder. Page 63 should give us his personal particulars as they were at that time." Graves flipped back through the register until he reached page 63.

"What is it sir?" Morgan asked, noticing a change in Graves's manner.

"The page is missing – ripped from its place to be accurate." He ran his index finger along the remnants of the page in the spine of the book. "Try Gould will you Morgan, the same year. I have a funny feeling that that page will be missing as well," Graves said almost resignedly. Morgan took the folder from Graves whilst he mulled over the implication. A few minutes later and Morgan confirmed his suspicions. Both men collapsed into the nearest chairs lost in their own disappointment. Several minutes later, a little deflated and dejected and yet still curious about the coincidence, they emerged from the Reading Room only to be met by the Club Secretary, who was keen for them to leave with the minimum of fuss.

"Ah, Inspector Graves, did you find what you were looking for?" Tyson said in hushed tones as two members of the tennis club walked close by.

"Not exactly Mr Tyson, but thanks for your cooperation," Graves answered as he passed by with Morgan toward the entrance. He stopped as the reached the door. "Oh, Mr Tyson, the break-in that you mentioned earlier–"

"There was no real harm done Inspector as I said. There's nothing missing and I thought I'd settle the cost of the repair rather than increase the club's insurance premiums since we spoke earlier," His features changed slowly from their usual smugness. "Were the registers defaced in some way?" he whispered suspecting the worst.

"Some pages have been ripped from one of the registers. Judging by the dust on the adjacent registers compared to the 1958 edition, I'd say fairly recently as well," Morgan replied.

"Bloody vandals," Tyson muttered. "Was that all?"

"It would appear so," Morgan commented, "but it was enough to stop our inquiries here, quite a coincidence that they were the pages we were interested in," Morgan stared at his boss wondering if he had spoken out of turn.

"Would you like to check our microfiche records instead?" the young receptionist interrupted. She had been half-listening to the conversation and made the offer almost as a knee-jerk reaction. She looked at the bewildered faces before her. "They were all converted, I believe, in1983 given their fragile condition, as a safeguard. The document reader is here in reception, behind me." She

In The Mood

motioned at a hooded piece of equipment behind where she stood. Tyson looked decidedly uncomfortable.

"My apologies gentlemen," he sighed at his receptionist, "I was on holiday at the time and I'd completely forgotten about the microfiche copies," he added sheepishly.

Both policemen stared at each other in disbelief then grinned at their stroke of good luck. Ten minutes later with the necessary tape rolls in place Morgan began focusing his search on the missing pages.

"Here we are sir. Members register for 1958, page 63," Morgan called out excitedly. The name written here is Hewitt, Frank, age 37 in 1958, unmarried, again at the time. Address is number 10 Canal Reach, Willenbury." Morgan had placed his notebook beside the document reader and was taking notes as he read from the screen.

"Gentlemen," Tyson whispered, urging them to keep their voices low. Morgan turned the dial on the projector again, slowing the speed as he reached page 86. The details for Ted Gould were also noted, only this time Gould, like Tim McDonald, was married in 1958. Morgan noted Gould's address and they thanked Tyson again for his cooperation then left to return back to the station.

"Do you think that they may still live at these addresses after all this time sir?" Morgan asked.

"I don't know Morgan. Either way, it's something we need to check out. At the end of the day, neither man may know the whereabouts of Tim McDonald or what happened to Robert Benson in 1960. They do, however, have a lot of explaining to do over what happened in 1953 at Harrington Hall orphanage. What was perceived to be a tragic accident at the orphanage over thirty years ago was arson and murder and for that reason alone we need to take this line of inquiry to its conclusion," Graves said as they made their way back to the car park.

"And if someone else now lives at these addresses?" Morgan replied patting his notebook.

"Then we may well have reached the end of the road constable, unless DI Wheldon has learned anything more from Benson." Graves said. "Morgan, drop me at home please. I want to pick my car up. I want you to pay a visit to the local records office at Willenbury and track down the birth, marriage – even death certificates if they are dead – for Hewitt and Gould and for their real names Turnberry and Grundy. Report back later today," Graves asked.

"OK sir," Morgan replied. The Granada erupted into life once more and Morgan steered it gingerly back toward the main road. There was a quiet moment as the car gathered speed. It was Morgan that spoke about something that had also been on Graves's mind for the last ten minutes or so. "Sir, the break-in and the removal of the pages were both fairly recent judging by Tyson's report of the break-in itself. I suppose they could have been connected." he thought.

"I've been thinking along the same lines myself," Graves replied pensively.

"Why now sir after all this time? Unless Benson's friends are aware of what we are doing," Morgan continued. Graves didn't offer any further comment, he just stared out at the road ahead mulling over their observations. There was plenty to consider on the way home.

17

Brackenridge House

It was mid-morning the following day. Graves had reversed his usual pattern of visiting the hospital at the end of the day by visiting his parents earlier that morning. It gave his mother a chance to freshen up while he took her place at his father's bedside. His father's condition remained the same throughout. Morgan was still preoccupied with a second visit to the council offices in the centre of the village where he was still trying to locate various birth, death and marriage certificates. He also had a debrief meeting to attend with the rest of the team back at the station after lunch and Graves was keen to find out what progress Wheldon had made over the last few days. Graves had left the hospital mid-morning and was on his way to the last known residency of Ted Gould, a leafy private estate that was a state-of-the-art development as Graves recalled when it was built in 1956. It was a long shot, but one he had to follow up on. He slowed the MG to a crawling pace turning smartly into the private estate, St. Michael's Hill, leafy woodlands with private roads leading to individually designed houses. Graves pulled up alongside the lodge that marked the entrance to the estate. A red nosed security guard, clipboard and pencil at the ready, suddenly occupied a stable type door with the upper section left open. Graves wound the window down and leaned out of the car slightly.

"Morning sir," the guard said, "can I help you?"

"Morning, I'm here to visit a Mr and Mrs Gould. I believe they live in Brackenridge House?" He questioned his own conviction as soon as the words left his mouth. "At least that was where they lived twenty-six years ago," he said to himself.

"Just one moment sir, I'll check the estate records." The security guard disappeared momentarily back inside the lodge. "I have no record of a Mrs Gould at Brackenridge House sir. You must be mistaken." he said reappearing several minutes later. He gave the impression that the best part of his job was dealing with nuisance callers trying to access an exclusive estate. Security was his responsibility. Wealthy people relied on him and even though the pay was paltry it gave him a sense of power. Stepping outside the office, he spread his sizeable frame as wide as he could in front of the four-barred gate – arms folded. Graves reached for his warrant card and waved it at the guard.

"I will need to speak to the owners whatever their name is," Graves replied. Begrudgingly, the guard stepped aside pulling the gate with him. It moved silently just far enough to allow the car through. As it passed by the guard called out.

"Straight to the top of the road Inspector and take the right fork, Brackenridge House is the third house on the left. You can't miss it. The current owner is a Mrs Valentine. It has two large stone lions marking the entrance to the property and a block paved driveway."

Graves waved his appreciation and moved slowly along the main spine road of the estate. His slow speed seemed appropriate for such a quiet, secluded and peaceful piece of countryside. He noticed more tree lined driveways, some with Mercedes or Bentleys parked on them. It was a far cry from Tower Hamlets in inner city London where the most people hoped for was a trip to the park at the weekends or a window box on the window sill of a high-rise block of flats.

This was the place to live when he was a boy, he recalled. The maturity of the surrounding grounds since those days only enhanced the look of the properties there now. Taking the right fork as instructed he travelled a short distance further before the MG pulled up alongside a nameplate attached to a brick pillar. Sat on top of the pillar a large stone lion as the guard described. The nameplate read, 'Brackenridge House' and a grill and button below it, suggested an intercom. He climbed out of the car and pressed the button it in anticipation. The little box crackled into life, before the metallic voice of an elderly lady came out of it.

"Yes, what do you want?" There was nothing friendly about the tone. In fact, it sounded irritated by the unwanted intrusion.

"I'm sorry to disturb you Mrs Valentine, I am a Police Inspector and I would like to speak to you about the former owners of Brackenridge House, a Mr and Mrs Gould I believe?" The intercom fell silent for a few seconds before the voice returned.

"Very well, but I insist on seeing your identification first. Oh, and can you leave your car on the road outside please? I hate oil on my driveway," she said firmly before a buzzing sound accompanied each metal gate as they opened together. Graves stepped through barely clearing them before they returned to their closed position.

"It must be something about gates on this estate, they have limited scope for movement," he thought to himself. He walked up the winding driveway, immaculate in its upkeep. Each topiary conifer mirrored its counterpart on either side of the drive. Beyond the trees, neatly kept lawns extending back to shrubbery and borders, all typical in their presentation and maintained to the highest standard. The house itself was a detached, mock Georgian house with a double garage. The block paved driveway meandered its way up to the garage entrance, broadening out to accommodate a number of cars for parking. A classic Rolls Royce Silver Shadow stood in one of the parking bays with the number plate 'VAL1'.

He had to admit to himself, if you didn't want oil on your drive you needed to have a quality car and she certainly had one. A sudden movement in amongst a large clump of Rhododendron bushes distracted his attention from the silver saloon. A figure garbed in an old pair of jeans, T-shirt, gloves, Wellington boots and a Fedora type hat knelt digging around the base of the shrub. It could have been Estelle McDonald from where he stood but then it could just as well have been the gardener. The figure's position prevented any attempt at any immediate introduction until he came within a few yards.

"Excuse me, could you tell me where I could find the lady of the house please?" The figure turned and revealed, to Graves's surprise, an elderly lady, probably in her late 60s. Her colouring suggested someone used to outdoor activities. Despite her advancing years she seemed sprightly for her age and agile in her movement. She eyed Graves pushing the brim of her floppy hat back to gain a better view of her visitor.

"I'm Mrs Valentine. Inspector Graves I take it," she crowed, peeling off her rubber garden gloves. Graves nodded, his hand already reaching toward hers. His free hand fumbled inside his jacket pocket for the warrant card she had requested sight of. They shook hands and then she took the card and satisfied herself that he was the genuine article. After a few seconds she squinted in the sunlight back at Graves, looking at the card once again briefly before passing it back to him.

"You have put some weight on Inspector since this picture was taken," she said, her features remaining unchanged matching her no-nonsense manner.

"I put it down to good food, wine and diminishing exercise with time and most important of all, it's an old picture," he replied, trying to keep discussions on a light-hearted basis.

"How exactly can I help England's finest?" she asked dropping her trowel into the flowerbed beside her. "Shall we have some homemade ginger beer while we talk? You look like you could use a drink Inspector." The harshness of her tone from earlier had relaxed more now in the flesh and he wondered if the metallic sounding voice that emanates from intercom systems was the reason. He nodded his appreciation. They walked along a footpath, passing through a wooden side-gate, it led them into the garden at the rear of the house. Part of the garden contained a conservatory as an annexe to the main house. Wicker furniture filled the room and on a central table sat a carafe of amber liquid and two glasses. "If you are wondering," she said, reaching for the container, "two glasses allows for unexpected visitors and the only reason that I stop working." She sat down, motioning toward an empty chair, before pouring the beer. "Now tell me Inspector, what is it exactly that you think I can help you with?" Graves looked at her giving her one of his appreciative looks.

"Well as I said over the intercom, I'm interested in the former owners of Brackenridge House. Their name as I mentioned earlier is or rather was a Mr and Mrs Gould. I need to speak to Mr Gould rather urgently as part of my current inquiries. I thought perhaps by chance that you might still have a forwarding address or that you recalled the estate agent that the Goulds used?" he explained. "That is assuming that you bought the house from the Goulds?"

In The Mood

"That sounds like a lot of *ifs* and *maybes* to me Inspector." she said frowning. Her eyes now fixed on the man before her, questioning his motives inside her mind before she spoke. "I am – or rather was – Phyllis Gould, Inspector," she confirmed, with a controlled smile. It was Graves's turn to frown this time. It was something he wasn't expecting. Yes she was about the right age, but even so. First the records at the tennis club, now this. He felt like he was using up his luck in one quick hit. "I never left the property Inspector. I divorced my first husband in 1978 just to formalise 18 years of his absence. I remarried 4 years ago taking my new husband's name. Unfortunately, Mr Valentine passed away 6 months ago." She eyed Graves in a way that reminded him of how Margaret McDonald had looked at him when he had asked her similar questions about her husband.

"I'm sorry to hear that Mrs Valentine." The offer of condolence was an automatic response from Graves, something he had become conditioned to as part of his job. Even so, he had picked up on the fact that Ted Gould was not only missing like Tim McDonald, but also that he apparently left his wife at or about the same time as McDonald left his wife and family and soon after Benson's death. His mind raced ahead over those few brief seconds, wondering about the circumstances behind Ted Gould's departure. Would the former Mrs Gould be willing to discuss such matters? From her change in tone over the mention of her first husband, a trait he had witnessed previously with Margaret McDonald, he didn't think so. How wrong was he?

"Have you found him?" She asked him. "If he is in trouble after all these years and he needs my help tell him to forget it," There was a degree of anger in her voice now that was steadily growing and she used both her hands to steady the glass to her lips. She cursed her lack of self-control slamming the glass down hard on the table edge so that it shattered, glass fragments and ginger beer suddenly sprayed in all directions. Graves put out a placating hand first then reached for a napkin. Fortunately, she appeared unhurt.

"Not exactly Mrs Valentine I'm not here to dredge up what may be painful memories, but I do need to ask some questions about the time your first husband left," Graves chose his words carefully. The incident was clearly still painful and her reaction similar in nature to Margaret McDonald's.

"That was over twenty-five years ago Inspector. I doubt my memory is that good particularly on events I have tried my best to erase since then," she replied.

"When did you last see your first husband Mrs Valentine?" he asked.

"September 30th 1959 at 10am," came the response without hesitation. A slight quiver in her voice was evident now, no doubt a product of the emotion that still existed. She managed a tight-lipped smile. Despite her inference about her memory, certain precious events and times have a habit of staying in every person's mind. "You see it was my 40th birthday. He had popped out, he said to get me some fresh red roses – something he always did on my birthday – and…" she hesitated, "…he never came back." Her hands gripped the arms of her chair as she remembered each

In The Mood

detail. "I checked at the florist in the village. He never arrived, even though he ordered them by telephone." She focused on a bamboo tree that was swaying gently in the breeze just outside the conservatory door.

"And you never heard from him or seen him since that day?" Graves asked, as tactfully as he could.

"Well," she said guardedly, "there was the letter." She adjusted her position on her chair and began to fidget nervously. She was clearly unsure about resurrecting this whole business.

"He wrote to you recently?" Graves asked.

"Not recently, no Inspector," she explained. Graves frowned at her, trying to understand her response. "He – or someone – wrote me a farewell letter a week after he disappeared." She continued. Again Graves felt more parallels emerging with Tim McDonald's disappearance and an alternative theory began to take shape inside his head. "The letter basically said that he had found another woman and that he was leaving me and that he was sorry." She looked vacant and distant. "Look at me, like a school girl after all these years," she said suddenly aware of Graves's stare and becoming embarrassed. Graves gave an understanding look, something he was getting good at by now, and let a few moments pass while she settled herself.

"You give me the impression that you didn't think that he was capable of writing such a letter from what you said?" Graves inquired.

She considered him carefully. "You see I knew Ted well enough back then. He didn't have the time to have affairs. Besides he loved me deeply. He told me so many times," she replied. "I never did understand what I had done wrong. I suppose that was the worst of it." Her voice tailed off quietly.

"Did you recognise his handwriting?" Graves inquired remembering Morgan's line of questioning with Margaret McDonald.

"Yes, as I said I think so, I mean at the time. The handwriting was certainly untidy compared to Ted's writing. In some respects it was similar and in others it was quite different. Would you like to see the letter?" she offered. Graves looked at her dumbstruck that she still had it and then nodded without speaking. She rose from her chair and disappeared into the main house. Graves decided to stretch his legs and wondered out into the garden. He speculated over things in his mind toying with the idea that perhaps McDonald and Gould had alone absconded a second time for reasons that remained unknown for now. Whether they had been involved in Benson's death was also unknown. Then again if Hewitt proved to be missing about the same time, it could present quite a different scenario. He pulled his overcoat close around his neck as the easterly wind with its chill factor found its way through a row of stout evergreen Leylandii hedgerows when Mrs Valentine reappeared.

"Oh Inspector," she called out as she came into the conservatory, clutching something between her hands. She sat down at the conservatory table as Graves made his way back across the lawn. "I keep the letter in here," she called out gesturing to a box that looked vaguely familiar from where he stood. "Cheap imitation I know," she called out, "but somehow it seemed appropriate given the way

I was treated." Then she lifted the lid of the box. Graves paused from several yards away as he recognised the odd whining melody that he had heard back at the station. "Here is the letter Inspector. There was no envelope, it was just pushed through the letter box." His attention was transfixed on the silver box that continued its melodious tones in continuous cyclic bursts. Phyllis Valentine noticed his stare and quickly slammed the lid closed.

"I'm sorry about that dreadful racket Inspector. I need to find a new home for the letter," she confessed. Graves shifted his attention to the letter and read its brief contents. Before he finished she volunteered a second sheet. "This was a draft speech that my husband was working on for the local party elections at the time in 1958. He always wrote them freehand and then had his secretary type them up. I compared them at the time and thought that they looked odd and then the anger took over as the implied adultery sunk in and I pushed it from my mind." Graves took the second letter and held them both up to the light. The style, layout and content of the Gould farewell letter was exactly the same as the letter Margaret McDonald had received from memory. Also, he was far from a handwriting expert, but even with his limited experience he could see differences in the letter formation and word spacing and how the writing in the Gould farewell letter leaned from left to right, unlike the writing in Gould's draft speech, which was more vertical.

The farewell letter was a competent copy, but nevertheless a copy in his opinion. "One for Ray Brightwell to take a closer look at," he said to himself.

"What do you think Inspector? Were the two letters written by the same hand?" she asked, standing behind his left shoulder.

"It's hard to say Mrs Valentine. Could I possibly borrow these papers and the box? I need an expert opinion on the letters and they can stay inside the box." He smiled pleasantly, hoping not to raise false hopes or even open up old wounds even further. Whatever the reason, her husband had been absent for twenty-five years.

"Err yes, of course, but please let me have them back," she said.

"Of course I give you my personal assurance. Oh, the music box Mrs Valentine?" Graves asked expectantly.

"It was a memento from Ted's war experience in the Far East, a dreadful thing if you ask me," she explained. Graves thanked her again before he left. Later that afternoon Graves and Morgan met back at the station.

"So what did you find out sir?" Morgan inquired. Graves sat at his desk, opened the bottom left-hand drawer and pulled out Phyllis Valentine's silver music box. "How did you get hold of that sir? I locked it away." Morgan asked, pulling at his drawer feverishly. He was relieved to see that his drawer was still locked.

"Actually this is Mrs Valentine's music box, the former Mrs Gould. Quite a surprise that she still lived there," Graves replied.

"Mrs Valentine?" Morgan questioned.

"Yes, she remarried," Graves informed him.

"Are the boxes important sir?" Morgan inquired.

"Not especially for now. They merely help to confirm that they all served together during the war at some

In The Mood

point in the Far East, but we knew that already." Graves reasoned. Opening the box he quickly retrieved the letter and speech before the music began in earnest.

"I want you to take these to Ray Brightwell and ask him to compare them to see if they were written by the same hand." He traced the writing on both sheets of paper with his index finger following the swirl of each letter. His mind recalled the farewell letter that Margaret McDonald received. "Can you also make sure that he includes Mrs McDonald's farewell letter from her husband as well and get him to compare it with Ted Gould's farewell letter? If my suspicious are correct, I am certain that the styles of the farewell letters are the same. Take both boxes as well and get them dusted for prints – you never know," he said hopefully.

Morgan read both letters belonging to Phyllis Valentine. "Do you think they were written by different people sir?"

"My guess would be yes," Graves replied, "but then I'm not the expert. One thing is for certain though, Mrs McDonald and Mrs Gould, as she was known then, received the same letter, word-for-word, probably on the same paper within six months of each other. The coincidence is too extreme to even contemplate. I expect Brightwell to confirm that they were crafted by the same hand."

For the next fifteen minutes Morgan explained how he managed to locate birth certificates for McDonald, Gould and Hewitt at the local records office. Not only were they much older according to their birth certificates than they were purported to be at the time of the fire, Morgan had also located their death certificates, which predated the fire, interestingly by only a few days. In addition and not surprisingly, the description on the death certificates didn't match those of Woollsey, Turnberry and Grundy. All three were of no fixed abode on the record suggesting that they might have been sleeping rough at the time of their death."So the three newly acquired identities at the time of the fire belonged to three tramps, probably living rough. The real Tim McDonald, Ted Gould and Frank Hewitt were found in the burned-out ruins of Harrington Orphanage and recorded on the death certificates as Woollsey, Turnberry and Grundy," Graves reasoned out loud. "Robert Benson, our bridge victim, isn't really Robert Benson if we follow the logic, which makes his identification the more difficult Morgan."

"What next sir?" Morgan asked.

"I'm going hopefully to visit the last known address of Frank Hewitt. You get Brightwell working on those letters. Tell him it's urgent and get the results for Mrs McDonald's letters from earlier. I promised Swallow I would put a draft report to him on what we have found out so far by tomorrow, so it would be useful to have a definitive answer on who wrote the letters by then," Graves said.

"I believe Wheldon is submitting a report as well for completeness although I did hear that his investigation had reached a dead end." Morgan confirmed Graves's observation from his earlier debrief meeting with the team. With that Morgan headed off back to County Labs. Graves had to start pulling together his draft report for Swallow before his visit to number 10 Canal Reach.

18

Canal Reach

It was mid-morning the following day when Graves finally left the station heading toward the little row of cottages that fronted Darlington Canal. A phone call to Willenbury Hospital had confirmed that his father remained stable. He had told his mother that he would visit the hospital later in the day and she seemed to accept the suggestion without protest, which concerned him. He was convinced now that her health was suffering and he decided he would visit as soon as possible.

Number 10 Canal Reach looked more like a small, two-up–two-down terrace house from where Graves had parked his car. It was one of ten similarly built cottages provided to house mill workers on the eastern outskirts of town. Most of the original mill produce was transported by barge before railways came along, as Graves recalled from local school history, along Darlington Canal. It was common practice to have workers housed by mill owners close to their place of work around the turn of the century to maximise productivity.

He stood at the entrance to the short narrow lane taking in each individual house wondering which would be the one he was looking for. The majority of the properties appeared well maintained with small but mature gardens, each painted cheery colours with dry-stone walls to separate each garden, denoting the boundary of each property. They all appeared to be looked after in the spirit in which they were originally built he noticed as he made his way progressively along the lane. They were all a credit to their owners – all except one. The house farthest away from his approach, the last in the row in fact appeared derelict from his vantage point. Both upstairs and downstairs windows were boarded. A gutter hung dangerously from the roof eaves, an accumulation of detritus weighing heavily, over a sparse front garden. He moved steadily down the lane, his eyes never leaving the rundown house. He knew somehow instinctively that this would be number 10 Canal Reach.

In The Mood

The number on the front door had long-since gone, but the image of number 10 still remained, ghosting through where the door had been varnished around them long ago. The front garden, not much larger than three yards square, looked tired and undernourished despite the autumnal month. Gangly rose trees desperate to be pruned waved around in the gentle breeze trying to snare anyone or anything that would venture too near. The garden gate was propped against the gable wall the hinges long since rusted through. He paused taking up a position that gave him a clear view of the front and side of the house, his eyes progressively looking beyond to other houses in the row in stark contrast. His thoughts were interrupted by the sound of a door bolt being drawn from inside the adjacent house.

The door opened and a little wizened old man appeared hands tucked inside his bottle green corduroy pants. He stood no more than five feet tall in his carpet slippers. His grey hair was cropped very short to the back and sides of his head and what little was left on top was kept in place by a generous amount of Brylcreem. His face was red, particularly his nose, which resembled a clown's nose, and his cheeks were hollow covered in short stubble. He eyed Graves suspiciously pulling his sleeveless cardigan tight around him more to keep the draft out than any heat in. He shuffled along his garden path to the gate and noticed Graves's briefcase under his arm. His lips parted revealing slightly yellow, uneven dentures.

"Are you from the council," he barked, saliva ejecting from the corner of his mouth. The shout was almost unexpected from such a slight frame. "It's a bloody disgrace it is. I've been complaining the best part of twenty years come next August about this house. It had squatters in at one time, but even they are choosey where they doss down these days. I put that timber on the windows to keep the rest of them out. That was about fifteen years ago." The old man began to cough with exertion and speaking in a cold frosty atmosphere and Graves decided to pick his moment.

"I'm sorry sir, I'm not from the Council. I'm a policeman," Graves replied.

The old man observed Graves afresh. Clearly the word *policeman* had rattled him, as was normally the case. "My name is Inspector Philip Graves." He looked for a further reaction, but none was forthcoming. "And you are…?" Graves asked.

"I haven't done anything wrong! What do you want to know my name for?" the old man demanded. Graves shifted his attention momentarily back to the house.

"I wasn't implying that you had sir. It is just a matter courtesy if we are to hold a conversation," Graves replied casually. The lit cigarette in the old man's hand was returned to its normal resting place at the corner of his mouth, where it hung limp, the ash almost twice as long as the cigarette that remained. His lip trembled as the cold wind blew down the lane, dispersing the ash. "I'm here to speak to Mr Hewitt, who according to my records lived here," Graves pointed at the boarded cottage over his shoulder, "about twenty-five years ago. Clearly he either doesn't live here anymore or he isn't too house proud." The old man took the butt of his cigarette between his fore finger and thumb and flicked it into the garden of the property in question. He smiled at Graves, his breath enough to convince any smoker to kick the habit.

"No one has lived in that house since he left Inspector. Twenty-five years would be about right. It was the same year I lost my Ethel to the big 'C'." His smile quickly vanished with the memory and his grimace returned.

"All three had indeed vanished at the same time. All four if I include Benson as well," Graves said to himself holding on to the thought for a few seconds. "Was he married, err Mr..." Graves began.

"Call me Bert," the old man interrupted before he began to chuckle and shake his head from side-to-side. He sat down on his front door step. "Married? That's a good one," he said prolonging his enjoyment. "There's no point getting married if you're a poof." He chuckled again more loudly this time until he began coughing wildly once more.

"What, he was a homosexual?" Graves asked. The thought had crossed his mind lately, given Lady Woollsey's comments about her brother and the lack of a spouse named in the tennis club records.

"I can see now why they made you Detective Inspector." Bert replied attempting sarcasm. "Yes he was a shirt-lifter. He used to bring his boyfriends here at weekends. Normally I would have said something, but Ethel was ill at that time and we didn't want the hassle." He pulled out a packet of Senior Service and lit another one. Cigarette smoke only made him cough more violently, but he didn't seem to mind. "I thought at the time Hewitt and his latest boyfriend had gone off on holiday together. Just as I was looking forward to some piece and quiet, his boyfriend turned up looking for him and knocking on my door. Needless to say I sent him packing. As I said before, I boarded up the windows to deter squatters and kids vandalising it on their way home from school. It's been like that ever since. Technically its private property and I expect the council is reluctant to get involved, but that doesn't help me and the value of my house." Graves made his way to the front window and strained to look through the joints in between each board.

"You seem to be suggesting that the house has remained in its original state for the last twenty-five years," Graves asked, his eyes now concentrating on the glass behind the boards.

"There's nothing gets passed you Inspector," Bert smiled, showing his jagged teeth. "Absolutely everything, you could say, it is a museum – a time capsule," the old man said.

"And no one has ever come forward? No relatives?" Graves asked, trying to persuade some of the looser boards to leave their position.

"No not one, but then either he is alone genuinely or he was disowned by them for being a nanny's boy?" he commented without pity.

"What happened to his post over the years? Graves asked.

"I use to go in and move it until it dried up after a few years, make the house look like it was lived in for the sake of any burglars and my own house. What letters there were I put in..." his words tailed off as he realised he'd been tricked into an unnecessary admission. "Oh very good Inspector. So I've been inside since Hewitt left.

In The Mood

I have to look toward the value of my property as I said, seeing as it is attached to it," he reasoned. He sucked hard on his cigarette and this time he blew out the contents of his lungs without coughing at all. Graves gave him his best disapproving stare before taking his leave, making his way to the top of the lane to the phone box he had spotted earlier.

"Hello," Graves said down the phone. "I need to speak to DC Morgan." There was a pause before telephone erupted into life again.

"Morning sir, I should be with you in about a half-hour," Morgan replied.

"Make it an hour and a half. I want to take a look inside Hewitt's property today. It's boarded up at present, but I am reliably informed that the contents are as they were in 1960, despite a number of break-ins," Graves said.

"Hewitt disappeared around 1960 as well?" Morgan queried.

"Yes, it would seem so," Graves replied.

"So they could all have been in it together? Killed Benson then disappeared like in 1953?" Morgan suggested.

"That would be the obvious theory, but something is wrong Morgan. I still maintain that it would have been unlikely that Benson would have ever been discovered, but for the accident. Also these men had set-up families and lifestyles – McDonald and Gould at least. Why throw all that away with Benson hidden in that concrete column?" Graves said. "Why not draft a more understanding personal note yourself to your spouse and family? Why would they draft each others' letters maybe and why make them so brief? No it won't do Morgan."

"I can arrange for a search warrant sir, although it could take some time to come through," Morgan offered returning to the subject at hand.

"Yes OK, but I'm going in anyway. I just need to see whether a farewell letter like the one that Mrs Valentine and Mrs McDonald received was delivered to Hewitt's house. If there was I'm afraid we may have reached the end of this investigation. Get here when you can."

Graves put the receiver down and looked back down the lane toward the derelict house. Bert had disappeared indoors and Graves took the opportunity to make his move. Outside No.10 again he probed areas of dry rot between the door panels and its frame. Someone had stuffed chewing gum into the door lock and there was a stench of dog faeces coming from the partially open letterbox. The small fan shaped glass window at the top of the door had been the subject of stone throwing yobs in the past. All but one shard of glass remained out of four panes.

"One little bastard did all that damage ten years or so back." Bert had reappeared and was standing behind Graves as he tried to apply pressure to the doorframe. "He went for an early bath in the canal." Bert grinned reliving the memory. "Him and his friends haven't been back since." The glee in his voice was self-evident and Graves smiled at the door, careful to keep his reaction from Bert. "You ain't going in there are you?" Bert asked. Graves switched his attention to the front window, pulling two boards from their position, ignoring the question. The glass was grimy and old tattered curtains hung all but closed except for about an inch gap. He cupped his hands to his eyes and tried to peer inside. It was no use though. "Just give the front door a good kick and you're in," Bert called from behind again.

With that Graves let fly with his size 10 brogues against what appeared to be the most solid part of the doorframe. The door shuddered under the impact and then opened a few inches. The origin of the smell a few moments ago, lay on the doormat just inside the front room. Graves edged the door inwards until he could move inside and stepped over the offending object. A welcome rush of fresh air followed him, purging the best part of twenty-five years of stale atmosphere. The light from outside illuminated part of the front living room. Some objects, like a writing bureau remarkably similar to his mothers antique, and a damp-smelling three-piece suite were easily discernable. It was only when he retrieved his pen-torch from his coat pocket that he picked out a fireplace, a television set that really did belong in a museum and a coffee table, all lurking in the shadows. Something as big as a small cat scurried out from behind the TV and into what Graves guessed was a combined kitchen and dining room. Rats never bothered him normally, not even during the drugs stakeout in London's Dockland, but this was a big bugger.

"One room at a time Philip," Graves said to himself, "and with a bit of luck I'll find what I am after and be out of here before this creature returns with its relatives." The little beam of light moved progressively around the darkened areas before he made a move towards the bureau.

By this time Bert had joined him at the front door and had missed the deposit on the doormat.

"Shit," he shouted as he hopped on one leg.

"Very astute of you Bert," Graves commented, his gaze now fixed on the lock of the bureau. "I'm not an expert on this sort of thing you understand, but I'd say recent shit, judging by the ripe odour and soft texture." Bert looked around outside as if to curse the first canine he saw, one arm on the doorframe to steady his animated actions.

Graves glanced at him momentarily. "I'm afraid he or she is long-gone by now and I wouldn't blame the dog in any case, unless it was a tall dog with a sense of humour that could get its backside up against that letter box," Graves commented with a wry smile.

"I'm not sure you should be in here anyway, " Bert growled, wiping the bottom of his slipper on the sparse grass outside.

"I'll tell you what," Graves answered, never taking his attention from the bureau. "If you ignore me breaking and entering, albeit as part of my duties, I'll ignore the fact that you've been in here in the past." Graves moved around the bureau examining it in every detail, choosing not to wait for a response. The light from his torch, now between his teeth, moved around the bureau, whilst he traced the contours of the wood grain with his hands until he found the button he was looking for.

"So it is like Mother's bureau," he said to himself.

"You can't prove I've been here," Bert croaked more nervously this time, still examining his soiled slipper.

"Oh, I would guess that your prints are in here somewhere and judging by the faded squares on the wallpaper and rings of dust on the bureau and TV some pictures and ornaments have disappeared in the past, no doubt adorning the furniture and walls of number 9 Canal Reach." Graves replied.

The colour in Bert's normally reddened face drained and he became more jaundiced-looking. He turned and mumbled something about all policemen being wankers and disappeared outside again. Graves hadn't wanted to antagonize the old man because there may have been more that he wasn't telling him. Earlier, Bert had said that the post had dried up after a couple of years. Whether he had opened any letters or not remained to be seen. He recalled from his parents' bureau that whenever the key was mislaid you could always open the front roller shutter by popping the button under the left-hand corner, rear leg. He pressed it and the shutter rolled back as if it was spring-loaded revealing various stacks of personal and business papers, some spilling out on to the floor. The majority of letters, bills, even an old Daily Mirror were dated as early as 1959 and one letter as far back as 1956. Some letters, predating 1959 were opened. Subsequent letters were not, which was a testament to Bert's self-control, Graves thought.

He scanned over them quickly. One of the letters had an airmail stamp from Peru, South America. It looked decidedly out of place. Carefully opening it, he made a quick mental note of the contents and placed it into an evidence envelope from his overcoat pocket for a full analysis back at the lab. He flicked through the remaining mail until a single sheet of notepaper fell to the ground.

Moments later he reappeared outside the cottage, pulling the door closed behind him.

"It is nice to be back in the fresh air," he said to himself.

"Found what you were snooping, I mean, looking for, Inspector?" Bert called from where he had propped himself against his garden wall.

"I'm not sure what I'm looking for Bert. That is half the trouble," Graves replied. "Incidentally, any idea who Juan Carlos is or was?" Graves asked recalling the name from the airmail letter.

"I'm not sure I should be telling you anything any more Inspector without my solicitor present. I might implicate myself and," he wheezed with the effort and the effects of the cigarette and chilly breeze, "I still haven't seen your search warrant yet." These last words seemed to give him great pleasure, the twinkle in his tired eyes giving him away.

"Perhaps," Graves said looking back up the lane again to where his car was parked hoping that Morgan might make a timely entrance, "your solicitor could come in handy when I ask you about access to the house, missing pictures and ornaments? Maybe," he continued, noticing the change in the old man's face, "I could also get a warrant that covers more than one house, once I have the fingerprint analysis completed." The old man looked agitated again and scowled back at the policeman without a word, but the message was clear enough.

"Juan Carlos, who was he in 1959?" Graves asked again more forcefully.

In The Mood

"Didn't I say he was a poof?" Bert growled not wanting to answer the question. Graves nodded. "Well this foreigner was Hewitt's boyfriend. He brought him back from holiday for three months before he went for good. On average I'd say a different boyfriend every six months. He must have liked his men dark and Latin-looking." He grinned at the comment usually used in conjunction with the opposite sex as far as he was concerned.

"Thank you Bert, you've been very helpful," Graves offered giving the old man a wave before leaving him to draw on what was left of his cigarette. The return gesture was not as friendly. "Oh, Bert," Graves said turning back. The old man squinted through the cigarette smoke staying quiet.

"Do you still have the music box?" Graves hadn't seen one during his brief search of the property and chose to play a hunch. Bert's cigarette drooped from the corner of his mouth even more still he offered nothing more. "An imitation silver music box, oh about so big," Graves said sizing it with his hands. "It plays an awful whining tune when you open it." Bert grumbled and turned, disappearing indoors. A few minutes later he reappeared clutching a third version of the same music box.

"Here," he snapped." I took it to cheer my wife up. It stopped working about the same time she did. Take it, I don't know why I kept it."

By the time Graves had reached his car, the familiar Ford Granada had appeared alongside it, a rather smug looking DC Morgan sat cross-armed on the bonnet.

"Glad you could make it Morgan, but I'm just about done here," Graves told him as he walked between the two cars.

"Sorry sir, I got tied up briefing DI Weldon back at the station," Morgan replied. "Oh and I got you your warrant," he continued. "Any luck here?"

"Mixed success," Graves said, pulling at the car handle. "I think I have another identical letter and another small silver music box, but no sign of Hewitt since 1960."

"A letter? So there must be a Mrs Hewitt?" Morgan surmised, remembering the now familiar style of the farewell letters to Mrs McDonald and Mrs Valentine.

"Ah well that is where the sender of these letters has made a mistake though I'm not sure if it benefits us," Graves replied through the open car door as he sat down in the driver's seat. He started the engine offering no further comment. Morgan leaned forward to compensate for the noise of the car engine. "Mr Hewitt was a homosexual, constable, I have it on good authority. He was never married. Obviously the sender of these letters didn't know that and just assumed probably that 'partner' meant a female partner," Graves explained. "The letters to McDonald, Gould and Hewitt are identical, I'll stake my pension on it," Graves concluded tapping Hewitt's letter on the dashboard.

"You're implying that someone else wrote these farewell letter sir?" Morgan suggested. Graves left the question unanswered. There was one way of confirming Morgan's observation.

"Let's get back to the lab and see Ray Brightwell. I'm keen to see the results from the other letters and get him to confirm my suspicions about this one."

"Are you still convinced that the boxes are unimportant sir?" Morgan asked. Graves lifted the silver looking box from his passenger seat and turned it around as if examining each side.

"I don't know why Morgan, but something intrigues me about them," He said thoughtfully. After a few seconds he snapped out his thoughtful mood. "It will come back to me eventually. Never mind the boxes for now." Minutes later both cars were heading toward the south of Willenbury town centre back to County Labs and Ray Brightwell. It was twenty minutes later by the time they arrived.

"Your letters are over here," Brightwell greeted them referring to the now familiar overhead projector set-up in the lab. "You are here about the letters I take it?" Brightwell asked clarifying his assumption. Graves nodded. "I'll give you what I've been able to ascertain and then an overall assessment and comparison of each specimen," Brightwell said, by way of an introduction.

"I have a third specimen for you to look at and compare against the other two farewell letters, but I'm sure that they are all exactly the same," Graves said. Brightwell eyed him warily. Several feet away, projected on to a white screen, Ted Gould's so-called farewell letter to his wife. Sat alongside it, his draft speech for the council meeting he never attended.

"The most striking quality of this piece of writing is the control and tension exerted by the writer in the forming of words and letters denoted by an apparent attempt to maintain verticality," Brightwell explained pointing at the farewell letter. "Also, the angularity of the individual letters themselves are strained and formed along an erratic baseline. I'd say you were looking at someone fighting against repressed emotions and possibly a compulsive personality disorder." Morgan looked puzzled at Graves who in turn shrugged his shoulders as Brightwell turned his back to both men. "Note the lower formation of the legs of letters 'p', 'f' and 'y' with full loops below the baseline. The abrupt and blunt ending of these loops indicates someone with a strong sex drive, which is frustrated by some possible inner turmoil.

"That must take account of most 16 to 18 years olds," Graves said mischievously. Brightwell looked at him disapprovingly before continuing.

"The writer possesses moderate intelligence, committed to their goals once set and works hard to achieve them. Above all else, this person has the qualities to persevere to a successful outcome in their chosen occupation, despite some underlying issues. The firm strokes that form the t-stems and strong t-bars suggests that this perseverance verges on stubbornness in the face of adversity and obstacles. Outwardly this person appears to be in control, but inwardly there must be something in direct conflict creating this inner turmoil I mentioned.

The sexual reference here could be something at the time the letter was written or even in this person's past, with angry connotations. If you had a sample dating back some time before the date on this specimen and the writing was consistent, I'd say it was something in this

In The Mood

person's past. Suffice to say, this person's counteracting qualities no doubt manage this underlying frustration, but only just. I don't suppose that you have an older specimen by any chance?" Brightwell asked. Graves shook his head. "I thought not," Brightwell said resignedly. He adjusted the specimen, checking the screen in front of him as he did to give the comparator the bulk of the screen.

"The second sample by way of contrast shows excellent verticality in the formation of words and the overall flow of the writing. The letters are well formed and forcibly constructed indicating someone with good self control, with a clear agenda and ambitions. The overall upright nature of sentence construction suggests someone doggedly determined in their outlook on life and their approach to it. Small angular writing suggests someone who is hard working, with good concentration and responsible qualities. A sort of figurehead that other people look up to. This person tends to deal with issues and problems in a practical way. I'd say he or she is unhampered by sentimentality or ties to the past as shown by the lack of lead-ins or excess flourishes in the way the letters are formed. I would say that this is a well-balanced individual, educated with good perceptive skills. He or she is well motivated and can be depended on to meet personal objectives. This person has a strong personality and has good team leader qualities," Brightwell said completing his assessment. "As far as a comparison is concerned and in my opinion, two different people have clearly written them. The formation of words and letters is quite different. As far as the person behind the pen is concerned there are similar qualities evident. I would go as far as to say the writer of the first specimen is almost trying to emulate the characteristics of the second. Either way they have been written by different hands – in my humble opinion," Brightwell concluded looking up at his guests. "Does this help at all Inspector?" he asked.

Graves was already going over the two samples on the screen at his own pace. The analysis bit always lost him in reality. He was sure that it all made sense to the experts, but it always sounded like psychobabble to him. He was interested in the bottom line. Having said this, the assessment of a one-time candidate in the local elections, Ted Gould the author of the second specimen, wasn't half bad considering the sample was given to Brightwell without any knowledge of who crafted it. Interestingly, if he was to accept this at face value, it also gave him some invaluable information about the real author of the farewell letter.

"Very useful thank you Ray," Graves said as he moved directly up to the screen. " What about the paper itself?"

Brightwell lifted both samples from the OHP. "The farewell letter has been written on common-or-garden note paper. There is nothing special about it as far as I can see. The handwriting is freehand obviously, done with a fountain pen. The ink is common black or *India ink* if you are from across the 'big pond'. It's made from a derivative of non-electric lamps based on carbon commonly called Lampblack. Various professions use this type of ink for its waterproof properties, other than that there is nothing special about it. You can buy it anywhere," he explained. "The second sample is written on a form of civil service notepaper, as indicated by the watermark at the bottom of

In The Mood

the sheet. The paper is good quality, as you would expect. Unlike in the previous example where the paper almost acts like a blotter, this ink sits prominently on the surface suggesting a high gloss finish, typical of quality notepaper. The ink again is common black, written with a fountain pen. Of course this does not confirm anything one way or the other. One author could merely have drafted one at work and one at home, using different paper sources. However, I still maintain that we are looking at two different people here, which is why there are two paper sources in my opinion," Brightwell concluded.

"Incidentally Inspector," Brightwell said as he took Ted Gould's draft speech from the projector, "the other sample letter you gave me belonging to err...Mrs McDonald. Graves nodded expecting no surprises. "Exactly the same as the farewell letter written to the former Mrs Gould in every respect, in other words, the same author," he said displaying it alongside.

"What about this one?" Graves said, pulling Hewitt's letter out of the envelope in his inside overcoat pocket. Brightwell took the envelope in his gloved hand and unwrapped it carefully on the workbench behind him.

"I don't think I need an acetate copy for this one Inspector. The three letters are almost certainly drafted by the same hand. There are some very slight differences, but within the normal parameters for handwriting, I would say definitely that the same hand wrote them. The writer appears to lack originality, but maybe that was the farthest thing on his mind when he was drafting it." Brightwell concluded. Both Graves and Morgan thanked Brightwell again for his valuable input before taking their leave. "Oh

Inspector," Brightwell called as the pair were at the door. "My analysis is of course set in time," he offered. Both men looked at him puzzled. "What I mean Inspector is my assessment is of the writers as they wrote these scripts. If some time has passed since and I had the same script to analyse again and it was a redraft by the same person now, the end result might be slightly different, you understand?"

"I see," Graves said as he put his hat and coat on. The inference by Brightwell was clearly that the author might have changed his or her personality with time. "I'll bear that in mind and thanks again." Outside in the corridor the pair strolled toward the exit in deep thought.

"Could it be possible that all three men were killed at or about the same time in a similar way to Benson and hidden in the same way and never found?" Morgan speculated. The same thought had gone through Graves's mind.

"Maybe they were found?" Graves replied tentatively, another option unfolding inside his head.

"Sir?" Morgan queried.

"Maybe they're in Hendon archive somewhere buried in 1960s records and maybe I didn't concentrate enough on good old-fashioned police work and conventional investigation initially with Benson before chasing up blind allies?" Morgan still looked at him perplexed. "I was never here to solve this case Morgan, in fact I wasn't even remotely interested in it until I made the most tenuous of links with my father's attack. I'm not even sure now if there really is one. I ignored more obvious lines of investigation convincing myself that DI Wheldon would cover those adequately. Maybe Wheldon has and then maybe he hasn't," he said cryptically. "I think it is time for us to re-examine everything on Benson afresh, perhaps reviewing Wheldon's progress along the way. If there are any clues as to what happened twenty-five years ago they will be with Benson," Graves said.

"I'm not sure I follow sir. "Morgan replied as they stepped outside.

"Benson wasn't expected to be found, I'll wager, so let us examine the evidence again. The murderer may have overlooked something because he or she thought that the body would never be discovered. I've always maintained that the environment was important to Benson's murderer, a premise that may come in useful if the other three men are indeed a statistic in Hendon Mews," Graves reasoned.

"You think that they were all killed in a similar way?" Morgan replied.

"It's a working theory," Graves said passively.

"I'm not convinced sir. DI Wheldon seems to have hit a dead end with his enquiries. At the team meeting earlier while you were at Hewitt's place it would appear that all dentists have been traced within a 20-mile radius of Willenbury Village around 1960. Only six are still trading, family businesses, and none have any records of a Robert Benson. Of course it's unlikely that this was his real name anyway, so checks are still being made with patients that fit Benson's dental records. I can review the notes and evidence so far if you think it will help?" Morgan volunteered.

"Good idea," Graves responded. "Can you get hold of an extra resource, someone you can trust to be discrete?"

I want you to get one of your colleagues to visit Hendon Mews tomorrow. If anyone asks why, he or she is working for me on some research to do with the case, nothing more," Graves continued, opening the door of his MG.

"The archive sir?" Morgan questioned.

"Remember what I said a few minutes earlier. If there have been bodies located around 1960 with the same or similar MO as Benson then you should find them at Hendon Mews. I want your friend to commandeer case notes and files for all bodies located in, say, a 10-mile radius of the village for years 1958 to 1962. He or she is looking for suspicious deaths that have never been satisfactorily concluded and the body never claimed by a loved one or relatives," Graves said. Morgan was busily scribbling notes in his notebook.

"I have someone in mind sir," Morgan offered closing his notebook, "someone used to research there."

"Fine! We'll meet back at the station first thing tomorrow and go over Wheldon's notes," Graves said. "I need to go now," he said checking his watch, "I'm expected at the hospital and I'm already late." They both climbed into their cars heading away from County Laboratories.

ooooo

As the MG made its way along the now familiar driveway leading up to Willenbury General Hospital, Graves suddenly felt a sense of guilt and selfishness overwhelming him. He had a natural aversion to hospitals and their environment; of that there was no doubt. The cold sweats, dizziness even now as the MG meandered its way toward the main entrance, it was inexplicable. There was nothing in his past to suggest a problem or occurrence that could have triggered such a reaction, but there it was. He'd avoided it during his days on the job. Now it hit him head on and he was finding it difficult to deal with just when he needed a heightened resolve. He was sure that Giles Prenton-Smythe would call it a problem of some kind triggered by a past event, a phobia. Maybe it was, but none that made any sense to him.

His reluctance to visit his father was as physical as it was psychological and impossible to defend from or explain to his mother. He sensed her disappointment during his last visit and as he entered the small private side room on the 2nd floor, the feeling of disappointment and rejection to him being there almost oozed out of her every pore. She didn't move at all as he entered the room, she sat motionless as if she was ashamed of the son she had worshipped all his life.

"How are you?" Graves asked her. She looked at him incredulously.

"Shouldn't you be asking how your father is?" she replied bluntly. She promptly pushed the lace handkerchief against her lined face once more like a child caressing its comfort blanket. Graves moved around the far side of the bed trying to choose his words wisely. It had taken him the best part of thirty minutes to step inside the one building he despised most of all, even more than the damp, derelict buildings on Canary Wharf, the scene of his nightmare. He'd chosen to take the stairs, not trusting the lifts for fear of a breakdown along the way. It was just as well because he had to pause on the first floor to visit the gents' toilets to splash water onto his face. He could just about stomach Jack Rowan's lab, probably because he didn't want to lose face with Rowan in particular, but hospitals, the scale of the building, all those white coats and beds and the smell of impending death, that was something else. At least in Rowan's lab the patients were already beyond death. Now in this room, alone with his parents the panic attacks had subsided and for once he could concentrate on why he was there, as his mother had just reminded him.

"I'm sorry I'm late. I had some business to take care of on the way," he had to admit. There was no use trying to hide it, he thought during his drive over.

"What business is more important than your father's health Philip?" she asked pointedly. He leaned across the bed and gently held his mother's hand. At first she was reluctant and evaded his touch, but her emotions soon got the better of her and she relented. "Why must you be in constant competition with your father?" she asked out of the blue. He looked at her a little shocked and was lost for words. This only seemed to enrage her even more.

"Oh come on Philip, you and your father have been competitors since you joined the police," she whispered in a hard tone. "You're out there now trying to solve the crime committed against him yourself, no doubt single handed, and why, when there is a whole team out there doing the same thing? Are they any less capable than the great Philip Graves? Do you consider yourself indispensable?" Graves sat down heavily on the chair beside the bed and stared at her, taken aback by the verbal onslaught. He began to realize that he perhaps had this coming and

In The Mood

he had to take it. She didn't relent choosing to seize her chance to let go of all her anger.

"I'll tell you why, so that you can say what a big man you've been solving the case when –" she paused, "*if* – he recovers?" She looked back at her husband. "Just so you've got one over on him. I never saw this side of you, Philip, in the past. Maybe I never wanted to. I always thought that your father was paranoid, perhaps even jealous of your career. Now I'm not so sure." The tirade stopped momentarily to allow more tears to escape. "You came here because I pleaded with you, not for any other reason," she blubbered. "This isn't a game anymore Philip! The stakes are the highest they have ever been; highest they will ever be in fact. You may never speak to your father again, even if you sit here every day, every hour, and every minute from now on. Spend some time with your father before you regret it and stop chasing shadows. What is done is done and we can't turn back time, however much we would like to." She looked lovingly at her lifelong partner. Her anger was ebbing now.

"With God's love and guidance, your father will recover. Whoever did this will be judged in due course .It doesn't have to be by you Philip. Let it go and let Gary do his job. Be here for your father, otherwise you may as well go back to London," she said pulling her hand away from his and placing a damp cloth across her husband's forehead.

She was wrong about his motive for coming. When he had heard the news about his father he was genuinely upset and concerned. He did have visions of never seeing him alive again and that was the prompt for his quick return. Yes he had arrived with the best of intentions, to be there for his father, first and foremost and to support his mother through this difficult time. Unfortunately human nature and professional curiosity had taken over, combined with his loathing for hospital environments, he'd allowed himself to be sucked into the investigation process. He managed to convince himself that the local plod needed an expert from The Met to help them out, all of which of course limited his exposure to Willenbury General, he had to admit to himself. His mother had seen right through him.

"Why don't you freshen up? I'll keep an eye on father until you get back," he offered. She frowned causing even more lines to form across her elderly face. "I'll come and get you if anything changes," he said softly. Running a hand over her wavy grey hair she was suddenly conscious of her appearance. Dabbing her eyes she stood without a word, walking backwards toward the door, never taking her eyes from the bed. She paused with the door ajar having second thoughts, before Philip smiled at her reassuringly. She left seconds later heading directly down the corridor toward the ladies room. Graves walked around the bed and sat gently where his mother had been keeping her beside vigil until a few seconds earlier.

"Well father, it's just me and you now for a few moments. You're a stubborn sod, almost as stubborn as me and I'm hoping that quality will get you through this. She would be lost without you; I never really appreciated how much until I saw her here tonight. For what it's worth, I need you as well. I don't know why we drifted apart the way we did over the years. I know we were never as close as perhaps we should have been and I don't know why to this day." He felt an emotion deep inside that was bubbling to the surface and a lump in his throat that was unexpected and he paused, swallowing hard. "I was never in competition with you for her affections – that's been abundantly clear since my return. She is your wife first and my mother second. Without the love between you two I wouldn't even be here," he whispered. Reg Graves remained motionless, his eyes closed, his breathing aided, the monitors showing no sign of change. Tears filled Philip's eyes and he fought hard to keep them in check, but it was no use.

"You stubborn old sod," he said quietly. Now that the tears were rolling down his face freely, he had to regain control of his emotions before his mother returned and feared the worst. "Don't give up," he said through the tears. "She needs you – I need you." Throughout he gently held his father's hand, unsure who was comforting whom exactly, when he felt the slightest of pressure across his fingers. The door catch clicked at the exact same moment as his mother returned feeling better for her trip along the corridor.

"Mother," he called out in as hushed a tone as he could muster," father just squeezed my hand," he declared, his eyes still glassy. She stared at him in disbelief at first, but his eyes betrayed something she hadn't seen in her son since he had been a boy toward his father. She knew what he was saying was genuine and she was even happier that her son had experienced it, despite her long vigil. They hugged and kissed each other with joy for what seemed like an age, Graves using one arm, the other still reluctant to let go of his father's hand. Hospital staff appeared conscious of the visual display of affection, rather than any disturbance they might have been causing and whilst mother and son continued their celebrations, a number of medical staff hurriedly checked the instruments for any change in their patient's condition. Satisfied with their appraisal, the lead nurse suggested enough excitement for one evening and Graves reluctantly let go of his father's hand. One visitor was more than enough overnight and that would always be his mother. It was nothing to do with hospitals anymore. Nothing would stop him seeing his father tomorrow: phobia, work, anything! The hour was late, after midnight at least. He didn't care though. He'd rediscovered something precious tonight and he felt like he was walking on air. God, he would sleep tonight, and tomorrow, he would wrap up his involvement with Swallow's team, pass the paperwork on to Wheldon and concentrate on his father's recovery and his parents' subsequent welfare as he realised he should have done from day one. Even the Yard and Gray would have to wait.

Several miles away earlier that evening Morgan had found PC Ben Rogers where he expected to find him in the Rope and Anchor pub playing darts for the local team. He'd briefed him over a pint on what DI Graves was after and Rogers had agreed to visit Hendon Mews on Grave's authorisation first thing the following morning.

19

Hendon Mews

It was 8am exactly as Rogers arrived at Hendon Mews, home of the Police evidence and archive storage unit for several CID departments shared and funded by three neighbouring counties.

"Morning sergeant, Constable Rogers – Ben to my friends. I've come to look at some files in your archive," the young officer announced as he entered reception.

"Oh you have, have you?" The response came from a much older looking man, stouter in build yet a formidable character. He leaned over the counter that formed the demarcation of his domain and the outside world. No one got past his counter unless he said so, irrespective of rank. He leaned back once more, his eyes still examining the presumptuous junior before him.

"Who sent you Rogers? I insist on a week's notice normally. I know my system and I like it that way." He gestured behind him with his thumb.

"An Inspector Graves, sir," Rogers replied. "He just said 'Get down to records at Hendon Mews and see Woody'. He said you would know where to look." PC Rogers wondered whether the sergeant might take offence to the 'Woody' reference, just as Graves might because he used it, but it was too late.

"Graves," the senior man said out loud. Rogers nodded. "Inspector hey?" Again the PC nodded. "It must be Reg's son? So the return of the prodigal – Graves of the Yard?" There was a slightly mocking tone to his voice, before it became serious again. Sergeant Alan Wood had fixed his eyes beyond Rogers as if he were reading the notice board on the wall behind. In truth his mind's eye had taken over and he was retracing past times in the local CID when young Philip Graves was no more than the young PC before him. "Well what is it you are looking for laddie? And the name is Sergeant Wood, even to my friends," he finally managed bringing his mind back to the present.

"I've been asked to look into all cases involving deaths of males where the bodies were never identified or claimed by a loved one or relative between 1958 and 1962," Rogers said in one breath. The more experienced police officer raised an eyebrow.

In The Mood

"Twenty-five years ago? You don't want much do you? Do you have anything else to perhaps narrow the search a little, constable?" The sergeant shook his head wearily and faced the wall behind him so that he had his back to Rogers.

"Sorry sir, cases that happened within a 10-mile radius of this village," Rogers added.

"I'm not sure that helps really laddie," he replied unimpressed. He sighed heavily, "let me see what I can do. 1958 would put the register..." his voiced tailed off as his eyes looked toward the ceiling. "Unfortunately, up there. The older the case the less chance it would be needed again, so it would sit up there," he said pointing at the rows of boxes on the topmost shelf. He reached for the stepladders and positioned them where he had indicated.

"How far back do your records go sergeant?" Rogers asked.

"As far back in detail as I have been here son – about twenty years. I spent the last three or four years documenting cases dating back from 1965 to 1955, so you might be in luck." He paused, as he was about to climb the ladder; an uneasiness had overcome him about Roger's request, something in the past that unnerved him a little. It was no use prevaricating he thought, he had to produce them. He climbed the ladder, each rung giving a groan under the sergeant's considerable bulk. He pulled down an A4 sized box from the top shelf. The date '1958' was stamped prominently on the front face. "Right son, the box contains registers, inventory of caseloads from the date shown. Beyond that secure door," he pointed to a wood stained door, half wood half with reinforced glass, "is where the evidence itself is stored. The only thing missing, in the case of murder, is the body. You will need an exhumation order for that. Postal addresses for each case should help you with your 10-mile radius constable." Opening the lid he lifted the first register placing it on the counter between them both.

"I'll leave you to it son. There's a table over there – make use of it," the sergeant said. "There's also brewing facilities just through that same door, but you'll have to get me to open it," he said guardedly. "Come and see me when you want to look at the actual evidence." With that he slipped through into the archive store to continue his daily duties. Rogers had already worked out his approach to the task. First a coarse sift of the circumstances surrounding cases that loosely fitted Morgan's briefing. Then look at the actual case files of those that were of interest followed by some copious note taking. Anything else presentation wise would be a bonus and might impress the man from the Yard later that day.

"Better get on with it then," he said quietly to himself.

20

A Chance Meeting

Tom Wheldon parked his Ford Cortina behind the Rope and Anchor pub in its usual spot – out of the way of prying eyes from station colleagues. He climbed out of his car, brushing the crumbs off his chest from the sandwich he had been eating along the way. Paying for beer was one thing. Wasting it on pub food was another.

"Why, it's sergeant Wheldon isn't it?" a female voice announced from behind him. He turned and was met by the curvaceous, Estelle McDonald just leaving the pub's rear exit and walking towards him. It was a cool, clear morning for the time of year and Estelle McDonald was dressed to combat the chill. She wore a fur hat and a three quarter length fur coat. Black fishnet stockings and calf length boots completed her alluring look. Her hands were tucked inside her pockets as she sauntered across the car park toward him. Wheldon hastily wiped away any evidence of his lunch from his beard with his handkerchief.

"Why Miss McDonald, what a pleasant surprise – oh and it's *Inspector*," he announced proudly. His imagination raced at what lay beneath the fur trappings. They shook hands and for a second he sensed a tightened grip from the young lady.

"Now you have a firm grip sergeant, I'm sorry, I mean Inspector. I like that in a man," she smiled. She leaned back against the dwarf wall that separated the parking area from the landscaped garden. Women like this barely gave him a second glance even when he was much younger so he was going to make the most of it.

"I've never seen you in the Rope before Miss McDonald." he said casually, trying to stare across the car park rather than at her.

"Oh, Estelle please," she purred. Unbuttoning her coat, she spread her arms along the wall, distributing her slight frame and allowed her head to fall back to take in the approaching midday sunshine. "Don't you just love sunny autumn and winter days Inspector? The sunshine just recharges your batteries until you're fit for anything," she said. Beneath the fur coat she wore a close fitting knitted pale blue dress, buttoned up the front and up along her slender neck. Wheldon's eyes were transfixed as

Estelle's ample bosom strained against their confinement. He reached for his handkerchief again, this time choosing to dab his brow.

"I'm afraid I've been stood up," she announced opening her eyes and facing Wheldon once more. "I was just leaving – dry of mouth and empty of tummy." She animated her comment by pointing to her open mouth with one hand, whilst rubbing her tummy with the other. Not for the first time since seeing her, something down below stirred as Wheldon's imagination took over.

"If you don't mind the company of an older man Miss McDonald. I'd be happy to buy you lunch. I'm just on my way in for a bite myself," Wheldon said, conveniently forgetting the sandwich he had just devoured.

"Why, that is a very kind offer Inspector Wheldon. I would be delighted to join you," she smiled. She stood and turned back toward the pub following his gesture along the path and into the Rope and Anchor.

"Actually darling, the pleasure is all mine," Wheldon said to himself.

"Call me Tom," he suggested as they took a seat in what the landlord liked to loosely call 'the best room', "at least when I'm off duty."

"And you are off duty now I take it?" she asked as she sat down on the bench seat behind the table. She took her hat and coat off and the sudden loss of body heat caused her to curl up on the seat with her legs tucked mainly underneath her shapely bottom. She pushed her boots off each in turn with the other foot leaving them discarded on the floor beneath the table.

"Yes," he said, when in reality he wasn't. An hour later, their meal consumed they sat finishing their drinks making light conversation, a pretext on Estelle McDonald's part before she broached her real reason for this so-called chance meeting.

"Thank you Tom, the meal was a lovely surprise," she said, that playful twinkle still evident in her eyes.

"So what are you working on at present? She asked, hitching herself higher on the seat revealing the tops of her black fishnet stockings, one of the clasps holding them in place making a brief appearance before it disappeared as she tugged her dress down again. Wheldon remained silent pretending to remark on the cloudiness of his beer whilst taking in the sight through his half-empty glass. Once again, he felt a sense of awakening down below, a luxury normally reserved for weekend porno films.

"I always wanted to be a detective, Tom," she continued, not waiting for a response. "You see I never knew my dad. He left us when I was young and I know that he is out there somewhere." Her happy-go-lucky mood changed with the mention of her father. "I know I can find him with the right help," she said sombrely. She stared at Wheldon expectantly, but his mind was on more primitive thoughts. "Those other policemen I met asked my mum and me about dad yesterday," she continued, giving Wheldon her best puppy dog eyes.

"Oh you mean Graves and his faithful manservant, Morgan?" Wheldon said sarcastically, trying desperately to keep his mind on the conversation. "I'm not really involved in the case you understand?" he added. Her face changed to one of disappointment.

"Perhaps I should speak to that nice DC Morgan?" she replied coyly, looking at her almost empty glass.

"Oh, err, what I meant to say was I don't get involved in the detail of what they are doing. I keep an overview of progress for my Chief Inspector, the legwork, I leave that to Graves and Morgan," he suggested trying to retrieve the situation. He was conscious that he was losing his credibility with this delectable young lady and decided to bend the truth to keep her interest. Her smile returned again.

"So you would know what all this is about regarding my dad?" she whispered over the table as she leaned forward. Wheldon leaned forward meeting her halfway.

"Well yes of course, "Wheldon stuttered slightly," but not the fine detail. That is back at the station currently being collated in a report being prepared by Inspector Graves for Chief Inspector Swallow," Wheldon explained, looking furtively away from Estelle McDonald's heaving chest. Perhaps another drink Estelle?" Wheldon asked before she could respond.

"You're going to get me drunk you are," she purred again holding out her glass. "A G&T refill please." A few minutes later, drinks replenished, she resumed her probing. "Why don't you pop back to the station, get a copy of the report and we could meet back at my place to discuss the contents," she said, a faint smile suddenly replaced by one of hope. Wheldon despite his preoccupation with the nymphet (at least he hoped she was) before him he knew that her suggestion would be a breach of procedures and would probably get him into deep shit. Before he could offer his apologies she continued. "I would be ever so grateful," she said leaning back once more against the backrest of the bench seat. Her movement caused her skirt to shift position again, her stocking tops making yet another brief appearance. Wheldon's eyes glazed over again at the sight and he found himself agreeing to her request without worrying too much about the ramifications.

"Well I suppose there wouldn't be any harm just to have a quick provisional look, just as long as it stays between us," he said, his serious look turning into a leering grin. "The price would be worth it," he said to himself as he took in what he presumed was on offer. As far as Wheldon was concerned, Graves had it all wrong anyway. Estelle's father had nothing to do with Benson, but if there was a chance of him getting-his-leg-over with a beautiful woman fifteen years his junior he could perhaps use his position close to the case to his advantage with no harm done, he convinced himself.

"I live at Little Crandon Cottage, about a mile outside of Chetley village on the Chetley road. It's 2pm now," she said checking her wristwatch. "Shall we say 5pm back at my place?" Wheldon nodded eagerly and the two left the pub together through the rear exit.

21

Hendon Mews Briefing

It was late afternoon the same day when PC Rogers returned from Hendon Mews complete with several files and a collection of 35mm slides, kindly loaned to him on pain of death, should he lose them, by Alan Wood. The archive as a whole contained amongst other things a collection of case photographs dating back to the mid 1950s. Whilst Sergeant Wood could be credited for pulling together the written archive, in all its various formats, the photographic displays were courtesy of Alfred Knowles, a latter day scene of crime officer noted for his meticulous eye for detail and recording his work more like a fashion photographer. Morgan had been warned in advance of Roger's arrival and had organised the small conference room inside the station for a brief presentation. With the projector carousel loaded, Rogers sat waiting for Graves and Morgan to appear. A few minutes later and both police officers duly obliged.

"Afternoon sir," Rogers said, aiming his welcome at Graves. Both Graves and Morgan nodded simultaneously. They were more interested in the projector and the stack of files and boxes on the table beside it. They both took an easy chair each at different sides of the room and settled back. It was Morgan who spoke eventually.

"OK Ben, "he said nodding at the projector, "when you are ready."

"Thank you Colin," he said nervously. "Just by way of a recap sir, Colin asked me to look at incidents involving missing persons between 1958 and 1962," he confirmed staring directly at Graves, "within a 10-mile radius of Willenbury village. As a result, I have spent the last 6 hours at Hendon Mews as you requested looking back over old cases that fit the criteria of unsolved murders involving bodies that were never claimed," Rogers explained. Morgan had kept the reasoning behind the research on a strictly need-to-know basis and Rogers didn't need to know. Graves just wanted someone to do the legwork. After all, it could all turn out to be for nothing, although Rogers's presentation material however suggested otherwise.

"My first sift was a coarse one to highlight all incidents of murder, reports of missing persons and suicides, between 1958 and 1962," the police constable explained.

In The Mood

Graves shot a concerned glance at Morgan obviously uneasy with Rogers's interpretation of what was expected of him. Suicides and missing persons certainly didn't fit the criteria, as both would more than likely have attracted some interest from a relative.

"There were 8 over this 4 year period. These were broken down into 6 murders, 4 in 1960 and 2 in 1961. There were 2 suicides, 1 in 1962 and 1 in 1959," Rogers explained. "The 2 suicides were misfiled sir, much to Sergeant Wood's embarrassment. The bodies were identified and claimed by relatives, days later after their deaths. That leaves the remaining 6 cases."

"How many of the 6 were reported missing by relatives and their bodies later claimed?" Graves asked. Rogers consulted his notes again cross-referencing each against the criteria requested by Graves.

"1 sir, again the report was only matched to the body some time later due to a clerical error and the file was never updated," Roger's confirmed.

"Right," Graves said convinced of his own convictions," tell me about the remaining 5 bodies PC Rogers, and I want a detailed description, until I say stop or unless you finish your briefing."

"Yes sir," Rogers replied. He changed his focus back to his notebook. "Well sir, case number 20/03/1961 occurred March 3rd 1961 and involved a tramp in his 70s found strangled on a building site just outside the village centre," Rogers began. Graves wasted little time cutting him off at the earliest opportunity.

"Skip that one," he called out from the back of the room. Rogers stared at him glumly.

"OK sir," he said regaining his train of thought, "the next case number 15/08/1960 involved the murder of a biker known to have been passing through this village on the 28th August 1960. It was alleged at the time and later confirmed that he belonged to a gang that had been having a running battle with a rival gang across this part of the country. It all came to a head here in Willenbury the following late August Bank Holiday evening," Rogers continued, clicking the projector into life. "The file says the victim was 23 years old…"

Again Graves stepped in. "Skip that one as well," Graves called out. Rogers glanced at Graves and then at Morgan, a frustrated look on his face, before he consulted his notes once more. He moved the carousel several times until the slide he wanted appeared.

"Case number 33/05/60. This is Willenbury Coal Mine sir, closed in November 1959 because it was uneconomical." A photograph appeared showing an aerial view of the general area. Rogers pressed the projector button once more and the screen displayed a wooded area surrounded by chain-link fencing. A sign hung from it with the words:

DANGER!
MINE WORKINGS
KEEP OUT!

"The Coal Board was to make the site safe soon after the fence you see in this picture was erected. Beyond the main gates is the lead shaft, which extends about a mile down below the surface. It should have been sealed and grouted up within weeks of the mine closing. Unfortunately, the closure was not well received by mineworkers and local employment was affected. They went on strike, which delayed access by outside contractors. The unrest meant that temporary fencing was placed around the site and timbers placed over the shaft opening and these temporary arrangements became semi-permanent." Rogers clicked the projector once more, showing striking protestors at the time, before moving to a slide showing the mineshaft entrance.

"In June 1960 a group of boy scouts camped out in Willenbury Woods to gain their Duke of Edinburgh Award or something of that nature." The projector clicked once more and the picture on screen showed a number of tents scattered about a clearing inside the wood. "This is the area regularly used by the Scout groups for the last twenty-five years. A small group wondered off and stumbled across a hole in the chain link fence eventually finding the entrance to the abandoned mine shaft." A third click of the projector showed several uniformed policemen peering through a smallish break inside what appeared to be a timber platform.

"This is the platform sir," Morgan commented. "It's unclear what happened next from the records. It seems the planks either gave way or someone had removed them. This is little Billy Kingham." Rogers clicked the projector, revealing a stout looking boy about thirteen years old, taken from an old school photo. "This was taken a week before he fell through the wooden staging that you saw in the previous photo. When they found him he was alive and in quite a state of shock and remained that way for months later, according to medical records. Police records detail how he was found very luckily on a ledge about twelve feet down from the top of the platform. At first it was thought that the fall and shock of a lucky escape was the cause of his distress, but rescuers found that the lad wasn't alone. Suspended on a rope in the centre of the shaft was a body or what was left of one. A man later described as being in his 40s. The body was half decayed and half eaten by rats. In fact, the body was covered in them when they rescued the lad. By this time he had stopped crying and he was just staring at the body."

"The environment and MO seem to fit, or at least they are very similar to Benson's," Graves thought and then he remembered about the rope knots. "The rope Rogers, what about the rope tying the hands and feet?"

"I was just coming to that sir, it wasn't considered important at the time, however, there were a few pictures on file that were restored and changed into slides." Rogers clicked the projector past a few more slides one last time to reveal a knotted section of rope holding together bones of what was once the forearms of a body. Both men winced at the sight. Even the bones had gnawed marks with whole fingers missing on one hand. " These aren't very pleasant to look at," Rogers said. "This is a shot of what was left from behind the body."

"And the knot is identical to that used to tie Benson," Graves declared out loud. Rogers looked at him blankly. "The old black and white photograph tells us nothing about the colour and texture of the rope though unfortunately," Graves whispered, but within earshot of his colleagues.

"Sir, I've taken the liberty of having that particular piece of evidence reanalysed for chemicals and lettering," Rogers exclaimed, aware of Rowan's work on Benson's case and pleased with his show of initiative.

"Excellent," Graves said. "What else have you got Rogers?" Graves pressed further.

"Case number 35/10/60 sir. This is Chetley Sewage Treatment Works," Rogers said, pressing the projector once more. The motor whirred into action from standby mode, displaying a photograph of a large rectangular concrete tank set in a rural background. "The date is 10th October 1960. This is the local treatment plant for raw sewage, as it was known then. The waste is processed through a series of tanks and filters. It comes in at one end as raw sewage and is eventually discharged back into local rivers and streams having been treated," Rogers explained. Graves had an uneasy feeling about where this was leading.

"The tank in the picture is a settling and filtration tank. The sewage is at its most raw state at this point. The sewage is held here for a period of time whilst the solids are broken down and allowed to settle. The, er, shall we say, less polluted liquid, is allowed then to pass over a weir where it is processed further with chemicals. The whole process relies on friendly bacteria and other living forms such as worms to break down the solids over a period of time until the liquid is in a puréed form." Morgan swallowed hard at the idea.

"I'll never have chocolate milkshake ever again," he muttered quietly.

"This is all very interesting Rogers I'm sure, despite the subject matter, but can you get to the point?" Graves asked impatiently.

"Please bear with me sir," Rogers pleaded. Graves sighed heavily and relented. "In September 1960, this tank was due for major refurbishment after a second, more modern tank had been completed elsewhere on the same site and waste diverted to it." There was a further click of the projector and the carousel moved around clockwise. "This refurbishment involved draining the contents of the existing tank, making good any repairs to the concrete walls, whilst replacing various automated parts used to turn the sludge at periodic intervals. You can just make out the huge paddles in the picture sir," Rogers pointed to the screen. Graves gave him one of his looks and Rogers decided to get straight to the point. "Basically, when the old tank was drained, maintenance workers found a human skeleton hanging from a rope. The rope had been hidden beneath the tracks that the paddles moved along and had been secured to a ladder bolted to the tank wall. The body was never formally identified, given its condition, and no one apparently ever came forward to say who it could be sir, despite wide publicity coverage at the time as in the previous case."

Morgan stood and walked up to screen. "Ben you said that the body was found hanging. Did you actually mean hanging by support or by strangulation?" Morgan inquired.

"No, it was supported. The skeleton appeared to have been supported around the rib cage and under what would have been the armpits. As with the previous case, the hands and feet were bound together at the back with the main support rope passing through it. Oh and yes the knots at the back of the body were the same type," Rogers offered, "it was about the only thing left intact."

Morgan turned, looking directly at Graves. "Strange this doesn't meet the criteria for the other victims," he suggested.

"Oh I don't know," Graves responded staring at the screen intently, "it's cold, lonely, frightening and there are plenty of creatures around albeit they're not rats in this case." Morgan glanced back at him uncomfortably.

"But the circumstances sir, he or she wouldn't have lasted ten seconds immersed in that stuff," Morgan said, his face contorted at the prospect even though he felt that he needed to ask the question.

"Colin," Rogers interjected, "it is possible based on the case notes actually. As well as the rope secured to the ladder they also found a length of rubber tubing. One end was tied to what would have been the mouth of the victim, his own lips I presume creating a seal from the outside environment. A rubber band attached it around the skull, according to case records."

"Wait you're telling us that the victim was alive when placed in….in that stuff?" Morgan asked.

"Speculation I would say, but based on the evidence, it would suggest that is what happened," Rogers replied. Graves glanced at Morgan this time.

"Maybe now we can assume that the MO was the same or near enough?" Graves suggested.

"But who would do such a thing to another human being?" Morgan gasped.

Rogers clicked the projector once more bringing both officers back to the matter at hand. "The last case is 39/01/61 sir," Rogers continued. "This is Chetley/Willenbury Railway Sidings, 4th January 1961. The depot is situated on the border between the two parishes and is or should I say was, an important distribution point for arable produce and fuel during the last war. It is disused these days with the general decline of the railways since the late 1950s, early 60s following the Beeching review." Rogers clicked the projector once more and an aerial view of the local rail network popped up on screen. "The main line runs along here," Rogers said pointing to the screen, "and is still in use even today, but the arterial lines feeding into the depot are pretty much overgrown and disused. Back in 1961 various rolling stock was stored there and left to rust.

One day in January 1961, several young boys playing hide and seek stumbled on a ghastly find. One of the boys decided to climb inside one of the disused tankers to hide. Anyhow, according to the case notes the lad used a rope he found hanging inside the tanker to lower himself down, until he hit the body tied to the end of it. The rope seemed to be covered in something slippery. It was described as having a waxy residue. He let go as soon as he hit the body," Rogers explained.

"The body was that of a man. He'd been tied hands and feet at the back of the body and yes it was tied the same way as the bodies at the mine and sewage plant sir," Rogers said anticipating the question. "There were no fingerprints sir, as per the previous cases, due to the condition of the hands. The tanker was already a frequent haunt for the local rat population given its former use transporting grain, now they had a body to eat as well. Interestingly, the rodent attention was mainly around the hands and arms again, possibly as a result of the animal fat."

"Animal fat?" Morgan repeated.

"Yes the records say that the waxy substance covering the hands and arms was animal fat," Rogers confirmed. Graves stood now, pacing up and down the room, absorbing the implications of Rogers's briefing in his own time. Even though it would be his last involvement in the case, he felt he needed to direct matters positively before handing over the reins completely to DI Wheldon.

"Do the ropes tying the bodies at the mine and sewage plant also have animal fat added?" Graves asked.

"Impossible to say at the sewage plant, but yes, now that you mention it, the body at the mine was treated the same way," Rogers confirmed.

Graves took the information in his stride. "Morgan, I want you and Rogers to go through these three particular files page by page and list all significant information that might lead to the identification of the bodies and any similarities with Benson's murder beside the way in which all four were bound. You remember I have some corroboration from the public records office that may tie these bodies to those of Woollsey, Turnberry and Grundy or if you prefer the bogus, McDonald, Gould and Hewitt. If the evidence is still not conclusive, I'm prepared to have the bodies exhumed if needs be," Graves said. Mulling over matters further in his mind he became aware of another implication now, one that had only surfaced in his mind as the finger of suspicion had shift to a fifth unknown person. "The same knot was used to tie each victim, one designed to tighten the more the victims struggled against their bonds. I would guess that the rope is the same as well in each case, possibly part of the ritual here rather than just using rope that just happened to be close at hand at the moment the abduction took place. Remember what I said earlier about the environment being important here," he spoke out loud, now focusing on Morgan. "If I am right, our perpetrator also has Navy connections to have access to this type of rope. It would also suggest why this person had knowledge of the more unusual types of knot."

"Sir, before you potentially go down the avenue of exhumation, you might want to try one more line of inquiry." Roger's interrupted eagerly.

Graves looked at the young officer, "I'm listening."

"Other than the similarity in the way in which these three bodies were found sir, the only other common denominator was the person who carried out the *post mortems*." Rogers suggested.

A look of recognition dawned on Graves's face as he cast his mind back and he didn't need it confirming. It fitted the time frame even if it predated his time at Willenbury CID.

"Thank you PC Rogers, I'll take it from here. You've both done some excellent work here today. Keep it up and get me some more detail from those files," Graves replied. "I need to see a certain pathologist about some old cases."

"One thing more sir," Rogers added, "Sergeant Wood was very reluctant to let me have these files at first. He relented after he made a phone call. It may be nothing," he suggested shrugging his shoulders. Graves took his leave soon after.

Within twenty minutes he had arrived unexpectedly at County Labs. The head of pathology was speaking into a handheld Dictaphone over his next subject when he noticed Graves standing in the doorway. There was a brief exchange between the two, nothing more than eye contact and Rowan knew this wasn't a social call.

"How is your memory Jack?" Graves asked surreptitiously as Rowan placed the recording device on a nearby trolley.

"As good as your memory my boy, if you are insinuating that I am too old again." Rowan replied managing a controlled smile.

Graves grinned, "No, kidding aside, I have a serious motive behind my question. 1960 Jack, I was about to join Police College," Graves announced.

"Yes, thanks to your father as I recall?" Rowan reminded him. The comment interrupted Graves's train of thought forcing his mind back to his ailing father. He needed to be done by the end of the day come what may.

"You were saying," Rowan probed.

"I asked one of the constables from the station to do some research into cases where bodies were discovered and never identified or claimed around 1960," Graves said.

"Do you think there is a connection here with your man Benson? Is that why your boy was sniffing around at Hendon Mews?" Rowan replied.

"Oh, so you know about that?" Graves said.

"It's a small, close-nit force fighting crime here Philip, you know that?" Rowan said playing his cards even closer to his chest. Rowan joined Graves at the door and the two walked back along the corridor to the exit and fresh air.

"PC Rogers pulled eight cases from the archive. Only three of them met the criteria that I was looking for. The sergeant in charge down at Hendon was, shall we say, less than helpful at first I believe. It was only when Rogers said he would speak with me that the sergeant decided to make a phone call. A few minutes later he reappeared and begrudgingly handed the files over. Rogers briefed us on the contents an hour or so ago," Graves explained. "Getting back to the case files, the pathologist on all three cases…" Graves paused turning 90 degrees to face Rowan.

"…was me," Rowan finished off his sentence, flicking his cigarette butt toward an old tin bucket with expert deftness. Graves looked at him momentarily, caught off guard by his candidness. The pathologist wheezed heavily before continuing, "when I said this was a close-knit force I was being literal. Everyone knows each other socially outside work, whether you're police or from the medical profession as you well know," Rowan continued. Graves was finding Rowan's train of thought difficult to follow and the look on his face must have said as much. "Sergeant Alan Wood is an old friend and was part of the investigation team twenty-five years ago on those three cases, replacing your father as I recall. Reg was ill with the flu at the time if my memory serves me correctly," Rowan recalled. "Alan rang me in a panic when Rogers mentioned your name and what you were interested in, so I told him to release the files and that it would be me that you would eventually come to see and so here you are."

Graves looked at the portly pathologist choosing to sit now, a puzzled look still etched on his face. "Jack, I merely wanted to know if these three cases were connected with Benson and his friends from the Navy," Graves explained. Rowan stared back him without comment.

"You know there is a connection?" Graves said firmly.

"I guessed that your inquiries at Hendon were probably tied into the bridge incident, though I have to confess when Alan spoke to me I was lost for a reason other than the similar timeframes. Then I reviewed my own copy of the files that young Rogers was researching..." Rowan continued and this time it was Graves's turn to interject.

"And you found similarities in Benson's MO, how they were tied, the environment in which they were found, coupled with the timing of their deaths. Why should Sergeant Wood be a so secretive about twenty-five year old case files though?" Graves said out loud the comment not necessarily aimed at Rowan. Before Rowan could react, Graves was already thinking about something else that Rowan had said that didn't sound quite right.

"And why would you have personal files on these three cases in particular Jack, which I might add is, if I'm not mistaken, strictly against the Lab's policy?" Graves asked pointedly.

Rowan looked Graves squarely in the eye considering his next words. "OK Phil, let's speak frankly. Twenty-five years ago I had my eye on the Head of Department post." He paused, his breathing laboured. "It was a hectic time, the department was being reorganised, posts were under threat and basically, the powers that be in the council wanted more for their money. You probably can't remember the Calder Review?" Rowan asked. Graves shook his head blankly.

"Well we had to make cutbacks and savings and yet still maintain a normal quality of service. It did result in what I would call less than a professional approach to cases that were, shall we say, not worth pursuing to a final satisfactory conclusion," Rowan said, his eyes now fixed again on Graves to gauge his understanding and reaction. Graves sat motionless not sure what to make of the revelation. Was all this washing of dirty linen really necessary for what he was after, he wondered? Before he could ask Rowan continued.

"Cases like the three you pulled from Hendon back in the 1960s were considered less important than other cases because of the scant evidence found and virtually zero public interest." Graves was about to protest when Rowan raised his hand, the smoke from his cigarette creating a blue halo momentarily. "Please, let me finish Phil. I carried out a full *post mortem* on all three men as with any other case. Evidence was presented, what little there was to the investigating teams and checks and inquires were made, but as I recall we hit a dead end on all these three victims. Oh, adverts were placed in local papers for relatives to come forward, but no one ever did. Murder by person or persons unknown was recorded and eventually, the cases were closed over time." Twenty-five years on, the senior pathologist was still less than happy with the way he was manipulated by local politics "I'm afraid I let others cloud my professional judgement back then and perhaps I knew that one day these cases might come back to haunt me, so I kept copies of the half dozen or so files in case I ever needed them as a safety net, so to speak, in any future defence of my actions."

"So the great Jack Rowan is human after all," Graves said to himself smugly. "OK Jack so we are in agreement. There is a possible link here between Benson and these three cases?" Grave's reiterated. Rowan nodded.

"That is all though Philip, having checked my notes and knowing what I know about Benson, it is only a possible link. I admit that the circumstantial evidence is pretty convincing and there is lots of it, but it is still not 100 percent," Rowan said quietly and with his usual authority.

"And if I can give you the original medical details for Woollsey, Turnberry and Grundy, could you review your files and see if the physical details match those in your files? "Graves asked. Again Rowan nodded.

"Good, I'll have Morgan drop them off within the hour. Can you let me know your thoughts the minute you have completed your assessment Jack?" Graves asked. Rowan could hardly object under the circumstances.

With that the two men parted company once more, Rowan to contemplate his old case notes in more detail, Graves back to the station to see what Morgan had discovered, if anything, from a more in-depth look at the files from Hendon Mews and Wheldon's case notes. There had to be something there possibly missed by Wheldon and his team?

22

Roger Gately, Borough Engineer

Morgan sat at his desk, the remnants of a doughnut discarded on a paper plate beside his in-tray. In his right hand he held a mug of tea, which he slurped from every now and then. In his left hand he held yet another rather dated black and white photograph. A dozen more were scattered across his desk, each overlapping the other and all on a similar theme – site photographs of Willenbury Bypass during construction. Graves sat at the opposite side of the room perplexed by recent events. His visit to see Jack Rowan had merely confirmed what he already suspected since his trip to Canal Reach. It seemed to him that a series of odd events had taken place, all interrelated, although he wasn't sure if or how his father was involved and yet here he and Morgan were apparently back at square one, actually looking at evidence considered and discarded by the elusive acting D.I. Wheldon. Morgan had spent the last few hours reviewing reports, files and bagged evidence considered by Wheldon's team to see if anything had been missed. Despite Graves's initial thoughts on Wheldon's ability, the man had proven him wrong in his approach and methodology that he used in his investigation. There were no oversights that Morgan could see and since his return to the office, Graves had to agree. However, this still left them at a dead end.

Rising from his chair, Graves strolled over to the window behind Morgan and stared out at the park where he used to play as a child. The rope swing hanging from the old Yew tree was still gainfully employed as a teenage girl was pushed backward and forward. By the look on her face and that of the boy who was pushing her Graves guessed them to be boy and girlfriend.

"Sir," Morgan said turning," DCI. Chambers from New Scotland Yard telephoned while you were out. He said he was just ringing to see how your father was. I gave him an update and he asked me to pass on his best wishes. I presume that was OK?"

"No that's fine," Graves said, still facing the window. "I'll ring him myself tomorrow." He turned around looking over Morgan's shoulder and his attention was drawn toward one of the photos on Morgan's desk. It was almost completely hidden by one of the dozen or so photos lying there, but the exposed portion had a young man's face on it, a face that he thought he knew from a long time ago. He pulled it free, turning it as he did. It showed various heavy earth moving equipment stripping the site in the background in readiness for construction, although it was a number of site staff positioned strategically in the foreground, one of the land surveyors in fact, that had caught his attention.

"Did any of Wheldon's team confirm where these photographs came from?" he asked Morgan. Morgan pulled out an inventory that Wheldon had created cataloguing the evidence by type, origin, date acquired and owner.

"A Mrs Winifred Cooper sir according to the inventory," Morgan replied. "There's a comment alongside the entry that says the photographs were her husband's, a Mr John Cooper. He was the original site agent for works." By now Graves had realised whom the man in the picture was.

"I take it Mr Cooper isn't with us anymore otherwise he would have been the one giving us access to the photos." Graves surmised out loud.

"From my limited time with DI Wheldon before you became involved sir I recall having been told that Mr Cooper passed away two years ago sir. Mrs Cooper was about to throw these away when we recovered them," Morgan confirmed. Morgan had noticed Graves's interest in the photograph and now it was attracting his curiosity. "Anything of interest sir?" he asked, expectantly.

"The man in the foreground in this picture, the one with the clipboard," Graves said placing the photograph back on the desk in front of Morgan," That is Roger Gately constable." Morgan looked back blankly at him.

On one of the few occasions Graves had been back for a family visit one of the headlines that hit him in the Willenbury Chronicle was Roger Gately's appointment to the post of Borough Engineer. "There is no reason why you should recognise the name. Roger Gately is the Borough Engineer based at County Hall – about a ten minute walk from here in fact," Graves said moving back toward the window. He stood there looking at the Victorian building in the distance peeping out above the tree line across the park. After a few moments contemplation Graves grabbed his hat and coat. "I'm popping out for a while. If Swallow wants me, tell him I'm pursuing a line of inquiry," he told Morgan.

"No mention about County Hall and Roger Gately then sir?" Morgan grinned.

"You don't want him having a coronary do you?" Graves said grabbing hold of the photograph, the door swung closed behind him. Nearly ten minutes later he was inside County Hall reception waiting in line behind an old lady with a King Charles Spaniel complaining about refuse collection. His eyes caught sight of a list of the various departments housed at County Hall and there prominently at the top was the title of Borough Engineer, accompanied by the name, Mr Roger Gately.

"Yes, can I help you?" A second bespectacled receptionist had appeared once it had become clear that the old lady had no intentions of being fobbed off.

"I'm here to see Roger Gately please," Graves announced bracing himself for a sharp intake of breath, given Gately's status.

"Do you have an appointment Mr..." she asked.

In The Mood

"Graves, Detective Inspector Graves," he replied reaching for his warrant card. "I have some rather urgent business to discuss with Mr Gately."

"Oh, the police," she said apprehensively. "I'll see if Mr Gately is available Inspector." Graves watched as she pressed various buttons on a large monitor in front of her until a low telephone dial could be heard. The elderly lady with the spaniel eyed him accusingly.

"I bet he gets better service," she mumbled. The tone of the line stopped and a crisp male voice responded.

"Yes, Roger Gately speaking?"

"Hello Mr Gately, it's Doris at the front desk I have an Inspector Graves to see you sir. He hasn't got an appointment, but he did say that it was rather urgent that he speaks with you. There was a brief pause as if Gately was contemplating an excuse.

"Did you say *Graves*, Doris?" Gately managed finally.

"Yes sir, his identity card says New Scotland Yard sir," she replied flicking the intercom switch backward and forwards.

"Send him up Doris, I have a free half hour as it happens," Gately replied before the intercom fell silent.

She looked toward the lifts. "If you take the lift Inspector, you'll find Mr Gately on the 8th floor. His secretary's office is directly ahead of you when the lift door opens. Mary, Mr Gately's secretary, will take you in to see Mr Gately in due course." Five minutes later Graves found himself in the much plusher offices of the council members. A tall slim brunette with the name 'Mary Abbott', on the lapel of her blouse had met him the minute the lift doors opened. She directed him behind her desk to a large teak panelled door. Knocking quietly, she waited a few seconds before entering.

"Sir, Detective Inspector Graves," she announced. The room was almost square in shape – Graves guessed about 15 yards by 15 yards – with window walls on one side and the rear of the room looking out over the park back toward Willenbury police station. Dusk was setting in and he could see the lights on the now reopened bypass looking fairly busy with rush hour traffic once more in the distance. Several feet in front of him was a large wooden desk stacked with at least a dozen files in columns of three. A number of chairs were positioned slightly proud of the desk each occupied by yet more files. Beyond this desk was a more typical office desk, equally as cluttered. The owner of the desk sat behind a copy of *The Times* newspaper; only the fingers on each page were visible from where Graves was standing.

"Bloody crossword," the comment came from behind the broadsheet before it was slowly lowered down on to the desk. A distinguished man, Graves knew him to be in his mid forties, moved his eyes from the newspaper, over the bifocals on the end of his nose focusing on Graves, then back to his newspaper again.

"Thank you Mary," he said, "that will be all for now." With that the door closed behind her as she left.

"Do you do *The Times* crossword Philip?" Gately inquired turning to the sports section.

"Sometimes," Graves replied taking in the rest of the office décor. "It depends on whether I managed the crossword in one of the tabloids and then whether I fancy a tougher challenge."

"Some anoraks try to beat their best time for completing it every day of the week. I haven't completed it once yet," he said as he folded the paper and placed it inside an open briefcase behind him. He clipped the lid shut turning on his executive swivel chair as he did, hands clasped in front him across the desk. At least three gold rings of various sizes reflected light from his desktop lamp causing small reflections of light to move about the ceiling above where he sat. "Then again, I am an engineer," he continued. "Now then Philip, it's been…oh, er…five years I would say since we last spoke?"

"Six years in December actually," Graves corrected him," at the Christmas Ball in this very building in fact."

"Why of course it was," Gately replied, stretching backwards and placing his hands on the back of his greying hair. "If memory serves me right you came to the ball with Peggy Morton as your guest." Gately continued labouring the point.

"I believe she is better known as Peggy Gately now?" Graves replied. Again Graves knew where Gately was heading and he was in no mood to spar with him over an old flame, even if it was the worst mistake he had ever made in his personal life.

"Ah yes too bad old boy. The better man won and all that," Gately just couldn't help himself. Graves would have loved to talk about Peggy longer, but Gately would have just turned the screws even more. Graves looked about him for a recent photograph of her, but he couldn't see any. Given the untidiness of the room though that was hardly surprising.

"I'd love to go over old times, but that isn't why I'm here Roger." With that Graves moved forward toward where Gately sat, still stretched out with his hands on his head. He took the photograph out from the plain brown envelope that he had brought from the station and dropped it in front of Gately. "Does that picture bring back any memories?" Graves asked helping himself to the only chair free of paperwork in the room, save Gately's own.

"My, my," Gately exclaimed, peering through his bifocals. "Gosh how the years roll by Philip. 1958/59 I'd say. It looks like the early days of the project if progress in the background is anything to go by. The 58/59 winter was a bloody cold one I can tell you. Freeze the nuts off a brass monkey. I always remember hearing the news that Buddy Holly had just been killed in that plane crash at the time we started to strip the site. Put on a few pounds as well since those days," he continued, passing the photo back to Graves.

"What was your role back then Roger in relation to this project?" Graves asked. Gately, as ever the wily old fox, wanted to know the ins-and-outs of Graves's interest before he was prepared to answer, even though he suspected the reason, especially having seen the old picture once more. He pushed his chair back and stood revealing the extra pounds that he had referred to a few moments ago.

"Too many council luncheons at the taxpayer's expense," Graves thought, but he kept his views to himself.

Gately stood with his back to Graves staring out of the window at the bypass in the distance.

"I presume this is about that body you found in the bridge – *Benson* I've heard him called?" Gately declared then momentarily lost in thought no doubt about his own involvement twenty-five years ago.

"As a matter of fact yes," Graves replied. "You were intending to come forward as a potential material witness in this case weren't you?"

"Are you suggesting that I had an involvement in the death of this Benson character Philip?" Gately asked, his voice becoming more defensive as he turned to face him.

"No, not at all, but you were working on the site at the time Benson was placed inside that bridge column and as yet we have no way of corroborating any of the facts back then or contacting any of those involved. Seeing your picture and knowing you back then was a fortuitous stroke of good fortune for me and the investigation team," Graves explained.

"I'm not sure if fortuitous is a word I would use Philip, but putting that to one side for a moment, you said that Benson was *placed*?" Gately replied. A frown played across his tanned face as he awaited a response.

"Yes, we believe he was alive when he was placed inside that column," Graves replied.

"Murder?" Gately volunteered and Graves nodded. Gately turned and gazed outside again, at the bridge in the distance. "That isn't as easy as you might think. He couldn't have been placed at ground level because of all the reinforcement therefore he must have been lowered eighty feet straight down. I thought you were inferring that he had just been pushed from the scaffolding perhaps and fell eighty feet?" Gately replied. Graves shook his head calmly.

"That was my initial thought."

"That puts a different complexion on things. Timing would have been everything for the body to have remained hidden right up to the placing of any concrete, suggesting someone with a basic working knowledge at least of the construction programme and processes involved," Gately pondered.

"Or just sheer opportunism?" Graves interjected.

"I think not. This took careful planning and an awareness of what was happening on site at a given point in time," Gately suggested.

"So you think someone close to the site itself at the time might be responsible?" Graves replied.

"It's a reasonable assumption," Gately said. "You see normal practice when pouring large batches of concrete into the ground is to get the area ready the day before the pour. It would be one person's responsibility to check the excavation the following morning prior to the concrete being placed to see if the area is still clean and free of debris or even wildlife that may have strayed into the hole overnight. Only then would concreting begin in a phased approach dictated by the design engineer's specification," Gately explained.

"So in an ideal world the person carrying out the final inspection would be able to help us if he or she is still around?" Graves suggested.

"Philip, this person may have been responsible for putting the body in there, who knows?" Gately replied.

"But why risk committing murder on your own doorstep, so to speak?" Graves speculated.

"Maybe the murderer was content that the body would never be found? Modern bridges are designed to last 120 years, "Gately offered.

"Yes so I've been told," Graves replied. "Perhaps it's a combination of that and being presented with an opportunity the murderer couldn't afford to miss," Graves suggested focusing on Gately.

"I'm not with you," Gately replied reaching for his pipe. He tapped it on the edge of the waste paper bin beside his chair before rummaging in his jacket pocket for his tobacco.

"The environment is important to our murderer. Why else go to so much effort and risk?" Graves said out loud. "Just like his contemporaries, Woollsey, Turnberry and Grundy." Gately frowned as if Graves was having a conversation with himself. "Sorry Roger, I'm expecting something from the pathologist's lab that will tell me Benson's death is connected to three other deaths all within 12 months of each other 25 years ago," Graves explained.

"How did Benson die in the end?" Gately asked, lighting the barrel of his pipe. He relaxed back in his chair waiting for an answer.

"He didn't suffocate. We believe the impact of the wet concrete caused his neck and backbone to break. I am reliably informed that death would have been immediate," Graves continued. Gately drew on his pipe preferring to stand now, acting furtively as he paced behind his desk.

"I was trying to keep an old friend out of this Philip," he said still unsure of his actions, "but you may wish to have a word with him. We worked on the project together as teenagers. I was the junior engineer responsible for checking the setting out of the works. Anthony Carson was a general labourer. Anthony must have covered every inch of that site during his time on the project," Gately said. "That's him in the picture in the background," he said pointing at Graves's photograph, which still lay on his desk.

"Why do I know that name?" Graves said out loud.

"Anthony Carson is a successful business man these days and a prominent member of the community. He owns three garden nurseries, the original one here in Willenbury, the other two outside the county. He's also a member of the Police Public Accounts Committee, which is where you may have heard his name before. If I was you I would tread carefully with your questions and how you put them to him."

Armed with this new development, Graves returned to the station to brief Morgan and pick up his car before visiting the hospital.

ooooo

It was getting a little late in the day to see Anthony Carson despite his curiosity. He was due back at the hospital and Carson would have to wait, maybe even Wheldon would have to interview him. This was his last night on the case, he said to himself.

"Sir, any luck with Mr Gately?" Morgan called out as Graves walked into the office.

"Another potential lead," Graves said unconvincingly. "Gately was the man in the picture, I was right about that. His knowledge of the bypass being built is limited, as you would expect, but he did seem to remember someone else who worked specifically on the project, a local businessman now and eminent community member," Graves explained. Just along the corridor in the kitchen, Tom Wheldon was helping himself to a coffee. He was wondering how to get the best out of his impending meeting with Estelle McDonald to get the outcome he had in mind, when he found the solution almost unfolding before him in the next room. He quietly listened to Graves's and Morgan's conversation. Ten minutes later, Morgan and Wheldon were up-to-date with the involvement of both Gately and Carson.

"Gately was reluctant to offer up Carson as a potential lead I suspect because of his political clout," Graves continued, "but we or should I say you," he corrected himself, "will have to interview him, probably tomorrow now. I'm winding up my involvement in the investigation tonight. Swallow knows about my intentions. It's yours and Wheldon's problem from now on."

"What is your opinion sir about Carson's involvement?" Morgan replied, taking his attention from the report he was typing and keen to milk Graves of all his insight before he left.

"Carson must have been one of the last people to probably work on that bridge before any concrete was placed. Proving it or just getting any useful information from him is another matter," Graves replied. "How far have you got with that report?" Graves asked, changing the emphasis slightly.

"Just waiting to add what you discussed with Mr Gately sir and that should be it. I would like to drop it into DCI Swallow's in-tray tonight as you agreed with him," Morgan said.

"What about Rowan's assessment of the three cases found by Rogers?" Graves queried.

"Dr Rowan is still finalising the paperwork sir. Off the record for now he did say that his review of his case files and the details provided by the records office at Hayes confirmed your suspicions. The body at the mine was that of Jack Turnberry. The body's features and hands were destroyed by rodent activity, but dental evidence, scars and an old leg fracture made identification conclusive. He came to the same conclusion with Jeff Woollsey I'm afraid, although he was more difficult," Morgan explained. Graves gave him a vacant look.

"Sorry sir, the skeleton at the sewage works – that was Woollsey. He had a metal plate inserted in his head in 1942 according to the Hayes medical records following an explosion on the Ulysses. It was one of the few things still left of Woollsey. Dr Rowan is due to get back to me any time now about the Chetley Sidings case," Morgan explained. Somehow the news didn't come as an earth-shattering revelation to Graves. He merely took the news casually. In his own mind, he didn't expect much from Anthony Carson, so they were back to square one, and his father, well his connection may never be known if there ever was one.

In The Mood

"OK," Graves said staring outside the darkened window, "take this down," Morgan began typing eagerly as Graves dictated .the missing final paragraph. Several minutes later Morgan had stopped typing and was carrying out a final check on his draft report to DCI. Swallow. Meanwhile, Tom Wheldon was fully up-to-date with their progress. It certainly gave him the ammunition he needed for his planned visit to Little Crandon Cottage later that evening.

The revelation about Estelle's father's death he would keep to himself until he had sampled what was on offer and even then he would force Morgan to offer the bad news, he thought to himself. To that end he would keep the report from the delectable Miss McDonald until he had been paid in full.

"You fell short sir of actually accusing this fellow Carson of being involved in Benson's death is my impression sir," Morgan observed.

"Only because he has yet to be interviewed and ruled out of our investigation. Gately's description of Carson's role on site puts him in the frame. No doubt Swallow will have a view on that given the politics involved when you have interviewed Carson. The final report may well read differently so it needs to be kept between Swallow, possibly Wheldon and us for the time being. If Carson knows nothing, or, he can't remember anything, then we are dead in the water with nowhere else to go and the report will need to be changed to reflect that," Graves said. "As for my father's potential involvement…" Graves went on to say on reflection when Morgan interrupted him.

"Oh, sir, your father!" he blurted out. There was a message for you while you were out to go to the hospital right away," He said meekly.

Graves grabbed his hat and coat without saying a word. He was already hurrying along the corridor when he called back, "Make sure that report goes in Gary's in-tray?" In the next-door kitchen, Wheldon had stepped back smartly behind the door as Graves passed by.

"Right sir, sorry sir," Morgan shouted. With that Morgan pulled out the last sheet from his typewriter and added it to the previous half dozen he had stacked neatly on his desk. "Time you were back at your flat with a takeaway," Morgan said to himself. Stapling the sheets together and collecting his own coat, he called in DCI Swallow's office along the way dropping the report into his in-tray before heading out of the building. It was only a matter of minutes before Wheldon appeared at the door into Swallow's office. A lecherous grin spread across his bearded face as he stepped inside scooping up the report from the tray.

"A quick photocopy and the original will be back in Swallow's in-tray before anyone else is any the wiser. If this doesn't get me anywhere with Miss McDonald nothing will and on the back of Graves's efforts, which makes it all the sweeter," Wheldon said out loud as he headed toward the photocopier.

23

A High Price To Pay

Tom Wheldon stood outside the front door of Little Crandon Cottage. Tucked under his arm the draft report jointly prepared by Graves and Morgan. He looked around him, conscious of the misdemeanour he was about to commit, but the sight of Estelle McDonald peering out through the window beside the front door was enough to convince him it was worth the risk.

"Ah, Tom you were quick coming back to me," she smiled at him seductively, twiddling the end of her blonde tresses with her fingers, which she wore loose now. She pulled the front door open a little wider and he stepped inside looking along the hallway into the kitchen ahead. His eyes moved upstairs toward the landing before he turned to face Estelle once more. It had only taken him a few minutes to find the report in Swallow's in-tray, copy it and replace the original. The remainder of his time was spent showering at home and putting on a change of clothes. A splash of Old Spice completed his brief preparations.

Estelle closed the door behind her, her back arched and pressed against the door so that she was facing Wheldon. The dress she wore at the Rope and Anchor had been replaced by a much longer lemon coloured short-sleeved dress. It was in the style of a sarong, with the cord around her slim waist tied in a neat little bow at the side. Her most interesting features as far as Wheldon was concerned fought against the restraining cotton that kept both prominent orbs in place.

"Shall we step into the dining room Tom? We can talk in there. I have some Chardonnay cooling in the fridge," she said, her eyes indicating the way. They walked down the hallway, Wheldon more than happy for his host to lead the way. It was only as they approached the door leading into the dining room that he paused, a slight hint of disappointment in his voice.

"Won't we disturb your mother?" Wheldon whispered half-heartedly.

She pushed the door open regardless and walked in. "I shouldn't worry, it's bingo night tonight. I have to collect mum later," she replied, stretching to lift two glasses from the kitchen cupboard above the breakfast bar. She passed the bottle of Chardonnay to Wheldon, "How good is your screwing?" she said, smiling, then bending down in front of Wheldon to retrieve something from the bottom most drawer. Wheldon followed her movement eagerly. She bent down as if touching her toes and this time it was the dress around her well-toned bottom that took the strain and for once he found his attention drawn to another equally alluring part of her body. Before he could answer she stood and turned in one movement offering him a corkscrew. Wheldon's trademark caddish grin returned and he took the implement without a word, placing the plain brown envelope on the breakfast bar beside the wine bottle. He gripped the neck of the bottle forcing home the corkscrew.

"Now Tom, what do you have in your envelope?" she asked. In contrast to Wheldon's eyes, hers had never strayed far from the slim brown envelope since he had passed through the front door. Allowing a playful smile to erupt across her face she lifted herself on to one of the three barstools that flanked one side of the breakfast bar, crossing her legs as she did. As in the Rope and Anchor earlier, the sudden movement caused the figure-hugging dress to reveal more of her legs than she had planned and she tried in vain to recover the situation. Wheldon watched her awkwardness becoming more and more aroused. Her fringe fell loosely across her eyes and she peered through it at him, one eye hidden behind it alluringly.

"I'm still not really certain whether I should be doing this Estelle?" Wheldon replied patting the envelope protectively. There was no real intention in his voice to keep it to himself. He was just reminding her of what he expected in return.

"Nevertheless, you brought it anyway," Estelle said, stroking her thigh. Wheldon watched her hand, wishing it were his.

It was enough for any negative thoughts to be cast aside. "This is strictly between us Estelle?" he said, pulling the stapled report from the envelope. Estelle's eyes followed its progress as Wheldon placed the report on the breakfast bar. The title on the covering page read:

CLASSIFIED
INVESTIGATION INTO THE DEATH OF ROBERT BENSON
AN INTERIM PROGRESS REPORT

"Are you aware of the basic details behind this investigation and how it relates to your dad?" Wheldon inquired managing to avert his gaze from his charming host momentarily back to the report. He'd spent ten minutes at home as he changed reading it carefully, particularly the executive summary, recommendations and conclusions in an attempt to sound informed and in overall control of the case and production of the report at this precise moment.

"Only what I learned from the daily papers. As for my dad, just a few vague questions from your colleagues that inferred they needed to make contact with him about this chap Benson. Fancy that after twenty-five years they come badgering me and my poor mum." There was a change in the tone of her voice that was changing the mood and he didn't care for it.

"I'm not sure that this is a good idea Estelle." Wheldon said turning the report over so it was face down on the bar. He had other things on his mind and he wanted payment upfront. Her female intuition picked up on this and she immediately changed her approach. She moved from her seat, sliding her hand toward the report. Wheldon instinctively pulled it towards him and she withdrew slightly.

"I'm sorry Tom, I didn't mean to be pushy and abrupt," she smiled pleasantly at him. "I'm a little wound up over this whole business. I've spent most of my youth and brief adult life trying to find my dad. I haven't had any luck so far and − well I thought − you might help me out?" she purred, rolling her sad eyes at him as she had in the Rope and Anchor earlier in the day. As if on cue, tears rolled down her cheeks, her eyes fixed on the kitchen floor before her. Wheldon suddenly felt compassion for the younger woman before him, instead of unbridled lust.

He put the report down, stroking her head gently. For a brief moment he was the missing father figure and she was the pining daughter in need of protection. She moved forward nestling her head into his chest protectively and he placed a comforting arm around her shoulders and squeezed gently. In this vulnerable state she was even more appealing to him in a perverse way. She raised her head slowly, almost reluctantly until their eyes were no more than a few inches apart. Thoughts rushed through Estelle's mind in those brief seconds. She knew that she would have to make the ultimate sacrifice if she was to see the report and decision time had come, but could she go through with it with a middle-aged, overweight, balding policeman? Wheldon merely firmed up on his earlier intention as soon as their eyes met. He placed his hands beneath her arms and lifted her, pulling her forward in one swift movement. Their lips met, hers hesitantly at first then as passionately as his and he squeezed her tightly. She pushed him back uncertain about her actions and saw that look in his eyes again. A look of suspicion and lust mixed together. She knew in that split second that there was no going back.

"Time to lie back and think of England," she said to herself. She pulled him hard toward her again this time with a veiled eagerness. Wheldon accepted her advances with equal enthusiasm moving his lips across her face and down her slender neck. Despite his age and physical appearance, he knew what to do and how to do it and the trouble was it wasn't long before she was beginning to enjoy it. He placed a hand of support at the small of her back as he pressed her against him. His sizable waistline prevented further progress toward his now fully aroused manhood. With his free hand he pushed the report from the breakfast bar and it tumbled on to the nearest barstool revealing the report's executive summary.

"Your report," she protested her voice trembling, his breath on her neck.

"To hell with the report," he exclaimed, "we'll get to that later." His lips found their way down toward her ample chest, which was heaving now more than usual from his attention. He let both hands grasp hold of Estelle's small firm bottom. The fineness of her dress made his touch feel as if the dress wasn't there at all. There was a surge from within him that he hadn't experienced since he was a teenager. His fingers slid down her slender legs and back up again toward her waist this time accompanied by her dress until he felt the texture of a strap, like the one he had seen earlier during lunch. His emotion increased and in his eagerness, he gripped her bottom firmer, lifting her on to the bar. He buried his head in between her breasts, his balding head delving deeply, his tongue tracing over every contour, his nose pushing against the dress to expose more of her tanned skin. Above his burrowing face Estelle braved his advances, strangely aroused by this less than appealing man.

Wheldon pulled frantically at the bow tied at her waist. The sight of Estelle's white stockings, basque and briefs clinging to her slender body was more than he could have hoped for. She sat slightly reclined her eyes fixed on his face, now showing a man almost possessed. Again she felt the need to leave, to run. He was just a dirty old man who couldn't believe his luck. In those few seconds her eyes caught sight of the report. She craned her neck without changing her position, her mind still torn between whether to run or grin and bear it, when she felt the clawing stubby fingers travelling across her legs toward her waist. One hand pulled at her briefs, whilst the other hand continued its progress pushing open the upper part of her dress and forcing its way inside her basque. One of Estelle's 44E breasts spilled out and Wheldon used the palm of his hand to massage it and hold it in place eagerly. She hadn't wanted to help his progress, it was his sheer strength and drive that caused her briefs to slide free. Wheldon couldn't wait for them to clear her ankles. He pressed his bearded face against the small patch of tanned tummy that was exposed between her basque and his next goal several inches below. She realised his intention and bit her lip hard.

"Was the price worth paying?" she kept asking herself. It was too late though. He moved his attention along her body his beard blending with the blond mound, now surprisingly moist with anticipation. Slipping both hands beneath her bottom he squeezed both her buttocks gently and her hips rose to the attention. She tensed in anticipation and expectation. He teased her at first, his tongue moving swiftly around the outside of her wet orifice, listening to her soft moans, until he chose to enter her as fully as he could.

Despite her initial revulsion he was obviously experienced in the art of arousal and foreplay, an area of sex, which she was hopelessly addicted to. She was gradually succumbing to the dexterity of his movements.

She began panting in time with the thrusting movements of his head as it moved in and out. She raised her legs in a frenzy of movement, above his head pulling hard on her knees to allow him maximum penetration. Just as she was about to peak with desire, Wheldon pulled away mercilessly and she cried out in protest at his poor timing. Wheldon had other plans, plans that he had been formulating in his head long before he had even entered the cottage, let alone the delightful Miss McDonald. She let her legs relax falling away, floppy as if the strength she'd had minutes earlier had left her all of a sudden. The blonde moist triangle between her legs was now coincident with the edge of the breakfast bar. She raised her head from the bar and looked at him, a sense of pleading in her eyes. Wheldon had already discarded his braces and was fumbling at the waist button of his pants. The button gave way, followed by the zip on his trousers. His stomach seemed to drop even further now without its support.

Estelle witnessed the spectacle and again she felt some initial revulsion. His trousers fell to the floor and he pulled desperately at what lay beneath his shirt until he found what he was looking for. His target was already known only his aim could be called into question. He moved forward toward her, his manhood surprisingly more prominent than his waistline, Estelle wasn't taking any chances clawing at the throbbing member just out of sight. She succeeded and it was his turn to moan with pleasure. She didn't wait for him to enjoy the initial experience, choosing to plunge him deep inside her. They both groaned again in unison before Wheldon placed both arms beneath her knees forcing her stockinged legs back toward her face until they rested on his shoulders. The effort gave Wheldon further penetration and he used it to full effect. Estelle groaned again wanting him to move more swiftly.

He chose not to disappoint her or himself and began to move, rhythmically timing his movements to coordinate with her erratic panting and spasmodic movements. He felt her legs tense and press tightly around his ears making his timing less predictable as he struggled to hear her mounting pleasure. Estelle gripped both edges of the breakfast bar, her head rolling from side-to-side, her passion, steadily increasing once more. Her long blonde hair lay over the surface of the bar, her breasts now bare and swaying from side-to-side with the increasing frequency of their movements. He let go of her legs allowing his hands to secure their movement. Estelle felt the rush of passion mounting inside once more hoping that her much older partner could hold on long enough to meet her needs. She glanced at his face, sweating, frowning, teeth clenched with every thrust inside her and she couldn't help but admire his staying power. She looked left, her head pressed against the cool surface of the bar, her eyes now fixed on the open report and for a brief second, she remembered why she was entertaining Tom Wheldon.

Would he renege on their understanding once he had had his way, she asked herself, unsure. She pushed at his hips slowing his stealth. At first he protested. She pushed him clear, turning as she did. She leaned across the breakfast bar her new position enabling her to see the report page more fully and she began to scan the front page quickly. Wheldon assumed she just preferred it that way pushing her dress up toward the small of her back. The sight of her raised his performance for one last effort.

He mounted her for a second time from behind and she groaned once more in appreciation. He gripped her shoulder with one hand, the other pulled at her hip. He resumed his steady, yet firm rhythm, the breakfast bar now taking the strain from their pleasure. He was determined to finish what he had started. Wild horses wouldn't stop him now. Despite Estelle's best efforts to read the report, Wheldon's feverish thrusting made it almost impossible. Their movement merely brought her own shudders of delight. It was no use, the report would have to wait. Her more frequent groans started at low pitch, picking up volume as her juices began to flow more freely. It was Estelle's turn to wince, through clenched teeth, her expression giving way to a cry of pleasure coinciding with that of Wheldon behind her. The report was no longer of interest to Estelle for these few moments. His hand slipped from her shoulder, pulling on her hair and on her hips until he had had his fill. Wheldon carried on thrusting long after Estelle had relaxed, satisfied and exhausted. She turned her attention once more to the report. She had to read the executive summary at least. Wheldon finally withdrew from her, collapsing in a heap against the wall behind him his now flaccid penis disappearing below his shirt and waistline.

She made no attempt to hide her partial nudity, choosing to reach forward she pulled the report closer. She'd made the ultimate sacrifice and now she was keen to bring their arrangement to an even swifter conclusion, despite her enjoyment. This wasn't the first time she had degraded herself trying to find her elusive dad. A deal was a deal though, even if the report proved to be less satisfying than the versatile Tom Wheldon. She was still lying face down across the breakfast bar, her wayward dress now covering her bottom and lower back. Wheldon still sat on the floor catching his breath, content to watch her antics and think about what he was doing only moments earlier.

"I'm afraid the report is a little inconclusive my dear," he finally blurted, out-of-breath, trying to scramble to his feet. He stood now pulling his trousers up and tucking in his shirt. "We have a few more leads to add to the final report before it is ready for issuing." She knew where his mind was leading and she didn't like it. "I could pop back in a week or so and we could go over the supplementary information when I'm sure we will have a final conclusion to the investigation," Wheldon said as he edged his way around the bar beside where she lay. She began to weep uncontrollably, like a little schoolgirl. Wheldon had hoped to give her the highlights from the report and string her along, perhaps even indulge himself with her further with some clever footwork. That would hinge on her not seeing the part of the report regarding her dad following Rowan's re-examination of the body found twenty-five years before at Chetley Sewage Works. As he moved beside her he realised that he was too late – the sobbing told him as much.

"You bastard, you knew my dad was dead before you came through that door," she managed in between the tears. Her fingers curled up with anger, the executive summary page torn from where it had been stapled together. "Who is Anthony Carson?" She demanded.

"Nobody!" Wheldon protested slightly alarmed at the connotations from the question. "Graves just identified him as someone around at the time your dad disappeared." The prospect of Estelle McDonald angrily confronting Carson filled him with trepidation.

"You haven't had any involvement with this report have you?" she glowered.

"I meant to tell you Estelle, about your dad, about the report, but things moved on a pace and before I knew it…well it was too late. I enjoyed it though and I know you did," he suggested, trying to justify his actions, but the leer in his voice remained in the background. Estelle hadn't felt like this for ten years at least. Used and treated like a piece of meat she lay discarded, the anger bubbling over inside her overshadowing her orgasm from moments earlier. This vulgar excuse of a man had misled her, like so many before him, like the doctor at her psychiatric hospital when she was only twelve years old. That same psychotic feeling from her past was beginning to surface again. Her eyes glazed over and suddenly she became calm almost quiescent. She stared at Wheldon and he became worried about her next move and the impact on his career.

"Come on love, it's not the end of the world. It's not as if your old man left recently and I expect this is not the first time you traded your wears to get what you wanted. Give me the report and I'll be on my way," he said dismissively now that he had had his way with her. It was time to cut his losses and if needs be, deny everything.

"You're right Tom, I'm being silly. I knew my dad was dead, I just didn't want to face up to it," she said staring directly ahead, avoiding his eyes. She pulled her dress about her shoulders as she slipped down from the breakfast bar. "Here let me staple the pages back together," she said opening the same drawer from where she had found the corkscrew minutes earlier. Wheldon turned away looking for his notebook that he dropped during those passionate moments. It would be the last thing he ever did. He never knew what hit him. The strike was clean, clinical with considerable venom and efficiency. His legs gave way first, his knees making hard contact with tiled surface. Despite the macabre scene, the satisfaction that was evident on his face from moments earlier was still there as it hit the floor with a sickening crunch. The back of his skull had been split from the base of his neck to the crown of his head. Protruding out of it at an angle with the majority of it embedded in his head, a butcher's cleaver that Estelle had retrieved from the drawer. Blood had sprayed out of the back of Wheldon's head creating a thick concentrated line along her dress from head to foot. The pressure slowly ebbed, replaced by a steady flow, which grew into a sizable puddle on the ceramic tiles around his head. Estelle pulled her bloodied wrap up tight around her, her eyes wild and strangely detached from her actions.

"Now then a quick tidy up and then I'm off to the garden centre to buy mum some roses to cheer her up," she declared, "from Carson's Nursery I think."

24

Grief and Sorrow

The sudden realisation of his father's passing hit him like an emotional sledgehammer. He never thought that his father was in any real danger. Fathers never are as far as their offspring are concerned; they're invincible. Now he was left numb apart from the gut-wrenching pain that often accompanies the loss of a relative or a close friend. He'd left his mother to mourn in peace. She wanted to be alone and he didn't blame her. It was the least he could do and this time it wasn't an excuse to distance himself from Willenbury General. He managed about a half mile from the hospital before he had to pull over, his vision too blurred, his grief too great and worst of all a sense of guilt and betrayal and the fact that he couldn't turn the clock back. He really did love his father he knew that now for sure yet it was too late to tell him and change things between them.

He lifted his head off the steering wheel pressing it hard against the headrest. The visor in front of him and the small mirror embedded within it gave away his tortured look. He hit the visor hard with his clenched fist, hoping the gesture would register some well-deserved pain and to push away the image he was now feeling ashamed of. He eventually calmed himself realising that he'd lost track of time. The little dashboard clock told him he had been parked for more than an hour by the time he regained some sort of composure. It was a little after 6:30pm and dark. The lack of street lighting along the country lane devoid of other traffic only added to his sense of emptiness. Pulling out of the lay-by, he decided he needed to return home. He was physically and emotionally exhausted and driving was not a good idea under the circumstances as he recalled from when he first arrived home. He needed to concentrate on something for those last few miles, but his mind wouldn't let him. A vision at his father's bedside at that tragic moment was fixed prominently in his mind, as was his sense of inadequacy.

"Why would anyone carry out such a vicious attack on his father?" He found himself echoing his mother's sentiments from their first meeting on his return home. Even his trained police mind couldn't rationalise an answer. Equally, he found it hard to accept that someone would lie in wait without a reason. His father had driven home directly from work. He hadn't been attacked outside some pub late at night or run into some football hooligans out to cause trouble. Robbery would have been the obvious motive, but then the gold dress watch was still in his waistcoat pocket when he was found. There were easier targets anyway with richer pickings, perhaps in the village? The family home was 1 of only 6 cottages situated in a quiet secluded cul-de-sac, hardly somewhere where you would expect a random senseless attack to take place or a regular throughput of would-be victims, even the time of day that the attack took place didn't make any sense…unless it was premeditated and done out of an immediate necessity." He found himself repeating out loud. His reasoned logic fitted the facts as they had presented themselves, despite it being implausible at first.

"What could my father have been involved in to warrant such treatment?" he said out loud. Then there were the sketches he had found in his father's study. It was at that very moment that something dawned on him, something that Rowan had said. He slammed down hard on the foot brake and the MG swerved left and then right on the loose road chippings scattering them on both verges. He stared out of the windscreen his eyes still wide and surprised, then filled with rage and anger. He knew he could have cleared up the matter by talking to his mother, but in her present state of mind he had no intention of questioning her. He resigned himself to that fact even as it passed through his mind.

"There was one other possibility," he said, almost in a trance, "I need to speak to Gary Swallow right away." With adrenalin now surging through his veins, he no longer felt fatigued and he certainly wasn't about to hand over the investigation to Tom Wheldon. Ten minutes later the MG left the narrow country lane heading west along the B531 back toward Willenbury village. He had a theory, nothing more. His destination and Swallow's office though were some distance apart, the police station in the centre of the village, whilst his destination was on the outskirts to the west several miles away. It had only taken him seconds to choose the latter with the intention of ringing Swallow from a telephone box once he arrived. The rush hour traffic was ebbing by the time he arrived, parking his car directly opposite the building he was now watching. He could see that people were still moving around inside even at this late hour from where the MG sat idling. Beyond, about 100 yards, on the same side of the road stood a red pillar-box that Graves could just make out in the darkness.

"Now then," he said to himself, "there should he a phone box somewhere close by." He slipped the gear stick into first and allowed the MG to inch forward until he drew up alongside the pillar-box. A side road appeared just beyond it and Graves indicated left, turning the corner. The MG's headlights picked out the familiar red phone box partly shrouded by a privet hedge on three sides. A few seconds later, he was inside contacting Swallow back at the station.

"Gary? It's Phil," Graves said crisply not waiting for a response and recognising the voice even as he asked the question. Swallow had heard the bad news already about Reg Graves and offered his condolences. His death was now a murder inquiry of a fellow officer and no stone would be left unturned according to Swallow in finding the culprit. Finally putting that to one side, he began grilling Graves about where he was and what the hell he was doing. He seemed a little more agitated than Graves expected given the news about his father. He had expected a more understanding tone.

"Never mind where I am for now," Graves butted in, "the day my father was attacked, the evening in fact, did he come to see you with a report?"

"Yes," came the reply down the phone, "but why, I mean how did you know?" Swallow asked, recalling that this had never been mentioned since Graves had returned. Swallow had wanted Carson and the committee keeping out of any Philip Graves witch-hunt. Memories of Swallow's first conversation with his old friend Superintendent Adam Gray had warned him what to expect from Graves's increasingly erratic behaviour, so he had been deliberately evasive about the committee's minor involvement with Reg Graves on the night he was attacked.

As far as Graves's theory was concerned his father had recognised something about the evidence that Rowan and Tranter had compiled about Benson and the Bedford Bridge incident. He'd taken the evidence – the draft report and photographs – and briefly studied it further at home, perhaps resulting in the sketches back at his study. Later that same evening armed with whatever evidence he thought he had, he left home, probably putting dinner off until later and drove across the village to see DCI Swallow about his findings. His mother could confirm his supposition about dinner later, but for now, Swallow's confirmation of his theory would have to do.

"It's not important for now," Graves retorted. "Who was with you at the time?" There was a slight pause on the other end of the line.

"Well, I was on the steps of County Hall, the meeting of the Police Public Accounts Committee had just finished. I'd say just about the whole committee were within earshot when your father turned up. I had to calm him down Phil and put him off until the following morning. It just wasn't the time or place. The committee had just bent my ear on last quarter year's expenditure," Swallow continued, before Graves interrupted him impatiently.

"How many in the committee?"

"Six," came the reply.

"And Carson was a member and present I take it?" Graves pressed.

"Why yes, in fact, he chaired the meeting," Swallow replied, becoming more and more perplexed about Graves's line of questioning, "oh and I need to talk to you about Anthony Carson myself," he added forcefully.

"So he will have overheard your conversation with my father?" Graves asked feverishly ignoring Swallow's last point.

"Err, yes as a matter of fact. That is why I had to stop him, it didn't look good having him rambling on about something that didn't make sense in front of committee members after such an acrimonious meeting," Swallow explained.

"And we wouldn't want that now would we?" Graves said to himself, annoyance growing by the minute to match his impatience. "Can you remember exactly what my father said – and I do mean exactly?" Graves emphasised. There was a sigh while Swallow gathered his thoughts, no doubt wondering why this was so important all of a sudden. He had important news of his own if he could get a word in.

"From memory, he pulled up at the foot of the Town Hall steps, leaving his car parked at an odd angle. He left the door open and the engine running and he raced up the steps toward us," Swallow recollected.

"Yes, yes, but what did he say?" Graves groaned allowing his impatience to become obvious now.

"He said, 'the body in the bridge…the tattoo…I know who it is," Swallow explained. "And then as if to undermine his own credibility, he said 'that it was impossible'. He looked visibly confused and bewildered. It was hardly the right message to be sending out in front of the committee, so I put him off until the morning to let him sleep on it. I dismissed the comment in my own mind and then the attack happened and well, I suppose I forgot all about it after Reg was admitted into hospital, it didn't seem important anymore."

"Fine, that's all I wanted to hear," Graves replied.

"Phil! Phil!" Swallow shouted down the phone, the second time pulling Graves out of his thoughts. "Whatever you're up to take care. We had telephone call from old Mrs McDonald three quarters of an hour ago. We dealt with the matter here under the circumstances. Her daughter is missing. She never arrived to pick her mum up tonight. She returned home alone only to find the cottage in some disarray. Things had been moved and some bits and pieces were missing, a sheepskin rug. Morgan visited Mrs McDonald at home after we said that we would have a look around initially to calm her nerves. Morgan spotted Tom Wheldon's Cortina parked a short distance back up the lane from the house. Once inside the old lady also gave him a notebook that she had assumed you had left behind when you and Morgan visited the cottage previously. It was Tom Wheldon's notebook though. In the kitchen Morgan found a copy of your draft report. There was a page torn out, the executive summary. Morgan gave me an idea what it said and I've since seen the original report and missing page here at the station, so the report at Little Crandon must have been a photocopy. It described Anthony Carson's possible involvement. What the hell has Carson got to do with all this Phil?" Swallow shouted down the phone. Graves thought back to when he and Morgan had penned the report. He turned his head and looked at the building opposite.

"I can't say just now Gary. I'm at Carson's nursery now, to have a chat with him," Graves replied. Swallow gave a dissatisfied moan down the other end of the telephone.

"I've got to go Gary," Graves protested.

"Wait, there's more. Morgan stayed behind at Little Crandon and we sent another two uniformed officers to help search the house with Mrs McDonald's permission. Estelle McDonald's bedroom is a shrine to her father. All the stuff old Mrs McDonald thought she had thrown out years ago was in her bedroom. Photos, letters, newspaper articles about his involvement with the council, Navy, everything," Swallow said. "Her mum didn't know because she has not been upstairs for five years due to her disability. The old lady said her sheepskin rug had disappeared from the dining room floor as I said earlier and there were scuffmarks on the kitchen tiles leading up to the back door. They decided to broaden their search outside. Thirty minutes later they fished Wheldon's body out of the septic tank at the bottom of the garden. He had a butcher's cleaver attached to the back of his head. There was mud and flattened grass across the back lawn between the back door and the tank at the bottom of the garden. Morgan found the bloodstained rug inside the tank with Wheldon. He was still partially wrapped inside it. It looks as if the rug was used to drag Wheldon's body to the tank and then he was pushed inside it." There was a pause that seemed to last an age before Swallow continued. "The old lady thinks her daughter has finally cracked. If she is correct Anthony Carson could be in real danger. I want you to stay there until I can get some uniform over there to provide backup." Graves acknowledged the request before replacing the receiver. Minutes later he was across the lane approaching the front door just as the place was closing for the day.

25

The Nursery

"I'm sorry sir, we are just closing," the teenage girl said through the half-glass door. It was 7pm and despite the later opening hours in the lead-up to Christmas that extra time had elapsed as well. Graves offered his warrant card up against the glass and the young girl squinted to read the small print through the pretend snow that had been sprayed around the edge of the glass. The prospect of being questioned by a policeman seemed to unnerve her and she backed off slightly.

"Not to worry," Graves said reassuringly, "I only want to speak to your boss," he said hiding his true emotions so as not to frighten the girl. Ideally, he wanted her out of there as soon as possible. He had enough to worry about just at the moment. She looked about her, her eyes catching sight of the large display board behind her. The manager at the top of the family tree was a Mr Daly.

"I'm afraid Mr Daly took the day off sir," she said with some relief in her voice, even though the door was locked.

"Actually, I need to see Mr Carson, the owner," Graves clarified. The name Carson made her even more jumpy, obviously someone she wasn't used to dealing with in person. She unlocked the door and let Graves in out of the cold night air.

"I'll try his extension sir, but I think he has someone with him at present – a lady," she replied lifting the receiver. Graves felt a certain amount of anxiety creeping over him, fearing that the lady in question could be Estelle McDonald. She tapped four digits into the phone and held her breath. She was no doubt willing her employer to be on his way home, until there was a break in the regular ringing tone of the line.

"Yes, what is it?" the voice came sternly down the line.

"I'm sorry to disturb you sir. I have a gentleman at the store entrance to see you. He's a policeman." She spoke keeping her eyes on Graves, his warrant card now in her hand. There was an inaudible response back as far as Graves was concerned. "Yes sir, the name is Inspector Graves from New Scotland Yard," she continued. Shortly after the line fell silent and she replaced the receiver. "Mr Carson said he will see you shortly sir. Can you see the door at the far end of the room?" she asked pointing at the door in question. Graves nodded. "He's working in the Propagating Room. He asked me to direct you there." Whilst Graves made his way toward the back of the room, the young assistant beat a hasty retreat letting herself out through the front door. She was out of sight before Graves had meandered his way between shelves of plant foods and herbicides. He tapped on the door and stepped inside the dimly lit room. He could just make out the hunched figure of someone with a table lamp focused on something of interest on a workbench at the far end of the room. The figure made no attempt to move, just offering a welcome hand gesture to step forward.

"Inspector Graves I presume?" the man's voice called out inquiringly as Graves made his way forward. With that the figure turned revealing a man in his early 40s garbed in a long laboratory style coat and rubber gloves.

"Forgive the interruption sir, I was wondering whether I might have a word with you about a case I'm working on? Your input may help with my inquiries." Graves asked. Carson had moved to the side, away from his workbench revealing the object of his interest.

"Winter Pansies I think?" Graves said without hesitation.

"Ah, a fellow horticulturalist," Carson acknowledged. Graves was anything but in reality. He'd seized an opportunity to break the ice on a subject that Carson was obviously interested in. What little he knew about plants he had learned as a boy with his father and that was precious little, given his short attention span as a youth.

"Not exactly sir, my father is or rather was the expert, I just recognised the cuttings," he said, his mood changing as the thought about his father's passing hit him again. Carson didn't seem to notice though. "He had rows of the same plant in his greenhouse at this time of year when I use to help him as a youngster," Graves continued regaining his train of thought. Carson leaned back against the bench smiling pleasantly as he pulled off his gloves.

"Me involved with the police and New Scotland Yard at that," he said, holding out a welcoming hand as he walked the few yards towards Graves. They shook briefly. "Whatever next?" he said casually.

"Oh the New Scotland Yard reference is a long story sir, suffice to say I'm working with the local CID on this inquiry, DCI Gary Swallow," Graves commented.

"Gary you say?" Carson said arms now folded, "He's a good man, well thought of by members of the Police Public Accounts Committee and the local community alike." Graves felt a gnawing at the pit of his stomach. Could he be wrong about Carson and was he in danger? Where the hell was Estelle McDonald? Brightwell's handwriting analysis of the farewell letters suggested someone dissimilar to Carson's characteristics, but the assessment was based on a letter written twenty-five years ago. "Now tell me Inspector, how can I help you with your inquiries – I believe that is the official terminology?" Carson said appearing to try and make light of their conversation.

"Well sir if you could cast your mind back twenty-five years," Graves began. Carson merely raised his eyebrows without uttering a word. "Your name was given to me by Roger Gately. He told me that you were involved in the construction of Willenbury Bypass around 1960, in particular, Bedford Bridge." Carson had begun to remove his coat as Graves was speaking and he paused briefly with one arm still inside the sleeve, before resuming. Throwing the soiled coat and gloves into a green bin he turned to face Graves.

"Shall we go into my office Inspector, it's much more convivial and I have some percolated coffee on the boil." Both men walked out through a nearby door and along a short corridor before turning left into a comfortably furnished office. The temporary nature of the storage areas, propagating rooms and greenhouses had been replaced by teak panelled walls and a bookcase full of all manner of gardening and horticultural text books. On the opposite wall a roaring log fire made use of what off-cuts were available from thinning out of the woods that populated the surrounding grounds. A rather nice mahogany writing desk and leather bound Queen Anne chair gave it all the look of an office of personal choice. In the corner of the room, beside the desk a coffee percolator gurgled ready and waiting.

"Coffee Inspector?" Carson said, reinforcing his earlier offer. Graves accepted courteously. Carson sat behind his desk pushing the cup toward Graves. "Willenbury Bypass you say?" Carson clarified. Graves nodded again. "Yes I seem to recall Roger and I did a brief spell of, shall we say, work experience as a couple of teenagers back then."

"Sir, you may have heard of the body discovered at the bridge nearly a week ago now?" Graves asked.

"Oh yes the body in the bridge. I heard something through my involvement with police matters. It must have been a gruesome discovery?" Carson replied, his cup masking his face as he spoke through the steam from his coffee.

"It was sir. I've invested some time over the last week or so looking into the matter. I won't go into the details sir, it wouldn't be appropriate whilst the investigation is ongoing. What I will say is that we came to the conclusion fairly early that the body must have been put there during the construction of the bridge. It would be impossible to have put it there any other way based on its condition," Graves explained.

"And due to my involvement at the time you were wondering whether I put the body in there," Carson said, his comment deliberately provocative and also a little tongue-in-cheek.

If only you knew, Graves said to himself. "No sir, you are one of the few people that were around at the time and still are today along with Roger Gately. The scheme records were lost when the council relocated to premises at County Hall in 1974 after a fire when most of them were destroyed. The main contractor has long-since gone into liquidation and a number of key individuals have either died, reside in rest homes or are untraceable. We simply don't have sufficient background knowledge of what happened all those years ago in any detail sir and certainly not about the victim," Graves said explaining his predicament.

Carson looked at his guest quietly. "I see your plight Inspector, but I'm not sure how much I can help you. You see apart from knowing Roger, I was a bit of a loner back then. I kept myself to myself and got on with my work. It was hardly intellectually challenging, but I needed the money to get me through college," Carson replied. He stood reaching toward an umbrella stand in the corner and pulled out a golf putter. The ball that went with it sat inside a crystal ashtray on his desk and he began aiming the ball into a makeshift hole made from an old plant pot. "Do you play Inspector? I find it terribly relaxing. It's my second passion after plants," he remarked sinking the ball with one shot. Graves shook his head. "You should you know. I get plenty of fresh air, it relieves stress and I get a good night's sleep. There's nothing like it. I even get to see the local flora and fauna as well around an 18-hole course."

Graves smiled again patiently. "You don't recall anything suspicious at the time then sir?" Graves asked. "Roger seemed to think that quality procedures for pouring new concrete were strict, requiring a last minute inspection of the ground before the concrete was poured. He suggested that you might have done the inspection yourself." He was moving into deeper waters now and aware that Carson was now wielding a golfing putter too close to him for comfort.

"I was hardly experienced enough back then to carry out such inspections and the responsibility that went with it, Inspector," Carson said, now reaching into the right-hand desk drawer. "As I said, I can't help you really. It was all a long time ago." He smiled, the sort of smile that told Graves he had outstayed his welcome.

In The Mood

"Do you smoke Inspector? " Carson asked as he rummaged in the top drawer of his desk.

"I used to, but I gave it up last year," Graves replied.

"Yes I don't blame you, it's a disgusting habit and one I am in danger of giving up on myself if I don't find my limited supply here somewhere. Ah," Carson said triumphantly. Graves was already standing and making his way to the door.

"Well I'm sorry to have disturbed you Mr Carson, I'll let myself out the front entrance," he said, when a familiar whining melody began to play, its origin, Carson's desk drawer. The realisation of what it was and the implication that it now presented seemed to hit both men at the same time. Graves turned instinctively, but Carson was already whirling the golf putter around his hand like a bandleader's baton menacingly.

26

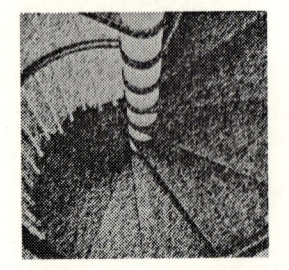

The Return to Harrington Hall

"Oh dear," Carson said, "how terribly careless of me." His tone was almost mocking in its delivery and yet he truly was angry at his own carelessness. "You seem to recognise the box and its terrible tune, but perhaps not the significance, although in fairness, you should," Carson said looking directly at him. Graves's eyes moved from Carson to the familiar silver box now sat on the desk beside where Carson stood. Carson slammed the lid of the box closed again barely disguising his anger.

"Benson's music box I take it?" Graves queried. Carson said nothing. "Put the putter down and let's talk about this," Graves said calmly. Carson didn't react. "You are waving that golf club at me, aren't you?" Graves asked. Carson eyed the putter and looked back at Graves.

"I'm afraid I can't do that Philip. I've worked hard to get where I am. I always knew that there might be a chance I'd be found out at some point in the future, albeit not by my own stupidity," Carson added, a certain irony evident in his voice, "so I have a contingency plan in place, which unfortunately I must now enact." The club, with its putter head, was now pointed at Graves to endorse the fact that he had no intentions of being interrogated any further. It was only then that Graves saw the remnants of a bloodstain smeared across the surface of the club head and it's dish-shaped profile that he made the connection with his father. He lunged forward so that it pressed hard against his chest.

"Easy now Philip, easy," Carson said standing firm. "Perhaps I owe you a little explanation before I go, seeing as you have evidently put the pieces of the puzzle together," Carson said. "Shall I set the scene first?" With that he pushed Graves back until he collided with chair he'd been sitting on, sending him sprawling. The golf club was then brought round in one swift movement taking the head off the desk lamp, the only form of illumination in the room except for that of the fire. The room was plunged into partial darkness. "Shall we step outside?" Carson suggested from out of the darkness. With that a rectangle of moonlight pushed its way through a doorway at the back of the room, one that Graves hadn't noticed upon entering the room. As he got to his feet, the fleeting figure of Carson disappeared through it into the night. Graves bounded toward the doorway, helping himself to one of the remaining golf clubs along the way. He stood there for a few moments peering outside allowing his eyes to focus beyond the shadows created by rows and rows of winter flowing plants and shrubs. He wielded the 9-iron club in front of him for protection.

"Come along Philip, you're keen to know what this is all about. Follow me and I'll enlighten you," Carson said in the foreground. Cloud cover had blotted out the moonlight, which had illuminated the nursery grounds initially. Now there was just a soft twilight glow. The noise from the High Street beyond was quiet now due to the late hour, leaving just Graves and Carson alone. "How did you find me so quickly Philip after the accident?" The voice seemed to echo from several hundred yards away now as if Carson had retreated further away. Graves guessed from the way Carson's voice was carrying that it came from the old ruined building beyond the immediate grounds of the nursery, the silhouette of which stood prominently as a backdrop against the soft pastel blue night sky.

"I've always known that you were a good detective Philip, I've never appreciated just how good. When I heard that you were investigating Benson's background part of me wanted you to hit a dead end. The other part of me wanted you to find out the truth and well, here we are. I never thought that you would make the connection with your father and piece it all together though," Carson continued, making no attempt to change his position. Graves ran forward weaving in between rows of small Christmas trees being grown for the festive season, the smell of pine needles filling the air as he disturbed several, before slamming heavily against the remnants of a brick wall, part of what was left of the old building's partially demolished gable-end. He paused breathing heavily, taking stock of his new vantage point. Behind him he could make out the odd lit room from within the nursery.

"Why attack my father?" Graves shouted angrily. "What the hell has he got to do with anything?"

"Ah, so there are still some missing pieces of the puzzle after all Philip? Carson repeated from inside the darkened shell of the derelict building.

"It had to be you, but I still don't know why, although I'm confident if I dig deep enough into your past I'll find a motive," Graves called out, peeping over the wall into the blackened building. The lack of immediate response made him hesitant though. "As to what convinced me you were involved, I had some help from Roger Gately, but what really sealed it for me was the music-come- cigarette box. There was only one not accounted for and that would have been the one owned by Benson. It's a nasty habit and one which you will probably live to regret."

"Yes that was sloppy of me," Carson said eventually in a reflective tone. "Why the hell I kept it I'll never know," His voice gave the impression that he had retreated even farther into the old building. "Are you sure that you want to dig deeper into my past Philip? You might not like what you find."

"Let me be the judge of that," Graves replied just as he scrambled over the three feet high wall into the nearest room loosing his footing as he did. He fell, rolling over bricks and rubble becoming disorientated. Clouds parted once more overhead and shafts of light shone down through the now vacant roof seemingly trying to search for him like a spotlight on a stage performer. He suddenly felt vulnerable and stumbled to his feet. Lurching forward he pinned himself against one of the remaining internal walls back into the shadows. Cloud cover intervened once more seconds later and the room fell into darkness again. He allowed his eyes to become accustomed to the darkness again and he became aware that he was in a kitchen area. The sinks and some of the worktops were still intact, despite the general condition of the room. A single doorway led out into a darkened corridor where no amount of moonlight could penetrate, using his pen-torch to guide his way, he inched his way along the wall gradually, as if he was trying rotten floorboards. He knew he was on the ground floor, but his mind was telling him to be cautious: these old buildings often had cellars.

"Why shouldn't I dig into your past? Scared I'll find out something more incriminating about you?" Graves called out, keeping the conversation going. He slipped out of the old kitchen and into a corridor. Now it really was dark, despite the little torch. Which way? He wondered, and what the hell lay in store for him?

"I have no objections to you delving into my past Philip. On the contrary, now that you're here, I insist. Shall we discuss it now while we play cat and mouse?" Carson said as if partly mocking the suggestion. Carson's timely reply prompted Graves to make a choice and he turned right, feeling his way along the walls of the corridor.

"I'd rather do it over a nice cup of tea in a dry, lit interview room back at the station," Graves said making further progress toward where he thought the voice originated from, although he soon found that the acoustics in the old building were misdirecting him at times.

"Can't do that old boy," Carson replied, "you see I don't intend to give myself up to you or anyone else. I would like to explain about Sergeant Graves though. I could have been long gone by now, but I need you to understand why and…forgive me." Graves froze, the anger from earlier in the evening returning. He clenched his fists wishing he could have just five minutes with Carson before a formal caution.

"You murdered him and for that reason alone I will put you away personally you bastard," Graves called out. "Come out into the open where I can see you, you coward." There was another uneasy silence.

"He died from his injuries?" Carson said eventually. His voice was low, a sense of regret in its tone.

"Only an hour ago," Graves barked angrily. "Don't try and make me think that you care."

"The one regret I have Philip is having to do that…I had no choice. I am truly sorry," Carson replied in an equally repentant voice.

"I don't need your apology or sympathy, I just want to know why and then I want you in custody." Graves called out into the darkness.

"OK, the why I can manage, but you won't like it," Carson remarked forcibly.

"As I said before, let me be the judge of that," Graves retorted.

"OK but before I do, a little light perhaps!" Carson suggested. There was a whining noise, hard to place at first, the sound of an engine firing into life. There was a flash of light briefly for a second and then darkness again as the engine made a noise like it was labouring before it died away completely. In that brief second he got an insight into the environment around him. It was instantaneous, but he was sure he was in a corridor leading to a large foyer area, the sort you walk into when entering a grand stately home. He had noticed the remnants of a winding staircase, the upper floors and roof gone showing the night sky, just like the kitchen area previously. The stairs came to an abrupt halt as if in midair. He staggered forward in the darkness blindly feeling his way along the walls of the corridor trying to visualise what he had seen during those brief few seconds. He tripped, stumbling face first desperately grabbing out in the darkness to cushion his fall. His hand seemed to slide along the surface of a door of some kind with a texture of polished wood. He was thankful to hold on to what must have been a handle of some sort just as he over balanced. Pulling himself upright, the door opened outwards with his efforts and there was a dull thud as something hit the floor just in front of him

He tried to assimilate these images in his mind to try and decide his next move until suddenly it became unnecessary. The engine – Graves guessed it to be a generator now – roared back into life and temporary floodlighting lit up the interior of the building like the lights at a football stadium. He found himself against a wood panelled wall at the end of a long corridor just as it opened up into a central foyer. The front door was now a mass of wood boarding nailed in place, probably to deter squatters and vandals at one time in the past from gaining entry, although he had found it easy to gain access himself. Behind him, the corridor became dark again outside the reach of the lighting. In the far corner of the foyer, high voltage light bulbs lit up the immediate area whilst casting shadows against objects set farther back toward the edge of the room and its arterial corridors. It was a bare shell, at least part of one the rest long-since demolished. It had no doubt been a grand house in its day. His attention shifted back to what lay before him. The door he had frantically caught hold of in the darkness was that of an old fashioned wardrobe. The contents had spilled out on to the floor before him and it was this that now engrossed him. He knelt down to where the still body of Estelle McDonald lay, checking for a pulse, but there wasn't one. She lay face upwards, her eyes lifeless and fixed on the night sky through the opened roof building. A single bloody puncture wound to the abdomen marked what Graves assumed had been the fatal injury.

"You see the tiled floor Philip, just in front of you?" Carson called out, as if ignoring Graves's grisly find. "If you would be so kind as to sweep the dirt and rubbish at the centre of the foyer to one side. The brush is leaning on the balustrade." Graves looked about him, but he still couldn't pinpoint where the voice was coming from. He moved across gingerly to the centre of the foyer, deciding to humour Carson, standing as requested; the sudden openness making him feel vulnerable again.

"Enough of these games, you may as well give yourself up," Graves demanded, spotting the brush. There was no answer. He decided to play along. Placing the putter down close by, he picked up the brush and used it to clear most of the rubbish and rubble that had accumulated over the years in one stroke, then he swept more slowly to clear away the fine dust. His first few strokes revealed the word 'TON' spelt out in mosaic tiles. For the first time since entering the derelict building his mind was drawn to something other than the apprehension of Anthony Carson.

"Keep sweeping," Carson called out from his hiding place. Graves swept more vigorously, humouring the potential madman. The word grew longer to read 'HARRINGTON'. After a few more strokes, the full name of the building came into view. 'HARRINGTON HALL'. He suddenly realised just where Carson had brought him, whether by accident or design remained unclear. "Back to the scene of the crime Philip. Now for that explanation," Carson said.

"What crime? The fire? Those poor bastards that Benson and the others burned to death?" he shouted.

"Once upon a time..." Carson began, ignoring him.

"You can't be serious?" Graves said to himself.

"...there was a man and a woman who were very much in love. It was during the war, early 1940s," Carson began. Graves was half listening whilst still looking about him for Carson's whereabouts. "They both came from the South of England. As a married couple, they moved around the country to meet his various postings as an RAF pilot. In 1943, Squadron Leader John Laine was posted to RAF Bellingham, it's about half way from here to London. Are you still with me Philip because this is very important?" Carson called out like a schoolteacher. Graves had moved around the foyer systematically, trying every conceivable hiding place that he could find. Despite his best efforts, Carson's voice gave Graves the impression that it was all around him.

"You won't find me yet Philip until I let you, so you might as well sit down and listen." Carson remarked confidently. Wherever he was hiding he could evidently see Graves clearly.

"On the evening of June 23rd 1943 the allied forces sanctioned a bombing raid over Hamburg. John Laine was one of the few senior pilots available. He was ordered to lead the attack from RAF Bellingham. Betty Laine, his wife, was heavily pregnant at the time with their first child or so they thought. Anyhow," he continued deciding not to elaborate further, "Squadron Leader Laine's plane and his crew went down in the English Channel on the return trip, just like Glen Miller did at the time and another reason why I don't like his music." Graves ignored the cryptic comment.

"John Laine's commanding officer, Wing Commander Frank Carter, promised John that if anything happened to him that he would break the news personally to his wife, which he duly did just as Mrs Laine telephoned the airbase for news about her husband's return. The shock proved too much for Mrs Laine and she collapsed in the phone box. Just as an aside, the telephone box opposite the nursery entrance quite by chance," Carson added. Graves recalled his conversation with Gary Swallow in that very call box not twenty minutes earlier.

"Ironically, Carter must have heard her cry out on the other end of the telephone and dashed out of the airbase to her aid. I've never discovered satisfactorily what happened next, just snippets from old newspaper cuttings and library archive. I suspect that the weather was bad that night, torrential rain perhaps, either way he never arrived to help her. There was a real panic at the time because Carter was involved in a top secret operation and like John Laine he was forbidden to leave the airbase while the air strike was taking place.

All sorts of theories were flying around at the time suggesting that he had defected or he was a spy, that he was responsible for the raid over Hamburg going horribly wrong and then months later they fished his car out of Lake Laffey about thirty miles from here. There were no trains running that night so he'd apparently taken the car trying to travel up at speed, apparently losing control on a bend. There was no local damage near the road and no evidence that he or any car had been there. The car sank like a stone. A local fishing boat snagged their nets on the car months later. Carter was still sat at the wheel, poor bastard, and you wonder why people like Benson get to live as long as they do? There is no justice in the world," he growled.

"How do you know all this? What has it got to do with my father's death, and Benson for that matter?" Graves shouted.

"I've had plenty of time to research the background into my true past." Carson replied. "As to why it is important and its connection with Sergeant Graves, you will have to be more patient. I've waited twenty-five years to get this off my chest. Now, where was I? Ah yes, I'm afraid Mrs Laine never recovered. Having given birth not to one child, but twins, she died soon after in a freak accident.

The twin boys were cared for at the hospital until the war ended and then they were relocated here, at Harrington Hall orphanage." Graves remembered his discussion with Charles Grimshaw about Harrington Orphanage, Benson and the others. His attention shifted toward what Carson was saying rather than finding out where he was hiding.

"This just happens to be where Benson and the others were employed between 1943 and 1953," Carson said, "but of course you already know that." Graves scowled a confused look. "Getting back to my story, the two little boys were happy in this huge adventure park with lots of other children the same age to play with until they were ten years old. That is when the sexual abuse started for some of the boys." Graves straightened, standing from where he had been sitting on the foot of the stairs. "I see that I have your full attention now – good." Carson continued. "The four men carrying out the abuse were selective – the younger the boys, the better. Easily intimidated and vulnerable boys were desirable." Graves knew instinctively who the four men were. "One of the quartet had a boyfriend who use to work at the local hospital mortuary at the time. He used to come and join them when Benson allowed it."

"Franco Russo?" Graves found himself saying.

"They use to threaten the boys with all kinds of unspeakable horrors and torture, if they did not give in to their demands. There routine was to choose whom they wanted on a given night then they would drug the cocoa of the boys in the same dormitory so that they would sleep throughout. The victim would know who had been selected. You see the tune told them that they had to come. The tune was always the same one, from those same silver-looking music boxes like the one that I clumsily kept hold of." Graves instinctively touched the bulky object in his overcoat pocket that he had picked up earlier as they both fled Carson's nursery.

"All the other staff were useless. I learned later that there was a scam at the time to, shall we say, misappropriate Government grants by housing more children on paper than there actually were in the orphanage. There was one person who befriended the children, a woman, a very nice lady from memory. She was the cook at the orphanage. She use to give extra food to the children when the other staff weren't looking. She found out about all the criminal activity and she told her fiancé at the time, who happened to be a young police constable. Somehow Benson had become aware that a raid had been arranged for the day of the Queen's Coronation." Graves was losing his patience now, despite how interesting the story was, and the way that it tallied with Charlie Grimshaw's account.

"So you are one of the twins that were abused by these men. You waited, oh, seven years after the fire to get your revenge and for some reason you were very particular about how you exacted that revenge," Graves pointed out in an attempt to bring matters to a head.

"Very perceptive of you Philip, but let's not run before we can walk now. Only one of the twins was submissive and easily intimidated back then and that just happened to be me," Carson replied from his hiding place. "Two weeks prior to the date of the raid, they seemed to leave all the kids alone. Then on the evening of the coronation, I heard the music box playing, coming up from the cellar

In The Mood

below. You see it was my turn again. I remember looking around the dormitory to see if anyone else was awake, even my twin brother, but mine was the only cocoa that wasn't drugged. This time I stayed and cowered under the bed sheets. After ten minutes or so I heard heavy footsteps coming up the stairs, familiar footsteps that I dread. The dormitory door opened so hard that it rebounded off the wall. I felt the sheets being literally ripped from me and I sensed Benson leering over me. He smelled of booze, sweat and he was almost drooling at the sight of me. He grabbed me around the neck and dragged me out kicking and screaming. No one else stirred – or so I thought at the time. If they had they would have suffered a similar fate," Carson paused giving the impression that he was reliving a tortured memory.

"He dragged me downstairs into the cellar rooms where the others were waiting. Oh, if you are wondering, the so-called staff were still celebrating the coronation at this stage drinking and playing loud music in the grounds outside so no one heard my screams. Ironically, Benson had been asked to keep an eye on the children's dormitory whilst the other staff enjoyed themselves. That was like putting a fox in charge of a henhouse. I'm not sure if the staff knew what was going on or just didn't care. I was pulled inside the cellar kitchen and told to lie face down on a large table. I knew the routine all right. This time I said no to myself, I simply couldn't do that again," Carson said defiantly in the darkness. Graves had mixed emotions at this point. If what Carson was describing really happened, he truly felt sorry for him, although it was no excuse to take the law into his own hands.

"Tell me Philip, ever had one up the rectum and one down the back of your throat at the same time?" Carson said graphically, the memory as painful now as no doubt it was physically and mentally to a boy of ten. Carson didn't wait for a response. "I wouldn't submit to what they had in mind. I had to be submissive you see or I was of no use to them, so they pushed me into a coal storage bunker adjacent to the room and closed the door shut until I changed my attitude. God it was dark and horrible. I'd been punished in there many times before you see. They knew I was terrified of the dark. I use to sleep in the end bed nearest the dormitory door to allow some of the moonlight to shine through. This was something else though. This was pitch black and what was worse, the bunker was also a storage place for cereal crops, which the orphanage grew as their own produce during the war." Graves thought about PC Rogers's briefing on the Chetley Sidings case and he winced inwardly. "The bunker was never cleared out properly and now there were rats – big bastards with incisors like razor tooth tigers. This time it was much worse, more horrific than you could imagine. Those images have been and always will be engrained in my mind Philip," His voice became monotone talking as if he was under hypnosis and then he seemed to snap out of it.

"There was an odour, an odour like no other. In later years I would know it as the smell of death. Once my eyes became accustomed to the very limited light I could make out the large mobile shapes scurrying around preoccupied with what appeared to be the origin of that foul smell. As a child I didn't make any sense of Benson's comment at

In The Mood

the time he threw me in that bunker. Something along the lines of, 'Do you want to join our guests? The rats could have you for dessert.' I remember his cruel laugh as he shone the torchlight inside at the rats and…four rotting corpses. The rats were ripping pieces of flesh from the bodies and I saw one scurrying off toward me with a hand in its mouth, just as Benson slammed the door closed. Anything was better than that – even what they had in mind for me. Do you recall the boyfriend I mentioned earlier? His name was Franco Russo," Carson said, relentlessly unfolding a tale that would be laughable if it weren't for the thread of logic running through it. Graves just stood and listened without a comment, strangely transfixed now by the account.

"Well he was a mortuary attendant at Willenbury General at the time and he supplied the cadavers that replaced Woollsey, Benson, Turnberry and Grundy. He figured that the planned cremation for the bodies would technically only have been delayed, given that they were burning down the place anyway. They dropped the bodies down the coal chute at the rear of the house in the early hours of the morning a week or so before the coronation. The whole thing was planned with the intention of already dead bodies taking their places, burnt beyond all recognition. You see with their service record in the Navy they were as good as convicted of abuse already and rightly so. They expected a lengthy prison sentence. Unfortunately, the fire that they had planned was started prematurely. Somebody attempted to rescue me just as they tied me to the table. Someone was banging on the door, outside in the corridor. The voice demanded that they let his brother go.

"The other twin?" Graves said.

"Yes Philip, the other twin who was too scared to help me earlier. He'd finally plucked up enough courage to try and save his brother. At first they all ignored the noise, then they began to panic, worried that other staff would return and hear, so Franco decided to investigate. They were all a bit pissed at the time, but not too pissed to screw me one after the other though," Carson paused, trying to compose himself.

"When Franco opened the door I remember hearing a scuffle in the corridor and then we all caught sight of the human torch as he staggered wildly, screaming, until he collapsed in the corridor. Franco's boyfriend, Woollsey, rushed to help him, to put the fire out, but he was already dead." Carson finished. A silence followed that could have lasted seconds or minutes. Graves suddenly felt uneasy about Carson's version of events.

"The old building never recovered after the fire. It was unsafe and suffering anyway from dry rot, so they closed it. All the children were relocated, scattered around the country." Graves's eyes moved about the foyer not really focusing on anything at all until they rested on the form of Estelle McDonald.

"She was as nutty as a fruit cake Philip if you are wondering," Carson remarked. Again he seemed to have an awareness of what Graves was doing and yet he was still hidden from view. "It was partly your fault with that report of yours, but mainly that other policeman. What was his name? Ah yes, Wheldon. Whatever happened, she came at me with a bread knife from out of nowhere demanding to know the truth about her beloved dad.

In The Mood

Anyway, she asked for the truth, so I gave it to her – the unadulterated version. She knew I was telling the truth as you do now. My account tallied with times and dates that she had become familiar with over the years." Graves recalled Estelle's involvement with her aunt Jessica's amateur sleuthing. "It was something in her eyes a crazed look when I finished speaking that struck me first. If I hadn't moved so swiftly an hour or so ago it would have been that bread knife across my throat. Fortunately she missed me, her momentum carried her forward, along with a little push in the back from me. She fell forward impaling herself on those iron railings that you must have passed outside on your way in here. Even then she was trying to reach me to throttle me with her outstretched hands. I stood just out of reach until the life drained out of her, literally, and then I dragged her in here and hid her in that old wardrobe for disposal later when it would be dark, then you arrived rather unexpectedly," he said almost indignantly.

As Carson finished speaking Graves pulled back a large piece of threadbare tapestry from the wall where it was still hanging, behind the partly demolished staircase revealing a doorway. As he expected, the door itself had long-since gone, burned away. Unlike other doorways he had been through though, this one had no cobwebs. The entrance to what lay inside had been used recently. He paused momentarily, flashbacks of his nightmare in his mind similar to the ones he had on his way back to Willenbury only this time they were happening inside the building he was standing in.

"I see that you found the door Philip," Carson called out.

Graves ignored the banter, choosing to drag one of the powerful floodlights across the foyer to the doorway. He propped the tattered cloth to one side pinning it with the lamp whilst angling the lantern through the doorway. Inside was a cast iron spiral staircase, which descended down as far as the light would permit his eyes to see before disappearing into the darkness once more. He paused again wondering about the wisdom of what he was contemplating and then he stepped down on to the first step. A vision of his nightmare came forward in his mind again, as the central column to the stairs gave a little and only the circular stone walls around it prevented it from falling over. The sound of cast iron against stone sent an echo down into the darkness below.

"Easy now Philip, easy. I don't want you falling," Carson's voice said out of the darkness below. "I haven't finished my story yet. I had intended to have this staircase ripped out and the cellar rooms filled in as part of my new expansion programme for the nursery," he continued indulging in his pet project. The stairs were badly affected by a fire from what Graves could see, probably the fire of 1953. Graves allowed Carson to ramble on, steadying himself he gingerly stepped slowly down the staircase, one-by-one, a hand on the central column and the other hand on the wall. By the time he dropped ten feet or so the light from behind him was disappearing fast. Reaching inside his jacket pocket, he retrieved his faithful pen-torch and shone it ahead of him.

The little beam of light partly picked out the first few yards along corridor, just as he stepped off the staircase. The corridor looked worryingly familiar. Darkened rectangular openings appeared at regular intervals as he moved forward along its length inch-by-inch. The walls were scorched with thick black soot and the smell of charcoal filled the air as his footsteps disturbed charred timber debris underfoot. The air was dank and stale typical of an environment below ground. Every now and then he stopped at one of the doorways and shone the torch inside. Each room was the same, just a mass of burnt objects vaguely resembling what was once furniture of some description. Ahead, he guessed about 100 yards, the silhouette of a person moved in front of the opening behind it. Graves shone the torch ahead, but the beam wasn't strong enough to pinpoint the form with any detail. Nevertheless, Graves couldn't help himself.

"Stand still!" he shouted, wondering if Carson would listen now that he had him cornered. In any event Carson obliged as if goading Graves to come nearer. Graves took a few steps and then brilliant white light illuminated everything. Flashes of his nightmare again invaded his mind more frequently now and he put his hands to his face, shielding his eyes until they adjusted to the bright light as he had done so many times in his nightmare. Seconds later Carson could be seen standing at the end of the corridor, his right hand resting on what Graves presumed was a light switch, his body a black shape against the powerful spot light behind him.

"Hello Philip, we meet again finally. Sorry about the lights, but I needed you to see this," Carson said, his voice carrying along the corridor. "Where I'm standing Philip is where Franco Russo fell, his clothes catching fire along with the rubbish. I was in the room behind me here tied to a table about to be sodomized again," Carson half-turned looking at the darkened room behind him.

"Look, whatever happened over thirty years ago must have been a terrible experience, a nightmare for you. Why my father though? I cannot condone your actions since. You have to give yourself up," Graves called out, his anger not as great this time.

"Yes, your father…why do I feel like saying, like father like son, in your stubbornness for the law?" Carson pointed out. "You know, had our friendly cook's boyfriend, the police constable, acted sooner the night of the fire it might have been so different and I could have had a happy family life. Had my brother got me out of this room instead of running we could have stayed together. Had our real parents lived it could have been so different Philip, so different. Now I have to go," he sighed, "just when we have become reconciled after so long. I just had to remind you what happened though, jog your memory, put your nightmares to rest, even if I have to live with mine. I'm sorry about Reg Graves, truly I am," Carson said, his voice petering out.

"What did you say?" Graves shouted up the corridor

"I'll have to go. You don't expect me to stay do you?" Carson replied.

"No you said, 'our real parents'," Graves reminded him, confusion reigning.

"Oh, I did. Well that's because you are my twin brother Philip," Carson replied in a matter-of-fact way.

"What?" Graves shouted.

"I appreciate this must come as a bit of a shock. I was in two minds to tell you at all, but today seems to be my day for putting my foot in my mouth for some reason." Graves stared incredulously at the figure before him.

"Your mum Philip – or should I say adopted mum – was a cook by profession. Jane Graves, formerly Jane Prentiss. Your adopted father was that certain young constable from all those years ago, the one who didn't quite react fast enough with his superiors to bring Woollsey and his friends to justice." Carson's voice took on an edge of bitterness that was filtering through his words. "Ironically, the same policeman that attended the traffic accident a week ago when Benson's body, or should I say Carson, his new chosen name, was found following that freak accident."

"I have no brother. You're lying," Graves rebuked him without hesitation. "You're trying to save your own skin with some fantastic fabrication, a made up story, one you had ready in case you were ever caught. You're crazy, barking fucking mad!" Graves gave the verbal tirade without pausing, as the full implication of what Carson had said gradually dawned on him." You killed my father because he didn't save you all those years ago?" Graves screamed.

"Don't be ridiculous Philip," Carson shouted, "your father recognised the tattoo on Benson's right arm even after thirty years." Visions of his father's sketches and Swallow's recollection of his meeting with his father on the night he was attacked crossed his mind.

"All four of them had the same tattoo done when they were in the Navy together. He almost killed himself trying to get the news to Swallow that night. I knew about the accident and the find, but as soon as I saw your adopted father bolting towards us shouting about a tattoo and Swallow referring to him as Sergeant Graves, I made the connection instantly. I had to think fast or face discovery. I couldn't let him talk Philip, you must understand?" Carson explained. Graves was stunned by the claim. Despite his need to say it was a pack of lies, there was something disturbingly convincing about what Carson was saying. "I went to your, er, father, to reason with him. His eyes that night were as wild as yours are now. He couldn't stop apologizing for all those years ago although he didn't know the half of it. Even so, he said he was a police officer, sworn to uphold the law and that the law would be sympathetic to my situation, again just as you are saying now. He turned his back on me as he did all those years ago and I suppose I struck out in frustration and to buy some time, to think perhaps, sell the business and disappear. I never meant to kill him Philip, you must believe me?" Carson said.

Graves was reeling from the revelations, still stunned by the elaborate story, which Carson had spun, each little twist managing to somehow fit the facts. Graves staggered backward, catching hold of the charred doorframe to steady himself. He neither had the strength or will to speak.

"Could it possibly be true?" Graves said to himself.

"When you disappeared upstairs the night of the fire Philip my torturers escaped as they had planned, through the cellar, the same way they had brought the hospital corpses down the coal chute. A child was reported to have perished, me, but no body was ever found. Sloppy police work if you ask me. They put it down to the intense heat, but it was inconsistent. After all, the other bodies were found burned beyond all recognition. Had they investigated further, my seven years of torment that followed the fire could have been avoided – but then I would say that wouldn't I?" Carson called out relentlessly. Graves still found the whole matter impossible to take in. He was dealing with a psychopath, he was convinced. Then again how did he know so much? And what about Carson's account and the way everything he had said fitted together?

"Benson returned to untie me when all the others ran. It was nothing to do with guilt or saving my life you understand. Benson had other ideas, which he must have hatched in his twisted perverted mind even as he fled the fire with the others. He then passed me off as his son living several miles away from here for the seven years that followed after the fire, somewhere where no one would know us. Of course the sexual abuse continued. It was the only reason for him saving me. What a mistake that turned out to be. As I got older, so did he and all of a sudden, I wasn't young enough anymore. That coupled with his loss of sex drive turned the sexual abuse into violent physical abuse. I've spent many an hour or two having bones set in the local hospital at the hands of that animal. For thirty-two years my sleeping hours have been plagued by the night of the fire. The fire, and that dark bunker, the rats, and those bodies," he continued.

"Don't you have nightmares about the fire, Philip? We are twins after all," Carson reminded him again now. Graves stopped his probing, the comment again registering inside his head as he thought about his own nightmare beginning to fall into sharp focus. He stared ahead blankly beyond Carson, thoughts racing through his mind, struggling to assimilate what Carson was saying any more. Carson continued though undeterred. "One morning when I was 16 or 17 he'd given me a kicking for being too mouthy and locked me in my room with no food or water. He returned 12 hours later stinking drunk, looking to carry on where he left off, only this time I'd had enough. He came crashing into my room hardly able to stand. I was behind the door waiting and as he passed by I hit him over the head with a chair. He lay still and for a few seconds I thought I'd killed him. Then his chest moved and I realised he was just unconscious. As he lay there all the memories came flooding back, the abuse from an early age, the hate that I had for him and his friends, you, and the life I could have had, and then that night again, inside the bunker. I couldn't stand to be in the same room with him and I dashed out on to the landing.

His room was slightly open, his private room. He had openly threatened to kill me if I ever went in that room and there I was, bravados running through me. I went in anyway, I had nothing to lose. There was nothing special inside, just letters and newspaper articles. I dismissed it at first, half-laughing at this sad man's existence, when a newspaper photograph caught my eye. It was Woollsey, a little older and using another name, but definitely him.

I delved a little deeper finding letters addressed to Tim McDonald and realised McDonald and Woollsey were one and the same person.

Benson had been blackmailing him over the last few years, which is why we always had money, yet Benson never worked. The gist of the letters basically referred to their colourful past. Each of the other three men were well-respected members of the community by then. Later, when I questioned Benson about it, having tied him up, he said he sat for nearly a day one wet Monday in May watching McDonald, until he left his office and met the other two at a shopping mall, just outside Chetley. With time and patience he hooked the other two and began a profitable blackmailing scam over the next two years. I should know, I took it over once I disposed of Benson. They had no idea he was dead and so I kept sending the letters demanding Benson's money. What do you think financed this nursery?" Carson announced pleased with himself.

"I've got some bad news for you," Graves interrupted, as if on autopilot. "Benson died much sooner than you anticipated. His neck and backbone was broken soon after you put him inside that bridge."

"That ugly fat bastard deserved worse, probably much worse than the other three, if I had my time over again…" Carson said reflectively,"…but I had to move quickly at the time."

"Tell me about the significance behind the ropes and the way they were all tied." Graves asked trying to satisfy his own curiosity and keep Carson talking.

"There is nothing to tell really. I used to be tied to the table in the room behind me using the same rope, rope that they had taken from the ship to secure their belongings when they were thrown off the Ulysses and out of the Navy. The knots, I would have thought that you being a New Scotland Yard detective would have worked that one out by now. They were used on me to stop me wriggling, just as I used them for the same purpose, more or less," Carson explained. "It seemed fitting that they should be tied in the same way. I of course told them of my intention when they each regained consciousness."

"What happened to the other men? Was the money not enough?" Graves called out again buying time as he slowly inched his way toward Carson.

"I was never greedy Philip. Just enough to part compensate me for years of abuse and set my business venture going. I couldn't help thinking that they were all getting off lightly though, particularly when McDonald, as I came to know him, challenged whether to pay me anymore. I gave him a full and final payment offer in return for all material that Benson had kept. We agreed to meet, he thinking that I was Benson by this time, at a place of my choice. It had to be my choice because I had more than an exchange of money in mind. We met out near the sewage works. Well, he turned up and I clobbered him from behind. It was as simple as that. The money went in my car, McDonald was tied up and I lowered him into that sewage tank. He wasn't pleased at all as he went in, but he did keep a tight hold on that rubber tube. The environment wasn't exactly what I had in mind but it was near enough, dark, unpleasant and pretty frightful." Carson ranted on.

"No rats but an adequate substitute," Graves said to himself.

"The tank was drained a few months later and his body was picked cleaner than a turkey frame at Christmas, so the papers said at the time."

"And the other two victims?" Graves pushed, inching forward further still as he kept Carson talking.

"It was all about finding a fitting place to get my revenge once I had made my mind up. I stumbled across the woods when I was looking at this place to extend the nursery. The woods are just over the hill to the rear of the orphanage you know," Carson said, wrapped up more and more by the sound of his own voice. "The old coal mine was ideal for my purposes and perfect timing just after the closure. Councillor Gould – as he called himself back then – was lending his support for the closure of the pit so it seemed. Only fitting that he should spend his last days there."

"But the body, the rats?" Graves said in exasperation.

"Yes perhaps I shouldn't have poured animal fat over the ropes and hands, but I didn't want them identified," he replied nonchalantly. Graves stared wildly at nothing in particular. His mind was busy dealing with the cruel insanity of it all.

"You know you traumatised the young boy that found him?" Graves called out.

"They shouldn't have been playing there, it was dangerous. What was the scoutmaster thinking of?" Carson remarked.

"Are you still a train buff Philip?" Carson said, as if deliberately changing the subject. "I used to have a little blue Flying Scotsman when I lived here and you had a red one. We use to pretend that if we prayed really hard at night that they would grow to full size while everyone else were asleep and take us away to find our parents. By the time I was twelve, I used to slip out of the house, away from Benson, and sit on the embankment at the old rail sidings with a packed lunch of jam sandwiches. All the trains that had been decommissioned were kept on disused lines there, rusting away. Anyhow, enough reminiscing, old Bertha as I used to call her had been parked up on Number 6 Line for some time and she was still connected to her last tanker. The storage tanker itself had long-since been emptied of its cargo – barley grain I think. I used to sit on the embankment throwing stones at the rats as they scurried backwards and forwards with stale grain across the top of the tanker back to their lair. I remember saying to myself, years later, that that would be an ideal place for one of them. I sent Hewitt a note supposedly from his friends asking him to meet them nearby to discuss Benson's blackmail. The rest you already know."

"That was your handiwork at the tennis club I take it?" Graves asked, changing the subject slightly as he moved further forward and referring to the break-in.

"I'd heard about the old photograph of Woollsey, Turnberry, Grundy, the tennis connection and your line of inquiry from Swallow. I couldn't take any chances. I had to dispose of the register records," Carson replied.

"But you forgot about the computer records, the copies," Graves added.

"I was never much good with these modern data capture methods," Carson said. Graves didn't know what to think.

"Where the hell is Swallow?" he wondered to himself, bewildered. Why had it taken so long to mobilise other officers…just like that night at Canary Wharf? He sat down heavily, his mind reeling from what Carson had said and then it hit him. A thought so compelling it must have been etched on his face even from where Carson was standing.

"You're beginning to remember," Carson called out. "If you are having nightmares they will be about this place." Graves ran his hand over his head, his eyes closed as more flashbacks pushed other thoughts aside.

"Tony McDowell…he died in a fire, but he was on the top floor of the old wharf building, a large room… and," he struggled with the images inside his head, "I didn't actually see him at the very end, the roof collapsed." He rubbed his temples vigorously as if the action might provide some more much-needed clarity. "My nightmare, the fire, it's inside a long dark corridor," he pulled his hands away from his face and stared at the lone figure who was claiming to be his brother and this time he spoke, just a whisper…"like this one."

"Would it help if I said that I kept the Christian name that they gave me at the orphanage, Philip, like you? You used to call me Tony back then. I prefer Anthony now, it adds a certain air óf respectability to my business and is more formal," Carson called out. Graves staggered to his feet, using his hands to steady himself. His nightmare and the detail related to him by Carson, it wasn't the death of Tony McDowell that had been haunting him, it never was – he never reached McDowell in time. It was a long buried memory from the past a long time ago. A time when he was a carefree ten year old, an innocent young boy playing with a twin brother he never knew about.

Just then the distant sound of police sirens made both men stir for the same reason. "Give yourself up, there's no point any more," Graves called leaning heavily on the corridor wall. "There's only one way out and that is passed me. By the time you do the police will have the place surrounded," Graves edged slowly forward again toward Carson when he heard a muffled banging followed by a noise that sounded like the splintering of wood and Graves guessed that the boarding on the front door had just given way.

"It seems like your colleagues have arrived Philip. Time for me to take my leave," Carson said calmly.

Graves looked at him wide-eyed. "Where the hell does he think he is going?" he wondered and then he guessed. The realization on his face must have again been visible to Carson. "The story is true. The coal chute, the one they used thirty-two years ago, to escape – Carson as a child of ten, my…my…brother," he found himself saying inside his head.

"I've got to go. Maybe we'll meet again either on this side of life or with mum and dad? Look after yourself and I'm sorry about Reg," Carson called out. Graves was already lunging forward as he had back in Carson's office when Carson clicked the light switch once more and the corridor was plunged back into darkness again. Graves went sprawling to the floor and for a brief moment snapshots of his nightmare invaded his mind again, this time the complete version. The corridor was alight with flames and he was shouting 'Tony!' only he really was this time – his brother – until it became an inaudible whisper from his lips. It was pitch black again. A wider beam of light penetrated the inky blackness picking out dust particles disturbed during Grave's fall.

"Sir, Inspector Graves?" the voice of DC Morgan, the owner of the torch, called out ahead as he made his way from the staircase toward where Graves lay dazed. He was quickly followed by more uniformed policemen. He'd already picked Graves out with his torch and feared the worst from where he was standing.

"I'm fine Morgan really," Graves protested. "Carson turned the light off when he heard you and I slipped, that's all," Graves explained climbing to his feet.

"Then he is still down here?" Morgan suddenly realised waving the beam of light along the corridor up ahead.

"Unfortunately, I suspect not, but feel free to search the place constable," Graves suggested brushing the soot and ash from his hands. Morgan moved steadily along the corridor wall tentatively toward the end room. "You'll find a light switch on your right, it's linked to the generator upstairs," Graves called out as Morgan reached the end of the corridor. There was a click and the corridor was bathed in light once more. Morgan stuck his head inside the end room cautiously waving his torch around.

"There's no one about sir, as you said. I'll get a SOCO team down here right away though, "Morgan suggested. "We can carry out a complete search later. In the meantime I will arrange for a search of the grounds to see if he is still in the area."

Graves didn't say anything. He knew it was a waste of time. He decided to return the way he had come. Back at ground level SOCOs had just arrived, while other uniformed officers ran around in the background armed with torches dipping in and out of overgrown areas of woodland that skirted the perimeter of the derelict house. The body of Estelle McDonald lay were it had been discovered awaiting the arrival of Home Office Pathologist, Jack Rowan. A nearby walkie-talkie crackled into life, as Morgan appeared a few yards behind Graves and the unmistakable voice of Gary Swallow could be heard demanding to be brought up-to-date.

"Sir, its DCI Swallow, I think for you," Morgan called out preferring his superior to explain what had happened. Graves kept walking though without a word, his mind elsewhere. He walked along the overgrown gravel driveway down towards the gates and the main entrance. A brother he couldn't remember, one he could or should have done more to protect, he kept saying in a mood of morose and guilt had turned into a psychopathic monster. Did he stand by and watch it happen all those years ago? Swallow would have to wait. He was in no mood to give half an account as fantastic as it sounded without corroboration and that could only come from one person. For once the word *mother* seemed foreign to him. As he left the main gates to Harrington Hall he recognised the place where he had lost control of his car the night he arrived back in the village. He even wondered whether his past link to Harrington had subconsciously triggered his first waking nightmare as he drove by. He looked about him dazed then realised that his car was parked at the opposite end of the estate.

27

Confession

Having skirted around the boundary wall passing the odd squad car en route to the scene, he arrived back outside the main entrance to Carson's Nurseries. As he put the key in the driver's door he caught sight of the phone box he had used to ring Swallow and his mind drifted back to much earlier times, forty or so years ago and Betty Laine, his alleged real mother, making that fateful phone call to RAF Bellingham.

Climbing into the car he stirred it into action and sped off in the general direction of Willenbury village. The

In The Mood

night had turned cold, colder than usual he feared after the shocks he been put through tonight. He glanced at his wristwatch. It was 11:30pm and way past his mother's normal bedtime, but something told him she wouldn't be in bed. Fifteen minutes later he pulled the MG to a stop behind the cottage that he had known as home for so many years. Discarded pieces of police tape used to cordon off the area where his father had been attacked by Carson, flapped about in the breeze, tied to pieces of garden fencing. Visions of the attack on his father flooded his head, only to be replaced by questions of whether he was his father at all. He shook the vision from his mind noticing the dim light from the kitchen. Running now, around the end of the row of cottages, he let himself in through the front door quietly. Jane Graves sat curled up on her husband's rocking chair, her limp head at an angle. A half-empty mug with the remnants of what looked like cocoa balanced precariously on her lap supported by three fingers. A picture of her family was cradled to her chest in her other hand. He looked at her reddened features and a lump appeared in his throat. The woman he had adored all his life, was she a stranger, biologically speaking? As if his presence had set off some silent alarm, she stirred.

"Reg?" she called out still half asleep. He moved across the room swiftly just in time to prevent the mug from falling over. "Oh Philip dear, where have you been? I was so worried about you. You looked really upset when you left the hospital. Have you eaten? I'll make you a sandwich and a nice cup of tea."

"I'm fine. You sit back and relax. I'll make *you* a cup of tea and then we can have a chat," he responded reassuring her. She smiled back at him, a sense of confusion behind it, as he filled the kettle and placed it on the gas hob. There was something in his voice that made the suggestion seem sinister.

"I would rather have had this conversation another time, when you are feeling better, but it's important to me just now," he continued from the kitchen.

"You're acting strangely Philip and it's frightening me I must admit," she replied looking back at him. Completing the task, he placed both cups on the coffee table between them.

"Whatever is the matter dear?" she pressed, evidently concerned about the serious tone in his voice. Graves sat on the settee in front of her choosing to keep his distance, something usually reserved for his father and she was aware of his body language.

"Please Philip, tell me what is wrong," she said, "I can't take much more tonight."

"Sorry, but I'm finding it difficult to know where to begin," he muttered looking into the open fire, a part of him still wanted to disbelieve Carson's story. He sensed the anxiety from her building so he decided to get straight to the point. "Tell me, truthfully, am I adopted?" He fixed his eyes on the elderly lady as her expression changed to one of abject horror. She had thought that there wasn't a tear left inside to shed anymore, but she was wrong. She raised her hands slowly cupping them over her nose and mouth. She began to rock gently backwards and forwards with hardly any noise from her lips at first. The sight was enough to confirm what Carson had been claiming for most of the last few hours was correct.

"So it's true then? Why did you never tell me? He asked, standing now, pacing about the room. He was angry, partly because of the deception and partly because everything else that Carson had said was more than likely true. Carson was his brother. What was more, he was the twin of a murderer.

"How did you find out?" she replied, the trembling in her voice stifled behind her hands.

"Never mind that for now," Graves snapped, his anger brimming over, "that part is of no importance."

"We meant to tell you, your father and me, but the situation never presented itself. You need to understand Philip about the circumstances surrounding your adoption, the fire?" she implored. The word *fire* hit him the hardest. It was the word he feared most of all. His world as he had known it was crumbling. "I promised, no, *we* promised – your natural parents," the words almost choked her, "that we would look after you, both of you, if anything happened to them." She stopped abruptly, her mind registering what she had said inadvertently. Her expression was enough for Graves.

"I know about Tony, I spoke to him tonight " he said interrupting her.

"He's alive!" she gasped.

"It's a long story, one we can sleep on," Graves replied, staring deeply into the coal fire now. He prompted her to continue.

"It was an uncertain time for everyone and your mother and father knew that. Reg and I planned to adopt you both after we were married and Reg had passed his sergeant exams. Then we would have had enough money to support a family," her voice trembled. I lived next door to your parents before I married Reg and we were good friends. I took the job as cook at the orphanage as soon as you and your brother were moved there. We thought we could keep an eye on you both while you were there until we could afford to adopt you. Then I heard rumours about the men that the principal had hired. I got Reg to look into the corruption and abuse, but the force was too late to react in the end," she said passively now. "He never forgave himself Philip. That is why he was so distant with you. Oh I tried to reason with him over the years, but his guilt, his pain over Tony was too much."

"They were all killed in the fire weren't they? Those you accused?" Graves replied trying to reign in his anger.

"Yes," she said hesitantly.

"Your father," again the word seemed wrong somehow now, "er, Reg, never got over being too late to save your brother. We were told that he died in the fire. He always loved you Philip as his own son, it's just that you grew apart, as you got older. You are competitive, just like your natural father," she tried to explain.

"Maybe I drove a wedge between you two?" Graves said out loud as he paced up and down. He began to wonder now whether the commitment to adopt, fulfilling a promise made to a young couple during the pressures that must have existed during the war, had driven his adopted parents apart. It all seemed to fit the circumstances of his relationship with his estranged father at the time. Maybe he needed safety and security after the shock of the fire in 1953, the loss of his brother, and he'd clung too much to her for comfort.

In The Mood

"No Philip, that's not true," she pleaded. Her reaction was natural, but her eyes betrayed something different.

"You and father will always be my parents, you must understand this," he smiled a little, "but now you need to tell me about John and Betty Laine," he said smiling. The look of despair in her face melted away and they both stood now, hugging each other as mother and son again.

"Oh," she said startled. "Whatever have you got in your pocket?" she declared. Something bulky had come between them and Graves knew immediately what it was. He put his hand inside his pocket and pulled out the imitation silver box that he had taken during his pursuit of Carson into the ruins of Harrington Hall. "I thought you'd given up smoking." his mother said disapprovingly.

"Don't worry, I have. It's a piece of evidence, a music box rather than a cigarette box, that I need to log back at the station, a very important piece of evidence," he emphasised reflecting on the events over the last few hours. Lifting the lid it played its now familiar out-of-tune musical piece.

"Evidence or no evidence I can't say that I like that version of the tune coming out of it," his mother scowled. He looked at her puzzled.

"Do you recognise it? It's been driving me mad since I first heard it."

"Why of course dear, but it's the worst rendition of Glen Miller's *In The Mood* I have ever heard," she said closing the lid of the box again. "I've heard quite enough thank you."

Graves considered the perverted minds that Benson and his friends must have had using that particular song title as a signal to entice young boys down to where the foursome lay in wait to feed their twisted ways. He also recalled Carson's comments about Glen Miller earlier and it all became much clearer. She linked his arm as they both sat down on the settee.

"When you came out of the fire you were in shock. The doctor at the time said he had never seen anything like it and that you may never recover. Fortunately, it only lasted twelve months, right through your 11th year at school and when you came out of it you remembered nothing of what happened. You could never stand being in hospitals after that," she explained. He smiled to himself as yet another revelation unfolded.

"We thought that it would be kinder to wait and tell you about the adoption later. You had repeated nightmares over the years that followed, always the same one, sometimes waking up three or four times a night screaming in a cold sweat. We decided not to tell you in the end in case it dredged up memories that might be better forgotten at least with the passage of time," she explained further. "The nightmares became less frequent as you got older disappearing altogether by the time you entered Police College and then you left to live in London. To my knowledge they haven't been back since." He chose to keep the real facts to himself. There was no use worrying her now it was all over.

For a moment he was lost in his own world. The memory he had subdued as a youth had been triggered again by the death of his former boss Tony McDowell. He'd simply misinterpreted Tony McDowell for Tony Laine, his twin brother, and the events at Harrington

In The Mood

Orphanage thirty-two years before. Had it not been for the discovery of Benson's body and its remarkable preservation he may never have known about his twin brother or his real parents.

"John Laine, your real father," she squeezed his hand gently, "he was an Air Force pilot, a Squadron Leader, a very handsome man who was married to an equally attractive young woman called Betty. They loved each other very, very much…"

About the Author

Paul Hupton is a life-long admirer of the styles of traditional crime writers, such as Agatha Christie and Sir Arthur Conan Doyle and contemporary writers such as PD James, Ruth Rendell and James Herbert. It is his interest in such authors and their attention to detail that has inspired him to write his first crime novel, In the Mood.

Paul has been married to Eileen for the last 25 year and they have 2 children, Jonathan and Luke. He holds an honours degree in engineering and is a Chartered Engineer, a part of his experience and background that he put to good effect in creating this intriguing story.

Paul considers this to be one of several cases for New Scotland Yard detective Philip Graves and he is already writing a second book on his adventures, with a third in the development stage.

He can be contacted by email at Paul@hutpon60.wanadoo.co.uk

Printed in the United Kingdom
by Lightning Source UK Ltd.
120247UK00001B/26